I0710545

UNDER THE BURNING STARS

ELEMENTAL ENCHANTERS SERIES

2

CARRIGAN RICHARDS

also by carrigan richards

Standalone Novels
Pieces of Me
Black Dove

Elemental Enchanters Series
Under a Blood Moon (#1)
Under the Burning Stars (#2)
When Darkness Fell (#2.5)
Under the Winter Sun (#3)
Under an Onyx Sky (#4)

January Dreams Series
January Dreams
Silent Dreams
Shattered Dreams

UNDER THE BURNING STARS

ELEMENTAL ENCHANTERS SERIES

2

CARRIGAN RICHARDS

Carrigan Richards Publishing, LLC

PO Box 3782

Suwanee, GA 30024

First published in the United States 2014

This paperback edition published 2024

Copyright © 2014 Carrigan Richards

All rights reserved. No part of this publication may be
reproduced, distributed, or transmitted in any form or by
any means, including photocopying, recording, or other
electronic or mechanical methods, without the prior
written permission of the publisher.
The story, all names, characters, and incidents portrayed in
this production are fictitious. No identification with actual
persons (living or deceased), places, buildings, and products
is intended or should be inferred.
Cover Art by Jake @ J Caleb Design

ISBN: PB: 979-8-98582-25-8-8; ASIN: eBook: B00LZ0REBW

Printed and bound in the USA

To Mom, who pushes me to do better.

Yet if hope has flown away
In a night, or in a day,
In a vision, or in none,
Is it therefore the less *gone*?
All that we see or seem
Is but a dream within a dream
—Edgar Allan Poe

PROLOGUE

Xavier Holstone gripped the cold iron bars of his cell, peering out into the moonless night. The rhythmic crash of waves against jagged rocks drifted up from the cliffs below, and the sharp scent of saltwater clung to the air. He ached to feel it. To breathe in the freedom of the open air and let the sun warm his skin again. But he wasn't free.

In due time.

His lips curled into a smile. Soon enough, he would have his revenge on those insolent Enchanters. They had slipped through his fingers last night, yes, but they wouldn't escape again. He knew where he had gone wrong. Devon had acted too soon, eager to prove himself without a real plan. And now, Devon was dead.

Good riddance.

Xavier shook his head, the bitter thought lingering. How had Devon ever been put in charge? *He*, Xavier, had done the real work. *He'd* spied on the Elementals, captured their precious Paramortal, and even taken four of the Elementals themselves. But Devon had underestimated them. Instead of following through with Xavier's orders and absorbing their powers so Xavier could take them to Caprington, he had hesitated. And the Elementals escaped.

The sound of footsteps echoed through the stone corridor. Xavier straightened, his hands gripping the iron bars, tension coiling in his spine. He forced the frustration out of his voice as he spoke.

"Have you come to let me out?" The words were tight, controlled.

"After the disaster you caused the night?" The voice was cold, unhurried, a dangerous edge curling beneath the surface. "You nearly killed her. And you know how much I need her alive. I need all of them alive."

Xavier rolled his eyes, grateful for the darkness that masked his impatience. Of course, Havok needed them alive. He'd been talking about it ever since he'd learned the truth about the Elementals. Six Enchanters. Six powers. It was all Havok cared about.

"I know what you need," Xavier muttered, more to himself than to the shadowed figure lurking on the other side of the bars.

"And yet," Havok's voice sharpened like a blade, "you keep acting like you don't."

Xavier's jaw clenched. One mistake. He'd made one mistake. And he wasn't going to kill the redhead last night. Far from it. Her fire intrigued him, drew him in. She was different. She'd understand him, once she knew the truth, once she realized why he did what he had to do.

Xavier's gaze flicked toward the silhouette in the gloom. His voice lowered, questioning. "Why do you even need them? We were born for this. We have the power to take the world without them."

Havok's response was swift, cutting. "Then tell me. How did they escape? How did you fail to turn the Paramortal into an Enchanter?"

Xavier ground his teeth together. "He's a mortal with protection magic. He shielded himself."

"And how is it," Havok's tone grew icier, "that Devon, in all his brilliance, used those wretched Ephemerals to create Halflings?"

Xavier's temper flared, but he kept it tightly coiled beneath his skin. "Those Halflings did plenty of damage. Twelve dead Ephemerals. You saw the carnage at the school. We need soldiers for the war."

Havok moved in the shadows waving a dismissive hand. "I'll decide what we need."

Xavier threw his hands up in mock surrender, though his blood simmered. "Fine. But if we move now, the Elementals won't see it coming. They're vulnerable."

There was a pause, thick with expectation, before Havok spoke again, voice measured, deliberate. "You've already cost me Devon. I need a new Enchanter. One who can absorb all of their powers. And in case you haven't noticed, our current Enchanters are not ready. Not yet."

The accusation dug deep, but Xavier swallowed his retort. Always his fault. Always the blame.

"Give it time," Havok continued, his tone gaining a dangerous, sinister weight. "The Elementals will be nothing but pawns when we're through. Their powers will mean nothing. And the rest of the world will fall at our feet. As it was always meant to."

The corner of Xavier's mouth twitched, imagining it. The world broken and bent before them. "When will you release me?" he asked, impatience creeping into his voice.

"You'll be freed when Sorcha and Garrison destroy this prison." Havok's voice dripped with malice. "Then we march on Savina and her coven. This time, we won't fail."

Xavier felt a thrill pulse through his veins. He could almost taste the chaos, the destruction that would follow. "I won't disappoint you," he murmured, eyes flicking toward the window where storm clouds smothered the sky. "Not again."

1

REVENGE

The acrid stench of smoke clung to the air, thick and suffocating, mingling with the scent of charred wood. The once-white house now stood as a blackened ruin, its charred remnants crumbling and fragile, a haunting reminder of all that had been lost. Ava Hannigan stood in the growing light of dawn, arms crossed tight over her chest, as if trying to hold herself together. The pile of ash and debris before her seemed to mock her silence.

The sky, a deep bruise of purple, began to bleed into pale streaks of bluish white. Another day rising, indifferent to the wreckage below. Ava's eyes burned, though she couldn't tell if it was from the smoke or the empty ache gnawing at her chest. A breeze stirred, pulling strands of her long, crimson hair across her face, but she didn't move to push them away. She stood rooted, staring at the charred remnants of what had once been a home.

It's gone.

The thought came to her with an eerie calm, like the quiet after a storm. The house—where her mother's ghost had lingered in memory, where the faint scent of her perfume sometimes filled the rooms—was now reduced to nothing more than ash. Ava imagined curling up on the old couch again, her father beside her, the world outside forgotten. But there was no going back now. There was no home to return to.

Only emptiness. A hollow, gnawing absence that settled deep in her bones.

At least she and her dad were alive. That was more than the families of the twelve bombing victims could say.

Her fists clenched, nails biting into her palms. *Xavier.*

She could see his face in the darkness, his cold eyes watching. He had been behind the destruction. His cruelty woven into every explosion, every death. And yet, there she stood, breathing in the smoke of his actions, while he rotted away in the Cruciari. A prison. As if *that* could hold someone like him. She should have killed him when she had the chance. It would have been justice. *Her* justice.

The Cimmerians had taken too much. The Elders thought it was over, but Ava knew better. She could still hear Xavier's voice, the warning that clung to her nightmares like smoke to the ruins: *This is only the beginning.*

But she would prove him wrong. She'd bring them all down. Every last one of them. Starting with the one who had taken her mother from her.

The first light of the sun crept over the horizon, casting the ruins in a pinkish-orange glow. It almost looked peaceful now, as if the fire had never touched it. But Ava knew better. The world didn't care about her grief or her anger. It would keep turning, keep moving forward, even if she couldn't.

She took a deep breath, wiped the moisture from her eyes, and let her hands fall to her sides. The ache was still there, raw and pulsing, but it no longer consumed her.

It was time to move on.

Ava arrived at Blackhart Manor, its steeples slicing through the bruised sky like jagged teeth. The gothic windows loomed like dark eyes, their glass cold and uninviting, casting fractured reflections of the brightening dawn. Raven statues crouched on the parapets, their wings half-spread, shadows stretching long and thin across the gravel path as if waiting for her to falter. A biting chill clung to the air, wrapping around her as the Manor seemed to swallow the light. This was home now. A place steeped in shadows and silence, where secrets were as thick as the ivy that curled along its stone walls.

She sighed, twisting her opal ring around her finger, an anxious tic she hadn't yet shaken. Uncertainty weighed heavily on her. Her dad would start looking for a new house soon, but for now, she was stuck with the ancient manor.

As she crept through the door, the grand halls greeted her with an eerie silence. The towering cathedral ceilings loomed like a dark sky about to break, their vastness pressing down on her. Every step seemed to echo, swallowed by the cold walls. The manor made her feel small, insignificant like a forgotten whisper in a place thick with untold secrets. And now, with so many people crammed inside, the atmosphere felt even heavier, more stifling. Each corner seemed to watch her, waiting.

Upstairs, she eased open the door to her room, slipping off her shoes with quiet precision. Peter lay in bed, his chest rising and falling in that familiar rhythm. Even in sleep, his brow creased ever so slightly, as if the nightmares still tugged at him. She slid into bed beside him, the warmth of his skin beneath her fingertips offering a fragile sense of comfort. Despite everything falling apart around them, his presence anchored her, kept her steady. But she knew the shadows of what had happened still clung to him.

Her mind wandered to Xavier, to the night everything had shattered. Trudy McVaine had taken Peter, held him captive in that damp, suffocating cellar. The memory of it made Ava's heart pound in fury. She loathed Trudy for toying with her, forcing her to relive her mother's death. The searing pain of loss pressed on Ava like a fresh wound. Ava hadn't even gotten the satisfaction of killing her. Trudy had slipped through her fingers, leaving behind nothing but venomous rage.

And Peter... Peter had seen too much. That night, he'd watched as she and her coven, in a desperate act, had taken an Ephemeral's life. He had been pulled into her world, his life forever changed because of her.

But now, they were together. In just a few days, he would give up his Ephemeral life and step into hers. He was willing to become an Enchanter for her. The thought filled her with a bittersweet ache, her heart swelling with love and fear. The cost of magic was high, and she couldn't help but wonder if it would be too much, even for them.

Peter stirred beside her, his eyelids fluttering open, revealing the familiar warmth of his chestnut eyes. A slow, sleepy smile stretched across his face, and Ava's heart ached at the sight. His dimples appeared, softening the worry lines that had begun to etch themselves into his features. That smile always made her feel like everything was okay, even when the world was falling apart around them.

"Good morning," he mumbled, his voice thick with sleep.

Ava smiled. "Hey."

"How long have you been awake?" His arm slid around her waist, pulling her closer. His skin was warm, the kind of warmth that seeped into her bones, momentarily chasing away the cold that always seemed to linger in the Manor.

"Not long," she lied, the truth too heavy to speak aloud.

She let herself relax into him, her fingers grazing the smooth curve of his jaw before slipping into his tousled hair. It was soft, silken, and she loved the way it felt between her fingers, how it grounded her in this moment, in *him*. Peter leaned down, his lips brushing against hers, a kiss so familiar yet still capable of sending a shiver down her spine. She felt the heat of his skin against hers, the gentle pressure of his lips, and for a moment, she forgot about everything. About Thomas, about the war, about the uncertainty that loomed like a dark cloud above them.

As Peter rolled on top of her, his kisses grew deeper, more insistent, and Ava's heart began to race. The heat between them intensified, and her necklace warmed against her chest, glowing softly in response to the passion that ignited within her. Her hands tangled in his hair, pulling him closer, as if holding on to him would make everything else disappear. His lips moved to her neck, leaving a trail of fire in their wake, each touch stoking a desire that sent her pulse hammering in her ears.

"I really enjoy waking up to you," he whispered, his warm breath tickling her skin. His voice was low, thick with emotion and something deeper, something raw.

Ava's heart swelled, but the pang of guilt followed close behind. She couldn't shake the fact that Thomas could feel her every emotion through the connection of their necklaces.

"You know someone's bound to catch on and tell my dad."

He pulled back slightly, a mischievous glint in his eyes. "I could always go back to my room," he teased, though the suggestion fell flat, his smile not reaching his eyes.

"No. Stay," she said quickly, the panic slipping into her voice before she could stop it. Her hand reached for his, her fingers curling around his like a lifeline.

His gaze softened, and he leaned down, kissing her gently on the forehead. "Always." His lips found hers again, soft and slow, but something shifted in the air. A sudden flash of anger flared deep in her chest, and her necklace glowed brighter, its heat sharp against her skin.

"Thomas." She pulled back, her breath catching in her throat.

He sighed, his hand cupping her cheek. "Will I feel that when I have my own necklace?"

"I'm sorry." She hated that her ex could feel her emotions, hated that she couldn't block him out.

"Don't be." Peter brushed his thumb against her cheek. "He hurt *you*, Ava. He'll move on."

She nodded, but the guilt still lingered, heavy and suffocating. She rested her head against his chest, tracing the lines of his skin with her fingertips, trying to focus on the steady rise and fall of his breath. "I just wish I didn't feel so guilty about it."

"He'll survive." His fingers threaded through her hair, the sensation soothing her in a way only he could.

But her mind wouldn't rest. It never did. "Did you sleep well?"

"Sorta. I woke up when you left, though. Where'd you go?"

Ava tensed. She thought she'd been careful, thought she'd slipped out quietly enough not to wake him. "I went to the library," she lied, but the guilt crept in almost immediately. She couldn't lie to him. Not about this.

"That's a lie. I went home."

His arms tightened around her. "I'm sorry."

"Don't be. It's okay." But it wasn't. None of it was okay. Not with everything hanging in the balance. "Are you nervous about the Initiation?"

He hesitated. "A little. But I'm more worried about my father."

"Savina's spell will keep him safe. No Cimmerian can even see his house."

"I know. But what do I tell him? He didn't even realize I had been missing for a month. Because … because they messed with his mind."

Ava reached up, her fingers brushing lightly against his cheek. "You'll figure it out. Your father loves you, Peter. It won't matter to him what you are."

His lips curled into a smoldering smile, the one that always made her heart skip. "You always know what to say."

She shrugged. "Just trying to help."

But the truth was, it all felt like sand slipping through her fingers. She could say the right things, offer comfort, but there were some things even she couldn't fix. The reality of the Initiation, of what they'd become was a line they couldn't cross back over. Still, she kissed him, letting herself drown in the moment, in him, not caring that Thomas could feel her happiness through their bond. Let him feel it. For once, this was hers.

Peter's fingers tugged gently at her tank top strap, his touch setting her skin alight with a heat that thrummed in her veins. But just as the desire to lose herself in him began to rise, he pulled back, breaking the spell. He shifted to the edge of the bed, running a hand through his hair.

"I should get home. My dad's probably freaking out."

Ava fought against the wave of frustration building in her chest. She didn't want him to leave, not yet. "Tell him the truth." She slipped behind him, wrapping her arms around his waist. She felt the warmth of his skin against hers. "You fell asleep here. And, well, then the house caught fire."

Peter's hand covered hers, their warmth blending together.

"You saved us," she whispered, her lips brushing the curve of his neck.

He chuckled, but there was a hollow note to it. "It was more of a team effort."

Ava's lips moved softly along his skin, her words heavy with gratitude. "You saved my father. And me. From the fire. From Thomas. From myself."

Peter turned, his gaze locking with hers, full of something deeper than affection. "I'd do anything for you, Ava." His voice was quiet yet laced with a fierce certainty that made her heart clench. He pressed a gentle kiss to her forehead, then slowly, almost reluctantly, untangled himself from her grasp. "But I really need to go. If I stay here much longer…" He trailed off, a bittersweet smile tugging at his lips. "I won't want to leave."

"I'll see you tonight." Her eyes followed his every movement as he dressed. His smile, sweet but laced with something more, lingered in the air as he quietly closed the door behind him.

The moment he was gone, the silence returned, drowning her. Her heart twisted, an uneasy knot settling deep in her chest. Was he second-guessing his decision? Maybe he was just scared. She could feel it, that creeping doubt, the fear of everything they were about to face. And who could blame him? He'd made a choice that would change everything.

2

BELONGING

The room was quiet. Too quiet. The kind of silence that pressed in on you, heavy and suffocating. Ava sat on the edge of the bed, staring blankly at the floor. She didn't want to go downstairs, didn't want to see the way they looked at her. The pity etched in their eyes would mirror what she had seen too many times before.

Her house had burned to the ground. She and her dad were homeless now. They were only being kind, she knew that. But kindness felt sharp, cutting into the fragile walls she'd built around herself since her mother's death. Since that freak lightning strike that had taken everything. People always looked at her the same way after—*poor Ava*. Like she was some fragile, broken thing. Like she didn't belong. It made her feel like a freak.

But what if their looks were different now? Not pity. Anger. After all, she had broken her oath and told Peter everything about their world. She'd caused a rift, splitting the coven. Half of them stood with her. The others probably wanted her exiled, cast out into the cold like some traitor. Maybe she deserved it.

She clenched her fists. *Stop.* Why was she so scared of them? Was it because she was still new to all of this? Or because she'd shattered their trust before she even had a chance to prove herself? The Elders certainly weren't impressed.

Ava tossed the blankets aside and swung her legs over the edge of the bed, her bare feet pressing against the cold wooden floor. The chill seeped into her bones, but it steeled her, made her feel awake. *I won't hide.* She would show them. She would show them who she really was, no matter how shattered or scared she felt.

She shuffled across the room to the closet, where, somehow, Savina had procured clothes for her—perfectly sized, neatly folded. How had she managed that so quickly? Ava wondered if Savina always kept clothes stocked in the Manor for emergencies like this. For moments when people lost everything.

A pang of sadness hit her. She shut her eyes tight against it. She *was* grateful for the clothes, for the roof over her head, for everything Savina had done. But she missed her own things. Her mother's books, the worn copy of *Edgar Allan Poe* that Peter had given her. The mixed CD he'd made for her that she played on repeat when she needed to drown out the world. Even the black hoodie she always wore, soft and comforting, was gone. And the silly stuffed animals her dad had given her over the years, reminders of better days. They were ash now, too.

She opened her eyes and scanned the new clothes, and a wave of gratitude threatened to overwhelm her. Composing herself, she grabbed a sky-blue shirt and a pair of jeans, quickly pulling them on. Boots, flats, or sneakers? She chose the black boots.

Once dressed, she made her way downstairs, the voices of others guiding her toward the dining room. She hesitated at the entrance, taking in the scene. Three elaborate crystal chandeliers hung above a long black wooden table, large enough to seat at least thirty people. Cast-iron pots sat in the center, filled with soup. Most of the bowls had already been emptied, pushed aside by those who had finished eating. The brick walls of the dining room gave the place a strange warmth despite the grandeur, and the stainless-steel kitchen behind the table gleamed with a quiet sterility.

Ava hesitated at the threshold, her chest tightening with the sense that she was an intruder there, like she didn't belong in this place, with these people. Yet, there was no turning back now. She had to step inside, face whatever waited for her.

Joss and Eric sat huddled together, their heads close, giggling over something. The soft murmur of their laughter felt almost foreign in the suffocating stillness that had settled around Ava. They looked … happy. She envied them. How could they seem so at ease, as if the world wasn't collapsing around them?

"Hi, Ava," Joss called out, her vibrant smile lighting up her face like the sun cutting through storm clouds. There was always something radiant about Joss, as if no matter what hell she had walked through, she managed to carry that brightness with her. It was impossible not to like her. Everyone did. Her patience, her relentless optimism, all of it felt enviable.

"Hey," Ava forced the word out, stretching her lips into what she hoped passed for a smile. It felt hollow, weak. She could only hope it didn't look as fragile as it felt.

"Did you sleep well?" Joss asked, her caramel skin practically glowing under the light of the chandeliers. Her dark hair was pulled back into a ponytail, and her mood seemed far too bright for someone who had killed Devon Maunsell the night before.

Ava shrugged. "Sure."

"You'll get used to it," Eric chimed in, tossing his crumpled napkin into his empty bowl. He stacked his bowl on top of Joss's and stood, offering her a lopsided smile.

But Ava didn't want to get used to it. She wanted to be home. Her *real* home. Not this strange place that didn't belong to her.

"It's not so bad once you settle in," Joss added, standing beside Eric, her arms wrapping around his waist.

Eric glanced down at Joss, his smile softening before turning his gaze back to Ava. "If you need to get out of here for a bit, come find us. We'll go somewhere."

The offer took her by surprise. They didn't seem angry with her. Not at all. "Thanks," she mumbled, the words feeling small and inadequate. But the knot in her chest loosened ever so slightly, a flicker of warmth that she hadn't expected.

Joss beamed, hugging Eric a little tighter. "Isn't he the sweetest?"

"Yeah," Ava agreed, and this time, the smile that tugged at her lips felt real, even if it was fleeting. It was a strange comfort, knowing someone would still help her, even when she wasn't sure she deserved it.

But beneath that fleeting warmth, the guilt lingered like a shadow. She had caused so much damage, broken so many rules. How could they forgive her so easily? And worse, how could she ever forgive herself?

Joss's light laughter followed as she and Eric disappeared into the kitchen, leaving Ava standing alone near the long black table. Her eyes drifted to the far end of the room, where her father sat with Savina. She blinked, her heart skipping. For a moment, her breath caught in her throat. *Mom?*

No. Her heart sank as reality settled back in. It was just Savina, her auburn hair and pale skin almost eerily similar to her mother's. Ava's chest tightened. Even though she'd inherited her mother's gray eyes, there was something about Savina's piercing green gaze that was colder, sharper. A constant reminder that her mother was gone, and no one, no matter how similar, could replace her.

Ava hesitated, watching them. They seemed deep in conversation, and she didn't want to interrupt. Just as she was about to turn away, her father looked up.

"Hey, sweetie," he said, voice soft and worn. The auburn hair that once defined him had given way to a dull, ashen gray, and the deepening lines around his eyes made him seem even more fragile. He looked so much older, as if the events of the past few nights aged him.

Ava moved closer, her steps slow and heavy. "Hey, Dad. How are you feeling?"

"I'm fine." Though the weak smile didn't reach his eyes. "Savina's been taking care of me, made sure I got some rest." He squeezed Savina's hand, an unexpected gesture that sent a ripple of unease through Ava. The sight of it still felt strange, even though they'd been friends for years. Somehow, it made everything more unsettling.

"Are you hungry, dear?" Savina's soft Scottish accent broke through the tension, her voice as gentle as ever. Ava had taken so long to trust her, always wary of Savina's secrets, her unreadable gaze. But over time, trust had come, even if there were moments when Ava questioned how much she truly knew about the mysterious woman who ran the Manor.

"A little," Ava muttered, though in truth, her stomach growled with hunger. She didn't want to admit how ravenous she was.

"Colden made a wonderful witches' brew this morning." Her father winked.

She blinked in confusion. "What?"

He chuckled softly. "Stew, honey. It's just a joke."

She rolled her eyes but couldn't stop the faint smile from tugging at her lips.

Savina smiled too, gliding from her chair with her signature grace, her long black robe sweeping across the floor like shadows following in her wake. "I'll get you a bowl, Ava. You must be starving."

Ava sat down heavily in the chair next to her father. The cold wood felt solid beneath her, grounding her in the whirlwind of uncertainty that had become her life. "You look exhausted," he said, concern etched into his face.

"I woke up a lot."

"Where's Peter?"

"He went home. He'll be back later."

Her father nodded, his brow furrowed in thought. "How's he holding up?"

"He's okay." Though she knew that wasn't the whole truth. Peter was struggling with more than he let on. "He's mostly worried about what to tell his dad."

Her father's lips pressed into a thin line. "That's not easy. But it can be done." He sipped his coffee. "I know this transition is hard. But we won't be here long. I'll find us a place."

Ava nodded, her thoughts drifting. Where would they even go now? The fire had consumed everything—their home, their memories, their sense of safety. What was left?

Savina returned with Colden, the scent of the stew filling the room, warm and inviting. Colden's dark eyes landed on her, and despite the warmth of his smile, he still unnerved her. His black hair and pale, almost translucent skin reminded her too much of his father, Corbin. But Colden wasn't Corbin. He'd proven that time and again. Still, the resemblance was hard to shake.

"Hello, Ava," Colden greeted her, his voice a soothing murmur.

"Hi," she managed, feeling a slight chill run through her as he spoke. He was gentle, kind even, but the shadow of his father always lingered.

Savina set the bowl of stew in front of her, and Ava inhaled deeply, the rich aroma filling her senses. She hadn't realized how hungry she was until the first spoonful of broth warmed her from the inside out. It was the first real comfort she had felt in days, maybe weeks. Before she knew it, she had emptied the bowl and was reaching for a second.

"That was amazing." She leaned back in her chair.

"Old family recipe," Colden said with a pleased grin. "I'm glad you enjoyed it."

Her father cleared his throat, setting down his empty coffee cup. "I can't thank you both enough for everything," he said, his voice thick with gratitude. "I'll start looking for a new place soon."

Savina gave him a gentle, reassuring smile. "Connor, there's no rush. You're welcome here for as long as you need." She squeezed his hand and turned her attention back to Ava, her green eyes soft but intense. "I'm terribly sorry about your belongings, Ava. But my library is open to you. I believe you may find some of your favorites there. Feel free to keep any book you wish."

Ava's heart fluttered at the mention of books. She hadn't realized how much she missed that simple comfort. "Thank you," she said, trying to keep the eagerness from her voice. The idea of losing herself in a story, even for a little while, felt like a lifeline.

Savina smiled warmly, then rose from the table with Colden, leaving Ava and her father alone again.

"It's good to see you smile," her father said. "You should do it more often."

Ava felt her smile widen, the first real one in what felt like days. "I will," she promised, though she wasn't sure if she believed it herself.

Ava lingered at the threshold of the library, her fingers grazing the arched doorway, as if seeking permission to step inside. The soft glow of candlelight flickered from the pewter chandelier overhead, casting dancing shadows along the towering shelves. The air was thick with the smell of old books, musty and rich, a scent that had always soothed her. The world outside could be falling apart, but here, in this sanctuary of forgotten stories, there was a strange kind of peace.

She walked further in, the sound of her boots a quiet echo against the marble floor. The shelves loomed high above, creating a labyrinth of knowledge, where every book seemed to hold its own secret. Her fingers brushed over the spines as she moved deeper into the library, as if the worn leather bindings could somehow anchor her to something solid. She inhaled deeply, filling her lungs with the familiar scent of aging pages, old mysteries, dark tales, and romances. Memories of her mother's voice reading to her flickering through her mind.

There was a rolling ladder, its wheels smooth against the polished wood, ready to carry anyone daring enough to reach the uppermost books. There were no walls, only endless shelves stretching into the shadows, making the space feel infinite. It felt like she could get lost there, and maybe that was what she wanted.

"Remarkable, isn't it?" A voice cut through the silence, low and controlled.

Ava startled slightly and turned. Gabriel stood behind her, half shrouded in the flickering light. His crystal-blue eyes locked onto hers, steady and piercing, and for a moment, she felt exposed, like he could see right through her. His dark hair, slightly mussed, framed his sharp features, and his shirt accentuated the lean muscles underneath.

He had saved her once, after all. Saved her from a Cimmerian who had been seconds from killing her.

"It is," she finally said.

Gabriel stepped closer, closing the book he had been holding. "I'm sorry about what happened. I know how hard it is to lose everything. But I'm glad you and your dad made it out." His tone was sincere, but there was something more there, something that made her stomach twist.

She turned away, feeling the sting of unshed tears. She didn't want to cry, not there, not in front of him. "Thanks." Her gaze fell back to the shelves, but all she could see were the books that had burned with the house.

Gabriel stepped closer, his presence warm at her back, and the air between them seemed to hum with something unspoken. "Savina really needs to organize this by author and not category. What are you looking for?"

She wiped her eyes before the tears could fall. "Edgar Allan Poe."

A small smile tugged at the corner of Gabriel's lips. "'Yet if hope has flown away in a night, or in a day, in a vision, or in none, is it therefore the less gone? All that we see or seem is but a dream within a dream.'" His velvet voice wrapped around her.

Her heart skipped a beat. It was the exact passage she had been thinking of. She turned to face him again, meeting his gaze, and for a fleeting moment, the world seemed to still. "That's my favorite poem."

"Mine too." His eyes held hers, as if searching for something there. He reached up, pulling a worn book from the shelf. Their fingers brushed as he handed it to her, a soft spark igniting where their skin met.

Ava opened the book slowly, the pages creaking under her touch. The smell of the old paper immediately brought back memories, making her feel as if she had traveled back in time. The tears welled up again, but this time, she didn't fight them. She let herself feel the loss. "Thank you."

"You're welcome."

She traced the cover of the book, her fingers lingering over the worn leather. "My mom used to read these to me. Every night. It's … all gone now."

"They didn't scare you?"

"No, I loved it. I guess I've always been drawn to the darker things. Every Halloween, I'd build haunted houses in my room with my parents. My friends would come over, and I'd make them go through it."

He chuckled, a sound that was low and genuine. "That doesn't surprise me. I've always been into that kind of thing too."

She raised an eyebrow, skeptical. "You? I can't picture that."

Gabriel smiled, his eyes twinkling. "My sister loved it. I used to do it for her."

Her smile faltered. "I didn't know you had a sister. Where is she?"

His expression darkened, a shadow passing over his face. "She's gone," he said, his voice hollow. "A long time ago."

Ava's heart clenched as memories of her own losses flooded her mind. "I'm sorry."

"It's fine." But his eyes told a different story. He looked away, as if the memory was too painful to hold onto.

They walked over to a small table near the fireplace, where the fire flickered low in the hearth, casting long, dancing shadows on the walls. Ava leafed through the book in her hands, her mother's voice echoing in her mind as she read the familiar lines. For the first time in what felt like forever, she didn't feel alone.

"Hey, we're here for the Initiation party," Melissa called from the doorway.

Ava glanced up, her eyes meeting Melissa and Lance as they settled into chairs across from her. The sharp scent of cigarettes clung stubbornly to Melissa's clothes, mingling with the lingering aroma of aged wood and candle wax that filled the manor's grand dining room. With her meticulously straightened blonde hair and heavy eye makeup, Melissa's piercing green eyes shimmered in the soft chandelier light.

"What time's it starting?" Melissa leaned back into a chair opposite Ava.

"Seven." Ava glanced at the antique clock perched on the mantel. "I didn't realize it was almost time."

"Where's the man of the hour?" Lance asked, his dark eyes scanning the towering bookshelves. Ava felt a flicker of gratitude towards Lance. He never held grudges, always been like a brother, just like Jeremy, who she missed.

"Home. Where's everyone else?" Ava asked.

Melissa shrugged, her lips twisting into a sarcastic grin. "Oh, they're being dramatic and avoiding you. Except Jeremy, of course, but you know how it is with him and Gillian. She's got him on a short leash." She rolled her eyes, clearly amused by the thought. "So, how was your first night in this giant mansion?"

"Fine." She paused. "Actually, I've been thinking … maybe we should all go to the memorial next weekend."

Gabriel lifted his head, his gaze sharp as it found hers. "The one for the victims of the school bombing?"

Ava nodded, feeling the idea settle over her.

Melissa's lips pressed into a thin line, her brow furrowing. "Are you sure about that?"

"Yes. We should go."

Melissa shifted uncomfortably, casting a wary glance at Lance. "I don't know, Ava. Do we really need to? Most of us didn't even know the people who died."

"So?"

"I mean … didn't people accuse us of being friends with Xavier? What if they still think we had something to do with the bombing?"

"Thomas and Gillian saved people that day," Ava said. "Plus, if we show up, maybe it'll help prove we didn't have a hand in it."

Melissa bit her lip, running a hand through her hair, clearly torn. "Look, I'm not saying it's a bad idea. I just don't see the point. You don't have to carry all that guilt, Ava. It wasn't your fault."

Ava shifted in her seat, the discomfort inside her growing. She knew Melissa was trying to protect her, but everything that had happened made it impossible to shake the feeling that she owed something to those who had died. She stared at her hands. "Maybe. But I need to."

Peter appeared through the arched doorway, his easy smile cutting through the dim light. "There you are." He crossed the room with a quiet confidence, the kind that always seemed to settle the whirlwind inside her. His presence always had a way of calming the storm inside her, even if just for a moment. "This place is a maze."

Ava's heart lifted slightly at the sight of him. "You get used to it."

Peter leaned in, his knee brushing against hers. "Still, I got lost like five times already. I'm pretty sure I ended up in the same hallway twice." His eyes glinted in the low light, that familiar warmth, but there was something else behind them. Ava didn't miss it, the flicker of doubt he tried to hide behind his usual grin. She couldn't blame him. It was overwhelming, this place, this life.

"I'm sure you'll learn your way around," Melissa teased, her sharp green eyes glinting with mischief. "Since Ava's staying here, you'll be back a lot. You know what the means." She waggled her eyebrows. "Was the bed big enough for you two—?"

"Mel," Ava warned, shaking her head with a smile, but her cheeks flushed despite herself.

Melissa grinned. "What? I'm just curious."

"You're impossible." Lance kissed her temple.

She gave him a lopsided smile and leaned closer to him. "Yeah, but you like it."

Ava couldn't help but smile. Melissa and Lance had always been playful, inseparable. They had their own bond, just like Joss and Eric. She envied that ease sometimes, the way they seemed so grounded in each other when her own world felt like it was constantly teetering on the edge of chaos.

"What exactly happens tonight?" Peter turned to Gabriel.

"All of the Halflings, including you, will be initiated," Gabriel said, his voice as steady as ever, but with a gravity that seemed to pull everyone's attention toward him. "It's a binding ceremony. You'll feel the connection with the coven, and it will feel overwhelming at first."

Ava turned to Peter, her stomach twisting with uncertainty. "Are you—?"

"Don't even ask." Peter gave her a look that spoke volumes. "Yeah, I'm nervous, but I've never been more sure of anything in my life." His voice was quiet, but the conviction was there, solid and unwavering. "I love you, Ava. That hasn't changed."

Melissa groaned dramatically, but there was no bite in it. "Okay, okay. We get it. Can we move on before I get sick?"

Ava shot her a playful glare. Peter squeezed her hand, anchoring her in the moment, even as the rest of the world felt like it was slipping away. His touch reminded her that no matter what came next, they were in it together.

Savina entered the room, her presence commanding immediate attention. "It's time," she announced, her voice carrying an authority that silenced the quiet conversations.

Peter stood, still holding Ava's hand, though now there was a tension in his grip. "Is this going to hurt?" he asked, his voice just loud enough to be heard, though it was clear he was trying to keep his usual bravado.

Gabriel smiled faintly, his expression unreadable. "No. But it's intense."

They followed Savina through the corridors until they reached the conservatory. The moment they stepped inside, hundreds of candles flared to life, casting the room in a warm, ethereal glow. The glass-domed ceiling reflected the soft light, creating a kaleidoscope of colors across the floor, the air heavy with anticipation.

Peter's breath caught as he looked up. "Wow."

Ava squeezed his hand gently. "Just wait."

In the center of the room stood the Elders—Savina, Aaron, Colden, and Maggie—while the rest of the coven gathered in a circle around them. Ava scanned the faces of the coven, which now included three new Halflings. Nicole had ditched her usual revealing clothes for a more modest T-shirt and jeans. Link had dyed his hair back to its natural blond. Seth still looked preppy, though his eyes darted around nervously, betraying his discomfort. Each of them had been through a traumatic ordeal, and Ava knew they were still adjusting. But at least they wanted to fight. Like her, they sensed this wasn't really over.

Her gaze shifted to Thomas and Gillian. Their anger seeped through the empathetic necklaces they all wore. How long would they hate her for telling Peter everything? She missed her friendship with Gillian, who had once been so kind but now radiated hostility. Ava couldn't shake the memory of Gillian's threat to mess with Peter's mind.

"We are here to bind ourselves together." Savina handed Peter, Seth, Link, and Nicole small black boxes, each containing a pentagram necklace. "These necklaces will protect you and allow you to empathize with every member of the coven. You will feel what they feel, though some of us can mask our emotions. The necklaces link and safeguard us all."

Peter opened the box, his brow furrowing as he studied the necklace. But he didn't hesitate. He slipped the necklace around his neck, the silver catching the candlelight.

Savina picked up a silver-bladed knife with a black handle. "This blood will bind us." She sliced her palm, letting the dark crimson drops fall into the pewter chalice below. The sound of blood hitting metal was unsettling, a quiet reminder of the price they paid for power. She passed the knife to Aaron, who followed her lead.

One by one, they offered their blood. Above them, the ceiling began to shift. An eerie, breathtaking spectacle Ava had witnessed so many times before, yet it still sent a shiver down her spine. Lance's blood summoned an orange sun, its fiery glow casting stark, sharp-edged shadows across the room. Ava's turn came, and as her blood mixed with the others, prisms of water shimmered across the ceiling, their reflections dancing like ghosts in the glass above. Thomas's fire crackled next, brief but intense, while Gillian's silver moonlight painted the space in soft, cold hues. Jeremy's swirling clouds followed, and Melissa's earth-bound energy added an almost primal weight to the air.

But when Peter and the other Halflings cut their palms and let their blood drip into the chalice, the ceiling remained unaltered. The stillness after the storm of power was jarring. Ava felt Peter stiffen beside her, the unspoken question hanging in the air. Why didn't anything happen?

With a calm and knowing expression, Savina moved forward, her voice piercing through the tension. "Before joining the circle, you must have absolute love and conviction." Her gaze swept over the newcomers. "This chalice now holds the blood of each of us. When you drink, you will feel a connection that cannot be broken."

Peter hesitated for a brief moment before taking the chalice. He drank, his throat working as he swallowed. He passed the chalice to Seth, who followed suit, though his grip was less steady. One by one, they drank, the silence around them thick and heavy, like the moment before a storm.

"Take each other's hands," Savina instructed. "And focus on your power."

Ava closed her eyes, drawing in a slow breath as her fingers tightened around Peter's. She could feel it—the energy in the room shifting, pooling, building. It moved through her like a wave, stronger than she had felt in a long time, as though the presence of the Halflings added something new, something potent. The air buzzed with power, thick and tangible. And there, within that current, was Peter's energy, a hesitant but undeniable force that hummed against her skin.

The pentagram beneath their feet began to glow, the light creeping outward until it encompassed them all, completing the Aureole.

"You are a Guardian," Aaron said to Peter, his Southern drawl always calm but commanding. "You protect not only us but yourself. Your body can regenerate, heal faster than any normal Enchanter."

Peter's brows furrowed. "How do I know it worked? That I have the power of an Enchanter?"

Colden's lips curled into a slow smile. "Look at your hand."

Peter glanced down at his palm. The cut, deep only moments ago, had sealed itself, leaving no trace behind. His breath hitched, eyes widening. "Whoa."

Savina stepped forward. "Nicole can manipulate ice. Link's gift is destruction—he creates explosions, shatters what stands in his way. And Seth is a Pathfinder—able to find what others have lost. People, objects, secrets."

Maggie's voice broke through, sharp and serious. "We'll begin training soon enough. But understand this, Peter. The full transformation will take two days."

"Two days?" Peter's surprise flickered across his face, the easy smile he usually wore now tinged with worry. "I can't train until then?"

"For now," Aaron said, "you need rest. When you wake, we'll start. But tonight, you've undergone a significant change. Don't underestimate its toll."

Peter and Ava exchanged a glance, a quiet understanding passing between them as the rest of the coven began to file out. The candles flickered overhead, casting wavering shadows against the stone walls. Aaron's words echoed softly as he lingered at the doorway, his smile warm. "Welcome to the Aureole, Peter."

As Peter and Ava left the conservatory, the air between them was heavy with unspoken questions. The silence stretched as they climbed the staircase, and Peter finally broke it, his voice low. "Why didn't the ceiling show anything when it was my turn?"

Ava looked at him. "Because it only shows true-blooded Enchanters."

Inside her room, Ava closed the door behind them with a soft click, the outside world fading away. She turned toward Peter, her fingers reaching for the pentagram hanging from his neck. The cool metal seemed to pulse beneath her touch, as if alive with the same energy coursing through them both. "I can feel you," she whispered, her voice barely louder than the distant hum of magic lingering in the air.

Peter's lips curved into a soft, tired smile. "I can feel you too. It's … almost overwhelming."

There was something in his tone, a wonder mixed with the slightest edge of uncertainty. She tilted her head. "What are you thinking?"

He let out a slow breath, eyes flickering with something raw and unguarded. "How amazing this is. The energy is incredible. I feel like I might explode. And … I'm a little dizzy."

Her heart swelled, her own pulse quickening in response to the emotions flooding through their connection. "Maybe you should lie down."

He nodded and slipped under the blankets. Reaching for her, he pulled her close, and she let herself sink into his warmth. She rested her head on his chest, and for the first time in what felt like forever, she felt grounded. Safe. His heartbeat was steady beneath her ear, anchoring her to the moment.

His fingers intertwined with hers. "What are *you* thinking?"

"I feel … oddly at peace. Having you be like me now. I'm not alone."

His grip tightened, a reassuring presence in the dark. "You don't regret this?"

She shook her head, her smile growing as she looked up at him. "No. I've never been so sure of anything." The connection between them was tangible, a thread woven from their very souls. The warmth of his love coursed through her, amplified by the bond of the necklaces. "Now I can *feel* what you feel for me. I've never been so happy."

Their lips met, and the world seemed to fall away. That familiar electric spark surged to new heights, their connection deepening in a way that words could never capture. Ava's necklace heated against her chest, echoing the fire of Peter's kiss. The intensity of it all—his love, the magic, the newfound bond—was overwhelming, but she reveled in it, letting it flood every corner of her being.

In that moment, nothing else mattered. Not the uncertainty of the future, not the looming threats, not even the choices they had made. There was only Peter, and the overwhelming comfort of his love, filling every crack in her heart.

With Peter by her side, Ava knew they could face whatever came next. Together, they were stronger than anything that might try to tear them apart.

3

MEMORIAL

The black, sleeveless dress clung to Ava's body like a second skin. Too tight, too confining. It itched against her, and the heels—though mercifully not as towering as Melissa's usual picks—still made her feel unsteady, off-balance. *Twelve people.* The thought pressed down on her chest like a boulder. Fire, smoke, Xavier's cold, merciless eyes as he dragged her down into that dark underground room. A shudder tore through her. *How could I have let this happen?*

Eight students. Four adults. Their faces haunted her, the memories swirling like smoke in her mind. Mrs. Duke, her calculus teacher, always wearing those giant red glasses that Ava had once complained about endlessly. Now, she would have given anything to sit through one of her lectures again. The thought sliced through her, and she blinked back the tears that threatened to blur her vision.

Peter embraced her from behind, his warmth providing solace from the memories flooding her. "Are you sure you want to do this?" His voice was quiet, low, filled with the same concern that had been in his eyes since the night everything changed.

"I have to." She tucked her pendant beneath the neckline of her dress and turned to face him. For a moment, her breath caught. Peter looked sharp in his suit, but it wasn't just that—there was something about the way he stood there, so solid, so unshakable.

He gently lifted her chin, his warm brown eyes locking onto hers. "This wasn't your fault, Ava."

She wanted to believe him. She wanted so badly to believe him. But the guilt twisted inside her, cold and gnawing. "I should've known what Xavier was planning. I should've stopped it. Even when they took you, I—"

"Stop." His voice was firm but gentle. "You couldn't have known. Don't blame yourself for things that were beyond your control."

"They were after us. They killed innocent people to force us to surrender."

"They killed because they're monsters. It was never about us. And they're not a threat anymore. It's over."

She nodded, though deep down, she wasn't convinced. The nagging sense that it wasn't really over, that the Cimmerians had more left to do, lingered in the back of her mind like a shadow. But she kept quiet. *Not now,* she told herself. *Not today.* "Thank you for being here with me."

"Always." Peter gave her that comforting, lopsided smile that made her heart ache a little less. "Are you ready?"

Ava took a slow, steady breath. "Yeah," she said, forcing the words past the knot in her throat. "Let's go."

As they made their way downstairs, Ava stopped short. Melissa, Lance, Thomas, Link, Seth, and Nicole were all dressed in funeral attire. It was strange seeing them like this, dressed so somberly, knowing how complicated their relationships were with those who had died.

Lance scratched the back of his neck, his dark hair just grazing his collar. "We're ready."

Ava met Melissa's sharp green eyes, opening her mouth to say something, but Melissa cut her off. "Don't. Not a word," she said, though her tone wasn't unkind. Ava understood. Melissa wasn't one for emotional displays. That was her way of saying they were here for her.

Ava nodded, grateful that they had come, and followed them outside to Lance's car.

"I hope we don't burst into flames the second we step inside the church," Thomas joked as they climbed into the SUV.

Ava rolled her eyes. *Typical Thomas.* He always used humor as a defense, but she couldn't help but wonder why he was even coming. Was it just because Lance was? Did he really want to be there?

The drive stretched in silence, thick with unspoken thoughts. Ava's mind drifted to Link, Nicole, and Seth. Each of them turned into Halflings by Xavier, and Link, the one responsible for producing the bombs. But no one could prove their innocence. It didn't matter to Ava. She knew they had been under Xavier's spell, manipulated like puppets, but would anyone else see it that way?

Link had struggled the hardest. He'd confessed to Ava more than once how the deaths weighed on him. His shame pulsed through the bond they shared, leaving Ava with the burden of his guilt alongside her own. The police had been baffled by the lack of evidence, no residue, no trace of a bomb. But Link's power was different, explosions came to him as naturally as water bent to Ava's will. His gift was a curse that no one but the coven could understand.

They're brave for showing up. Ava admired that about them. Even though they weren't at fault, they carried the tragedy with them. Today, standing before the families of the victims, would test the courage they barely clung to.

Peter's hand slid into hers, the warmth of his touch seeping through her skin. His eyes met hers for a fleeting moment. *We can do this,* he seemed to say, but the storm of doubt lingered beneath the surface.

When they arrived at the church, the world seemed to still. Eyes turned toward them—accusing, fearful, uncertain. Ava had anticipated the stares, the cold disbelief. Their necklaces marked them as different, even at school, but now, after what Xavier had done, it was as if the town saw them as complicit in his crimes. The necklaces weren't just a sign of power—they were a scarlet letter.

Ava lifted her chin, the sorrow in her chest growing heavier. Despite the bitterness of the moment, the day was achingly beautiful. The kind of summer day where the air hummed with the promise of life, flowers blooming, the sky a perfect, uninterrupted blue. And yet, all she wanted was to vanish into that expanse, to be anywhere but there. By the water, at Melissa's pool, anywhere but standing on the edge of this reckoning.

But she needed to be there, for them. To pay her respects, to show her face, even if blame was reflected in the eyes of the crowd.

Thomas approached one of his old football teammates, but the guy barely acknowledged him before walking away.

Melissa crushed her cigarette on the ground, her face tight. "We shouldn't have come."

Ava frowned.

"Let's just get this over with," Link grumbled, eyes downcast as they walked into the crowded church. The soft hum of the organ did nothing to soothe the tension in the room.

Ava couldn't shake the feeling that they were being watched, judged. Every sideways glance felt like a dagger aimed at their backs. The room was suffocating, heavy with the scent of flowers and loss. So many lives gone, their names etched in stone on the memorial outside.

Ava and the others took up an entire row in the back. She caught sight of Valerie Hammond, Peter's friend, glowering at her from across the room. Once her eyes fell on Peter, her eyes widened in shock. Valerie had never liked Ava, never understood what Peter saw in her. Now, her eyes were full of accusation, as if Ava had personally lit the fuse that destroyed their world.

Ava squeezed Peter's hand to stop herself from playing with her ring. As the service droned on, a girl from school with her leg in a cast, hobbled to the front to sing "Amazing Grace," her voice trembling over the weeping crowd.

Link shot up from the pew and bolted out the door. Ava hurried after him.

Outside, the sunlight was too bright, too cruel. Link was bent over on the pavement, hands gripping his knees, shaking. "I killed them," Link said through sobs, sinking to the concrete. His voice was hoarse with guilt.

Ava knelt beside him, her heart heavy, but she didn't know how to fix it, how to make the nightmare end. "You didn't do this," she whispered, but her voice was too soft, too hollow to reach him.

When Peter, Nicole, and Seth appeared, Nicole immediately pulled Link into her arms, her own tears streaming freely.

"This wasn't your fault," Seth said.

Link glared at him, eyes bloodshot and filled with raw pain. "Don't patronize me," he growled. "I knew what I was doing. I should've fought harder. I should've—" His voice cracked, and he sagged against Nicole. "I swear, I'll kill Xavier for this."

Ava stood frozen, guilt curling tight in her gut. This was her idea. She had pushed them to come, thinking it would give them some kind of closure, but now it was unraveling before her.

Peter's hand found hers again, his grip grounding but laced with tension. He leaned in close. "Stop blaming yourself." But how could she stop? This was her fault.

Thomas emerged, his expression hard, jaw clenched. "Great idea, Ava. Really."

"You didn't have to come," she shot back.

"Then why did you?" a voice demanded.

Ava turned to see Trent Gattis, flanked by Jonah Sanders and Drew Foley, stood with their arms crossed, eyes burning with barely contained fury.

Thomas squared his shoulders. "Justin was my friend, too."

Trent sneered, pointing a finger at Link, Nicole, and Seth. "Those freaks killed our friends. What gives them the right to be here?"

"It's not what you think," Thomas warned, voice low and dangerous.

Jonah's face twisted with grief and rage. "Those freaks bombed the school. They killed my sister." His eyes flicked to Ava, hard and accusatory. "And you were there."

Her heart raced. She had been there, but not like that. She'd tried to stop it. "We didn't—"

Trent inched closer, narrowing his eyes. "My girlfriend saw you. Crouching like you knew the bombs were coming."

Ava opened her mouth to protest, but the words wouldn't come. How could they twist this so easily? The guilt, the doubt all surged forward, crashing into her like waves.

Peter tightened his grip on her hand. "Let it go, Trent."

His gaze hardened. "Why are you even with them, McNabb? Joined their cult now?" He pointed at the pentagram hanging around Peter's neck. "What makes you any different from Xavier?"

"You think we helped Xavier?" Ava asked, incredulous.

Jonah's eyes darkened. "Of course you did. You're probably protecting him, too."

"We got injured in the bombing, too."

Trent arched an eyebrow. "Funny how there's not a single scratch on you, yet you were right there."

Jonah lunged at Seth, tackling him to the ground. Chaos erupted. Fists flew, and Link was in the middle of it, swinging wildly. Ava tried to pull Trent off Seth, but he shoved her aside, backhanding her across the face. She stumbled, tasting blood on her lip, her anger flaring hotter than the sun.

In a flash of desperation, she pictured Trent drowning, gasping for air. His eyes bulged as he dropped to his knees, choking.

Peter's power surged, overpowering Ava. Trent gasped, breaking free from the invisible grip, coughing and wheezing on the ground.

Ava's heart clenched, anger boiling beneath her skin. Why did Peter stop her? Trent deserved to feel what they felt, what they had all lost.

Trent staggered to his feet, wiping blood from his mouth. "This isn't over," he spat, venom dripping from his words. "You'd better watch your backs."

Just as they disappeared, Melissa and Lance exited the church with the crowd.

"What the hell happened?" Melissa rushed to Ava.

"Nothing." Ava wiped the blood from her lip and turned to Peter. "Why did you stop me?"

"Are you kidding me?"

Melissa cut them off, waving toward the car. "Whatever this is, you can argue about it later. Let's get out of here."

The Manor was quiet as dusk began to settle. Everyone had gone home. Ava was the only one in her coven staying at the Manor, and the thought made her feel a pang of jealousy. She and Peter went upstairs to her room, and as soon as she sat on the bed, she kicked off her heels, wincing at the ache in her feet.

Peter stood nearby, hands on his hips, biting his lip. He was still fuming.

"What is it?" Feeling his anger and disappointment, she sensed the storm brewing between them.

His face hardened. "I can't believe you."

"What?"

"You're not supposed to use your powers against them. They're Ephemerals, Ava."

She set her jaw. "Then why were you fighting them? I was only trying to help you."

"You were about to kill him," he said, his voice rising.

"No, I wasn't!" She sprang to her feet, her heart racing.

"You're supposed to protect them. Isn't that your job?" She didn't miss the underlying accusatory tone and felt the sting of his words.

"It's hard to protect them when they think we killed all those people, Peter. They hate us."

"They're just angry. They don't blame you, not really."

Her hand shot up to her necklace, gripping the pendant. "They found this symbol in Xavier's hideout. They've already linked us to the bombing."

"But you had nothing to do with it," he countered. "You can't control what they think."

"That doesn't stop them from accusing us. Trent thinks we're protecting Xavier. He's convinced we're part of it."

His eyes softened, but he was still upset. "Who cares what they think? They don't have any proof."

"It won't matter when they decide to hold a witch hunt and come after us. You don't understand. They're looking for someone to blame."

"You're overthinking this. Nothing's going to happen. You're supposed to protect the Ephemerals, not turn on them. I thought you of all people would stand by that."

"I do, but we have to protect ourselves too! If they turn on us, what then?"

"Would you have killed him if I hadn't stopped you? Enough people have died because of what you are."

She recoiled as the words struck her chest like a dagger. "Are you blaming me? For not stopping Xavier in time? Or because this wouldn't have happened if I had joined him?"

He ran his hands through his hair. "I didn't mean that."

Ava's eyes burned with unshed tears. "You're one of *us* now, Peter. Or have you forgotten already? He wasn't just blaming me. He was blaming you, too."

The lines of tension in his jaw loosened. He looked at her for a moment, his chest rising and falling. "I gotta go."

"What? Where?"

"I just … I just need to get out of here. Sorry." He rushed out the door.

Ava clutched her necklace as Peter's anger and regret pulsated through it. Her heart raced, matching the rapid beat of his emotions. Every throb echoed in her chest, amplifying the confusion that clouded her thoughts. Was he regretting his decision? Did he resent her now? She couldn't help but fear that their love was slipping through her fingers. And with each passing moment, the ache in her heart grew, a constant reminder of the choices they had made and the uncertain future they now faced.

4

FALLING SHORT

Sitting alone in an unfamiliar room wasn't how Ava had imagined spending her summer. But neither was grieving lost friends or watching others recuperate in hospitals from a school bombing. *Could be worse,* she reminded herself, though it didn't make her feel any better.

She lounged on the window bench, still in her pajamas, with a book resting in her lap. The curved roof above the bench made it feel like her own little bubble, one of the few places where she could hide from everything. She'd grown to like it, even if it was a small comfort.

Peering through the window, Ava looked out at the towering oaks and maples that framed the view, their leaves dancing in the soft breeze. Below, the garden bloomed with vibrant roses, gardenias, and azaleas, flowers Savina had grown with magic. Normally, the colors would have brightened her mood, but today all she could feel was Peter's resentment and anger. It sat heavy in her chest, gnawing at her nerves.

Movement in the garden grabbed her attention. Kira was watering the plants, moving quietly among the blooms. It was ironic that someone who generated poison was in charge of tending the garden. *Who does she even talk to?* Ava wondered. Other than Maggie, Kira kept to herself. Elusive. Content. Or maybe just shy. Ava wasn't sure.

For a brief moment, Kira looked up and held Ava's gaze through the window. Ava quickly looked away, feeling as if she'd been caught doing something wrong. She sighed, twirling her ring around her finger. *I can't just sit here and sulk.*

Determined to shake off the gloom, Ava changed out of her pajamas and slipped out of her room, eager to escape to the library. She found Link hunched over a table, books and notebooks spread around him in organized chaos.

"Hey." She plopped down in the chair across from him. The velvet cooled against her skin.

Link looked up, his brows furrowed with concern. "You and Peter okay?"

Ava suppressed her irritation. She hated how exposed she felt, how everyone could sense her emotions. "Yeah," she said, trying to sound nonchalant. "He just needs time to think, I guess."

"About what?"

She shrugged, but her fingers tightened around her pendant. "I think he's second-guessing everything. His decision … this life."

"At least he got to make a decision." Link winced, rubbing the bridge of his nose. "Sorry. That came out wrong."

"You aren't wrong." She leaned over, eyeing the mess of books. "What are you working on?"

"Trying to piece together what happened when Xavier took me. I get these flashes, like memories, but they slip away before I can grab hold."

"Why do you want to remember?" she asked.

Link leaned back, running a hand through his hair, his gaze distant. "Because if Xavier said anything about Devon, or if someone else was pulling strings, we need to know. We might be able to stop whatever's coming."

"The Elders said it's over."

"Do you believe that?" He met her eyes. "Devon was weak. There's no way he was in charge of the whole operation. And it wasn't him who turned me."

"How do you know? Didn't your memory get erased?"

Link nodded, his jaw tightening. "Yeah. But I keep seeing … black hair. I don't know if it's a person or just a blur, but it's there." His frustration seeped into his tone. "I just wish I knew what happened to me."

Her heart ached for him, but there was nothing she could say that would make it better. "The only person who could tell you is Xavier, but I doubt he'd give you any answers."

Link gave her a half-smile. "You think I'm crazy, don't you?"

"No," she said. "Honestly, I've been having the same thoughts. Taking down Devon felt too easy. It's like they wanted us to think it was over."

"Exactly. And if someone else was pulling the strings, why would they let Devon take the fall?"

Her pulse quickened as she recalled something from before. "Havok," she whispered. "He mentioned Havok. Trudy did too."

Link froze, his face paling. "Havok… That name … It's familiar." He cursed under his breath. "It's right there, but I can't grab it." His frustration pulsated through the necklace.

"I'm sorry. I can't imagine how hard this is for you."

Shrugging, his expression hardened. "Life hands you lemons, right?"

Her mind drifted back to the memorial, the grief etched in his face. "I'm sorry about the memorial. I shouldn't have made you go."

"Don't be. I knew it'd be tough, but I needed to go. Some of those people … I knew them."

Ava nodded. "I tried to stop Xavier that day. But I had no idea what he was planning. I feel like it was all just a diversion to capture us."

"It was. For a while, anyway." Bitterness crept into his words. "But why didn't he take you all straight to whoever's behind this? Why hide you away?"

"Maybe he wanted to get all of us at once. Or maybe he needed more time. Who knows?"

"I still can't believe they took Xavier to the Cruciari," Link muttered. "Feels like he got off easy."

"I want him to suffer. Like we have." The words tasted bitter, but they were true.

"He probably will," he said. "The Cruciari's no joke."

Ava shook her head, her mind flashing to Devon. "Devon escaped last year. If people can break out of that place, how secure can it really be?"

"Maybe he had help. Someone on the inside."

Her skin prickled. "Xavier claimed to have helped Devon, but later said it was a joke. What if he wasn't lying?"

They sat in silence for a moment, uncertainty hanging between them.

After a long pause, Link bit his lip. "Can I ask you something?"

"Sure."

"What did Trudy show you that night?"

Ava wasn't expecting the question. Her heart skipped a beat as the memory resurfaced—her mother's death through the eyes of the killer. She swallowed hard, her voice shaking slightly as she spoke. "She made me see my mother's death. From the killer's perspective. It felt like I was the one who…" She couldn't finish.

"Why would she show you that?"

"To distract me. And it worked." She shook her head, trying to push the memory away. "She's gotten away twice now."

"You can't let her get to you. We'll find her."

Ava met his gaze, something shifting inside her. "She knows who killed my mom. She's the only one who does."

Link was quiet for a long moment, then nodded. "What if we help each other? You want answers, and I need to know who turned me. We work together."

"What's your plan. Interrogate Xavier in the Cruciari?"

Link's expression didn't waver. "Yes."

"I was joking."

"I'm not." His eyes gleamed with determination. "Come on."

"We can't just break into the Cruciari."

"Why not? Who says we're not allowed to go?"

"The Elders would never let us. And it's dangerous."

He arched an eyebrow. "I think we can handle it."

"Link—"

Nicole, Joss, Eric, and Gabriel entered the library.

"Hey, we're starting training soon," Nicole said. "Where's Peter?"

Ava glanced away. She hadn't heard from Peter since their fight. "He had to go do something."

"Let me know when he's back. He needs to start training," Eric said.

"I'll call him," she mumbled.

Nicole smiled sympathetically. "I'm sure he's just with his dad. Come on, Link."

"Are you coming with us?" Link asked Ava.

"No. I promised Melissa I'd go swimming."

Link closed his books and gave her a knowing look before following the others out.

She stayed behind, watching them leave. *Maybe going to the Cruciari wouldn't be so bad.* She quickly shook the thought. *What am I thinking? It's impossible.*

Still, the idea lingered. Could they get answers from Xavier? And if they did find him … could Ava stop herself from killing him?

5

UNFORGIVEN

The moment Ava entered Melissa's house, the inviting aroma of fresh linen greeted her. The walls were covered with photos of Melissa, her parents, and the rest of the coven, smiling through the years. Melissa's parents had always welcomed Ava like family for as long as she could remember. The house had been a second home to her.

"Hey there, Ava." Mrs. Rollins smiled, pulling her into a hug. The strong lilac scent from her perfume overwhelmed Ava. Mrs. Rollins always wore way too much of it. "Melissa's outside already. Would you like some water?"

"Sure," she said.

Mrs. Rollins opened the refrigerator and pulled out a cold bottle of water. Despite her age, she could easily pass for someone in her thirties. "How have you been holdin' up? Melissa told me about the memorial."

Ava took the bottle, feeling the chill against her skin. "Yeah … I thought it was the right thing to do, but now I'm not so sure."

Mrs. Rollins placed a comforting hand on her shoulder. "You had the right intentions, sweetheart. But you know how some people are. They just want someone to blame. What they don't know is the real culprit is already locked away."

"I just wonder how long all this is going to last."

"I can't say it'll blow over soon. But you're strong. Just keep a low profile this summer and let things settle."

"Thanks."

"You girls have fun. I've got some errands to run."

"Okay, see you later." Ava pushed through the sliding glass door, and the heat wrapped around her like a thick, smothering blanket. The air was heavy with humidity, clinging to her skin and making each breath feel like it was drawn through syrup. She barely made it a few steps before cooling the air around her, her powers cutting through the oppressive heat like a cool breeze off the ocean.

Melissa lounged in a wooden chair, wearing a fluorescent green bikini, and bobbing her head to some heavy guitar music. "Oh good, you're here. So, what's up with Peter?"

Ava sighed, setting her pool bag down next to a chair. "He's fine." She had texted him before driving over, telling him and Seth about the training, and his vague reply—*we'll try*—had annoyed her.

Melissa raised an eyebrow, visible even behind her oversized sunglasses. "Sure, he is."

"He's just … lost. He needs time to adjust."

"He'll get there." Melissa lit a cigarette and exhaled a cloud of smoke. "But, no offense, I didn't think he'd transition into this life easily. Everything's so new to him. Maybe he should talk to your dad. He made the choice, after all."

Ava slumped into the chair. "I don't know if he's more upset that I used my powers against Trent or if he regrets the whole thing."

Melissa took a drag from her cigarette. "That was stupid, by the way."

"I know. But what was I supposed to do? Let them beat each other up?"

"Yes. They're boys. They'll get over it."

"But they're so much stronger than Ephemerals. They could have seriously hurt them."

Melissa shrugged, blowing out another cloud of smoke. "Maybe you should've tried breaking it up without using your powers."

"I did." She touched her lip where Trent had hit her. "And look where that got me. Peter knew what he was getting into. I warned him. And now … he regrets it."

"I doubt that."

"He should," a voice snapped from the sliding glass door. Gillian's anger hung thick in the air, as stifling as the heat. "Why is she here?" she spat, glaring at Ava. "I thought it was just going to be the two of us."

Melissa stubbed out her cigarette, rising to her feet with a sigh. "Because you two need to get over this ridiculous drama."

Ava narrowed her eyes at Gillian. "Are you seriously still mad about this? What exactly are you so pissed about?"

Gillian's eyes blazed. "Are you really that clueless?"

"Come on, guys." Melissa stepped between them. "You've been friends forever. Ava did what she had to, and I get that you feel betrayed, but she didn't do it to hurt you."

Gillian crossed her arms, refusing to meet Ava's gaze. "She put all of us in danger by involving Peter."

"He was already involved," Ava said. "They kidnapped him, Gillian. Was I supposed to just stand by and let them turn him?"

"You're the reason they took him!" she shouted. "You practically handed him over. Maybe it wouldn't have been such a bad thing if he'd joined them."

"Gillian!" Melissa snapped, looking both disappointed and furious.

Ava's breath caught in her throat, her shock morphing into a white-hot fury. "I can't believe you just said that. If you can't accept that Peter is one of us, then maybe we're not friends anymore."

"We haven't been friends in a long time, Ava," Gillian retorted coldly. Her eyes flashed with something darker. "And maybe you should ask Peter where he really stands. From what I've heard, he's not as committed to this life as you think. Maybe he'd be better off with the Cimmerians."

Melissa placed a firm hand on Gillian's shoulder. "G, stop. This isn't helping."

But Ava had already had enough. The air around her seemed to vibrate with her anger as she turned away. "I'll see you later, Mel."

"Ava, wait—" she called after her, but Ava didn't stop. She grabbed her bag and stormed out, slamming the sliding glass door behind her.

Her mind whirled, thoughts crashing into one another as her heart pounded in her chest. How could Gillian say that? After everything they'd been through, how could she not forgive her? And the way she spoke about Peter ... Was it true? Was he really unsure about being an Enchanter?

Ava's heart pounded as she drove, tears prickling her eyes. *How dare Gillian blame me for Peter's kidnapping?* But no matter how angry she felt, a bitter truth clung to her—Gillian wasn't entirely wrong. If Ava had kept her distance from Peter, the Cimmerians wouldn't have targeted him in the first place.

She angrily wiped the tears from her face, gripping the steering wheel tighter. No more mistakes. She'd been reckless, and it had cost them all. She needed to be better for her friends, for Peter. There was no way she could face the Cruciari now. She couldn't get anyone else hurt.

No more risks. No more failure.

The cabin sat quietly, shadows stretching long in the fading daylight. No sign of movement, just as Ava expected. *Perfect.* She needed the solitude, the silence. All she wanted was to escape to the waterfall, the one place that still brought her comfort.

As she made her way through the summer forest, the air was thick with the scent of pine and damp earth. The trees stood tall and silent, their leaves rustling softly in the breeze, as if nature itself was holding its breath for her. Her footsteps crunched against the underbrush, the only sound breaking the stillness, yet she welcomed the isolation.

When she reached the waterfall, she paused, her gaze following the water as it tumbled over smooth stones, cascading down in silver ribbons into the river below. The golden light of dusk shimmered on the surface, making the water glow, and for a moment, everything else fell away. The ache in her chest, the anger that had simmered beneath her skin, none of it mattered there. The waterfall beckoned to her like an old friend.

Ava climbed onto the large, familiar rock, the cool stone solid beneath her bare feet. She closed her eyes, took a breath, and jumped, letting gravity take over. For a few heartbeats, she was weightless, suspended in the air as if time itself had slowed. Then the rush of cold water enveloped her, pulling her deep into the crystal-clear pool below. It was a shock to her system, a cleansing chill that chased away the heat and tension clinging to her.

For a moment, she stayed beneath the surface, suspended in the quiet, where the world above seemed far away, unreachable. Only there, beneath the water, did she feel truly free.

She took a deep breath, the familiar sensation of breathing underwater taking over. She remembered how panicked she had been the first time it happened, but now it felt like second nature, like a part of her soul had always belonged to the water.

Wash it all away. That's what she wanted. To let the water cleanse her, to drown the annoyances, the frustrations, the guilt over Peter, and the loneliness that agitated her. She wished the water could block everyone else's feelings, shield her from the constant flood of emotions she picked up from her Aureole.

Night had already fallen by the time Ava returned to the Manor. *Not home.* It would never feel like home. She glanced at her phone for what felt like the millionth time, but still, there was no message from Peter. Her stomach tightened, but she wasn't going to text him first. Not this time.

Normally, she would've spent her Saturday night hanging out with her friends at their usual spot in town, but everything had changed. Her Aureole couldn't stand to be around her, and apparently neither could Peter. Plus, the rest of the town blamed them for the bombing. *It's better to stay in tonight.*

Ava made her way to the dining room but stopped short at the table full of people. *Great.* She hadn't expected everyone to be there, but she didn't want to be rude either. Besides, she knew her father would be happy if she joined him.

"Hey, sweetie." Her father smiled, rising from his chair to offer her a seat before Aaron slid over to make space.

"Hey, Dad." She forced a small smile as she sat down.

"How are you?"

"I'm okay." She hoped no one would ask about Peter.

"Where's the rest of your Aureole?" Joss scooped a spoonful of casserole onto her plate before passing the dish to Ava.

Ava shrugged. "I don't know."

Joss frowned. "I heard Gillian and Thomas are still upset."

Ava passed the dish to her father, her frustration rising. "Yeah. Lucky me."

"I don't get why they're still holding a grudge." Nicole grabbed a roll from the basket. "I mean, I get Thomas being mad, but he's always been kind of a jerk to you. I remember that even before all of this."

Nicole's short, freshly cut hair framed her face, making her look sharp and confident despite the tension everyone had been feeling lately. She seemed at peace with being part of the Aureole, something Ava wished she could share.

"He must've known things weren't great," Joss added.

Ava felt her irritation grow as they continued talking about her situation. *Can't we just eat in silence?*

"I'm sure Ava doesn't want to talk about it." Link smirked, nudging Nicole.

Joss blushed, embarrassed. "Sorry, Ava. I didn't mean to bring it up."

"Yeah, me too," Nicole added, looking guilty.

Ava sighed, her anger softening. She couldn't be mad at them. They were just trying to help. "It's okay. I'm sure Thomas will get over it … one day." *I hope.*

"How was the memorial?" Eric asked, and the tension in the room grew.

Ava shifted in her chair. "It was … tense. None of us were really welcome."

Joss frowned. "Why not?"

The muscle in Link's jaw twitched. Nicole placed a hand on top of his.

"They think we had something to do with the bombing. And because of … who we are."

"That's ridiculous!" Joss cried, her eyes widening in disbelief. "Don't they know you were trying to help them? Why do people have to be so judgmental, whether it's about skin color, Enchanters, or anything else? People can be so cruel."

Ava was touched by Joss's passion. She hadn't expected such a fierce defense. It reminded her that not everyone was quick to judge or blame.

"It's not just Ephemerals, either," Joss continued, her words gaining momentum. "Enchanters can be just as bad, thinking they're better than everyone else. And blaming you guys for something you had no control over? That's just so—"

Eric fanned her with his hands, grinning. "Easy, Joss. You're starting to smoke."

She let out a small laugh. "Sorry. I just get worked up about this stuff."

With a slight grin, Gabriel shook his head. "You'll have to excuse her. She likes to get on her soapbox."

"Well, it's true!" Joss retorted playfully, earning some laughs around the table.

"Well, I have something that might cheer you up," her father said. "I found us an apartment."

"Really?" She smiled, the idea of leaving the Manor sparking a glimmer of hope.

"Yep. I know it's not a house, but I didn't want to deal with all the hassle. It's in the city, though." His grimace mirrored her feelings about city life.

The city wasn't ideal, but at least she wouldn't be stuck at the Manor forever. She smiled, trying to stay positive. "That's fine. When do we move in?"

Her father's face softened with a hint of hesitation. "Not for a while, unfortunately. It's the only place I found that was both nice and affordable. But it won't be ready until November."

November? Ava's heart sank. She'd be stuck there for six more months? She swallowed her frustration. Her dad had tried so hard for them. She couldn't be mad at him. "That's great, Dad. I can't wait."

Across the table, Gabriel caught her eye, his expression unreadable. Ava wasn't sure how long he'd been watching her, but it sent a small chill down her spine. His calm control always intimidated her, the way he could lock down his emotions so tightly, she rarely had any idea what he was thinking.

"The city's not so bad," Eric said. "It'll be a change of pace, but you'll adjust." His tone was light, but Ava caught the way his eyes flicked toward Gabriel, as if they shared an unspoken conversation.

Ava shifted uncomfortably. "Yeah, I guess so."

Gabriel leaned back. "It's not like you'll be stuck here alone. You'll have us."

His words echoed in her mind, a subtle reminder that Gabriel and the others would forever be there.

"Yeah," she muttered under her breath.

Eric glanced up from his plate. "How's Peter handling all this?" His tone was casual, but the question hit like a slap.

She stiffened, glancing down at her phone, though there were still no messages. "I wouldn't know. He hasn't exactly been around lately."

Gabriel raised an eyebrow. "Still no word from him?" His voice was calm, but there was an undercurrent of curiosity, not accusation.

Her stomach twisted. The last thing she wanted was to discuss Peter, especially in front of everyone. She shrugged, trying to keep her voice neutral. "He's … processing things."

Gabriel's gaze stayed steady on her. "Is that what you're telling yourself?" His words were measured, but his tone softened slightly, as if he was trying to understand rather than attack.

Her fingers tightened around her fork, the metallic scrape against her plate the only sound as the room fell silent. She fought the urge to snap back, feeling everyone's eyes on her.

"I'm sure Peter just needs some space," her father said. "He'll come around."

Ava forced a tight smile. "Yeah. Maybe." But she didn't believe it. And from the way Gabriel was watching her, she knew he didn't either.

Dinner couldn't have ended fast enough. Ava stood from the table, her mind swirling with frustration. She needed space, a quiet place to think, away from everyone's questions about Peter. She slipped down the hallway toward the library.

But footsteps followed her, soft and steady. She didn't have to look back to know who it was. Gabriel had been watching her all night, his calm, indecipherable gaze trailing her more than she cared to admit. It made her wonder, not for the first time, why he—and Joss and Eric, for that matter—still bothered to hang out with her. No one else seemed to anymore.

Her Aureole kept their distance. Peter had all but disappeared. Yet here they were, this small group, sticking around for reasons she couldn't quite figure out.

As she reached the entrance of the library, Gabriel's voice broke the silence. "Ava."

Pausing, she slowly turned to face him. "Yeah?"

He stopped a few paces away, his eyes soft but still guarded. "You okay?"

She let out a breath, crossing her arms. "Why wouldn't I be?"

He inched forward, his lips twitching into a small, knowing smile. "I can think of a few reasons."

"Is this you being concerned?" she asked, her tone teasing but with an edge. "I didn't know you did that."

He raised an eyebrow, clearly amused. "I have my moments."

Ava leaned back against the wall, her arms still crossed. "And what about you? What are you doing lurking around here on a Saturday night? Don't you have plans?"

Gabriel's smile widened just a fraction, his eyes gleaming with that calm control. "What, and miss the chance to see how *you're* doing?"

She rolled her eyes, but there was a slight warmth spreading in her chest. "You must be really bored then."

"Or maybe I just know where to find the most interesting company."

Ava's lips curved into a small smile. "So, what's your excuse? Feeling emotions all day must be exhausting."

Gabriel shrugged, leaning casually against the doorframe. "It has its perks. Like knowing when someone's lying about being 'okay.'"

Her smile faltered, her heart skipping a beat. "You're saying I'm not a good liar?"

"I'm saying I can feel what you're feeling," he said, his voice quieter now, more careful. "I've tried not to, believe me. But with you … it's hard to block out."

Her breath caught in her throat, and she looked away for a moment, unsure how to respond. "Why didn't you tell me sooner?"

"I didn't want to push you. I figured you'd talk to me when you were ready."

She swallowed hard. "I'm still not used to people knowing how I feel. It's … a lot."

"You're not alone, you know."

She met his gaze again, feeling the tension between them, the unspoken words hanging in the air. There was a playfulness to their banter, but underneath it, something deeper.

"So," she said with a teasing smile. "No wild Saturday night plans for you then?"

Gabriel chuckled, the sound low and warm. "Not tonight. Looks like I'll have to settle for the library. Or…" He tilted his head, eyes glinting with challenge. "I could crush you at training."

Ava scoffed, raising an eyebrow. "You think you can take me? Try me."

Moments later, they stepped out into the cool night air, the training grounds behind the Manor bathed in the soft glow of stars just beginning to twinkle. The fresh scent of earth and pine filled Ava's lungs as she breathed deeply, the familiar stir of energy rising within her. She knew Gabriel had suggested training to help take her mind off everything, and to her surprise, Joss and Eric had eagerly jumped at the idea.

"All right, who's ready to get their butts kicked?" Eric teased, stretching his arms with a wide grin.

Joss rolled her eyes but smirked, small sparks of electricity crackling along her fingertips. "You mean your butt, right? I'm not the one who's gonna end up on the ground."

Gabriel stood off to the side, calm and relaxed. His eyes flicked toward Ava, and she caught the briefest hint of a smile. "You guys talk a lot for people who can barely keep up."

"Oh, it's on," Ava said. If there was one thing that could pull her out of her head, it was a good sparring session. "Let's see who's left standing by the end of this."

They formed a loose circle, the open space around them buzzing with potential. The air grew thick with energy as each of them prepared, their powers quietly building beneath the surface.

Gabriel was the first to step forward, teleporting to the center of the circle in a blink. "Let's start simple. No powers for now. Just reflexes."

"Reflexes?" Eric raised an eyebrow. "I thought we came out here to have fun."

"You'll have plenty of fun when you're dodging electricity," Joss said, crackling sparks dancing around her hands.

"Not yet," Gabriel said with a calm smile. "Just speed. Dodge this." And with that, he teleported behind Eric in the blink of an eye, tapping his shoulder lightly before vanishing again.

Eric gave a frustrated groan, turning just in time to see Gabriel reappear behind Joss, smirking. "You've got to be quicker than that."

Ava lunged toward him, her water magic rippling around her as she moved. But he teleported out of her reach, reappearing a few feet away, his expression still calm and controlled.

"Too slow," he teased.

"Fine. Let's see how you handle this."

In an instant, she summoned water from the moisture in the air, a swirling current forming at her fingertips. With a flick of her wrist, she sent a torrent of water rushing toward Gabriel, but he vanished just as the wave reached him, reappearing on the other side of the clearing.

"You're going to have to do better than that."

"Oh, I plan to." Her grin widened as she prepared for another round.

Sparks flew from Joss's fingers as she aimed a crackling bolt of electricity in Gabriel's direction. But once again, he teleported out of the way, this time reappearing behind her.

"Can't hit what you can't see," he said.

She scoffed, her eyes narrowing as she sent another bolt toward him.

Meanwhile, Eric had multiplied, his duplicates spreading out across the clearing, ready to surround Gabriel from every angle. "Try teleporting your way out of this!" he called, his copies moving in sync toward him.

Gabriel's eyes flicked between the copies and the others, calculating. In an instant, he teleported again, dodging Joss's electricity and sidestepping Ava's water blast before appearing on a rock above them all, grinning.

"Come on, Gabriel!" Ava called, breathless with excitement. "Stand still for once!"

"You know I'm not gonna make it easy." He grinned, teleporting to the ground, effortlessly dodging every attack.

Ava's magic flared to life as she sent another wave of water his way, swirling the currents to encircle him. But just as the water reached him, Gabriel vanished, teleporting out of its path in the blink of an eye and reappearing a few feet away, completely dry.

"Too slow."

Ava blinked, momentarily frustrated. "Okay, now you're just showing off."

Gabriel chuckled. "I thought that's what you wanted."

Eric grinned. "We've got to step it up if we're going to take him down."

Ava glanced between them all, the air between her and Gabriel crackling with tension, competitive, but something more, unspoken. Her pulse quickened, but she kept her cool, not ready to let Gabriel have the last word.

"I'm just warming up." She narrowed her eyes and flicked her wrist again, summoning another stream of water, this time more focused. Gabriel blinked away, but as he reappeared, the water just grazed his arm, droplets splashing against his sleeve.

"Ha! Got you."

Joss and Eric erupted in cheers.

Gabriel glanced down at his damp sleeve and smirked. "Lucky shot."

Ava grinned, her pulse quickening with excitement. "Next time, I'll do more than graze you."

Gabriel let out a warm and low chuckle. "We'll see about that."

Exhausted, Ava wandered into the library and found Link hunched over a table, notebooks and loose papers scattered around him like a battlefield of unanswered questions. The sight had almost become routine, but the tension in the air between them was anything but.

She slipped into the seat across from Link. "Still at it?"

Link sighed, tossing his pen into the crease of an open book. "Yeah. Not getting anywhere though."

"I'm sorry," she murmured, knowing it wouldn't help, but saying it anyway.

He leaned forward, lowering his voice. "Xavier knows something, Ava. We should go."

Her chest tightened. "It's not a good idea," she whispered back. *It's dangerous. Reckless.* "I can't keep being reckless. What I did at the memorial—"

"Was necessary." His eyes were sharp, studying her like she was a puzzle he couldn't solve. "Is that why Peter's upset?"

"No," she lied.

Link stood abruptly, motioning for her to follow. He led her deeper into the library, away from any prying eyes or wandering ears. His voice dropped to a near whisper, urgent, pleading. "Come on, Ava. Xavier's the only one who knows everything. I've been searching for answers in these books for days, and I'm hitting walls everywhere. We can't keep sitting here, doing nothing."

"What do you expect to find?"

"I don't know. Anything." He raked a hand through his hair. "The books only talk about Corbin, the horrible things he did. That he was Savina's stepfather and Colden's father. But what if there's more?" He paused, lowering his voice further. "You don't think Corbin's still alive, do you?"

Ava shook her head. "No. A lot of people saw him die, Link. He's not coming back."

"Then who's running things? Devon was never on Corbin's level. Someone else is pulling the strings, and Xavier knows who it is."

"I agree that there's someone else. But even if we went to the Cruciari, Xavier wouldn't tell us anything. Why would he?"

"Maybe we could bribe him."

"With what?" Ava raised an eyebrow. "You really think he'd sell out whoever's in charge for a few favors? He doesn't care about us."

He let out a frustrated groan. "I've thought about it from every angle. I even tried to find out more about your mom's killer, but I keep hitting dead ends. Xavier might be our only chance."

"He won't help us. I know he won't."

His voice dropped to a whisper. "Then what? We just sit around and wait for whoever's in charge to come for us again? Or worse, go after more innocent people? I'm telling you, we have limited options. We either try to get answers from Xavier, or we look for a Necromancer."

Ava almost laughed, but the look on Link's face told her he was serious. "A Necromancer?"

"Yeah, apparently, they exist. But do we really want to go down that road? The only other option is Caprington, and you know how dangerous that is. I'd rather take my chances at the Cruciari."

She took a deep breath as the decision pressed down on her like a stone. They were running out of options. Savina had given her nothing. Colden might know more but asking him could mean walking into a storm she wasn't ready for. And Peter... *Where is he when I need him?*

She missed him, and maybe, just maybe, if he were there, he could help them decide. Things were supposed to be easier with him as part of the Aureole, but nothing had gone the way she'd planned.

Link watched her closely as though waiting for her resolve to crack. "You're thinking about it. We should just go. We can get the answers we need."

Ava met his eyes, and her heart sank. "I can't. Even if we got to Xavier, what makes you think he'd help us? We're the ones who put him in the Cruciari. He'd rather kill us than help us out. And who knows how sane he is after all this time. Besides, how would we even get there?"

"I've been studying the map, but..." Link trailed off. "Maybe Gabriel—"

"No. I'm not bringing him into this."

"You know I'm right, Ava. And I'm going, with or without you."

His words caused her stomach to lurch.

Link walked past her, his footsteps fading into the shadows of the library. She hated feeling like she was trapped in an endless cycle of impossible choices. No matter what she decided, someone would get hurt.

But going to the Cruciari? Could they really pull that off? Could she face Xavier again and trust herself not to do something she might regret?

Trembling, she struggled with the decision that loomed over her. *What if I make the wrong choice?*

———⟨ 6 ⟩———

THE CITY THAT CARE FORGOT

The next morning, Ava tossed off the blankets, her body stiff from an uneasy night. Sleep had been elusive, full of fragmented dreams that left her feeling more exhausted than rested. She reached for her phone, hoping—*needing*—to see a message from Peter, but the screen remained frustratingly blank. Her stomach knotted with that familiar, sinking feeling.

Maybe I should text him. But her stubborn side reared its head. *If he needs space, I'll give it to him.* She wasn't about to chase after someone who clearly didn't want to talk. Still, the growing silence between them scared her. *Did Dad ever treat Mom this way?* Did he ever regret it? Did her mom have the same hollow ache in her chest?

With a frustrated sigh, Ava gave in and dialed Peter's number.

After two rings, he answered. "Hey."

"Hey," she replied, her voice softer than she'd intended. It almost sounded vulnerable.

A heavy silence stretched between them.

"Are you okay?"

"I'm fine," he answered, though his tone said otherwise.

She swallowed hard. "Do you want to come over today? We could go swimming or something."

"I'm actually hanging out with Seth."

Of course you are. Her heart sank, the rejection cut deeper than she'd expected. "Okay," she managed, trying to keep her voice light, unaffected. "I just wanted to check in."

"We're good. I'll talk to you later."

And just like that, the line went dead. Ava stared at the phone for a second. *We're good?* The tightness in her chest flared as she tossed her phone aside. *We're not good. You're avoiding me.*

She stood, pacing her room as her emotions churned. *I need to get out of here.* The more she thought about Peter, the more the hurt twisted into anger. She clenched her fists, wanting to scream, to break something, anything. She hated this feeling, this limbo between them.

But being alone was nearly impossible in the Manor. It was full of people who knew too much about her, about Peter, about everything that had happened. Privacy felt like a luxury she couldn't afford. She wished, just for a moment, that she could disappear, escape the constant pressure and eyes watching her every move. Maybe she should stay at the cabin.

With one last frustrated sigh, she changed into a black tank top and shorts. If she couldn't escape her thoughts, she'd at least escape the walls closing in around her.

Deciding to escape to the waterfall, Ava quickly grabbed her shoes, her body still stiff from the intense training the night before. She headed downstairs, determined to shake off the lingering exhaustion that clung to her muscles.

"Ava," Colden's voice called from behind her.

She stopped, turning to meet his dark eyes. His usual calm demeanor was intact, long black hair tied into a low ponytail, the black robe-like button-up he always wore billowing slightly as he moved. "Yes?"

"Are you leaving without breakfast?"

She shifted uncomfortably. "Yeah, I'm not really a breakfast person," she lied. She just needed to get out.

"You should reconsider," Colden smiled. "It's important for your strength."

"Maybe tomorrow."

"Nonsense." He chuckled, lightly placing a hand on her arm. "Come join us. It'll only take a minute."

Reluctantly, Ava followed him into the dining room, mentally cursing her luck. The table was already set, and to her surprise, it wasn't a large crowd—just Gabriel, Joss, Eric, and Natalia. *Where is everyone else if breakfast is so important?* She suspected this was Colden's way of trying to include her.

"Morning." Joss smiled, her violet eyes glinting.

"Hi," Ava said.

"There's plenty to eat, but if you'd like something fresh, just let me know," Colden said.

She eyed the table with plates of eggs, bacon, sausage, grits, and potato hash spread out in a feast far too grand for just five people. "This is fine, thanks."

Colden nodded and quietly left the room.

As Ava sat down across from Gabriel, he glanced up from his plate, a smirk already forming. "Well, well, look who survived last night's training. Feeling sore yet?"

She rolled her eyes, trying to suppress a smile. "Barely."

"I'd offer you a rematch, but I'm not sure you're ready for round two."

"Don't tempt me." She narrowed her eyes with mock defiance and spooned a small portion of eggs onto her plate.

With Natalia's icy presence lingering in the background, she felt more like an outsider than ever. Ava's skin prickled with discomfort. Ava poked at the eggs, her appetite long gone.

Joss took a sip of coffee and leaned toward Ava. "How are you?"

"I'm fine. You?" She wanted to avoid any deeper conversation. Something told her Joss could feel her sadness about Peter.

"I'm good," Joss said. "I'm sorry about everything that's been going on. It's a lot to handle."

Ava shrugged. "It's okay."

Eric reached for a sausage link. His plate was nearly empty, but he seemed intent on finishing everything on the table. "Doing anything fun today?"

"We're going to New Orleans today," Joss said. "That is, if we can get Gabriel to leave his precious library."

He smirked. "I'm not in the library right now, am I?"

Ava felt a stab of envy. "It must be nice, being able to go anywhere, whenever you want."

He opened his mouth to respond, but Joss jumped in, laughing. "Oh, it's amazing."

Eric playfully tousled her hair. "Let the man speak."

Gabriel chuckled, his blue eyes sparkling, and Ava felt a twinge of guilt for even noticing how attractive he looked when he smiled like that. "It is amazing. You should come with us." He met her gaze.

Why would they want me to come? She hesitated, unsure of how to respond.

Natalia finally spoke, her tone cutting through the room like ice. "I'm sure she has other things to do."

Joss rolled her eyes. "Do you?"

She had planned to escape to the waterfall, maybe help Link with his investigation, but … New Orleans sounded tempting. Still, Natalia's presence made her feel unwelcome. "It's fine. I don't want to intrude."

"You're not intruding," Joss insisted. "We invited you. Come on, it'll be fun! Don't let Miss No-Fun over there stop you. Invite Peter."

Ava felt a twinge of sadness at the mention of Peter but quickly hid it. "I don't know—"

"Joss, it's too many people already," Natalia said sharply. "I wish you wouldn't invite others without asking."

Ava shifted uncomfortably. Natalia's disapproval was clear, and it stung more than it should have. "It's really okay. I'll just—"

"Don't leave!" Joss pleaded. "We'd love for you to come."

"If she doesn't want to go, don't force her." Natalia rose from her chair and left the room with her coffee and newspaper.

Feeling awkward, Ava stole a quick glance at Gabriel. "Have I done something to her?"

"No," Eric replied. "She's just … crabby."

Gabriel shrugged. "Don't worry about Natalia. I don't."

Joss waved a hand dismissively. "Seriously, forget her. Are you coming or not?"

Ava hesitated. *Maybe I could use the distraction.* "I don't want to cause any rifts—"

"Rift schmift." Joss laughed. "You'll be fine. You wanna invite Peter?"

The knot in her chest tightened again, but Ava smiled, pretending it didn't bother her. "He's busy."

Joss shrugged. "His loss."

They began clearing the table, and as Ava brought her dishes into the kitchen, Colden smiled warmly at her. "I'll take care of these. Go have fun."

Ava smiled, surprised by the genuine warmth in his voice. Maybe she'd misjudged everyone. Maybe she wasn't as alone as she thought.

"Ready?" Gabriel held out his hand. His easy smile mirrored the one he'd worn last night during training, when he'd teased her effortlessly.

She took his hand, closing her eyes. *Just for a day. One day to forget Peter, to forget everything. Maybe I can let go, just for a little while.*

A second later, they stood in an aisle between towering mausoleums, the walls of tombs lined with flowers, pictures, and rosaries. The morning sky hung low with gray clouds, casting a somber mood over the scene. *Not exactly a lively start,* Ava thought, glancing around the famous cemetery.

"What a downer, Gabe," Joss teased, nudging Eric as she started walking. "A cemetery is where you wanted to start?"

"No one saw us materialize out of thin air, did they?" He smirked.

Joss rolled her eyes dramatically, but Ava could tell she wasn't too bothered.

"This is the famous Saint Louis Cemetery." As Ava stood there, she was struck by the eerie hush in the air.

"Number one," Gabriel added.

She shook her head, smiling slightly. "I think I'm with Joss on this one. Starting off in a cemetery is a bit of a downer."

He chuckled, his eyes warm as he glanced at her. "Yeah, sorry about that. I knew it wouldn't be crowded."

"It's fine. I'm teasing." She shrugged. "But cemeteries aren't really my thing, to be honest."

Gabriel looked thoughtful for a moment. "Didn't think of that. But before we leave, would you like to see Marie Laveau's mausoleum?"

"Who?"

His eyes widened in mock disbelief. "You don't know Marie Laveau? The Voodoo Queen of New Orleans? Come on, little grasshopper." He gently took her hand and guided her to a whitewashed mausoleum, where sets of three X's had been etched into the stone. Beads and rosaries hung from the door's handle like offerings to a long-gone queen.

"What do the X's mean?" Ava asked.

"People draw them, hoping she'll come back and grant them wishes."

"Why would she grant wishes to people who vandalize her tomb?"

He laughed, a rich, deep sound that seemed to shake the lingering gloom of the cemetery. She found herself smiling despite everything. "Good point. People are weird. So," He tilted his head, "what do you want to see next?"

It was a loaded question. "I don't know. I've never been here."

"Well, there's a lot to explore." His eyes lit up with enthusiasm. "How about we grab a mid-morning snack first?"

She found herself laughing quietly at his sudden excitement. It was refreshing to see him relaxed and not always weighed down by responsibility. *I could probably stand to do the same,* she realized, feeling a small knot of tension ease in her chest.

She'd let herself follow Gabriel's lead, just to see where the day took them.

Once they met up with Joss and Eric, they headed to a famous street-side café. Ava had never heard of the place, but when the beignets arrived—piping hot and dusted with a thick layer of powdered sugar—she understood why it was so popular.

By the time they finished, they were covered in powdered sugar.

"I think I need a bath." Joss wiped her face with a napkin.

"Here, you missed a spot." Eric reached out and touched her cheek, leaving a fresh smear of sugar.

Ava bit her lip, trying not to laugh. Gabriel glanced at her, a knowing grin tugging at the corner of his mouth.

"What?" Joss asked.

Eric shrugged. "Maybe it's an inside joke."

"You put sugar on my face, didn't you?" Joss narrowed her eyes, but her mock seriousness didn't last long.

Unable to contain herself any longer, Ava burst into laughter, and soon Gabriel and Eric followed. Joss scooped up a handful of sugar and flung it at Eric, getting it all over his hair and eyelashes.

Some of it landed on Ava, too.

"Hey, don't drag me into this!" she laughed, brushing sugar off her arms.

But it didn't stop there. Eric retaliated, and even Gabriel, usually so composed, got caught up in the moment, tossing sugar at Ava. Soon, all four of them were covered in powdered sugar, laughing so hard they had to stop before they got any on the other patrons.

They left the café, still brushing sugar off their clothes and hair as they strolled through Jackson Square. The square was alive with the vibrant sounds of New Orleans. Musicians playing jazz on street corners, artists painting colorful scenes, and tourists snapping photos.

As they wandered through the French Market, Ava marveled at the endless array of souvenirs—masks, dolls, shirts, all kinds of trinkets reflecting the city's rich culture. She glanced up at the intricate wrought-iron balconies that lined the French Quarter, many decorated with beads and fleur-de-lis, and took in the beautiful blues, pinks, and yellows of the townhomes.

This place is incredible. The blend of French Creole architecture with its vibrant colors and Victorian influences reminded her a little of Blackhart Manor, only much more alive.

As they passed a group of street performers, Ava caught herself smiling, really smiling, not the forced kind she'd been giving everyone lately. The energy of the city, the music, the art was contagious. For the first time in what felt like forever, she felt lighter.

They finished their day with a short ride on the steamboat *Natchez*, where they ate Cajun cuisine and listened to more jazz.

As the steamboat drifted along the river, Ava leaned against the railing, gazing out at the water. The setting sun cast a golden glow over the city, and the soft hum of jazz music filled the air. For the first time in a long while, she felt at peace.

"You seem like you're enjoying yourself," Gabriel's voice came from behind her.

She glanced over her shoulder to see him approach, his usual serious expression softened by a small, genuine smile.

Ava smiled back, surprising herself with how easily it came. "I am. It's been a while since I've had a day like this."

He stopped beside her, resting his arms on the railing. "I'm glad. I wasn't sure if today would help you relax or just be a distraction."

"Maybe both." Her gaze drifted over the calm water. "But I needed it. Thanks for inviting me."

"You don't need to thank me." His eyes flicked toward her, a light smile playing on his lips. "It's nice to see you having a good time, though. You've been carrying a lot lately."

His words lingered in the air between them, sinking into Ava more than she expected. There was something about the way he said it, like he truly saw her, saw everything she'd been bottling up. Warmth spread through her chest, and for the first time in a while, she didn't feel like she had to hide behind a shield of strength.

"I guess I didn't realize how much I needed to get away."

His smile widened just a fraction, his crystal-blue eyes catching the last rays of sunlight. "Well, you deserve it. And, for what it's worth, you're pretty fun to be around when you let yourself relax."

Ava chuckled, brushing a strand of hair behind her ear. "So are you." She glanced at him from the corner of her eye. Being around Gabriel made her feel lighter, like maybe everything wasn't so overwhelming after all.

They stood in comfortable silence for a moment, the gentle lapping of the water and distant jazz music creating a peaceful atmosphere. She found herself thinking how easy it was to be with him, to let go, even if just for a little while. For once, Ava felt like she could breathe.

By nightfall, the sky was clear and a deep shade of blue, stars twinkling above. Ava felt pleasantly exhausted. Her legs ached from walking all day, but her heart felt lighter than it had in weeks.

"We should go to the Metropolitan," Joss suggested with a grin.

"What's that?" Ava asked, not quite ready for another wild adventure.

"It's a dance club. So much fun."

"I'm not much of a dancer, and I'm also only seventeen."

"When do you turn eighteen?"

"November."

Joss waved her hand dismissively. "I'm sure we could get you in."

Ava turned to Gabriel, feeling awkward. "If you wanna take me back so you all can go, you can."

"Nonsense," Joss insisted, shaking her head.

Eric chimed in. "Why don't we visit Sophia and Caroline? We haven't seen them in a while."

"Ooh, that's a good idea," Joss agreed, her excitement growing.

"Who are they?" Ava asked, feeling more out of place with each suggestion.

"Old friends of ours," Joss said.

They walked into the Garden District, and Ava marveled at the beauty of the historic homes. Timeless double-gallery mansions lined the streets, with their arched wrought iron balconies and vibrant, colorful facades. When they arrived at a beige home surrounded by an iron fence, Joss opened the squeaky gate, and they climbed the steps.

Joss knocked on the door, and a tall woman with curly black hair answered, her brown eyes lighting up.

"Joss!" She pulled her into a hug before doing the same with Eric. Then, her gaze landed on Gabriel. "Oh, how is my Gabriel?" She kissed him on the lips, lingering for a second longer than necessary, making Ava shift uncomfortably.

"Mmm. It's so good to see you all." The woman's gaze finally shifted to Ava. "And who is this?"

"Ava," she introduced herself, shaking the woman's hand.

Recognition crossed her face. "Ah, you're one of the special ones." She smiled warmly. "I'm Caroline. Come in, honey."

Ava followed the group inside, the house dimly lit with beautiful chandeliers and walls adorned with portraits. The ambiance felt as heavy as the history that lived within the walls.

"I hear Joss," a raspy voice with a Southern drawl called from upstairs. A red-haired woman descended the staircase, her black off-the-shoulder blouse and jeans emphasizing her confidence. She immediately hugged Joss and turned to Ava with a curious smile.

"I'm Sophia," she said.

"Ava."

"Good to meet you. You all are just in time. We're heading to the club soon. Well, some of us," she added with a laugh. "Rene isn't much of a dancer."

"Neither am I," Ava mumbled, feeling increasingly out of place.

"It's easy." Sophia flashed a grin. "Just shake your hips, and if you eye a guy just right, he might buy you a drink."

Ava offered a weak smile. She was ready to go home.

They moved into the parlor, which was filled with plush but well-worn furniture. Ava sat next to Gabriel on the loveseat, only half listening to the conversation between Joss, Eric, and Caroline. Her thoughts wandered, growing more uneasy by the minute.

"Is she an old girlfriend?" she asked Gabriel.

He laughed. "Caroline? No. She's with Sophia."

"Ahh."

A few minutes later, Sophia returned with two men. One had blond hair and a scar down his face, dressed entirely in black. The other, a man with a shaved head and dark glasses, gave off a hipster vibe in his skinny jeans. The blond man's gaze lingered on Ava, sending chills down her spine.

"This is Rene," Sophia said as the man with glasses raised his hand. "And this is Marcel." Marcel nodded but kept his eyes trained on Ava, making her uncomfortable.

"So, how does it feel to be the woman who killed Devon Maunsell?" Caroline asked Joss.

"It's … okay, I guess. If it weren't for Ava, he'd probably still be here."

"I think we should celebrate," Sophia said with a mischievous smile. "Shots, anyone?"

Ava tensed. She wasn't in the mood for socializing or celebrating.

As the others moved to the back of the house, Gabriel stayed behind. "No shot for you?" she asked.

He shrugged. "Not really much of a drinker." Leaning in, he whispered, "Besides, I can tell you're uncomfortable."

Her cheeks reddened with embarrassment. "Sorry."

"There's nothing to apologize for. Let's go hang out on the porch instead. You can hear the music playing."

She nodded gratefully and followed him outside to the iron bench beneath the windows. Marcel and Rene trailed behind them, but she focused on the distant jazz music, trying to ground herself in its rhythm.

"What's it like being an Elemental?" Marcel asked.

She jumped, and crossed her arms. "It's fine, I guess."

"Which one are you?" His eyes narrowed.

"Water."

"What would Devon want with you all?"

Her pulse quickened. "To use our powers. But he's dead, so it doesn't matter now."

"I don't believe that. And I can tell neither do you."

"I didn't say anything otherwise."

"You've seen death," he said.

Her breath caught in her throat. "What?"

Gabriel shifted beside her, his body tensing slightly, but Marcel continued as if he didn't notice. "You've experienced death … it haunts you."

Her fists clenched. "What are you getting at?"

"It was your mother, wasn't it?" Marcel's eyes seemed to lose focus, his voice grew quieter. "She was murdered."

"I don't want to talk about it."

"There's something else." His eyes turned a ghostly white.

Her heart raced, and Gabriel subtly inched closer.

"I see her … standing next to Corbin."

"What?" Ava's voice shook, disbelief and rage flooding through her.

"She was a Cimmerian."

Fury surged through her, and before she could stop herself, she slapped Marcel hard across the face. "How dare you?"

In an instant, Gabriel's strong arms wrapped around her, pulling her back before she could strike again. "Ava, calm down," he whispered urgently in her ear.

Rene intervened, worry lining his features. "What happened?"

Marcel blinked, his eyes returning to normal. His face was full of regret as he looked at Ava. "I … saw something. It wasn't clear."

Ava struggled against Gabriel's grip, her breathing fast and shallow as tears blurred her vision. "My mother was *not* one of them."

"Breathe," Gabriel whispered again, holding her tighter. His steady presence was the only thing keeping her grounded.

She inhaled deeply and, slowly, her tension began to ease. Gabriel loosened his grip slightly, and she wiped away the tears.

"Marcel, sweetie," Rene said, "why would you say that?"

Marcel shook his head, still looking bewildered. "It was just an image. It might not have been real."

Ava turned to Gabriel, her voice barely above a whisper. "Please take me home."

"We're sorry, dear," Rene said.

"I'll be back," Gabriel said. "Tell Joss and Eric." He took Ava's hand, and she closed her eyes. When she opened them, they were standing in the backyard of the Manor.

For a moment, they stood in silence, the night air cool against her skin, but Ava's mind was still racing. She realized she was still gripping Gabriel's hand tightly, as if it was the only thing steadying her.

"I'm sorry for that," he said, his voice gentle, soothing. The calmness in his tone made her release her grip, though part of her wasn't ready to let go.

She looked up at him, her chest still tight with confusion. "It's not your fault. Why would he say that about my mom? What did he mean he 'saw something'?"

"Marcel is a Percipient," he explained. "He picks up images or memories from people. But the images aren't always true, and sometimes they get jumbled. Tonight, he just took it too far."

She shook her head. "He made me feel so uncomfortable. He wouldn't stop staring at me."

Gabriel gave her a small, apologetic smile. "Yeah, he does that. It's his way of getting to know someone, but … he comes on too strong."

"That's an understatement."

His smile widened just a little, a flicker of amusement breaking through his otherwise serious expression. "I really am sorry. We should've warned you."

Ava let out a sigh, the tension starting to unwind ever so slightly. "Thanks for bringing me back." She started to walk away, but something made her pause. She turned back, her gaze meeting his. "And Gabriel?"

"Yeah?"

"Thank you for today. I really needed it."

"Anytime." A quiet concern lingered in his eyes. He hesitated. "Do you want me to stay for a bit? Just in case you need to talk or … if you don't want to be alone."

The offer caught her off guard. She almost said no, her instinct always to push away, but something about the way he stood there, waiting patiently, made her reconsider. The idea of not being alone for once didn't seem so bad.

"Maybe for a little while."

Gabriel's expression softened, relief flickering in his eyes. "Of course."

They sat together on the bench outside the conservatory, the silence between them comfortable, as the cool night air wrapped around them like a shared secret. For the first time in a while, Ava felt like maybe she didn't have to carry everything on her own.

After a while, Gabriel returned to collect Joss and Eric, and Ava made her way into her room, her mind swirling with thoughts of Marcel's bizarre words. She was about to sit down when she noticed Peter sitting on the window bench. Her heart skipped a beat.

"Peter," she said, surprised.

"Hey." He stood and walked toward her. "Where've you been?"

"New Orleans."

He raised an eyebrow. "Oh? For what?"

"Just needed to get away."

"How did you—?"

"Gabriel."

"Oh." His tone shifted, though he tried to mask it.

An awkward silence hung between them, something that hadn't been there before. Ava felt her stomach knot, unsure why being around Peter suddenly felt different.

Stepping closer, he let out a sigh. "I'm not mad at you, Ava, and I don't regret this at all. I freaked out, and I'm sorry. I just ... never thought I'd have to protect myself against people I've known my whole life. And when they saw the necklace, they looked at me like I was some kind of freak."

"I know. That's something we've had to deal with for a long time. But you can't just leave when things get tough. I told you this wasn't going to be easy. I thought you understood that." Ava's voice softened, though she couldn't shake the frustration in her chest.

"I do understand. It's just … harder than I thought it'd be." Moving closer, he placed his hands on her shoulders. "I'm sorry for how I acted. I won't run again."

Ava searched his eyes, needing more than just his words. "This isn't over, Peter. I don't care what the Elders say. We haven't seen the end of all this, and I need to know you're fully in this with me."

He cupped her face between his hands, his gaze unwavering. "I'm with you. I love you, Ava. I'll always protect you." He kissed her, and the familiar electricity buzzed between them. She had missed him, the warmth of his lips, the way he touched her as though she were the only thing in his world.

His soft lips gently glided along the curve of her jawline, leaving a trail of tingling sensations in their wake. As his kisses continued, her heart quickened its pace, the rhythmic thud echoing in her ears. "I've missed you," Peter murmured, his voice filled with longing. He pressed her back against the door, his hands slipping to her waist as their kisses deepened, igniting a fire within their souls.

Her heart raced, her body responding to him, but then … it hit her.

Thomas's anger. His sadness.

Peter groaned, resting his forehead against hers, their breath mingling. "This sucks."

She sighed. "It really does. We need to figure out how to block it."

Peter nodded, his fingers still lightly brushing her skin. "It's exhausting. Maybe Lance and Melissa know how to deal with it."

"I'll ask. They've somehow managed to keep their emotions under wraps."

He leaned in, pressing one more gentle kiss to her lips before pulling back. "So, how was the trip?"

"It was nice. I've never been to New Orleans. The city feels so alive, like it has its own heartbeat. It was exactly what I needed … until the end." She bit her lip. She didn't want to ruin the moment, but she needed to talk about what had happened with Marcel. "Something weird happened, though."

Peter frowned. "What do you mean?"

She recounted her interaction with Marcel. "He started talking about my mom, about how she was a Cimmerian."

"A dark Enchanter?"

"Yeah," she nodded. "I … slapped him. I couldn't help it. He said he saw it in some image, but Gabriel thinks it was just confusion. Marcel's a Percipient. He reads images from people, but they're not always real or clear."

"Are you okay? You're tensing up." He reached for her hand.

"I just don't understand why he'd say something like that. My mom couldn't have been one of them. Could she?"

"No way. There's no way your mom was anything but who she said she was. Marcel probably just picked up on something random."

"That's what Gabriel said too." She sighed. "But it got under my skin."

Peter squeezed her hand. "We'll figure it out. Don't let it mess with your head." He smiled. "How about we go on a real date tomorrow? Just us. No interruptions."

"A real date?"

"Yeah," he grinned. "I'll pick you up at seven. You need a break."

Her heart warmed at the idea, but she couldn't shake the lingering heaviness. "That sounds nice."

He kissed her once more. "I'll see you tomorrow."

"You aren't staying?"

"I would love to, but I shouldn't. I'll see you tomorrow."

As he left, her chest tightened as Thomas's emotions filtered through her once again. She wanted to message him, to tell him to stop being angry, but she didn't. Instead, she closed her eyes and sank onto the bed. Despite the exhaustion, her thoughts drifted back to Marcel's words, and no matter how much she tried, she couldn't shake the feeling that something was wrong.

Who was he to call her mother a dark Enchanter? There was no way her mother would ever stand next to Corbin Havok. That was impossible.

But then her mother stood in the sunlight, her smile radiant and warm, her familiar gray eyes full of life. The memory was so vivid. Ava heard herself laughing, the sound light and carefree.

And then, everything turned cold.

The light vanished, swallowed by shadows. Her mother's smile shifted into something twisted, menacing. Her eyes lost their warmth, replaced by an eerie, emotionless gaze that sent a chill through Ava's veins.

Ava jerked awake, her heart racing as she clutched her necklace. Every time she closed her eyes, she saw the same thing. Her mother, dark, changed.

She had tried to sleep, tossing and turning, staring at the clock as the hours slipped by. But sleep was impossible. Could Marcel have been right? No. He had to be wrong. Her mother couldn't have been a Cimmerian.

Still, a nagging fear twisted in her gut, and no matter how much she tried to convince herself otherwise, it wouldn't go away. She needed answers. Something to put her mind at ease. Maybe if she researched Percipients, she'd find proof that Marcel's vision wasn't real.

Slipping out of bed, she made her way to the library. The darkness of the night still clung to the world outside, but dawn would break soon. When she entered the library, she found Link slumped over an open book, fast asleep. She gently nudged his shoulder, and he jolted awake, eyes wide with confusion.

"Sleep well?" she asked.

He rubbed his face groggily. "What time is it?"

"Almost four."

"Ugh." He yawned. "What are you doing up?"

"Can't sleep." She settled into the chair across from him. "I need to find some information about Percipients. Have you read anything about them?"

Link stretched, glancing at the scattered books around him. "Yeah, a little. Why?"

Ava hesitated. "How accurate are their visions? Can they be wrong? Or could they see something random that isn't true?"

"From what I've read, they see things related to the person or someone connected to them. But the details are pretty accurate, I think. It didn't mention them being wrong."

Her heart sank a little at his words. What if Marcel had seen something real? What if her mother had been involved with Corbin? No. She couldn't accept that. It just didn't make sense. But if she wanted to stop the nagging doubts, she needed more than assumptions.

"I had a rough night. I think ... I think we should go to the Cruciari."

Link's eyes widened in surprise. "Wait. You're serious?"

She nodded, though a knot of uncertainty twisted in her chest. "I need answers, and I don't think we're going to find them anywhere else."

"What changed your mind?"

She shook her head, not ready to share the full extent of her fears. "I just ... I can't sit around and do nothing. I need to know the truth."

He studied her for a moment. "Okay. When should we go? We'll need to prepare."

"Soon. But we need to keep this quiet. No one can find out. Not even Nicole or Peter."

Link's gaze locked with hers, his expression serious. "Agreed. We leave no trace."

"We can't rush it," Ava added. "I don't know when exactly, but it has to be the right time. We can't mess this up."

He leaned back in his chair, running a hand through his hair. "I didn't think you'd ever agree."

"Maybe you were right."

"Whatever happens, we'll face it together."

Doubt still gnawed at her. She didn't know what they would find at the Cruciari, or if the answers would bring any peace. But one thing was clear: it was a step she had to take, no matter the cost.

7

DATE NIGHT

"I look ridiculous." Ava tugged at the hem of her dress, trying in vain to make it cover more of her legs. Standing in front of the oval full-length mirror, she frowned at her reflection.

Melissa groaned in frustration and slapped Ava's hand away. "Would you stop? You look amazing, and Peter's gonna love it."

"We're going to see a movie. Why do I have to dress up like this?"

"Omigod. Didn't Thomas ever take you anywhere nice?"

"Maybe once."

"Well, it's good to see you dressed up. And stop adjusting the skirt."

"It's too short." Ava pulled at the dress again.

"That's the point." She rolled her eyes. "You've got great legs. Show them off."

"Whatever. Where are my shoes?"

Melissa grinned mischievously and held up black patent shoes with long skinny heels that looked more like weapons. "These beauties."

Ava recoiled in horror. "No way. I'm not wearing those."

"Why not?"

"Because I'll tower over Peter, and I don't wear heels. Ever."

"Well, you do tonight. Come on, he'll be here any minute." Melissa pushed the shoes toward her.

"Fine." She reluctantly slipped them on and wobbled as she stood. "If I break my ankle tonight, I'm kicking your butt."

"You'll be thanking me by the end of the night." Melissa gave a knowing smirk.

Ava gave her a skeptical look, her cheeks warming slightly. "You know Peter liked me before … all this." She gestured to the short leather dress and the dangerously high heels. The whole outfit felt like a costume.

"And now he won't be able to keep his hands off you." Melissa's sly grin grew wider.

"We're not … doing that. But how do you and Lance hide it from everyone else? The emotions, I mean."

Melissa lifted a shoulder. "I don't know. We just tune everyone else out and only focus on what we feel. I guess people ignore us now that we've been together for so long. But you and Peter? You're new, and with Thomas hating him … it might take some time to block that out."

"There has to be a way, though. We can't feel the Elders or Gabriel's coven. Just their presence. Why can't it be the same with everyone?"

"I know it's hard, but don't let it overwhelm you. Practice blocking it, like the moment you feel it creeping in. Push it away and focus on your feelings. It's all about controlling your own energy. The more you push them out, the less they'll intrude."

Ava bit her lip, trying to absorb the advice. "I'll try. But I swear, Thomas's anger is like a wave. It's so hard to ignore."

Melissa sighed, her expression softening. "Yeah, he's intense. But don't let him ruin your night with Peter. Focus on what *you* feel, not what Thomas is projecting. You and Peter deserve a good night."

She glanced at herself in the mirror again, smoothing the dress down one last time. "Okay. I just hope I survive these heels."

"You will." Melissa gave her a playful wink. "And trust me, Peter's going to be speechless."

The doorbell rang, and Ava's pulse quickened when Mrs. Rollins answered. Peter's familiar voice carried through the house, making her nerves heighten. Melissa's excitement about the evening only added to the pressure.

Ava walked out to meet Peter in the living room.

"Wow." He raised his eyebrows, his smile making her cheeks flush as Melissa nudged her from behind.

"Thanks." But she still felt exposed in the short dress. "Are you ready?"

"Yeah."

"Have a great time!" Melissa grinned widely.

Rolling her eyes, Ava led Peter outside into the humid June night. The rhythmic hum of cicadas filled the air. He opened the door for her, and as soon as she settled into the passenger seat, he shut it. Sliding into the driver's seat, Peter started the engine.

"You look great." He glanced at her as they pulled away.

"Thanks. I feel weird, though." She tugged at the dress again. "This dress is too short for a movie."

"Well, you still look great."

Ava smiled back, but the unease lingered. "Doesn't this feel … kind of weird?"

"No. Why?"

"I don't know … With everything that's happened, and now we're going on a date. It just feels strange."

"We deserve to be happy, Ava. Sometimes that means taking a break and enjoying the moment. Let's just have fun tonight."

She nodded, trying to ease the knot of tension in her stomach. "You're right."

"So, what's it like staying at the Manor?" he asked.

"It's … kinda weird. The only time I'm alone is when I'm in my room. I miss it being just me and Dad. But he's been busy with the Elders, so it gets a little lonely."

Peter smirked. "Maybe I'll sneak in through your window sometime."

She playfully hit his arm. "You could just stay. Savina has a room for you."

"Yeah, but my dad's been wanting me home more lately. I don't think he'd be cool with me disappearing all the time."

"Have you thought about how to tell him everything?"

Peter's smile faded. "Not really. Nothing's going on right now, so I figured it could wait."

Ava frowned. "I'm not so sure. I don't think it's really over. If Devon was in charge, why would he have only used a few Halflings and Enchanters to attack us? He knows how powerful Savina's coven is."

"Didn't the Elders explain it, though? Everyone who's a threat is locked away."

"Except for Trudy. I bet she ran back to Caprington to gather more followers."

"You sound paranoid."

A snide remark formed on her lips, but she swallowed it down. "I'm still going to find out who killed my mom."

"I know. And I'll help you." Peter squeezed her hand. "But let's take tonight for ourselves, okay? We deserve a little peace."

Ava turned to the window, thinking about the disturbing dreams she'd been having, the dark visions of her mother. She could feel her eyes sting with unshed tears. Peter must have sensed it because he gently tipped her chin up.

"She wasn't a Cimmerian, Ava. Your mom was a part of this coven. She was with your father. Don't let what Marcel said get to you."

She nodded, but her heart still felt heavy with doubt. "Percipients aren't usually wrong."

"Usually. But it's not absolute. We'll figure it out. I promise."

She nodded, and Peter kissed her.

Dinner felt like a step back in time, to before everything changed. They laughed and talked, and for the first time in a long while, Ava felt something close to normal. It was so different from the strained, silent dinners she had with Thomas. Being with Peter was easy.

But when they arrived at the movie theater, the peaceful moment shattered.

"You think you're welcome here?" a voice snapped from behind. Ava turned and found herself face to face with Trent and Drew, their eyes full of contempt.

"What do you want?" she asked, trying to keep her voice steady.

Trent sneered. "For you two freaks to get the hell out of here."

Her blood boiled. She was sick of being treated like a criminal. "We have as much right to be here as you."

"No, you don't," he hissed, stepping closer, his fists clenched. "I suggest you leave before we make you."

Ava squared her shoulders, refusing to back down. "We got hurt by those bombs, too. Stop blaming us."

His eyes darkened with rage. "You're just as guilty as Link and Nicole. You're no better. And don't use your dead mom as an excuse for what you've done."

Ava clenched her fists, heat rising from her necklace beneath her dress. "Say whatever you need to justify your hate, but we're not leaving."

An icy liquid splashed over her, drenching her dress and sending a chill down her spine. She gasped, realizing Trent had dumped his drink on her. Anger surged, and she drew back her hand, ready to strike, but Peter's grip closed around her wrist, stopping her mid-motion.

"Come on," he said, his voice tight. "Let's go."

Trent and Drew laughed as Peter led her away. Ava wanted to unleash her power, to show them she wasn't weak. But Peter's grip kept her grounded.

Outside, she kicked off the heels, too angry to care. "Why are you always protecting them?" she demanded, storming ahead.

"Ava, we've talked about this. You can't hurt them."

"But they can hurt me?"

He grabbed her arm, pulling her back. "I didn't say that. But you have to let it go. Don't give them the satisfaction of seeing you lose control."

"You just stood there while they poured Coke all over me!"

"I'm scared of what I might do, okay?" he shouted, surprising her. "I don't want to hurt anyone, and I don't want you to either. The Elders didn't make me an Enchanter so I could terrorize humans. You need to learn restraint, too."

Ava's shoulders slumped, and her anger melted into exhaustion. Tears pricked her eyes. Peter took her hand, his touch soft now.

"Come on," he said gently. "I have a better idea than a movie."

Ava glanced at him, unsure of where he was taking her. But when they arrived at the cabin, she began to relax.

The waterfall's soothing sounds and the cool night air felt like a balm on her skin. Peter stripped off his shirt, and Ava couldn't help but admire the way his muscles rippled in the moonlight. He caught her staring and grinned.

"Ready?" He held out his hand.

Ava smiled. "Melissa's not gonna like this."

"She'll get over it. Besides, you need a bath."

Gasping, she playfully pushed him. As he snatched her wrist, the sound of their bodies hitting the water echoed through the air. She pulled him closer, their bodies entwined in a dance of desire, and she breathed into his mouth.

When they surfaced, Peter's lips met hers with a fervor that set her senses ablaze. He held her close while her legs wrapped tightly around his waist. He gently pressed her back against the rugged surface of a boulder, and she felt the coolness against her warm skin.

Their gazes locked, and she could see the intense yearning in his eyes.

Whispering along her jaw, he declared, "I love you, Ava. They won't hurt you. I will protect you." The words, like a soothing melody, echoed in her ears.

For a fleeting moment, she wanted to tell him about the Cruciari but didn't. She wasn't sure why. Maybe she feared him telling her what a bad idea it was. But would he protect her? Even from the Ephemerals?

8

NOTHING LEFT TO SAY

Wind billowed around Ava, whipping her hair into a stormy frenzy, as the electricity coursed through her veins, throbbing with power. She stood on the hill, watching the woman unpin bed sheets from the line, sloppily rolling them into a basket. A small smile curled on Ava's lips as her heart raced with the idea of revenge. One lightning strike. That's all it would take.

She raised her arms to the sky, summoning the storm, but before she could strike, cold hands grasped her wrists, holding her firm. White, veiny hands. Comforting in their power, pulling her toward an irresistible darkness.

Ava gasped awake, her pulse racing, her breath short and ragged. The familiar knot of fear twisted in her stomach as sweat dripped down her forehead. She clutched her necklace, the cool metal grounding her in the sweltering room, and focused on cooling herself with her power.

The same dream. Every night for a month. Ever since Marcel.

Wiping her damp face, she tried to shake the eerie feeling clinging to her skin. Marcel's words haunted her. Could her mother have really been a Cimmerian? A wave of nausea washed over her as the thought sank in.

Her phone buzzed beside her, snapping her out of the spiral. She grabbed it, finding texts from Gabriel and Melissa.

Gabriel: *You okay?*

Melissa: *hey you alright?*

Her fingers hovered over Gabriel's text, tempted to answer him, but her phone buzzed again. Peter's name flashed across the screen.

"Are you okay?" he asked.

She took a steady breath. "Yeah. Just another dream."

"The same one?" Concern filled his voice, but it was a concern she'd heard before, one that always stopped short of going deeper.

"Yeah."

"What do you think is bringing them on. You've been thinking about your mom a lot?"

Not like I have a choice after what Marcel said. "A little. But not like this."

"Maybe it's just stress."

Ava rolled her eyes. *Stress.* That seemed to be Peter's explanation for everything. Ever since their date night, he'd gone back to barely being around. It felt like he was slipping further away. He wasn't even practicing his powers. And now, with her and Link planning to sneak off to the Cruciari, Peter felt more like a distant worry than a partner.

"Want me to come over?" he asked, but she knew he didn't want to.

"No," she said, trying to sound firm. "You've got your camping trip with Seth. I'll be fine." She didn't want Peter involved, not when she was about to dive into something dangerous with Link.

"I can cancel. Seth would understand," he offered, but there was something half-hearted about it.

"No. It'll be good for you guys. You need this."

"I'll miss you."

"You too." She ended the call, staring at her phone for a long moment, a knot of unease tightening in her chest.

Glancing back at the texts from Gabriel and Melissa, she quickly typed a response to both: *Yeah, just a bad dream.*

Tossing the phone aside, she lay back down, staring at the ceiling as her thoughts raced. *Answers. I need answers.*

When the first rays of sunlight peeked through her window, she forced herself to get out of bed. She dressed quickly, pulling on a pair of jeans and a T-shirt, trying to keep her mind focused. The Cruciari held more than just secrets. It held her mother's killer. She was sure of it.

And today, she was going to find out the truth.

Ava hoped to find Link without running into anyone else as she made her way to the library. The last thing she needed was someone stopping her. As soon as she entered the library, she froze.

Jeremy was there, sitting with Gabriel, Link, and Nicole.

"Ava!" Jeremy grinned, standing to hug her.

She hugged him back tightly. "I didn't know you were coming."

"I snuck out before Gillian woke up. It's good to see you. I've missed you."

"I've missed you too," she said. "But I can't stay long. Link and I have plans."

"Oh. What are you two up to?"

"Yes, please tell us what your plans are," Gabriel said in an all-too-knowing voice.

Her stomach dropped. She glanced at Link, whose guilty expression said everything. *He told.*

Shaking her head, she stormed out of the room, heading toward the conservatory. As soon as she made it outside, she kept walking.

"Ava, wait!" Link called after her, but she ignored him, her pace quickening. He caught up, grabbing her arm. "Ava, listen. I didn't mean to—"

She whirled around. "Why did you tell him, Link?"

"Gabriel guessed. He wanted to know why we've been acting so secretive."

"And you couldn't just lie? This was supposed to be between us!"

Gabriel approached, his tone calm but firm. "Ava—"

"I don't need a lecture right now," she said.

"I'm not here to stop you. I'm here to help. You don't understand how dangerous the Cruciari is."

She glared at him, crossing her arms defensively. "I know how dangerous it is. Believe me, I didn't want to go. But I need to know the truth about my mom. Besides, why do you even care? The Elders say everything is fine."

His expression softened, but his eyes remained sharp. "Because I've been there. I know what happens when things go wrong. And if you lose control, they will throw you in a cell without hesitation."

She felt the tension building, her pulse quickening with anger and fear. "I don't care."

"Well, I do," he snapped, his voice more intense than usual. "Once you're inside, there isn't a guarantee that you'll get out."

Ava clenched her fists, trying to control the storm of emotions rising within her. Gabriel's words struck a chord she didn't want to acknowledge, but deep down, she knew he wasn't wrong. She turned away, staring at the tree line, her voice quieter but still laced with urgency. "I *need* to go, Gabriel. Link and I both do. Please." She back at him, pleading. She rarely asked for help, but this was different. This was her only chance to find out the truth about her mother.

Gabriel met her gaze, conflict flickering in his eyes. His hesitation only deepened her desperation.

"Please," she repeated softly. "I can't do this without you."

He sighed, running a hand through his hair. "Fine. I'll take you. But you *have* to follow my lead. Exactly."

Jeremy and Nicole exchanged concerned looks behind them but remained silent, adding to Ava's sense of isolation. She knew they cared, but it wasn't their burden to carry. It was hers.

The five of them began walking away from the Manor, the summer heat pressing down on them like a heavy blanket. Though the sun beat relentlessly on her skin, it did nothing to chase away the chill creeping up Ava's spine, winding its way through her body like an ominous warning.

"Why can't you teleport us?" Link asked Gabriel.

"I will once we get out of eyeshot of the Manor," he replied.

"Would they ask why you teleported?" Ava asked.

"Probably."

"Why? Aren't you free to go wherever you want?"

Gabriel hesitated for a moment before answering, "Yes, but Aaron worries."

She halted, causing the others to stop and look back at her. The knot of unease in her chest tightened. "Worries? About what? Is there something you aren't telling us?" Her tone was sharper than she intended, but Gabriel's vague responses only heightened her suspicion.

His eyes swept over the group before settling on Ava. "Aaron has his reasons. And I'm not keen on letting him know we're doing this."

Ava crossed her arms. "That's not an answer."

His voice softened. "It's the only one I can give right now." There was something in his tone, something almost pleading, urging her to trust him.

Even though she was frustrated, she didn't push him further. The look in his eyes were a mixture of caution and something unspoken. Whatever Gabriel was keeping from them, it was clear now wasn't the time to dig deeper. She'd have to figure it out later.

They resumed walking, but Ava's mind buzzed with questions.

Jeremy fell into step with her. "How are you and Peter?"

"We're good, but he's been struggling with everything. And it doesn't help that the Ephemerals keep terrorizing us."

"I'm sorry."

She sighed. "Peter's still scared."

"Of course, he is. His entire life has changed. But that doesn't mean his feelings for you have."

"What have you and Gillian been doing this summer?"

"Not much of anything really. We hang out at Melissa's like usual."

A wave of sadness hit Ava. "I haven't seen any of you all summer, except Melissa. Now … it feels like I've been forgotten." None of them even knew she was going to the Cruciari. Or why for that matter. Or that she'd been having nightmares for an entire month. Or why she needed information about Percipients. Had she really burned all the bridges?

"It's not like that. Gillian's been hogging Melissa and me, and Thomas has been hanging out with Lance. I think some of us just assumed you were happy because you have Peter now."

"Of course, I'm happy with Peter. But that doesn't mean I don't miss you. I feel so disconnected from everyone. Peter is trying to adjust and help Seth out. Melissa's busy with Lance and Gillian."

Jeremy placed a reassuring hand on her arm. "I get it. We've all been caught up in our own things, but it's not because we don't care about you."

"Thanks, Jer. I've really missed you this summer."

"I've missed you too."

Once they were out of sight of the Manor, Gabriel turned to face them. He didn't even try to hide the fear in his eyes, which only made Ava more unsettled. A cold knot of doubt formed in her stomach. *Why am I doing this?*

"Before we go," Gabriel said, "you need to understand something. Your powers will not work inside the prison or anywhere near it."

Ava's heart skipped a beat. She exchanged a worried look with Link, Jeremy, and Nicole. Her mind raced. No powers. She wasn't sure how to process being completely vulnerable.

"The prison is surrounded by water," he continued, "and the area is enchanted to suppress any elemental powers. We'll have to take a boat across. The only way in or out. "The guards won't tolerate any missteps. We'll be under constant surveillance, and if they even *think* something's off, they'll lock you up without a second thought. There's no arguing, no pleading."

Ava swallowed hard, her pulse quickening as Gabriel's warnings sank in.

He took a breath, his gaze shifting between them. "And one more thing. Once we get inside, do not, under any circumstances, speak to any of the other prisoners. They're not just locked up. Most of them are being tortured, broken. They've lost their minds. I'll be surprised if Xavier can tell you anything useful."

Her stomach churned with fear, and for a brief moment, she wondered if it was a mistake. Tortured. Broken. She hadn't imagined it would be this bad. Xavier might not even be capable of answering their questions.

"And if anything goes wrong," he said, his voice dropping to a near whisper, "you won't get out."

The silence that followed was heavy, each of them digesting the gravity of what they were about to do. Gabriel's words heightened her doubts.

But she had to know. She *needed* to know the truth about her mother, even if it meant walking into the heart of darkness.

"Do you all understand?" Gabriel asked.

Everyone responded with a quiet "yes," their voices tinged with unease. Gabriel's gaze swept over them before he nodded. He instructed them to touch him.

Link, Jeremy, and Nicole reached out first, their hands lightly gripping his arm. Ava hesitated, her heart racing as she stared at his outstretched hand. This was it. There would be no turning back once they crossed the threshold into the Cruciari.

Finally, she took a deep breath and placed her hand in his. Gabriel's warmth was unexpectedly comforting, grounding her just enough to calm the storm swirling inside her. She wasn't alone in this, at least not entirely.

"Hold on," Gabriel said quietly.

In an instant, the world around them shifted, and the suffocating weight of what was to come settled even deeper in her chest.

When they arrived, a fierce gust of wind assaulted her face, stinging like a whip. They stood atop a towering embankment, their gaze fixed upon the small rowboats tethered to the docks. Several vigilant guards kept watch, their eyes scanning the surroundings. Across the tumultuous sea, the Cruciari emerged, a formidable stone fortress encircled by menacing jagged rocks. The relentless ocean waves relentlessly pounded the shore, as if nature itself sought to dismantle the place. Overhead, seagulls soared in circles, their piercing cries echoing through the somber, overcast sky. Ava's hair thrashed about wildly, while the once soothing scent of the salty sea air now carried an unsettling premonition.

Beside her, Link seethed as he glared at the prison. "It would be so easy to bomb it right now," he muttered through clenched teeth.

"Your powers don't work here," Gabriel reminded him.

Link scoffed. "How did the Cimmerians escape before? Did they pull a Monte Cristo and come up with some elaborate plan to escape or something?"

Gabriel chuckled slightly. "Maybe."

"I wish we had a morphing ability," Nicole said, and Ava winced at the memory of the last morphing Enchanter they'd encountered. Thomas had burned him alive while he was still in her father's form. The image would forever be seared into her mind.

"Let's just get this over with." Ava moved forward.

They made their way down the incline, where a burly guard with an eye patch watched them warily. "What's your business?" he asked in a gruff voice.

"We're here to see Xavier Holstone," Gabriel said, his usual calmness edged with tension.

The guard smirked. "He sure is a popular one."

"Who else has been here to see him?" Ava asked before she could stop herself.

"I'm not allowed to share that information."

Ava opened her mouth to argue, but Gabriel shot her a warning look. "That's fine. We're ready to go," he said.

The guard led them to a small boat, and Gabriel leaned down to whisper to Ava as they boarded, "Don't ask questions."

"Why?"

"I'll explain later," he murmured.

The boat rocked violently as they set off across the choppy waters. Ava gripped the sides, trying to steady herself. Nicole wasn't as lucky. She leaned over the edge and retched into the sea. The guard laughed.

As the waves grew more violent, Ava exchanged a worried glance with Link. "Isn't it too early for hurricane season?" She eyed the looming clouds.

The guard grunted. "It's like this all the time. The sea's designed to drown people."

A cold chill ran down her spine. Drowning. The one thing she always believed she could survive. But not there.

The boat finally reached the Cruciari, its towering walls looming like the skeletal remains of some ancient beast. As Ava climbed out, her feet landed on slick stone steps that led up to the fortress. Cold, oppressive, and foreboding, the Cruciari felt more like a crypt than a prison. The jagged, narrow windows allowed little light inside, casting long shadows that seemed to cling to the stone, suffocating the space in eternal darkness.

Ava's skin prickled with unease as they entered the fortress, the thick iron doors groaning as they opened to admit them. Their footsteps echoed in the cold, damp corridors, the air thick with a staleness that seemed centuries old. The scent of mildew and rot clung to everything, and the walls, slick with moisture, glistened under the flickering torchlight.

As they descended deeper into the Cruciari's belly, the air turned frigid, causing them to shiver uncontrollably. Cells lined the stone walls like forgotten tombs. Inside, the prisoners—Cimmerians and others alike—were pale, gaunt, their faces etched with years of imprisonment. Their eyes were hollow, lost to whatever horrors they had endured. Some whimpered softly, their bodies huddled against the walls like beaten animals. Others stared out with an unsettling, animalistic curiosity, tracking Ava and the others as they passed.

Ava's gaze locked onto one prisoner, a blond woman who met her eyes with an intensity that made her shiver. For a fleeting moment, there was something there. Recognition? She couldn't be sure.

"This is Xavier." The guard stopped before a dark, damp cell. "You have five minutes."

Ava's breath caught in her throat as she looked into the shadows. Xavier Holstone, once a charismatic and commanding figure, was now nothing more than a broken shell. He sat hunched in a dark corner, his face marred by deep gashes that crisscrossed his skin like a twisted map of suffering. His eyes, once sharp and cunning, were dull, clouded with madness, though a faint flicker of something sinister remained. A long, scraggly beard hung from his chin, tangled and filthy. His clothes were torn and stained, hanging loosely on his emaciated frame. Ava barely recognized the man who had once terrorized them.

"Well, isn't karma a bitch?" Link glared at him.

Xavier lifted his head slowly, squinting at them through the gloom. His lips curled into a faint, deranged smile. "You look familiar," he rasped, his voice raw from disuse. His eyes focused on Ava, and something flickered like mocking recognition.

"You know exactly who I am," she said coldly. "You told us this wasn't over. But from where I'm standing, it looks like it is."

Xavier's lips twitched into a sickly grin.

"Why us, Xavier?" Link demanded. "Why did you choose us?"

As he leaned forward, Xavier's gaunt face caught the dim light, and his expression twisted into a grotesque parody of amusement. "I don't know what you're talking about," he said, his voice dripping with mockery.

"Don't lie to us!" Link clenched his fists.

Xavier's laughter was low and ragged, more of a wheeze than a sound of true delight. His crazed eyes narrowed. "You really think you're special, don't you?"

Link's jaw tightened, and he turned to the guard. "How do you get information out of them?"

The guard crossed his arms, unfazed by the rising tension. "We have our ways. But the more we torture, the more they forget who they are. It's a delicate balance."

"I need answers," Link said. "Torture him. I thought that's how we'd get what we need."

The guard squared his shoulders and smirked. "If you've got a problem with the way we do things here, take it up with the Elders."

Link charged toward the guard in fury, but Jeremy held him back just in time. The prisoners in the nearby cells burst into hysterical, deranged laughter, their cackles echoing down the corridor like the cries of the damned.

"Take him outside," Gabriel said firmly to Jeremy and Nicole, his voice calm but commanding.

"Come on." Nicole tugged at Link's arm, guiding him away from Xavier's cell.

Ava remained behind for a moment, her eyes still locked on Xavier. He met her gaze, that faint, unsettling smile still lingering on his cracked lips. Xavier was broken, but there was something in his eyes that made her skin crawl, something that whispered this wasn't over.

"Tell me who killed my mother," she demanded, her voice cold and steady.

He grinned, his lips curling with dark amusement. "I'm not the one you should be asking." His eyes flicked past her.

She followed his gaze to the blond woman in the adjacent cell. Her hands gripped the bars as a twisted, sadistic grin spread across her face.

"It was me," the woman said, her voice dripping with malice. "I killed your mother."

Ava's breath hitched. "What did you say?" She crossed toward the woman, her body tense. Gabriel moved beside her, already on edge.

The woman rolled her head lazily, her matted blond hair falling in dirty clumps around her face. Her teeth were yellowed, but her eyes glimmered with wicked delight. "I watched her die," she purred slowly, savoring each word. "She betrayed us, and it was such sweet justice."

"Betrayed you how?" Ava's voice shook, anger boiling just beneath the surface.

The woman's grin widened, her eyes gleaming with cruel satisfaction. "I took pleasure in her death. And I watched you cry over her like the pathetic little girl you were."

With a cry of rage, Ava lunged at the bars, her body trembling with fury. Gabriel seized her and pulled her back, his grip firm but careful.

"No!" Ava struggled against Gabriel's hold as the woman laughed cruelly. "I want her dead!"

As the guard advanced, his narrowed eyes sent a silent message of caution. He pressed his fingers to the woman's forehead. She screamed, clutching her head in agony before collapsing to the ground, whimpering as the laughter died on her lips.

"You need to leave," the guard said. "Now."

Ava's heart pounded as she stared at the woman, now lying motionless on the cold stone floor. "She killed my mother. She deserves to die," she said, her voice shaking with anger and pain.

"That's not up to you," the guard said.

"Who is she?" Ava demanded.

"Leave," the guard repeated.

"I want to talk to the warden," she insisted.

The guard chuckled darkly, his laugh filled with disdain. "You naïve little girl. You think you can walk in here and demand an audience with the warden? Only the Elders speak to him. Now, I suggest you leave before I make you."

Gabriel stepped in again, his hand still gripping Ava's arm gently but firmly. "Come on, Ava. We're done here." He tried to pull her away, but she stopped just short of the guard.

"You don't have everyone locked up. There are others still out there who won't stop until they kill us all. Are you even looking for them?"

"It has ended," he growled. "Devon was killed. You were there. Don't you remember?"

Ava froze, her pulse quickening. How did the guard know she had been there? Everyone knew the Elementals had been involved in Devon's death, but how did he know *her* specifically? "How do you know I was there?" she whispered.

"Leave. Now." He motioned for them to climb the stairs.

She shook her head. "How do you know I was there?"

The guard's eyes darkened, his expression turning menacing. He seized Ava's arm with a crushing grip. "You need to learn when to keep your mouth shut," he snarled, yanking her closer. "One wrong move, and I'll throw you in a cell right next to them."

Ava's heart slammed against her ribs as she struggled in his grasp. "Let me go!"

The guard's grip tightened.

Gabriel moved instantly, stepping between them, his presence commanding. "That's enough," he said, his voice low and dangerous. He gripped the guard's wrist with a quiet strength that made the guard hesitate.

The guard glared at Gabriel but didn't release Ava, his grip lingering in a show of defiance.

"Let. Her. Go," Gabriel repeated, his tone now sharp, a deadly calm settling over him.

With a final glare, the guard released Ava, shoving her away with a grunt. "Get out of here. All of you," he growled. "Before I change my mind."

She stumbled backward into Gabriel's waiting arm, her pulse still racing as the guard's dark eyes bore into hers, a silent promise of what could have happened.

Gabriel's hand on her shoulder was firm but reassuring. "We're leaving. Now."

Ava's mind whirled with adrenaline, her anger still simmering beneath the surface, but she didn't resist as Gabriel pulled her toward the stairs. The guard's cold, unwavering stare followed her, a chilling reminder of the thin line she had just crossed.

How did the guard know who she was? He had recognized her, but how? Was he helping some of the Cimmerians stay hidden? Had he helped Devon escape before? And what about the blonde woman, the one who had so cruelly claimed to have killed her mother? The woman's sadistic grin and venomous words echoed in Ava's mind. She had found her mother's killer but had been powerless to do anything about it. What kind of justice was that place serving?

The journey back across the turbulent waters was silent, except for the relentless pounding of the waves. Gabriel's eyes never left Ava, as if he were holding back a lecture, waiting for the right moment to unleash it. But he didn't say a word. The silence in the boat was suffocating.

The tension in the air was thick as they emerged from the Cruciari. Gabriel wasted no time once they had teleported back, his face tight with anger. He turned sharply toward Ava and Link, his eyes blazing.

"What the hell were you thinking?" he snapped. His calm, measured demeanor had cracked, revealing the raw frustration beneath.

Ava flinched at the intensity in his tone, but her resolve only grew stronger. "She killed my mother, Gabriel. I wasn't going to stand there and let her get away with it."

"And what exactly were you planning to do? Attack her? In the middle of the most dangerous prison we've ever set foot in?" His voice was sharp, cutting through the air like a blade. "Do you even realize how close you came to being thrown in a cell yourself?"

"I had to know the truth. You don't understand—"

"I *do* understand, Ava!" He moved closer, his eyes boring into hers. "But charging at a prisoner in a place like that? That's not bravery. That's reckless! And you, Link," he turned, fixing Link with a glare, "you're just as guilty. You were supposed to keep a level head, and instead, you were ready to fight the guards. Do you know how many ways this could have gone wrong?"

Link shifted uncomfortably under Gabriel's intense gaze. "I know, but I couldn't just stand there and let him treat us like that. We deserve answers, and I thought—"

"You thought wrong," Gabriel said. "We're not in a position to make demands, and you nearly threw away your one chance to find out anything." He ran a hand through his hair, exhaling sharply as he tried to reign in his anger. "You think the Elders would've come to rescue you if things went south? They would've left you to rot in that prison, and I wouldn't have been able to stop them."

Ava's anger faltered at his words. She hadn't thought about the full consequences. She hadn't considered how easily everything could've spiraled out of control.

Gabriel turned back to her, his voice softening, but the frustration was still there. "I understand why you're angry. But you can't let that anger drive you to make reckless decisions. It almost cost you everything today."

She swallowed hard, letting his words sink in. She stole a quick glance at Link, but he averted his eyes, leaving her overwhelmed with guilt. Gabriel was right. They had both let their emotions take over. She had let her rage blind her to the danger.

"I'm sorry," she muttered. "I didn't mean for it to get so out of hand."

Link sighed, rubbing the back of his neck. "Yeah, me too. I just … I thought we could handle it."

"I don't want apologies. I want you to understand how serious this is. We're dealing with people who won't hesitate to break us if they get the chance. Next time, we might not be so lucky."

Ava nodded, her anger now replaced by a heavy sense of regret. "I get it."

Link nodded as well, his face serious.

Gabriel's shoulders relaxed slightly, but the worry in his eyes lingered. "Good. Because if either of you pulls a stunt like that again, there might not *be* a next time." He took a deep breath, glancing between them, his voice gentler now.

"We're in this together. But if we're going to survive, we have to be smart. No more reckless moves."

Ava and Link exchanged a look before nodding in unison.

Suddenly, the warmth of their necklaces flared to life. A flood of emotions—panic, pain, and anger—surged through the bonds of Ava and Jeremy's Aureole, washing over them like a tidal wave.

Ava's hand flew to her necklace. She met Jeremy's worried eyes.

Something was happening. Something terrible.

9

RETALIATION

The night was thick with tension, a heaviness in the air that made Ava's chest tighten as they materialized in the woods. The second they arrived, she felt a surge of rage, terror, and unbearable grief coursing through her. Thomas's pain hit her hardest, but it was Melissa and Gillian's fear that lingered in the pit of her stomach.

The orange glow of flames lit up the sky ahead, black smoke billowing upward like dark tendrils. Her heart plummeted.

"Oh no…" Ava broke into a run, the others right behind her.

She tore through the trees, branches whipping at her face, until she burst into the open. Flames swallowed Thomas's house, the heat scorching even from this distance. Embers crackled in the air. Black smoke curled around the sky, choking it with ash.

Ava's breath caught in her throat as she scanned the scene. Gillian screamed and darted toward Jeremy, throwing herself into his arms. Melissa stood with Lance, both covered in soot, their faces streaked with ash and shock. The sight of them, shaken but alive, should have been a relief, but the sight of Thomas, clutching his mother, sent a chill through her.

Where's his father? The question gnawed at Ava, but deep down, she already knew the answer.

"Is everyone okay?" Gabriel's asked as his eyes darted over the wreckage.

Melissa nodded, tears streaming down her cheeks. "Thomas's father…" Her voice cracked. She buried her face in Lance's chest. "We didn't think we'd get out."

Ava's throat tightened as she hugged Melissa and Lance, but the numbness in her chest refused to leave. She turned her gaze to Thomas, standing like a statue, gripping his sobbing mother as if holding onto her was the only thing keeping him anchored.

"I'm sorry, Thomas," she said, unsure if her words would reach him through his grief.

He met her gaze for a fleeting moment, his eyes brimming with tears and raw, uncontainable rage. She knew that look too well. The same fury had consumed her when her own home burned.

"What happened?" Gabriel asked.

"We were watching a movie," Lance said, his voice hollow. "then there was an explosion in the back. It all happened so fast. The house—it went up in flames in seconds."

The wail of sirens broke the uneasy quiet, followed by the flashing lights of fire trucks and police cars. First responders surged forward, pushing the crowd back as firefighters worked to control the blaze.

Ava's phone buzzed, but she ignored it, too numb to care. Instead, she crossed to Gillian, who stood with Jeremy. "Are you okay?" she asked, but Gillian's icy glare stopped her cold.

"She's fine," Jeremy said, his tone soothing, but the sting of rejection lingered.

Ava felt more like an outsider with each passing moment. She swallowed hard and turned toward Thomas.

Savina and Aaron had arrived, speaking to Thomas and his mother. Thomas's shoulders were hunched, his face streaked with soot and tears, as he held his mother close.

"He's gone," Mrs. Arrington kept repeating, her sobs filling the air.

Ava's heart twisted painfully for them, for the loss they couldn't even process yet. Thomas and his father had never seen eye to eye, but now … there would be no more chances. Even without their shared bond through the necklaces, she could feel his fury and guilt and pain reverberating in her bones.

It felt like hours had passed since they first arrived at the burning house, and after Thomas and his mom answered questions from the police, declined ambulatory services, Savina turned to Gabriel. "Take them back to the Manor. They shouldn't stay here."

Thomas barely reacted. His mother sobbed against his chest.

"I'll be back for you," Gabriel whispered to Ava, his eyes lingering on her as if he was trying to say something else. Sympathy, maybe, but there was something more, something unresolved between them.

"I'm fine," she said, her voice barely steady.

"Be careful."

Gabriel disappeared with Thomas and his mother, Savina, and Aaron, leaving Ava's thoughts spinning. Was this part of Xavier's warning? Had they misjudged the true threat?

Her eyes drifted back to the towering flames. Who else was out there, pulling strings?

The sound of laughing, cruel and out of place, snapped her attention to the edge of the crowd. Trent, Jonah, and Drew stood there, high fiving each other like they'd just won a game.

Burning with anger, she stormed over with Melissa, Lance, Gillian, and Jeremy close behind.

"What could you possibly be celebrating?" Gillian wiped her tear-streaked face.

Trent scoffed, his lip curling into a sneer. "This is karma, Piggy. What goes around comes around."

"We didn't bomb the school!" Gillian shouted, her fists trembling as Jeremy held her back. Her eyes flashed with barely controlled fury, her breath coming in ragged bursts.

"Did you do this?" Ava asked.

Jonah's laugh sliced through the tension, sharp and cruel. It was a nasty sound that echoed in the pit of Ava's stomach. "Why would we need to? You witches are the ones playing with fire. Maybe your spells backfired."

The air crackled with sudden movement. Trent's fist shot out, colliding with Drew's face with a sickening thud. Drew's nose crunched under the impact, blood spraying in a bright arc. Time seemed to slow for a moment as the blow set off a chaotic chain reaction. Jonah lunged at Trent, fists swinging wildly, and within seconds, the three were tangled in a vicious brawl, fists flying, grunts of pain mixing with the dull thuds of bodies hitting the ground.

Ava realized with a start that it was *Gillian's* doing. Her powers pushed the boys to violence, the energy radiating off her like static in the air. The metallic scent of blood hung thick around them as punches landed with brutal precision. Drew's face was smeared with crimson, blood oozing from his broken nose. Jonah's lip split open as Trent threw another punch, spraying blood across the ground like rain hitting pavement.

Flashing red and blue lights danced across their faces, casting jagged shadows in the chaotic scene. The piercing wail of sirens grew louder, the flashing lights of ambulances and police cars bathing the area in pulses of harsh, electric light. The sound of engines idling, the clamor of people shouting orders—all of it pressed in, adding to the suffocating tension.

"G, stop." Jeremy pulled her back. "Let it go."

"They almost killed us!" Gillian cried, her voice raw. Tears streamed down her face, and her fists were still clenched.

Jeremy tugged hard, and with one final gasp, Gillian released her hold on them. The boys froze mid-swing, stumbling backward, confusion clouding their eyes as they blinked in disorientation, blood dripping from their faces. The fight drained out of them as quickly as it had started.

Trent wiped the blood from his split lip, glaring at Ava and her group with wild eyes, his breath ragged. "What the hell are you trying to do to us?" His voice shook with anger and fear.

Ava met his gaze. "You should probably leave us alone, or this won't end well for you."

Lance took her hand. "Get in the car. Don't antagonize them."

"Ava should drown them all," Gillian muttered bitterly under her breath.

Heat rose inside Ava's chest. "Why should we protect them?"

As they walked away, Trent threw one last look over his shoulder. "This isn't over. No one in this town cares if something happens to you."

She let Lance steer her toward the car, knowing he was right. And Gabriel's warning about being reckless hit her hard. How much longer could they keep pretending to protect people who hated them? How much longer could they endure it?

Reluctantly, she slid into the back seat, the image of Thomas's house burning to the ground flashing in her mind. The charred remains, the thick black smoke choking the air, and Thomas's devastated face was still so fresh, so raw. *He's lost everything.* Her chest tightened. She could feel his confusion, his anger, his disbelief that something so terrible could happen to him, to his family.

She slammed the door hard enough to rattle the windows. "Are we seriously just going to let them get away with this?" The frustration in her voice barely concealed the guilt gnawing at her. *We didn't protect him. We couldn't stop it.*

Melissa sat in the passenger seat, lit a cigarette, and took a long, deliberate drag. "We don't even know if it was them." She exhaled smoke as if trying to clear the tension.

"They just *happened* to be in the neighborhood at the exact moment Thomas's house burned to the ground? That's a pretty big coincidence." Her phone buzzed in her pocket for the fourth time, but she ignored the call. It wasn't important. Not right now.

"Maybe the Cimmerians made them."

The suggestion hit Ava like a punch to the gut. "What? Why would you even say that?"

"I don't know," Melissa said. "I just … do."

"That's not an answer, Mel." Ava's voice sharpened as she leaned forward between the seats. "Why would you think the Cimmerians are behind this?"

She flicked the cigarette out the window, her lips pressed into a thin line. The silence between them thickened, heavy and uncomfortable.

"What aren't you telling me?" Ava asked, her suspicion growing. "Is something going on?"

Lance sighed heavily and shot Melissa a warning look. "Nothing's going on, Ava. Drop it."

Her pulse raced. She could feel something *off* between them. The secrecy, the hesitation. It felt wrong. "No, there's something. You're both acting weird. Melissa, why did you say that?"

"Just forget I said anything, okay?"

Ava was stunned by the sharpness in her tone. Since when did Melissa keep things from her? They used to tell each other everything. Ava stared out the window as the flashing lights from the police and ambulances faded in the distance, her heart sinking deeper. *Why isn't she telling me?*

Her thoughts returned to Thomas. She'd felt his pain, seen the loss in his eyes. *How many more people are we going to lose before this is over?*

But now, sitting in that car, surrounded by people who were supposed to be her closest allies, the divide between them felt wider than ever. Something was happening, something that none of them were willing to share. And as the realization sank in, a cold wave of doubt washed over her.

She wasn't sure if she could trust them anymore.

10

THERE GOES THE NEIGHBORHOOD

Ava finally sent Peter a quick message, assuring him of her safety and promising to explain everything later. She tried not to dwell on the fact that Peter hadn't even offered to come home.

Melissa's strange comment about the Cimmerians, coupled with the tense way she and Lance had acted, still rattled her. Maybe she was paranoid, but she couldn't shake the lump in the back of her throat, making her feel like she was about to unravel.

She thought about telling them about her recurring dreams or Marcel's chilling vision, but it wasn't the right time. She didn't want to talk about her mother. Not yet. Not like this. Not when her friends barely escaped a fire that claimed Thomas's dad.

The library seemed like a good escape, but the low hum of chatter in the air told her it was far from quiet. The room was crowded, and Ava wasn't in the mood to be around people. Why did everyone have to congregate in the library?

She hurried past the aisles, searching for solitude at the very back. Maybe she should have gone to the waterfall instead.

But she sank to her knees in the quiet corner and gave in to the tears she had been holding back all night. *Mr. Arrington was dead.* How many more lives were they going to lose? And how could she have stooped so low, threatening to kill an Ephemeral? Especially after Gabriel's warning. She had always been better than that. What was happening to her?

Ever since that night with Marcel, she had felt a shift inside herself. She had never been the type to threaten a mortal, yet she had done it without a second thought.

"Are you all right?" a familiar voice asked.

She looked up, blinking through her tears. Gabriel stood a few feet away, eyebrows lifted in sympathy, his crystal blue eyes locking onto hers.

She wiped her cheeks, trying to regain composure. "Yeah," she lied.

He nodded slowly, as if giving her space to retreat if she wanted it. "Sorry. I didn't mean to bother you."

"It's okay."

Gabriel turned to leave, but something inside Ava twisted. She didn't want him to go. "Gabe?"

He paused and turned back toward her. "Yeah?"

Ava swallowed, the words catching in her throat. "I'm sorry about today. You were right. I was naïve, and I wasn't thinking."

Gabriel's expression softened. He moved closer and sat across from her on the floor with his forearms on his knees. "You don't need to apologize, Ava. I shouldn't have been so harsh either. But I wasn't expecting you or Link to lash out at the guards or prisoners."

Sighing, she drew her knees to her chest and wrapped her arms around them. "Neither was I. It's just ... that woman claimed to be my mom's killer. And Trudy is still out there. It feels like nobody cares."

Gabriel's eyes darkened. "I get your frustration. But lunging at a prisoner won't help you. And it won't change what's happened."

"I wish she was dead."

"It won't bring your mother back."

"I know that." Her breath hitched. "But it doesn't feel like the punishment fits the crime. It never will."

"I'm sorry," he whispered.

A heavy silence enveloped them.

"Why can't we ask the guards questions? Why is it such a big deal?"

"Because they see it as a challenge to their authority," he said. "To them, you're a young Enchanter questioning their ability to do their job. They take that seriously."

"I wasn't trying to challenge them."

"I know. But the Cruciari isn't a place for questions. They don't care about personal vendettas or justice. Their only concern is keeping the prisoners locked up."

"But Devon escaped," she pointed out.

"And they've increased security since then."

Ava sighed, leaning her head back against the bookshelf. "How did that guard know I was there when Devon died?"

He shrugged, but his face betrayed a hint of uncertainty. "Word travels fast in our world."

"Yeah, but not about my appearance. What if the guards are hiding something? What if they helped him escape?"

"That's a stretch, Ava."

"It's not just that. They're not torturing the prisoners. They're protecting them."

"You're letting your anger cloud your judgment. Just because that woman claimed to be your mother's killer doesn't mean she's telling the truth."

Ava clenched her jaw. "She was telling the truth. I know she was. And Xavier knew us. He wasn't as insane as he pretended to be."

"I think you're reaching. I understand why you want someone to blame but be careful. Don't let it consume you."

She fell silent, staring at her hands. The frustration, the confusion, the grief was all too much. Gabriel was right, but it didn't make her anger any less real. "I've been having dreams," she blurted, her voice small. "Ever since Marcel's … vision or whatever. Every single night I dream about my mom's death. But in them, I'm the one killing her. Just like Trudy's vision."

He blinked, surprised. "Have you told anyone about this?"

"No. I don't know who to tell. It would hurt my dad. Savina won't tell me anything."

There was a long pause. "I'll help you, Ava. We'll find the answers, but going to the Cruciari won't solve anything. I know you, Thomas, and the others want revenge, especially after tonight, but it's not worth it. Trust me."

"Why wouldn't we retaliate? After everything that's happened, I'm surprised the Elders are just sitting back doing nothing."

Gabriel's expression darkened. "You think they're relaxing? They don't want a war on their hands. No one does. Believe me, you don't want to go after the Cimmerians."

"Why not?" Something about his tone made her wonder if he was hiding something. Was he … protecting the Cimmerians? That thought twisted uncomfortably inside her, making her question her own instincts. *Why am I so quick to blame everyone?*

"They're stronger than we are." His eyes narrowed as though he was carefully choosing his words.

"They're all locked up. Isn't that what the Elders said?"

He exhaled, rubbing the back of his neck as if the burden of everything rested there. "Yes. But they're not just sitting there doing nothing. The Elders are working constantly to keep us safe."

She tilted her head, scrutinizing him. "Do you think it was the Cimmerians who burned down Thomas's house?"

"I really don't know. But the Ephemerals seem to think they had a reason for doing it."

"I can see them targeting Link or Nicole after what happened with the bombing, but Thomas? Why would they go after his family?"

"You think it was the Cimmerians."

"What other possibility is there? Whoever is in charge of the Cimmerians still wants us, the Elementals."

"In charge? Ava, there's no one left," he said firmly, with a determined look in his eyes.

"You can't believe that."

"I have to." He looked away. Maybe he didn't want there to be anyone else. Neither did Ava.

"What about Trudy?" she asked. "She's not doing this alone. I know she wouldn't."

He ran a hand through his dark hair. "You're right. Trudy's not the type to work solo. But we haven't heard anything from her since Xavier was locked away. And Devon is dead. Whoever's left, if anyone, wouldn't have the power to lead a revolution."

She wasn't convinced. Something was off, like they were on the brink of something bigger. Someone had to be out there, waiting in the shadows. "What about Havok?"

"Havok? Wasn't that what Devon called himself?"

"Yeah."

"Devon probably just wanted to use the moniker."

Ava shrugged. "I don't know. All of this is too much. All I wanted was to learn who killed my mom, and now it feels like everything is unraveling. What if the Cimmerians really are after us? What if they're using our parents as pawns?" Her voice broke, betraying the fear she tried to keep hidden. "I just don't know what to do."

Gabriel moved beside her and gently rubbed her back. His eyes locked onto hers, steady and grounding. "Take a breath, Ava."

She obeyed, drawing in a deep, shaky breath. The knot in her chest loosened slightly, but the overwhelming uncertainty still loomed. "How are you always so calm?"

"Years of practice," he replied with a faint smile. "You can't keep torturing yourself like this. Maybe we should practice more. Just in case. It'll help everyone stay focused, and more importantly, keep our heads clear."

She nodded, feeling the tension beginning to ebb away, if only a little. "Okay."

Gabriel smirked, his usual playful demeanor returning. "Besides, we need a rematch anyway."

"Why? Can't stand the idea of a girl beating you?"

He cocked an eyebrow, a spark of challenge in his eyes. "You didn't beat me. You grazed my shirt."

"Is that a challenge?"

"Maybe." He smiled, but for a fleeting second, his eyes flickered with something else, something deeper.

"I really don't deserve your friendship. But I appreciate it."

His brows creased. "Why do you think that?"

"Because I keep making mistakes. I don't always listen. I don't know what I'm doing half the time, and I feel like I'm dragging everyone down."

He was quiet for a moment. "Ava, we've all made mistakes. But you're doing the best you can, and that's enough. You care, you try. That's what matters." He paused. "I don't think you need to worry about whether you deserve my friendship. You do, by the way. And besides, it's not something you have to earn. I'm here because I want to be."

Her chest tightened, but this time it wasn't from fear. Gratitude washed over her, dispelling the loneliness that haunted her. "Thank you."

A genuine warmth shone in his eyes as he smiled. "Anytime. And remember, you're stronger than you think. We all are."

Ava nodded. The storm of emotions still swirled inside her, but with Gabriel beside her made it more bearable. Maybe, just maybe, they would get through this.

Wandering through the dark woods, Ava followed a glowing white light. She was barefoot, but the harsh debris of pine straw and sticks under her feet didn't bother her. Her necklace warmed and glowed. It was cold outside, but she couldn't make herself warm for some reason. She wanted to know what she was following.

The ball of light stopped, and Ava looked around. She was in a witches' circle with stone markers at each point of the pentagram. She stood in the center and all at once, the ball of light exploded, and fire outlined the pentagram shape. Embers rained down over Ava.

This is your destiny, a voice said, but there was no one else around.

She couldn't move. The fire grew into walls, keeping her enclosed in a circle. When Ava looked ahead through the orange waves, her mother walked through the fire toward her.

"Mom?"

Her mother cupped Ava's chin. *"My child, you are the one to end it all. You must join them. Give yourself to him."*

"What are you talking about?"

"Join them. This is your fate."

Ava woke with a start. The pounding in her chest wouldn't stop. She'd never had a dream like that about her mother. What was she talking about? Her fate? Who was she supposed to join? She couldn't have been talking about Corbin, could she? Was her mother trying to send messages to her? How was that even possible?

Or was it just Ava's mind cracking?

11

PROVOCATION

The funeral for Thomas's father was held in a small, somber chapel. The air was heavy with grief and the scent of freshly cut flowers. Soft sobs filled the room, echoing off the walls.

All they ever did was attend funerals.

The rest of the week had crawled by each day heavier than the last. The dreams that haunted Ava continued to unsettle her, filling her with thoughts she couldn't shake. What exactly was her destiny? To protect her coven by any means necessary even against humans?

She shook her head, trying to dispel the dark thoughts that clouded her mind. It didn't help that Peter and Seth were still away. Bonding, or whatever they were calling it. Peter's constant absence stung. She had tried asking Melissa and Lance about the secrets they were clearly keeping from her, but they refused to say anything. Had she driven a wedge so deep that even her best friends didn't trust her anymore?

Ava reluctantly walked into the large parlor where the meeting was being held. Thick tension lingered in the room. Thomas stood against the wall, arms crossed, his face carefully neutral. But Ava could feel the simmering anger beneath his stoic expression, the raw guilt gnawing at him like a wound that refused to heal. She sensed his pain, radiating from him like heat. It hit her hard, an overwhelming wave of emotions she could barely process.

She slid beside Melissa, who reeked of stale cigarette smoke. Lance stood nearby, his fists clenched tight, his frustration crackling in the air like static. His anger was more obvious, sharper, and it made Ava uneasy.

"How are you holding up?" Ava asked Melissa quietly, trying to distract herself from the storm of emotions swirling around her.

"I'm okay, I guess. Where's Peter?"

"Off with Seth," she muttered, barely able to keep the annoyance out of her voice.

"They know these meetings are mandatory, right?" Melissa raised a brow.

"Yeah." She sent a quick text to Peter, hating that he wasn't there. Everything was spiraling, and he wasn't there.

As the Elders moved to the front of the room, a quiet hush fell over the space.

"As most of you know, we've had an attack on one of our own," Savina began, her voice steady and measured. "We need to clear the air."

"There are rumors that Cimmerians were involved," Aaron continued, his gaze sweeping the room. "This is not true. There is no threat from the Cimmerians."

Ava's stomach twisted, her pulse quickening. *No threat?* Thomas's anger spiked at those words. His guilt and pain surged alongside it, almost drowning her. His father was dead, and they had almost killed him too.

Before she could stop herself, the words burst out of her. "No threat? Thomas's father is dead. They almost killed four members of our coven. How is that *no threat?*"

Aaron's eyes narrowed, his calm exterior cracking just slightly. "There is no danger from the Cimmerians," he repeated, this time with an edge of frustration. "We understand what you're all thinking, and I want to assure you, the police are investigating the Ephemerals who were involved."

"The police?" Ava spat. "What good will they do?"

"They won't help us," Lance growled. "They still blame us for the bombing. They think we're the problem."

"There were no charges," Aaron insisted. "This was an act of revenge by the Ephemerals, not Cimmerians."

Lance's jaw clenched. "How do you know it wasn't the Cimmerians? How can you be so sure?"

Aaron didn't flinch. "The Cimmerians are either imprisoned or dead. This is over."

"Except Trudy," Ava said. "She was there when my house burned down. They're not all gone."

Chatter rippled through the room, voices rising in fear and confusion.

"Enough!" Aaron's voice cut through the noise like a whip. "There will be no further discussion. You have nothing to worry about."

Lance's fists balled tighter, his knuckles white with tension. "So, we're just supposed to sit here and take it? Let them push us around? Kill us?" His voice shook with barely controlled rage.

"Revenge solves nothing," Colden said. "Ignoring their attempts at provocation is the only real strength."

As the Elders left the room, an atmosphere of anger and unspoken fears lingered, enveloping Ava. Everyone was on edge, unsure and afraid. Thomas hadn't moved from his spot, but his silence spoke volumes. She could feel his pain—an unbearable, crushing weight—and it made her stomach twist in knots.

"I'm still going to practice." Lance pushed away from the wall. "I'm not going to sit back and let them walk all over us. We'll figure out who did this, Thomas."

Glancing at Thomas, Ava's heart ached. His remorse pressed down on her through the bond of the necklace. He didn't speak, but his silence was telling. He wasn't just angry, he was drowning in guilt. Guilt she didn't fully understand, but it was there, heavy and suffocating. "Me too," she said. She wasn't about to let Lance fight the battle alone. Others in the room voiced their agreement, pledging to stand behind him. But she couldn't shake the feeling that something was deeply wrong, and it wasn't just the Cimmerians or the Ephemerals. It was Thomas's silence, his pain, and it scared her.

After a moment, she made her way to him. His eyes met hers, and for a second, all the anger seemed to drain out of him. He pulled her into a tight embrace. The suddenness of it caught her off guard, but she wrapped her arms around him, holding him as he trembled.

"I never understood it before," Thomas whispered. "I feel like such an asshole for the way I treated you after your mom died."

Ava's throat tightened. "It's okay."

"No, it's not. I didn't get along with my dad, but he was still my father." He pulled back slightly, looking her in the eye. "I didn't even get to say goodbye."

"I know. I'm so sorry, Thomas. I know how much it hurts. But I'm here for you. I always will be."

In that moment, she finally caught a glimpse of the depth of his sorrow, as his eyes softened and revealed the pain he had been silently carrying. "Thank you. I didn't realize how much I needed that."

She nodded, blinking back her own tears. "Do you want to practice?" She hoped to offer him a distraction from the pain.

"Yeah, I think I need that." He started to walk away.

"Thomas."

He paused, turning to face her, the sadness in his eyes still unmistakable. "Yeah?"

"I just wanted to say … I'm really sorry. I never wanted to hurt you."

He sighed heavily but didn't look angry. "I know. I don't hate you, I never did. It's just … hard. I'm not going to pretend like everything's fine, because it's not. But I understand why you chose him."

Her throat tightened at his words. "You do?"

He nodded, running a hand through his hair. "Yeah. I wasn't always the best for you. I get that now. I care about you a lot, but I couldn't give you what you needed. Peter … he can. And it should be me to apologize."

His honesty caught her off guard. "I didn't mean for things to turn out like this."

Thomas offered her a sad smile. "It's okay. I'm still hurting, yeah. I won't lie about that. But I get why it happened. You needed something more, and I wasn't it."

"You still have me as a friend, though."

"I know. I just … I need a little time. I need space to deal with all of this. But I don't hate you, Ava. I could never hate you."

She nodded, feeling the sting of unshed tears.

Thomas managed a small, bittersweet smile before stepping back, the tension between them not entirely gone, but softened by understanding. "Let's just focus on training, okay?"

"I'll be out in a minute. I just need to call Peter."

He turned to walk away, but there was a subtle change in his demeanor, as if a burden had been lifted from his shoulders, even if just a little.

Maybe her coven wasn't as distant as she feared. Maybe, just maybe, they would forgive her, and maybe she could forgive herself too.

Ava jogged up the two flights of stairs, her mind spinning with the day's events. She opened the door to her room and froze. Peter was there, waiting for her. The tension in her chest grew as he hugged her. Something was off. His embrace felt mechanical, his lips cool and distant. His eyes barely met hers.

"What's wrong?" she asked softly. "Where've you been?"

"Seth and I were just hanging out." The lack of warmth in his voice sent a chill through her. There was a distance between them, and it wasn't just physical.

"Why weren't you at the meeting? You can't keep distancing yourself. People are starting to notice that neither of you have started practicing. I can't keep making excuses for you both."

Peter's jaw tightened, his eyes flickering with something she couldn't quite place. "I never asked you to. Seth's just having a hard time, that's all."

Ava softened, but her irritation still lingered. "Are you sure it's just Seth? You can't keep skipping meetings and training. We need you. I know you're struggling with everything, but don't shut me out. We can figure this out together."

Peter's eyes finally met hers, and for a moment, there was pain there, something deeper than his usual calm. "Why didn't you call me?"

"When?"

"The night of the fire. I called you so many times, but you never answered."

A knot of guilt tightened in her stomach. "I'm sorry. Everything happened so fast. There wasn't anything you could've done. I wasn't hurt—"

"That's not the point, Ava." His voice grew firmer as he cupped her face, gently forcing her to look at him. "Don't you think I'm important enough to call when something like that happens?"

She swallowed, resisting the urge to snap back. She was tired, too tired to argue. "You were busy… You haven't exactly been around much. I didn't want to worry you. It's no big deal."

"It *is* a big deal. Ava, no matter what's happening with me, if you're in danger I want to know. I could've been there. I *should've* been there."

Her heart ached at how weary he sounded. "You can't protect everyone."

"I know that." His hands fell from her face as his shoulders slumped. "But that doesn't mean I won't try."

Ava's chest tightened, her frustration ebbing at the toll everything was taking on him. "Then you have to start training. No more skipping, okay? You can't protect anyone if you're not prepared."

He nodded, but it wasn't convincing. "Do you think it was the Cimmerians who burned Thomas's house?"

"I don't know." Ava moved to sit on the edge of the bed. "They burned down my house…"

Peter sat beside her, their shoulders barely touching. His brow furrowed as he stared down at his hands. "Here's what I don't get. They used fire on Thomas's house. Doesn't fire obey him? Like how water listens to you? Why couldn't Thomas stop the fire? He got everyone out except his father."

The question hung heavy between them, unsettling. Ava hadn't considered that before. "You think … you think Thomas left him there on purpose?"

Peter shook his head, eyes wide. "No, of course not. I just think it's weird, that's all."

"Maybe it wasn't a normal fire. Maybe it was controlled … like with a spell."

"Maybe." Peter shifted beside her. "Do you think some of the Cimmerians escaped?"

"No," she said, but deep down she wasn't convinced. "But I do believe they're still out there, and just as dangerous as Devon was."

"Is that why you're pushing for everyone to train?"

"That, and you newbies need it," she teased, trying to lighten the moment, though her heart wasn't fully in it.

Peter smiled faintly, pressing his forehead against hers. "Just … don't shut me out, okay? I need to know you're safe. I want to protect you, Ava."

"Same goes for you. Don't leave me out."

Their lips met, the kiss deep, a promise woven between them. Ava's fingers twisted into his shirt, pulling him closer. The warmth from his body mirrored the heat building inside her. Peter's hands moved gently over her skin, his lips trailing along her jaw. She melted into the moment, her necklace heating as her body responded.

A sharp knock at the door startled them, and Ava jerked upright.

The door cracked open, and Gabriel's voice slipped through. "Whoa, sorry."

Peter sat up quickly, running a hand through his hair. "No, it's okay, man. We're on our way out."

Gabriel nodded. "All right. See you out there."

As the door closed, Peter groaned, pulling Ava to her feet. "Well, that was embarrassing."

She laughed, her heart still racing. "Yeah, just a bit."

He squeezed her hand. "Come on. Let's go train."

They stepped out into the large practice field, where all the Enchanters were already training. The air hummed with the low murmur of energy, and the rhythmic sounds of power clashing and echoing across the open space. Ava's gaze found Thomas, her eyes lingering on him for a moment. Relief washed over her, seeing him participating.

Practicing would do them all good, though. It was a way to keep their minds sharp and ready for anything. The last time Ava wasn't prepared, it nearly cost her life. She could still feel the phantom pressure of the witch's hands around her throat, choking her as she fought for air. If Gabriel hadn't intervened, she wouldn't be standing there now.

Gabriel approached her and Peter, his face hard and emotionless. "Ready?" His voice was curt, lacking the usual lightness.

"Sure," she replied, though his icy tone unsettled her.

"Is he okay?" Peter asked under his breath, his eyes following Gabriel's retreating figure.

"I'm not sure." Her lips brushed Peter's in a quick kiss before she moved to follow Gabriel. Her heart quickened, unease swirling in her chest.

"Okay, so what—" An unseen force hit her square in the chest, knocking her off her feet. She hit the ground hard, the impact jarring through her spine. Blinking in shock, she searched the field for any sign of an attack, but Gabriel had already vanished. *What the hell?*

She scrambled to her feet, brushing dirt from her clothes, but was knocked down again before she could catch her breath. Her body slammed into the earth, harder this time. The air was forced from her lungs in a painful gasp. Ava's head swam with confusion. This wasn't their usual training. It felt too personal, too aggressive.

Her frustration flared. She pictured Gabriel submerged in water, her powers surging in response. She willed the water to take control, to stop him. But nothing happened. Gabriel reappeared, standing a few feet away. His eyes were cold, distant. She sensed something in him had shifted.

"Come on, Ava. I don't have all day," he snapped.

Her stomach churned at the harshness in his tone. What was going on? "Have I done something?"

"You're wasting my time. You're weak, and you need to learn to focus."

Her temper flared, and heat spread through her chest. The words stung, cutting deeper than she wanted to admit. She didn't know why he was being so cruel, but it ignited something fierce inside her. Her powers surged, and she imagined him drowning again. Still, nothing happened.

Frustrated, she whirled around and was slammed against a tree. The bark bit into her back, the impact knocking the wind out of her. Gabriel was in front of her in an instant, his hand wrapped tightly around her throat. His eyes, usually steady and calm, were wild, intense.

A moment of fear passed before anger set in. "What is wrong with you?" she gasped.

"I didn't come out here to chit-chat," he growled, his grip loosening slightly but his gaze never wavering.

"Why are you being such a jerk?" Power buzzed under her skin, ready to explode if she lost control.

"You think your enemy will be nice and friendly?" he retorted, his voice harsh, but beneath it, there was something more vulnerable, though he hid it well.

"I didn't think *you* were my enemy."

For a split second, something flickered in his eyes, regret, maybe, or guilt, but it disappeared just as quickly, swallowed by his anger. Releasing her, he retreated to his initial position, his expression hardening.

Ava's heart pounded with a mix of anger, confusion, and something she couldn't quite name. Why was he acting like that? Was it part of his tactic to make her stronger, or was there something deeper going on?

The next time Gabriel moved, she didn't hesitate. The familiar flow of water surged through her veins, and with a swift motion, she sent a blast of it straight at him, knocking him off his feet. He hit the ground, coughing, but didn't acknowledge her victory. Ava didn't offer any comfort either. They trained in silence after that, no words exchanged, just the sharp rhythm of their movements and the thick tension crackling between them.

At one point, Gabriel knocked her down again, but this time, his hands lingered on her shoulders a moment longer than necessary. Their eyes met, and Ava's breath hitched. There was something in his gaze, something deeper, intense, like he was seeing her for the first time.

"I think it's time for a break," he muttered, his voice flat, but his eyes told a different story. He jumped to his feet.

Her pulse raced as she sat up on the ground. "What's wrong?"

"Nothing." He didn't even look back as he walked away, leaving her sitting there, staring after him, her mind tangled in confusion.

Ava made her way over to Peter, who was chatting with Eric. Her thoughts were scattered, her gaze flickering across the training grounds. The knot of worry tightening in her chest refused to loosen, but she forced herself to focus as she approached.

"Are you okay?" Peter asked.

"Yeah. Just tired."

"It's been a rough few weeks." Eric offered her a small, sympathetic smile, the exhaustion clear in his own eyes. "Totally understandable."

She nodded, but her gaze strayed across the field again, landing briefly on Gabriel, who was standing next to Joss and Natalia. His usual calmness had been replaced with something more distant, closed off. Her stomach twisted with concern. *He's different tonight.*

"Is Gabriel okay?" she asked.

Eric shrugged. "As far as I know. Why?"

"I don't know. He seems … different tonight."

"Oh. That." Eric gave a knowing smile. "He pulls this act on all of us. Likes to push us harder than necessary sometimes, but it's just his way. Thinks it's hilarious to catch us off guard." He winked before walking off toward Joss, Gabriel, and Natalia, leaving Ava's question unanswered.

Her eyes lingered on Gabriel for a beat longer, watching the way his gaze flickered toward her before turning away, almost as if avoiding her. *Why won't he look at me?*

Peter's hand gently squeezed hers, drawing her attention back to him. "Are you really okay?"

Ava sighed, her heart heavy. "I am," she admitted, though her mind was still elsewhere. "I guess I'm just worried."

"We'll be fine." He gave her hand another reassuring squeeze. "I'm trying so hard to get stronger, to get used to all of this. It's all so new, but it's also incredible. Sometimes I feel like I'm invincible." His lips curved into a small smile. "Did you feel that way when you first started?"

Invincible? I'm not sure I've ever felt that way. "At times, yes," she said, her tone lighter now. "How's training with Maggie?"

"She's tough. Doesn't cut me any slack for being new, but honestly, that's good. At first, she just helped me figure out what I could do, but then it was straight into action. It's wild, Ava. Maggie can literally transform her body into weapons. She turned her arms into Sai daggers. How crazy is that? She even cut my hand, but it healed back like nothing happened. It was surreal."

She gasped. "She cut you? Did it hurt?"

"Yeah, but only until it healed." He shrugged. "It's still … hard to wrap my head around. But I feel bad for Joss. She's training with Gillian, and Gillian controlled her mind a few times, made her shock herself."

"Ouch. Gabriel overtook me a few times, too."

"Does anyone train with Savina?"

"I don't think so. I'm not sure how we would even fight someone who can read every move we make."

Peter released a sigh. "How are we supposed to do this? Fight people like them?"

"Savina says the trick is to catch them off guard or block them out. You have to clear your mind, make it unreadable. It's tough, but Gabriel's good at helping with that." Her words trailed off as her eyes flicked toward Gabriel again, unable to resist. "The key is focus."

"Wow. Sometimes I wonder if I'll ever get the hang of this."

The worry in his voice tugged at Ava's heart, and guilt flared in her chest. She hadn't meant to drag him into this world, this chaos. "I'm sorry. I never should've pulled you into this world."

He cupped her face gently, his eyes steady and filled with quiet resolve. "We've been through this. This is what I want."

Her heart swelled at his words. She brought her hand to his cheek, running her fingers over his smooth skin, and looked into his warm brown eyes that were so full of determination despite the challenges.

Peter leaned in and kissed her softly, then whispered in her ear, "I love you, Ava."

Her eyes fluttered shut, and she melted into his embrace. For a second, their worries vanished, leaving only the comforting embrace of his arms and the caress of a gentle breeze.

Their moment was interrupted by a surge of emotions from the Aureole. Ava felt Thomas's sadness and jealousy and Gillian's simmering anger wash over her. She sighed, pulling away. "I have to talk to her."

"You should wait until she cools off."

"I can't keep avoiding her." She scanned the field until she spotted Jeremy and Gillian. She made her way over to them. "Can we talk?" she asked Gillian.

"I don't have anything to say to you." Her eyes narrowed.

Jeremy stepped in, adjusting his glasses. "Gillian, come on. Talk to her."

"Why are you so angry with me? You know how important Peter is to me. I thought you understood."

"He doesn't belong here, Ava," she shot back. "You lost my trust when you brought him into this without telling us. You don't get it. You broke something between us."

Her words felt like a slap. "I didn't mean to—"

"No. You didn't think. You never do. And now look at what's happening. Have you even noticed how much Thomas is hurting?"

"That isn't fair."

"Yeah, you pushing him aside for Peter isn't fair, and now you don't even see how much he's suffering."

Gillian's anger hit Ava like a scorching flame, intense and unyielding, as searing as Thomas's fire. In a moment of reflection, Ava realized Gillian was right. She hadn't made it easy for her coven to trust her, but she was at a loss for how to fix things, unsure how else to handle the growing divide.

"We'll talk about this later." Jeremy stepped between them as Savina and Aaron approached the group.

"I'm glad to see you all practicing." Savina's eyes swept over the group, and everyone gathered closer to her and Aaron. "I think it's time we rotate partners. This will give you a chance to test your skills against different powers."

Ava tensed, her stomach twisting with unease. Who would Savina pair her with next?

Savina moved down the line, pairing the more experienced witches with the newcomers. When she finally stopped in front of Ava and Natalia, a chill washed over her. She stifled a groan. Of all the people…

Natalia smirked, her eyes narrowing in on Ava like a predator sizing up prey. "I hope you're better than your ex." Her hand rested casually on her hip.

Ava bristled. "That's a little insensitive. He just lost his father."

"I really don't care what you think."

"Aren't I immune to your singing?"

The smirk on Natalia's face deepened into something more malicious. A shrill, ear-piercing screech erupted, reverberating through the air and slicing into Ava's mind like a dagger. Her skull was being violently torn apart. Overwhelmed by the excruciating pain, she crumpled to the ground, dropping to her knees and desperately clutching her ears. The agony engulfed her senses, rendering her unable to utter anything but a muted cry, while a warm trickle of blood slowly seeped from her ears.

The screech finally ceased, leaving Ava gasping for air, her body shaking in agony. She lay on her back, dazed, as her hearing slowly returned.

"Ava, are you okay?" Peter rushed to her side, helping her sit up. Her head throbbed, and the concerned faces around her blurred.

"I'm fine," she managed to croak, though her body trembled from the shock. She wiped the blood from her ears, feeling the eyes of the others still on her.

Peter turned on Natalia, fury in his voice. "What did you do to her?"

Natalia shrugged. "We're supposed to be practicing. She needs to know what to expect."

"She isn't supposed to feel pain like that," Gabriel cut in, his voice cold. His sudden defense of Ava surprised her, but she was too disoriented to process it fully.

Natalia folded her arms, unbothered by the confrontation. "She should've been prepared."

Ava stood, shaky but determined. "I'm fine. It's nothing." She squared her shoulders, trying to shake off the vulnerability.

"You're weaker than I thought," Natalia said.

The insult stung, but Ava clenched her jaw and reminded herself of Gabriel's advice. Stay focused, stay calm. Letting anger take over would only make her exposed. She needed to prove her strength. "No. I'm new, but I'm not weak."

She thrust her hands forward, water surging from her palms and slamming into Natalia with enough force to knock her off her feet. Natalia hit the ground hard, gasping as Ava pinned her with a cold, unrelenting grip around her throat.

Natalia's eyes bulged in shock, her hands flailing, but Ava held her firm. "I may be new, but I'm stronger than you think. And I'm not someone you can underestimate."

Natalia stopped struggling, her face turning pale. Slowly, Ava released her grip, stepping back with a measured breath.

"Nice. Catfight," Eric's voice called from behind, clearly trying to break the tension.

Ava turned, her irritation flaring. She blasted him with a jet of water, knocking him to the ground. "Don't push me today, Eric," she said, though her lips twitched in a faint smile.

He held up his hands in surrender, a grin on his face. "Lesson learned."

But Ava didn't laugh. She was tired. Tired of being bullied, tired of constantly defending herself. She stood tall, her back straight, and faced Natalia once more, her resolve unshaken. She would not let anyone, not Natalia or anyone else, bring her down.

12

STORIES

Training with Natalia made Ava feel stronger. She was tough, relentless, and always challenging, just like Gabriel. Despite their mutual dislike, Ava couldn't deny that training with her was effective. Natalia had taught her to always be ready, to anticipate attacks even if she couldn't predict them, and to be precise and focused. It was a lesson she needed.

After a few grueling hours, the weary Enchanters gathered inside for dinner, the fatigue evident on their faces.

"That was intense." Melissa nudged Ava as they sat down at the long dining table. "Is Natalia afraid of you now or what?"

Ava smirked. "Not afraid, just ... aware I'll fight back."

"What did she do to you?"

"You didn't hear it?"

"No. We were busy with our own thing, then suddenly you screamed, and you were on the ground with your ears bleeding."

"She screeched. This loud, awful noise inside my head. It felt like my brain was going to explode."

Melissa winced. "Yikes. Sorry."

Ava shrugged, trying to shake off the lingering discomfort. "It's part of training."

"By the way," she added, leaning in, "don't listen to Gillian."

"She's right though." She dropped her gaze.

"No, she's not. I just don't get why she still has such an issue with Peter. She should be over it by now."

"Has she been acting strange lately?"

Melissa hesitated, tucking her hair behind her ear. "Yeah, actually. She'll be mid-conversation and then just … stop. It's like she's lost in thought, and I have to pull her out of it. And some days, she won't even leave her house."

"That's … weird. Have you asked her about it?"

"I tried. She brushes it off like it's nothing." Melissa paused, lowering her voice. "She's also been making some pretty harsh comments about the Ephemerals."

"Maybe it's just her way of blowing off steam, given everything that's happened."

"Maybe," Melissa said, but the doubt in her eyes was hard to miss.

Joss approached the table with a smile as she placed bowls in front of them. "Colden's making goulash. It's really good. How was training?" She sat down across from them, her face marked with small cuts and a rash.

"Eric and Gabriel are tough," Melissa answered. "But it was cool. Gabriel helped me learn how to create a shield with rocks and dirt. Does Eric ever mess with you with all those duplications?"

"Sometimes, but I get back at him." She smirked.

Melissa leaned forward. "Are your eyes really that violet, or are you wearing contacts?"

Joss laughed. "They're real. People ask a lot, but I don't mind."

"Those cuts on your face … what happened?"

Ava rolled her eyes. "Mel, seriously?"

Joss didn't seem bothered. "Jeremy got a little carried away with his wind abilities. Felt like my skin was peeling off, but I'll go to Savina after dinner, and she'll heal me right up."

Peter, Lance, and Jeremy joined them at the table, and soon everyone began serving themselves from the large pots of goulash. Conversations buzzed around the room.

"How does it feel being an Enchanter now?" Joss asked Peter, crumbling crackers into her bowl.

"It's … strange." He glanced at Ava with a small smile. "But extraordinary at the same time."

Joss's eyes lit up. "It's amazing, isn't it? You two have this intense connection. It's rare for Ephemerals and Enchanters to be so … in sync. You're definitely meant for each other."

Ava's heart warmed at the compliment, but her amulet heated against her skin. Thomas's jealousy flared in her mind, and she remembered Gillian's harsh words. She gripped Peter's hand under the table.

Joss's face fell. "Oh no, did I say something wrong?"

"You didn't," Melissa interjected. "Thomas is just … going through a lot. We'll all get through this, though."

Joss nodded, but her expression remained apologetic. "I hope so. He'll find his way, I'm sure."

The library was the one place where she could breathe, the quiet hum of magic and knowledge weaving through the rows of old books. As she passed Jeremy, Link, and Nicole sitting at one of the tables, she zeroed in on the shelf that held the Edgar Allan Poe collection. *Perfect.* She wanted to relax, escape for a moment.

"Your book is right here," Gabriel's voice came from behind her.

Ava froze for a second. Slowly, she turned to see Gabriel standing there, holding out the very book she had been reaching for. His hair was damp, and the faint scent of soap and juniper drifted off him. He looked calm, casual even, but there was a distance in his eyes that unsettled her.

"Thanks." Ava warily took it from him. "I didn't see you at dinner."

"Yeah. Eric and I went out for a bit." His tone was casual, but there was something off in the way he avoided her eyes.

She nodded, unsure what to say. The awkward tension left a heaviness between them. *Did I do something wrong?* She couldn't shake the feeling that he was still angry with her about the Cruciari. *Maybe he hasn't forgiven me. Maybe he hates me now.* The thought tightened her chest, making her wish she could ask him directly, but she was too afraid of the answer.

"Well, thanks for the book."

Gabriel didn't step away. Instead, he sighed softly, his voice dropping. "Ava, I'm really sorry about earlier."

She glanced up at him, surprised by the apology. His usual calm, controlled expression had softened, but the guarded look in his eyes was still there, unsettling her. *Maybe he's just saying this because he has to.*

"I wasn't myself. And I took it out on you. That wasn't fair."

"What was the matter?"

"It's nothing. Just … personal stuff. But that's no excuse for how I acted. I'm sorry for being a jerk."

She hesitated, unsure if she should press him for more. *Does he mean it? Or is he just covering up how he really feels?* She wanted to ask, to dig deeper into what was bothering him, but she feared it would only make things worse.

"Thanks." She forced a smile.

Gabriel offered a brief, almost relieved smile in return, though it didn't quite reach his eyes. Without saying more, he turned and walked toward his usual spot by the fireplace, leaving her standing there, holding the book that now weighed heavier in her hands.

Ava's thoughts spiraled. *He's still angry, I know it.* Would things ever go back to how they were before the Cruciari. *So many people are angry with me.* It wasn't just Gabriel. There were others too. And the more she tried to fix things, the more everything unraveled.

Pushing away the negative thoughts, she made her way over to join Jeremy and Link at one of the tables.

"I learned so much today," Jeremy said, excitement lighting up his face. "I'm getting better at controlling my powers, focusing them on just one person at a time. It's amazing. Joss is way stronger than she looks. Once she gets going, she can create currents of electricity like nothing I've ever seen. She shocked me a few times, but I got her back," he added with a grin.

Ava gave him a small smile, grateful for the distraction. "She told me at dinner how impressed she was with you."

Jeremy beamed.

"You seemed to have made a new friend today," Link said with a sly smile. "Was Natalia upset?"

Ava sighed, shaking her head. "Probably. She hates me."

"She doesn't hate you," Gabriel chimed in from across the room. "She just doesn't warm up to younger witches easily."

Jeremy raised an eyebrow. "Didn't she used to be one herself?"

"She did." Gabriel shrugged. "But some things don't matter to her."

The conversation hit a lull until Link broke the silence, his tone shifting. "I still can't believe we didn't get any answers at the Cruciari. What a waste of time."

Jeremy leaned forward. "What exactly are you trying to figure out?"

"Someone had to be behind everything. Devon wasn't smart enough to mastermind all of this."

Jeremy nodded thoughtfully, removing his glasses to clean them with the edge of his shirt. "Maybe Devon just got impatient, messed up in the end."

Link shook his head. "That's what bothers me. Why would someone with a plan like his just screw it all up at the last second?"

Joss bounded into the room, her smile brightening the space. "There you are, Gabe!" Her energy was infectious, but uneasiness settled over Ava as her gaze flickered back to Gabriel, who remained quieter than usual.

Gabriel chuckled, though it seemed half-hearted. "Where else would I be?"

"What are you all talking about?" Joss glanced around the table.

"Same stuff," Link replied. "Do you think it was Cimmerians who burned Thomas's house?"

Ava hesitated, choosing her words carefully. "I have my suspicions. But what if the Elders are right? What if the Cimmerians are controlling the Ephemerals?"

Jeremy nodded. "That's possible."

"Like how we were controlled?" Link asked.

"No, not Halflings," Ava clarified. "But what if they're using the Ephemerals?"

"What do you think, Gabriel?" Link turned to him.

"It could be any number of things."

Joss pursed her lips. "Maybe it's Hunters."

Link's brow furrowed. "Hunters?"

"They hunt Enchanters," Gabriel explained as he moved toward the table. "Cimmerians, Ephemerals—it doesn't matter to them. They've been gone for a long time, though."

"Maybe with everything happening, they're coming back," Joss suggested.

Ava's heart sank at the thought. *Another threat?* The idea of Hunters returning unsettled her even more than the Cimmerians. Just as the anxiety began to edge its way inside her, Gabriel's hands gently rested over hers.

"Take a deep breath." His touch comforted her despite the awkwardness.

Ava did as he said, inhaling deeply and exhaling slowly. *So much is happening, and I can't control any of it.* "How do we find out if the Hunters are really back?" She pulled her hand away from Gabriel's, though part of her longed for the comfort. "I mean, do you think Drew and his friends are actual Hunters?"

"We spy on them, of course," Joss said with a mischievous grin.

"What? Like, sneak around?" Link asked.

Joss nodded. "Gabriel and I can do it. They've never seen us, so we won't draw suspicion."

"Why not us?" Ava asked.

"They already know who you are. It's easier if we go," Gabriel explained. "Besides, don't you all have school starting again soon?"

Link groaned. "Next week. But why bother?"

"Because Savina insists on normalcy." Joss stifled a laugh. "She wants you all to live like everything's fine."

"Normalcy?" Ava scoffed. "There's nothing normal about us. Going back to school is asking for more bullying, more trouble."

"Especially after what I did," Link muttered, guilt heavy in his voice.

"There comes a time when you can't be afraid anymore," Gabriel said. "Let them think what they want. You're stronger than you know."

Link shook his head. "Easy for you to say. You didn't blow up a school."

Gabriel's gaze softened, the hint of something more in his eyes as he spoke. "You're right. I didn't. But I've done things I regret, things I couldn't control. That doesn't mean we run from who we are."

Jeremy adjusted his glasses, sighing. "We're supposed to protect them, but instead, we're the ones being hunted."

Joss offered a small smile. "You're all stronger than you think. No one can take that away from you."

A heavy silence descended. Ava knew there was more to discover, more lurking beneath the surface of their world. She had to find out who killed her mother. Maybe spying on the humans would help, or maybe she needed to dig deeper into the Cimmerians.

"Have either of you been at war with Cimmerians before?" Link asked.

"Yeah," Joss and Gabriel replied simultaneously.

Ava exchanged a glance with Link and Jeremy. "What happened?"

Gabriel leaned back in his chair, his face darkening. "We were trying to stop Corbin from starting a war with the humans. We lost a lot of people in the process. Corbin was always one step ahead. He knew us better than we knew ourselves. They used illusions, manipulated our minds, morphed into people we trusted. Objects came at us out of nowhere. It was chaotic, and we weren't ready." He paused, eyes distant. "That was almost eighty years ago."

Link shook his head. "Corbin was trying to wipe out the Ephemerals and anyone who got in the way?"

"Yeah," Gabriel said.

"What about my mom?" Ava asked. "Were there revolutionists?"

Gabriel frowned, searching for an answer. "I don't know."

Link shifted. "What about Caprington?"

"What about it?" Gabriel asked.

"What really happened there? From what I've heard, the village thought Corbin was a good guy. So did everyone else. Then his sister Veronica visits, they go to Caprington, and suddenly Corbin comes back and starts unleashing hell on the citizens."

"No one knows exactly what happened at Caprington," Joss said. "We do know Veronica killed her husband. He was a Hunter. He got involved with the wrong family, and it ended badly."

"But they had a child," Ava pointed out.

"It was all part of their deception," Gabriel said.

"And no one knows what made Corbin snap?" Ava pressed.

"Not even Savina and Colden know the full story," Joss added, her voice taking on a somber note.

But Ava doubted that. How could they not know?

"Do you think a Hunter killed your mom?" Link asked Ava.

She swallowed hard. Only she and Gabriel knew what had really happened at the Cruciari. "It was a Cimmerian," she said softly. "I think she killed my mom out of revenge. Maybe my mom betrayed someone."

Concern flickered across Link's face. "How do you know that?"

Ava waved off the question, not ready to dive into the details of the encounter or the visions that haunted her. She glanced at Gabriel, who had turned his attention back to the fire. "Did Corbin ever try to take any of you?"

Gabriel hesitated. "Maggie and Kira. Kira's power is incredibly dangerous. She can kill instantly with venom. If Corbin had that, he could've wiped out anyone without leaving a trace."

Link frowned. "But didn't Corbin have a similar power?"

"Yes, but Kira's is faster," Gabriel said. "Corbin's poison took time, days, sometimes weeks. He wanted to build an unstoppable army to do to the Ephemerals what he thought they did to him. But according to Savina and Colden, the Ephemerals never attacked him."

"And since he died," Joss added, "there have been Cimmerians trying to rise to power, but none of them have been as dangerous as Corbin."

"Like Devon," Link muttered.

"What made Corbin so powerful, other than his age?" Jeremy asked. "Was it his followers?"

Gabriel seemed to hesitate, his jaw tightening. "That, and his tactical mind. In the beginning, Savina wasn't as experienced as she is now. She wasn't as strong."

Ava leaned forward. "But now, the Cimmerians know there's a coven of Elemental Enchanters backing Savina. If Corbin was desperate to build an army, who's to say others aren't doing the same? What if Devon was just the beginning? A test?"

"The Elders would know if something like that were happening," Joss said confidently.

Ava narrowed her eyes. "Would they?"

"Of course," Joss replied, but there was a hint of doubt in her voice now.

"I think the Elders are hiding something from us," Ava said.

Joss raised an eyebrow. "What would they hide? They're just as overwhelmed as we are."

The room fell into an uneasy silence. Ava glanced at Gabriel, who sat deep in thought. There was so much she didn't know about her mother, about the Cimmerians, about whatever forces were rising against them. Maybe Marcel had more answers, but the thought of confronting him sent a shiver down her spine.

"Who's the strongest witch you've ever faced?" Link asked.

Joss grinned. "For me, it's anyone who can control water." She cast a playful glance at Ava. "But I haven't faced too many others besides you and your mom."

Gabriel's expression darkened. "Sorcha."

Ava exchanged a glance with Joss, who nodded grimly.

"What can she do?" Jeremy asked.

Gabriel's jaw clenched, a muscle ticking as he answered. "She can cast a sleep spell that leaves you powerless. It's the worst feeling in the world."

Ava, Jeremy, and Link stared at him in shock.

"Weaken you how?" Ava asked.

"To the point where you have no power left. It can take months to recover."

Her mouth fell open in disbelief.

"But Aaron can restore your strength, right?" Jeremy asked.

Gabriel shook his head. "Aaron can amplify power that's already there. But with Sorcha's spell, there's nothing left to amplify."

"Does it come back?" Ava whispered.

"Eventually."

The door to the library creaked open, and Natalia stepped inside. Ava tensed.

"Gabriel, I need to talk to you," Natalia said, her tone clipped as she stood at the entrance.

He gave a small nod, pushing his chair back. "Have a good night. Try not to worry too much." His eyes briefly lingered on Ava before he followed Natalia out of the room.

"I think I'm gonna head out." Jeremy stood up and gave Ava a one-armed hug.

"Yeah, me too," Link added, his face tired. "I'll see you all in the morning."

Ava and Joss murmured their goodnights, the air still thick with the unanswered questions hanging between them.

"Does Natalia know how to clear a room or what?" Joss teased with a smile. "Just kidding."

"Are Natalia and Gabriel ... together?"

Joss let out a sharp laugh. "No way. They're more like brother and sister."

"Then why does she seem to order him around so much?"

"She orders everyone around." Her smile faded a little as she hesitated. "She ... doesn't really like you. She's not thrilled that Gabriel spends time with you."

"What? Why does it matter? You hang out with me."

Joss shrugged. "That's just how she is. I wouldn't waste too much time worrying about it."

But she knew Joss was holding something back. "It's okay. I get it. I'd probably feel the same way if I were in her shoes."

"How do you think the new Enchanters are handling all of this?"

"I guess okay. I haven't really talked to Seth or seen him much here, but Peter's helping him. Nicole and Link are just trying to figure things out. I can't imagine what they're going through though."

"I know. I mean, I didn't even know I was an Enchanter until I was sixteen. But for them, being kidnapped and suddenly turned into one? I can't imagine."

"Wait, you didn't know you were an Enchanter?"

Joss shook her head. "Nope. When my parents died, my aunt and uncle took me in, and they wanted to keep me away from the Enchanter world. But eventually, even they couldn't stop it."

"Were they not Enchanters too?"

"No, they were Drolls," Joss said, referring to powerless Enchanters. They were rare, and Ava had only known one. Colden. "They tried to shield me from it, but strange things started happening, like me staying warm in the middle of snowstorms or electrocuting myself when I took a shower. That's when they finally told me the truth."

Ava winced. "That must've been terrifying."

"It was. I had no idea what was happening, and it wasn't until I was older that I really understood."

"Did you have an Aureole then?"

"I did. But after we were introduced as kids, I never saw them again. I didn't even understand what it was until much later."

"So how did you end up with this Aureole?"

Joss's face softened into a smile. "Eric. We met in school, and it was like love at first sight." She rolled her eyes, a playful glint in her gaze. "We both knew we were different, but back then, it was hard to trust anyone. One minute, Enchanters were your friends, and the next, they were ready to turn against you."

"I know what you mean."

"It took time, but eventually, I became part of their Aureole. Aaron says that our love strengthens the bond, and I believe it. Other than Savina and Aaron, we're the only couple in the group. It's kind of cheesy, but I wouldn't trade it for anything."

"It's not cheesy at all. You're lucky to have that."

"I am," Joss agreed. "And I know you feel the same about Peter."

At the mention of Peter's name, a mix of warmth and doubt stirred in her chest. "Yeah, I do. It's incredible having him with me now, but…" She trailed off, unsure if she should say more.

"But what?"

"I feel conflicted. I broke the rules, Joss. I lost the trust of my Aureole, and I don't know if I'll ever get it back. Thomas and Gillian … they still haven't forgiven me. And Gabriel hates me."

"Why do you think that?"

Ava's heart sank. She couldn't bring herself to tell Joss the full truth about the Cruciari. Instead, she waved her hand dismissively. "It's just a feeling."

"Well, I seriously doubt he hates you. As for Thomas and Gillian, they'll come around. It just takes time. And Natalia … well, that's probably why she's been cold to you. She thinks you're a bit naïve, and maybe…" She paused. "A little selfish."

The word stung more than Ava expected, but she couldn't deny the truth in it. "Selfish," she repeated quietly, the word hanging between them. Maybe she had been more focused on Peter than she should have been.

"Hey, don't take it too hard. She was cold to me at first, too. She'll warm up eventually. Just focus on what matters. You've got Peter, and you're still part of the Aureole."

Ava nodded, but the heaviness remained in her chest. "You're right."

Joss smiled, giving her a reassuring nudge. "Exactly. Gabriel and I will keep an eye on things, see if we can dig up anything on the Ephemerals. But for now, let's get some rest. It's late, and tomorrow's going to be another long day."

"Thanks, Joss."

As they made their way upstairs, Ava found herself not wanting the conversation to end. Joss had become someone she could really talk to, like Gabriel, and it felt good to have that connection.

Joss stopped in front of her door. "I'm all the way down at the end. But if you need anything, feel free to knock the door down until I wake up."

"Thanks. I will." Ava laughed softly, touched by the offer.

Joss leaned in and hugged her tightly. "See you in the morning."

When Ava slipped into her room, she found the lamp still on and Peter asleep. She changed into a soft shirt and shorts before sliding under the blankets. As soon as she clicked off the light, Peter stirred and wrapped his arm around her, pulling her close. He kissed her forehead sleepily.

Joss was right. She didn't need to worry so much. Peter was there, part of her world now, and she felt incredibly lucky. For the first time in a while, Ava let herself relax in his embrace, knowing she wasn't alone.

━━━━◆13◆━━━━

FIRST DAY BACK

Peter pulled into the parking lot, and Ava's anxiety grew with every step closer to the school. Ava stepped out of the car, the crisp morning air doing nothing to calm her nerves. She twirled her ring around her finger, trying to distract herself from the sinking feeling in her stomach. It was hard to believe it was already September. She didn't want to be there, and she could feel the same dread radiating from Peter beside her.

Melissa, Lance, Link, Nicole, and Seth were already waiting for them by the entrance, each of them looking just as uneasy.

Link let out a long sigh. "I can't believe we're actually back here."

"I can't believe they rebuilt it so quickly." Melissa took a long drag from her cigarette.

"I really don't want to be here," Nicole muttered, her voice trembling. She hugged herself tightly, and Ava could see the fear in her eyes. It hit her hard. This place wasn't just a school anymore. It was a reminder of everything they had lost.

Link gently unclasped Nicole's arms and took her hand. "I'm not leaving your side today," he promised, his voice soft but firm.

Melissa flicked her cigarette to the ground and stomped it out. "We can do this. It's our senior year. We have every right to be here, just like everyone else. Let's show them we're not scared." Her voice was determined, but Ava could sense the underlying tension in her words.

Ava slipped her hand into Peter's, holding on tightly. "She's right. We'll be okay," she whispered.

Peter gave a small nod. Together, they made their way toward the newly constructed part of the school. The building smelled fresh. New paint, new floors, but the stares from the other students were cold, sharp, and unforgiving.

The shiny gray walls and bright lights seemed to highlight every glance, every whispered word. Ava envied how Melissa and Lance walked confidently, as if the glares and jeers didn't touch them. But Ava knew better. They were all targets, and no matter how many times they explained they were victims too, no one seemed to believe them.

"I feel like I'm going to have a panic attack," Nicole whispered behind Ava.

As they passed through the hallway, students stopped and stared. The usual morning bustle—the clatter of lockers, the laughter, the chatter—faded into silence as Ava and her friends walked by. The tension was suffocating, but eventually, the noise picked up again as if the school forced itself back to normalcy.

The group split up to head to their separate classes, and Peter stayed with Ava as they walked toward her locker. The tension was like a shadow following them, the whispers growing louder with every step.

"I'll see you at lunch." Peter glanced around warily.

Ava grabbed his face, turning his attention back to her. "Ignore them. I know it's hard, but we're just as innocent as they are."

He gave her a small nod before kissing her softly. Then, with a deep breath, he turned and walked off, braving the gauntlet of angry glares alone.

Ava took a deep breath, steeling herself as she made her way to her English class. She slipped into the back seat, close to the door, hoping to go unnoticed. For a moment, no one said anything as they filed into the room. A girl dropped into the seat next to her. Ava barely recognized her, but she couldn't help but be reminded of Kristen Miller, Xavier's first victim.

A loud smack echoed through the room, making Ava jump. She turned toward the noise.

Drew sat in the seat in front of her, a sinister smile spreading across his face. "Well, hello there, Ginger," he said.

Ava rolled her eyes, unwilling to play his game. "Like I haven't heard that one before."

He turned back in his chair and rested his arms on her desk. "Where are all your little buddies? They finally ditch you?"

"They're in class, just like everyone else," Ava shot back.

"So, what's it like being a witch? Can you cast spells? Make someone fall in love with you? Curse people?"

"Why don't you come to my secret lair, and I'll show you?" The look of unease on Drew's face brought her a small bit of satisfaction.

"You're full of it," he muttered, but there was a flicker of doubt in his eyes.

She laughed softly. "You're seriously asking me about witches? You really are paranoid."

His eyes darkened, and he leaned closer, his breath foul. "You act like you're better than everyone else. But you're just a sad little freak."

"And you're just a scared little boy who only feels strong when he tries to hurt others."

His jaw clenched. "You better watch it, or your house won't be the last thing that burns."

"I'd need a house for that to happen."

Drew's laugh was sharp and cruel. "Oh, right. You're too poor for a house now. That's hilarious."

She kept her voice steady, refusing to let him see how much his words stung. "My house burned down in the same attack that bombed this school. The same one that injured us all."

Drew's smile faded, replaced by a look of suspicion. "You expect me to believe that?"

The bell rang, but he didn't move. "What did you have to do to become a witch, huh?"

"You're not letting this go, are you?"

He shrugged. "I'm just … fascinated."

"You sound like an idiot. Maybe you should see a shrink."

Drew grabbed her wrist, his fingers digging painfully into her skin. "You're playing with fire, and you don't even know it. None of you deserve to be here. You should be locked up. Or worse."

Ava stared at him, forcing herself to keep her breathing steady, her heart pounding in her chest. "Let go of me." She wanted to drown him.

He held her gaze for a moment longer before releasing her. "I wouldn't keep showing your face around here if I were you. But if you do … well, you'll be the center of the next bonfire." His smile was sickening.

He finally turned around to face the front, and she rubbed her throbbing wrist. She took a deep breath, trying to shake off the encounter. The day had barely started, and already, she felt exhausted. But no matter how much they pushed, she wasn't going to let them win. She couldn't be reckless.

When the bell rang, Ava followed the stream of students out the door, hoping the tension would eventually ease, but she doubted it. The stares, whispers, and glares followed her down the hallway like a shadow. She stepped into her government class, trying to shake off the unease, but it clung to her.

As she sat down, a group of girls across the room caught her eye. They were staring and whispering, their laughter sharp and cutting. Ava recognized two of them—Valerie Hammond and Amanda Russo. Peter's old friends.

Great. Her stomach twisted with unease. She could already imagine the rumors they were spreading.

Valerie stood up and made her way toward Ava, her eyes flashing with anger. Ava braced herself as Valerie stopped in front of her desk, towering over her in a weak attempt at intimidation.

"What do you want?" Ava's voice was steady, though irritation simmered beneath the surface.

Her gaze turned icy. "Whatever you did with Peter, give him back."

Ava let out a small laugh, more out of disbelief than amusement. "Excuse me?"

"You heard me. He was kidnapped, and now he's suddenly hanging out with you and your freak show of friends."

"Same with Seth," Amanda chimed in from behind Valerie.

Ava leaned back in her chair, resisting the urge to roll her eyes. "Maybe you should talk to Peter and Seth. It was their choice."

Valerie's eyes narrowed. "You think Peter and Seth are stupid enough to just *choose* to join your little cult? I know you did something to them. And we know it was you and your friends who bombed this school." Her voice dropped to a low, harsh whisper. "You're a heartless bitch."

Ava's hands tightened into fists under the desk, but she forced herself to stay calm. *Keep it together. Don't let them get to you.*

Valerie waited, as if daring her to snap, but Ava remained silent, refusing to give her the satisfaction of a response. After a tense moment, Valerie let out a huff of frustration and turned away, Amanda trailing behind her.

As they walked off, Ava exhaled slowly. The accusations, being blamed for the bombing, for Peter and Seth's choices, had become a cruel mantra at this point, and she knew it wasn't going to stop anytime soon.

Homeschooling doesn't sound so bad right now. She pushed the thought away. They weren't supposed to run from their problems. But what were they supposed to do when the very people they were meant to protect turned on them?

The weight of that question settled heavily on her shoulders as she faced another long day of whispered accusations and simmering hatred.

As soon as class ended, Ava found Peter waiting by her locker. His face mirrored the frustration and tension she felt inside. She reached for his hand, giving it a reassuring squeeze, and he returned it with a sad smile. Neither of them spoke as they made their way to the new cafeteria.

The cafeteria looked almost identical to the old one. Same high, warehouse-like ceiling, same gray concrete walls. The only real difference was the newness of the paint, the brightness of the lights, and the tension that hung in the air.

"At least they could've made this place look different." Ava scanned the room. The familiar unease tightened in her chest as they moved through the lunch line.

After getting their food, they sat down with Melissa and Lance. Ava couldn't help but notice that Gillian, Jeremy, and Thomas were absent. It stung more than she wanted to admit.

"Well, today sucks a big one." Melissa picked at her salad. Her tone was light, but her expression said otherwise.

Ava stabbed at a piece of lettuce. "Yep. Drew Foley's in my English class and already threatened me."

"Fantastic." Melissa sighed. "Trent did the same in my science class. I really need a cigarette."

Lance gave her a disapproving look. "We'll go out in a second."

Link, Nicole, and Seth approached the table, trays in hand. "Can we sit here?" Link asked.

"Of course." Melissa moved her bag to the floor.

They sat down and exchanged uneasy glances, like they were waiting for something to happen.

Ava surveyed the room again, noticing the hushed conversations and hostile glances directed towards them. "It's so somber in here."

"Well, did you expect it to be all puppies and rainbows today?" Melissa shot back, her voice tight.

"I was just making an observation," she muttered.

Link leaned forward, resting his arms on the table. "Does Savina realize what we're actually going through? This isn't normal bullying. We're not welcome here, and it feels like we're constantly in danger."

"They can't hurt you," Melissa said firmly. "You have to remind yourself that none of this is your fault. None of us were responsible. You had no control, and until you believe that the Ephemerals will keep badgering you."

Nicole chewed on her bottom lip. "Has it always been like this for you all?"

"Like what?" Ava asked, already knowing the answer.

"The constant stares, the whispering…"

"Unfortunately, yes," Ava replied. "Maybe not quite this bad, but people have always gossiped about things they don't understand."

"I don't know how you deal with it," Nicole whispered.

"You learn to ignore it." Melissa shrugged. "It's hard at first, but eventually, it fades."

"Just don't let them walk all over you," Ava added. "The moment they see weakness, they'll take advantage of it."

Nicole nodded, though she still looked apprehensive.

"Where are Thomas, Gillian, and Jeremy?" Seth asked.

Ava sighed. "Still avoiding us. Well, Peter and me, mostly."

"They'll come around," Melissa said between bites of her salad, though her tone wasn't convincing.

Seth frowned, his gaze distant. "I wish I could say the same about Amanda. I've been trying to figure out how to talk to her. Maybe if I told her about everything, it would change her mind. How did you do it, Ava?"

"She was so wishy-washy for a long time," Melissa smirked at Ava. "You were practically obsessed with Peter for a while."

Ava shifted uncomfortably. "Really, Mel?"

"What? It's true."

Seth turned to Peter. "What was your reaction when you found out about Ava?"

Peter gave a small shrug. "At first, it was surreal, but it didn't matter to me. I love her."

Ava's heart warmed at his words, and she smiled at him.

Melissa groaned. "Okay, lovebirds."

Ava shot her a playful glare. "Please, like you and Lance aren't obvious, always sneaking off into the woods."

"At least we're private about it." Melissa grinned.

"We try to be," she muttered under her breath.

Seth asked, "You really don't think I should tell Amanda?"

Ava hesitated. "I don't think it's a good idea. Not yet at least."

"Why not?" he pressed.

"She won't understand. They were pretty nasty to me when I tried sitting with them one day. Things got ugly." *And today.*

Seth frowned. "That's because Valerie has had a thing for Peter for a really long—"

"Seth," Peter interrupted, his tone sharp.

"What? It's not exactly a secret." He raised an eyebrow, unfazed.

Ava felt her frustration rise, a knot forming in her chest. She had always suspected Valerie's feelings but hearing it out loud made it sting more. She pushed down her discomfort. "I don't think that's the reason," she said, trying to steer the conversation in another direction. "They accused me of worshipping the devil because I was wearing my necklace. Valerie and Amanda were relentless."

Peter let out a tired sigh. "They were stressed. Seth had just been kidnapped."

Ava stared at him. "That doesn't excuse how they treated me."

"They're not bad people," Peter said. "Maybe if we all hung out, you'd get to know them better."

"Maybe I don't want to get to know them."

Peter looked taken aback, hurt flickering in his eyes. But Ava couldn't shake the resentment bubbling inside her. Why was he so quick to defend them? They had made her feel like an outsider, like she didn't belong. She had kept quiet about Valerie's snide comments earlier, but now she wondered if Peter would even believe her if she told him.

She stiffened, a strange sense of detachment creeping in. *Why do we bother protecting them? They're weak…*

"Ava?" Melissa's voice broke through her thoughts.

"What?" she snapped, her voice harsher than she intended.

"What's going on in that head of yours?"

"Nothing. I'm fine."

"Come on, you don't have to keep it all inside," Melissa coaxed.

"Maybe I don't feel like sharing my every thought with everyone."

Melissa held her hands up in surrender. "All right, all right. I get it."

Guilt settled over Ava like a heavy blanket. "Sorry," she muttered. "It's just—"

The bell rang, and the cafeteria erupted in noise as students rushed toward the doors, leaving their conversation unfinished.

Peter took her hand as they walked through the crowd. Tension coiled inside her, like a storm waiting to break. It was going to be a long time before anything felt normal again.

14

WHERE THE DEMONS HIDE

Glaring at the back of Drew Foley's head, Ava's mind swirled with violent thoughts she barely recognized as her own. Images of his skull smashing against the desk or him drowning, suffering the way Xavier had, flashed before her eyes. The anger brewing inside her was new. Darker, sharper.

Gabriel and Joss had assured her that Drew and his gang weren't Hunters, just angry, petty boys seeking revenge. But their torment had been relentless for two weeks now. Ava was convinced they had started the attacks on Thomas's house.

Drew twisted in his seat, the smug look on his face making her blood boil. "Now that I think about it, I think your mom deserved to die," he sneered. "I mean, if she had lived, she would've seen her pathetic daughter bomb a school."

Ava's grip tightened on the edge of her desk, her knuckles turning white as her vision blurred with rage. Before she could stop herself, the words spilled out. "Maybe it was a good thing your friends died," she hissed. "So, they wouldn't have to see what a pathetic loser you turned out to be."

Drew's face darkened, and for a moment, something flickered behind his eyes—shock, hurt, fear. But it vanished quickly, replaced by his usual sneer.

"I can't wait until the bonfire this Friday," he spat.

Ava's heart pounded, but she leaned forward, her voice dangerously low. "Me either. Can't wait to see you try to burn us. We're crazy, Drew, and you never know what we'll do."

For a second, fear flashed in his eyes. It was almost satisfying. Almost.

What am I doing? The realization hit her like a wave of cold water. *What's wrong with me?*

She couldn't believe what she'd just said. The hatred, the violence. It wasn't her. Or at least, it hadn't been before. Was she becoming like the Cimmerians? Her thoughts had been sharper, crueler lately, like bitterness was seeping into her blood. Ever since Marcel had mentioned her mother, the line between who she was and who she feared becoming had started to blur.

Was she turning into something worse?

And the nightmares of her mother hadn't stopped. She shook her head, trying to banish the thought. She didn't hate all Ephemerals, just certain ones. *Just the ones who deserved it, right?*

But the nagging voice in her mind wouldn't leave her alone. *Was Mom a Cimmerian? Is that why I'm having these thoughts?* She needed answers. Maybe Savina or Aaron could tell her. Or even Colden. But then Link's ridiculous suggestion about the Necromancer crept into her thoughts. *Could Necromancy even work?* The idea was laughable ... wasn't it?

The bell rang, jolting her from her thoughts. She hurried out of the classroom, trying to leave the darkness behind, but it clung to her like a shadow. As soon as she stepped into the hallway, she spotted Peter waiting by her locker.

"Hey," he said softly. "Are you okay?"

Ava leaned against the cool metal of the lockers, her chest tightening. "Sure."

"Drew piss you off again?"

She let out a humorless laugh. "Yes. I'm not sure how much more of him I can take."

Peter reached out, brushing a strand of hair behind her ear. His touch was warm. "I know what you mean. Why don't we hang out tonight? Just the two of us."

"I'd like that."

He smiled, showing his dimples for the first time in what felt like ages. That smile was enough to lift the heaviness, if only for a moment. He kissed her gently, and with that, she felt a flicker of hope, like she could breathe again.

But her necklace grew warm, the familiar sensation of someone else's emotions seeping in. Gillian's anger. And … guilt? Ava's brow furrowed as she exchanged a confused glance with Peter. *Guilt?* Maybe Gillian was finally starting to realize how silly it was to be mad at Ava for being with Peter.

Ava looked up as Jeremy rushed toward them, his face pale with worry. "Have you guys heard?"

"Heard what?" Peter asked.

"Trent Gattis went to the mall today and shot a bunch of people before turning the gun on himself."

Ava's heart dropped, her jaw going slack. "What?"

"It's all over the news. He killed four people and injured two." Jeremy shook his head in disbelief.

Peter frowned. "Why would he do that?"

Jeremy glanced around and lowered his voice. "This has to be the Cimmerians. They must have manipulated him somehow. Redirected his anger or compelled him to do it."

Ava's stomach churned, but she shook her head. "No. This wasn't a Cimmerian attack. Trent did this on his own." The words tumbled out harsher than she intended. "He couldn't hurt us, so he took his anger out on others."

Both Jeremy and Peter gave her a confused, almost disbelieving look.

"You can't be serious." Peter's brow furrowed. "Why would you think this wasn't the Cimmerians? You were the one who thought they might've been behind burning Thomas's house."

"I never said that!" Ava shot back defensively, her pulse racing. "And Aaron already told us it wasn't the Cimmerians. They're all locked up."

Jeremy placed a hand on her shoulder. "Ava, are you okay?"

"I'm fine!" She pulled away from his touch. "I've gotta go."

She stormed past them, her footsteps echoing in the now-emptying hallway. Confusion curled inside her. *Why are they so quick to pin this on the Cimmerians? It's the Ephemerals who are waging war against us, not the Cimmerians. Trent's actions were driven by his own distorted rage. He did what he thought needed to be done, and those people deserved it.*

Ava halted, frozen, the door to the stairwell halfway open. *What the hell was that?* Why was she defending Trent? Defending the Cimmerians? It felt as if someone else's thoughts had seeped into her mind.

Her fists clenched as her pulse quickened, the roaring sound of rushing water engulfing her senses. It was trickling down her arms, dripping onto the tiled floor. Ava bolted down the stairs, panic bubbling inside her. *I'm not turning into a Cimmerian. This isn't me. These aren't my thoughts!*

She shoved open the door to the next floor, leaning against the cool wall, gasping for breath. Slowly, the water stopped. Her heartbeat steadied, but the fear lingered. What was happening to her?

The rest of the day was a blur, whispers of the mall shooting swirling around her. People couldn't stop talking about Trent. No one could make sense of it, but most chalked it up to trauma from the bombing, how it pushed him over the edge. Ava wasn't sure what to think anymore.

At lunch with Peter, she forced a smile and explained her earlier reaction. "I was just … trying to take what Aaron said into account. If there *are* Cimmerians out there, we've got to worry, right?" she said, her voice sounding more certain than she felt.

Peter seemed to accept her explanation, though she could still see the unease in his eyes. Strangely enough, he didn't press the matter, and Ava felt a pang of guilt twisting inside her as she held onto her secret.

As Ava pulled up in front of Peter's house, dark, ominous clouds loomed overhead, hinting at an impending downpour. The crisp autumn breeze gently brushed against her skin, sending a shiver down her spine. With each step towards the door, a peculiar sensation washed over her, as if unseen eyes were fixed upon her every move. She scanned her surroundings, straining to catch any glimpse of a lurking presence, but found nothing out of the ordinary.

Peter answered the door with a smile, pulling her inside. His lips crashed against hers, and her heart pounded against her ribcage. She kissed him back, but the desperation in the way he clung to her made her heart race for the wrong reasons.

He pulled away, breathless, his eyes searching hers as if looking for something just out of reach. "You should probably come inside," he muttered, guiding her up the stairs. Once in his room, he sat on the edge of the bed, pulling her onto his lap with a sense of urgency she didn't quite understand. His lips pressed against hers, almost desperate, and his hands slid up her back, grazing the skin where her shirt ended. She kissed him back, trying to keep up, but it was clear. He wasn't just kissing her. He was avoiding something. She could feel it. Something was wrong.

Pulling back, she studied his face. "Peter, what's wrong?"

He sighed, and she slid off his lap. "It's just everything. School sucks. Dad keeps asking why I'm not hanging out with my old friends anymore. And then there's what you said about Valerie and Amanda…"

Her stomach tightened. She knew where this was going. "What about it?"

His eyes darkened. "Did you really mean that? You don't want to get to know them at all?"

Ava hesitated. She didn't want to fight, but she had to be honest. "Yes, I meant it. I don't think it's a good idea for Seth to get involved with Amanda either. Not right now."

"Why not?"

"Because they hate us, Peter. They've made that perfectly clear. It's not just Valerie and Amanda. Every Ephemeral in school looks at us like we're the enemy."

"They don't hate us," he argued, standing now, pacing. "They're just confused. If we explain it to them, maybe they'll understand."

"You *can't* tell them what we are! Do you remember how much trouble I got into just telling you? What it did to our coven? I broke their trust for you."

"So what? You just don't want me to be friends with them. That's what this is really about, isn't it?"

Her temper flared. "Are you serious right now? You think I'm just being some controlling girlfriend?"

He stopped pacing and crossed his arms. "I'm just trying to find a balance. Seth is miserable, Ava. He didn't want this life. He only stayed so Savina wouldn't erase his mind because he wanted to be with Amanda. And now he's stuck. I just … I feel like I'm being pulled in so many different directions and I don't know how to fix it."

She stared at him, the words sinking in, each one cutting a little deeper than the last. "Maybe I'm not part of what you want to fix." She stood up.

"Ava don't twist this," he groaned, running a hand through his hair. "It's not you. It's everything else."

"I can't stand here while you keep pulling away." She crossed her arms, feeling a mix of hurt and anger rising inside her. "Are you regretting your decision too?"

"Don't start with that. You know I'm not."

"How am I supposed to know? You've been acting like you still want to be one of them."

"Them? Do you even hear yourself? I *was* one of them! Now you sound like the people we're supposed to be fighting against."

Ava's breath hitched, a sharp pain shot through her chest. "You think I sound like a Cimmerian?" The accusation hit her hard. He knew about her nightmares. He knew what she feared.

Regret flickered in his eyes. "Ava, I didn't mean—"

"Yeah, you did." She shoved past him. "I can't believe you'd say that." She charged downstairs and outside, the rain pouring down in thick sheets. She didn't care that her clothes were plastered to her skin, water dripping from her hair.

"Ava, come on!" he called after her, grabbing her arm to stop her. "Don't do this. Just come back inside."

She wrenched her arm free, the cold rain mixing with her hot anger. "Why don't you call your precious friends? If you're so desperate to keep them in your life, why don't you tell them what's really going on? Maybe they'd love to hear how we bombed the school or that I'm some witch who 'brainwashed' you."

He blinked, caught off guard. "What? What are you talking about?"

"They said it to my face, Peter. And you're still defending them."

"I just don't believe they'd say something like that." He shook his head, water dripping from his hair.

Her heart dropped. He didn't trust her. "Of course. They're so *perfect* in your eyes."

"That's not true. Ava, I care about you. Can we please just go inside and talk?"

The rain poured harder, but she shook her head. "No. I'm done talking. If you don't believe me, I don't know what else to say."

"Ava, don't go like this!" Peter grabbed her hand, his voice pleading but still edged with frustration. "I'm sorry for what I said."

She pulled her hand free, shaking her head again. "You might be sorry now, but you still don't get it." Her voice broke, the hurt spilling out despite herself. "Maybe you never will."

She climbed into her, her hands trembling as she shut the door. Peter stood there, alone in the rain, watching as she drove away, the downpour swallowing his figure in her rearview mirror.

As she sped down the road, her mind swirled with Peter's words, each one echoing in her head like a dull throb. Did he really think she was becoming like the Cimmerians? Or was she just paranoid, letting her fears twist her reality? The thought burrowed deeper with every mile. Her grip tightened on the steering wheel, knuckles white, as flashes of memory—of the nightmares, of the things she'd said to Drew—surged to the surface.

Ava swallowed hard, her chest tightening as doubt crept in. Was she really losing control? She had felt the darkness rising inside her lately, the anger, the violent urges that weren't hers. But was it really as bad as Peter seemed to think? Could he see something she couldn't?

The rain came down in thick sheets, blurring the road ahead. She was too lost in the spiraling questions that gnawed at her mind.

15

BAD MOON RISING

For the past thirty minutes, Ava's phone buzzed on and off, the screen lighting up with Peter's name, but she refused to answer. Tears blurred her vision as she angrily wiped them away, driving aimlessly through the rain-slicked streets. She knew her frustration and hurt were leaking out for everyone in the coven to feel, but she didn't care. Not tonight. She didn't want to explain herself, didn't want to hear their reassurances.

The rain had stopped, but the cold air clung to her skin, seeping into her bones. She shivered but didn't bother using her powers to warm herself. She couldn't summon the energy. The hollow ache in her chest refused to subside. As she drove, the low fuel light flickered on the dashboard, making her groan. *Of course.*

The nearest gas station was in the opposite direction of the Manor, miles away from where she wanted to be. She hated stopping at stations this late, especially ones that felt as deserted as the road she was on now. But she had no choice. She turned the car toward the station, her heart sinking.

When she pulled up, the station's bright lights flickered, casting eerie shadows in the cool, damp night. The neon *open* sign buzzed softly, but the place felt lifeless, the air still and unnerving. As she stepped out of the car, the quiet swallowed her, and the distant hum of the lights sounded like a warning.

As she stepped out of the car, the twang of a country song blared from the gas station's speakers. Something about a red solo cup. She hated country music. Her phone buzzed again in her pocket, but she didn't bother looking at it. Instead, she focused on pumping gas.

As she finished, her heart sank when a black truck pulled up to the other side of the pump. Jonah and Drew got out, and the moment their eyes met hers, Ava stiffened. She couldn't escape them, not even there.

As Jonah pumped gas, his face became red and tight with anger as he glared at her. "Look who it is."

With his eyes fixated on his phone, Drew finally glanced up. His expression darkened. "Hey, killer."

Ava's pump clicked off, and she quickly returned it to the base, her nerves prickling. She moved toward the back of her car, but Drew was already there, blocking her path.

"What do you want?" she asked, keeping her voice steady.

Drew smirked. "What are you doing here?"

"What does it look like?"

"What did you do to Trent?"

"Nothing. Stop blaming us for everything and look at yourselves. You burned Thomas's house. Trent killed innocent people. You're not the victims here." She tried to move past him, but Jonah stepped in her way.

"What do you want?" she repeated, her voice sharper now.

Jonah tightly grabbed her arm, his eyes blazed with intense hatred. "Come take a walk with us."

She jerked her arm free. "Not a chance."

A hard jab to her side made her suck in a breath. Her heart pounded as she glanced down at the gun now pressing into her ribs. Drew stepped closer, his smirk gone, replaced with something darker, more dangerous.

"I think you need to come with us," Jonah growled.

Her pulse raced, but she refused to show fear. "Let go of me."

A flash of lightning cracked across the sky, illuminating the gas station in a stark, white blaze. Ava flinched, her breath catching in her throat as a wave of memories crashed over her. Her mother's voice echoed through her mind. *Destiny awaits you, Ava.*

Her mother's face flashed before her, the memory vivid and haunting. She could almost see it again. The moment the sky had split open, and her mother was struck by lightning. Ava squeezed her eyes shut, trying to block out the image, but it was too late. The vision overwhelmed her, a cruel reminder of everything she had lost. The ground shifted beneath her feet.

When she blinked, she was no longer at the gas station. She was in the woods. The air was cold and damp, and Jonah and Drew stood in front of her, a gun still pointed at her chest.

Her head swam. *How did I get here?* The feeling of lost time was unsettling. Her body tensed, her heartbeat erratic. No one knew where she was.

"You don't want to do this." She trembled.

Jonah advanced, his face contorted with rage. "It's your fault she's dead. You and your friends killed my sister."

"What are you talking about?"

Tears welled in his eyes. "Trent killed those people because of you. He was trying to get revenge, just like we will. You all deserve to die."

He raised the gun and smashed it across her face. Pain exploded in her head, and warm blood dribbled down her chin, the metallic taste filling her mouth.

"You bombed the school. You killed them. You think we're just going to let you walk away from that?" Jonah's voice cracked, but his grip on the gun tightened. "We're going to kill every last one of you."

Ava's head throbbed as her vision blurred. "It wasn't me. It was Xavier."

"Shut up!" Jonah swung the gun again, knocking her to the ground. "I know you made Trent do it. Don't lie to me."

Her thoughts raced. They were going to kill her. It didn't matter what she said, Jonah had made up his mind. Desperation clawed at her, her body shaking with fear and anger. *Kill them.* The thought slithered through her mind. *This is your destiny. End this.*

Ava blinked, horrified by the voice in her head. But before she could process it, Jonah was raising the gun again.

"Jonah don't do this," Drew said, sounding less confident now. "We can't kill her."

Jonah's face was wild with fury. "Watch me."

Her necklace warmed, and energy surged through her body, a simmering force begging for release. Her focus narrowed to Jonah, blocking out everything else. A pulsating power coursed through her veins, echoing in her ears. She pictured him submerged beneath churning waters, thrashing desperately for air. His bulging eyes and flaring nostrils betrayed his panic. Veins on his neck swelled, his face turning a fiery shade of red. With a gasp, he clutched his throat, his mouth agape, desperately clawing for precious breath. The gun slipped from his grasp as he crumpled to the wet ground, writhing in agony.

"What are you doing to him?" Drew shouted, backing away.

Ava's focus didn't waver. *Let him drown.*

A gunshot rang out, and a sharp, searing pain tore through her stomach. She doubled over, clutching the wound, her vision going black around the edges. The pain was unbearable, twisting and radiating through her body like fire.

She had to get out of there. She tried to stand, but her legs buckled. Every breath was agony. She could hear Jonah and Drew moving closer, but she couldn't see them. Her body trembled, her energy slipping away.

Clenching her jaw, she reached out with her power one last time, imagining them both submerged in water, drowning. They choked and gasped, but her strength was fading fast.

With a final, desperate effort, she let go, collapsing onto the ground. The world around her blurred, her heartbeat slowing as darkness crept in. She blinked through the haze.

The sound of footsteps echoed in the woods. Panic surged through her, her body frozen in fear. She couldn't move, couldn't fight anymore.

A voice broke through her haze. "Tyler, over here!"

Ava's pulse quickened as she strained to hear.

"It's Jonah and Drew," Tyler replied, his voice low. "Stay back, Beth."

"Are they … are they dead?" Beth's voice trembled.

Ava's heart dropped. *Dead? No. No. No.* She hadn't meant to kill them. She wasn't even sure how it happened. It was all a blur. A mess of anger, fear, and power surging through her.

"I think so." Tyler moved closer. "I don't know about the girl. She's still breathing."

Beth gasped. "What do we do?"

"We need to call 911. Come on."

Their footsteps faded, leaving Ava in silence. Relief flooded her, but it was fleeting. Her mind was a swirl of confusion and fear, and her strength was waning fast. She pressed a hand to her stomach, feeling the warm blood seep through her fingers. She was running out of time.

I can't die here…

With shaking hands, she fumbled for her phone, ignoring the blood on her fingers as she unlocked the screen. Ava's vision dimmed, but with the last of her strength, she dialed the only person who could help her now.

"Gillian," she gasped into the phone, her voice barely audible. "I need your help."

16

AS I LAY DYING

As Ava lay under the burning stars, their chaotic pattern dancing in the dark sky, the wind cut through her. Her heartbeat slowed, her breaths shallow. Holding her bleeding wound, she didn't want to move. She still couldn't make sense of how she'd ended up there, maybe just behind the gas station, in the woods where high schoolers partied. But there was a block of time missing, gone after she saw her mother.

Then it hit her. *Trudy McVaine.* The name echoed in her mind like a curse. Trudy, the same woman who had controlled visions in Ava's mind before. Had she warped this one too? Ava's mind spun as the pieces slowly started to fall into place. The image of her mother, the disorienting moments afterward. None of it made sense until now. Trudy had to be behind it. *Of course she was.* Had she been manipulating Ava all along, trying to push her toward something darker? Her stomach clenched as a terrifying thought crossed her mind. *What if she made me kill Jonah and Drew too?*

Was she out there now, watching, waiting for her next move?

Ava doubted it. The piercing sound of sirens shattered the stillness, growing louder, closing in. Ephemerals had found her first. *Will Gillian get here in time?*

She needed Gillian to compel the police, the paramedics, anyone who would question how two human bodies lay next to her, dead by drowning in the middle of the woods. *I killed them. I murdered them.*

Tears streaked down her cheeks, burning with guilt. What would Peter think? Or her father? Would Aaron strip her of her powers? Would she be cast out of the coven?

She could barely keep her eyes open as the flashing lights painted the night red and blue. *I don't want to move. Let me disappear…*

The voices grew closer, crowding her. Faces hovered over her, but she couldn't focus. A female paramedic with a tight ponytail leaned over her, a flashlight blinding Ava's already weak vision.

"Can you hear me?" the paramedic asked, her voice far away.

She nodded weakly.

"What's your name?"

"Ava!" Gillian's panicked voice pierced through the chaos. She pushed past the officers, her eyes wide with shock at the blood. "Holy crap, you're bleeding so badly."

"Ma'am, step back—" the paramedic started, but Gillian's fierce glare stopped her.

"She's my friend." She kneeled beside Ava.

Ava met Gillian's gaze, hoping, *praying*, that she could understand without words. *I killed them.* The words screamed inside her head. She needed Gillian to know, needed her to *fix* this.

Gillian's expression shifted, the pieces falling into place. She lowered her voice, her tone hard. "I'll take care of it."

Ava closed her eyes briefly, relief mixing with the pain.

Gillian leaned closer to her ear. "I'll call Savina."

Her eyes shot open. "No … don't…" Her voice was barely audible, but the panic was clear.

"Why not?"

"Please … just don't…" Ava's heart hammered in her chest, the idea of facing Savina unbearable. She wasn't ready to face the judgment. Not yet.

Gillian exhaled sharply, rolling her eyes before pulling out her phone. "Fine," she muttered, but Ava wasn't sure she trusted her. Gillian dialed, her voice low as she spoke into the phone. "I found her. She's been shot—yeah, the paramedics are taking her to the hospital." Her eyes flickered back to Ava, softening with worry. "I don't know the details yet. Okay, see you soon."

She ended the call, gripping Ava's hand. "Why didn't you call her first?"

Ava's heart sank. *Savina.* Gillian *had* called her. *Was she really out to get me?*

The female paramedic returned with a stretcher, her face tight with urgency. "Okay, Ava, we're going to lift you. This might hurt."

"I don't … want to go to the hospital…" she tried to say, her voice fading.

"Honey, you have to," the paramedic insisted. "You'll bleed to death if you don't."

Ava's grip on Gillian's hand tightened, desperation in her eyes. "Don't let them take me."

Gillian's frustration cracked through her worry. "They're trying to save you. I'll be right behind you. Just let them help."

She didn't want to let go, but her body betrayed her. Her strength was slipping, and as the paramedics lifted her onto the stretcher, she felt her connection to the world weaken.

The paramedic gently placed an oxygen mask over Ava's face, the cool air easing her ragged breaths. She met Gillian's eyes one last time, hoping she'd keep her promise.

Gillian mouthed, "I'll fix this."

As the paramedics wheeled her toward the ambulance, the pain overwhelmed her. Ava closed her eyes, surrendering to the darkness.

When her eyes flickered open, Ava was disoriented. It was dark, but the room was warm, and the bed felt familiar. Her hand was being held, and she instinctively squeezed it. The person next to her stirred and gasped.

"Ava," Melissa's voice broke through the haze, soft but filled with relief.

Relief washed over Ava as she blinked, trying to focus. "Mel…" She tried to sit up, but a sharp, stabbing pain shot through her stomach, forcing her back down with a cry.

"Easy, easy," she soothed, gently pushing her back onto the bed. "Just lay back. You're safe."

Ava did as told, her mind trying to piece together what had happened. She winced as memories of the night rushed back. Jonah, Drew, the gun, the vision of her mother, that voice in her head. It all felt like a blur. "What's going on? Where am I?"

Melissa clicked on the small bedside lamp, filling the room with soft light. Ava recognized Melissa's room. It had been a long time since she'd been there. She glanced at the familiar poster of Bradley Cooper plastered on the ceiling and couldn't help but wonder how awkward that must be for Lance.

"You're at my house." Melissa said.

"Why … why am I here?"

"I brought you here. You don't remember?"

She shook her head slightly, trying to focus through the lingering fog in her mind. "I remember getting shot. The paramedics … the stretcher."

"You were in surgery. They got the bullet out. When you woke up, I took you here. You told me you didn't want Savina to know, so I didn't tell her."

Ava's heart skipped a beat. "But … I thought Gillian told her."

"She hasn't. At least, not that I know of. She called and told me what happened. I felt your fear, Ava, I was trying to find you all night. You didn't answer your phone. I didn't know what to do until Gillian called. What happened?"

Ava's chest tightened as the memories crashed back. Drew and Jonah, the gun, their lifeless bodies. Fresh tears welled in her eyes as the horrifying reality hit her again. She had killed them. Her breath caught in her throat. They had threatened her, but still, they didn't deserve to die. That voice urging her to kill them. She'd *wanted* to kill them.

"What is it?" Melissa asked, concerned.

"Nothing."

The door creaked open, and Gillian stepped inside, her expression tight, eyes guarded. "Oh, good. You're awake."

Her voice was brisk, almost clipped. "Everything's taken care of. The hospital thinks you were shot by some random guy, and the shooter ran off. The police don't remember seeing you, and neither does the couple who found you." She hugged herself, the confident facade cracking as her fingers fidgeted, and she bit her lip.

Ava felt the anxiety rolling off Gillian and knew how much she had hated cleaning up the mess. "Thank you, Gillian."

"Don't thank me," she snapped. "Why didn't you want Savina to know? This is … this is *serious*, Ava. I'm not going to get in trouble for something you did. I had to clean it up. What if I get caught?"

"G, seriously," Melissa said. "Chill out, okay? She was shot by two Ephemerals. You ever think of self-defense?"

"She didn't have to kill them, though!" Gillian shouted. "She had a choice. And now we're all caught in the middle of this mess."

"You weren't there," Melissa countered. "You don't know what happened."

Ava flinched as their argument swirled around her, the burden of their words weighing her down. She didn't want them fighting, not over her. She hated that her actions had caused this. She had been reckless, again. No one would forgive her now.

Melissa turned to her. "Everyone's been worried sick about you. We have to let them know you're okay."

"No," Ava said quickly, her heart racing. "Don't tell anyone I was shot."

"What? Are you crazy? Why won't you let Savina heal you?"

Tears welled up again, the guilt too much to bear. "Because I killed them, Mel," she whispered, her voice trembling. "I didn't mean to. It just … happened. I didn't even realize it until the couple found us. Please don't tell anyone. They'll banish me."

Melissa's face softened. "Ava." She pursed her lips as she thought. "We'll figure something out. But you need to heal. You need to let Savina take care of you. People are going to ask questions."

Ava shook her head, her voice trembling. "No. I can't."

"What happened? It was self-defense, right?"

She couldn't answer.

Gillian crossed her arms, her face pale. "Great. So now we're all lying for you. I hope you realize what you've dragged us into. I'm not going to get kicked out because of this."

"Get out," Melissa snapped. "You're not helping."

Gillian's eyes flashed with anger, and she made a disgusted sound before storming out of the room, slamming the door behind her.

Ava stared at the closed door. "If she hates me so much, why did she even help?"

Melissa sighed, sitting beside her. "She doesn't hate you. She's just mad. She's angry because she knows you made the right choice but won't admit it. But I keep feeling her guilt."

Ava's voice broke. "I didn't know what to do, Mel. They pulled a gun on me. They forced me into the woods, and … I blacked out."

Melissa eased onto the bed, gathering Ava in her arms. "It's okay. You're a lot stronger than they are. How did they get you in the woods? What happened?"

"I don't know. I had a vision of my mom again. It had to have been Trudy who planted it. She must've done something."

"Trudy? There was no sign of her."

"It had to be her," Ava insisted, her eyes closing tightly. Her hands went to her throbbing head, trying to chase away the tormenting sensations. Despite the gunshot wound confined to her stomach, the ache spread through every inch of her body.

"Peter's on his way. What do you want me to tell him?"

"Nothing," she whispered, the ache in her heart returning. Their fight … his words. He was right. She was becoming a Cimmerian.

"You can't hide this from him."

"I can't tell him what I did, Mel." Ava's voice was raw, her guilt too heavy. How could she face Peter, especially after what he'd said?

"Just get some rest." Melissa stroked Ava's hair gently. "I'll be right here if you need anything."

Ava slowly blinked her eyes open, squinting as the bright sunlight flooded the room. Bradley Cooper's familiar, smirking face on the poster was above her, and she rolled her eyes. She felt a warm, familiar weight beside her.

Peter's arm was draped around her waist, and the dull ache in her stomach reminded her of everything she was trying to forget.

He stirred, his body tensing slightly, as though he'd been awake, waiting for her to open her eyes. "Ava?" His voice was soft, laced with concern. "Are you okay?"

"I'm fine," she lied, shifting slightly, only for a sharp pain to slice through her abdomen. She quickly masked the wince, hoping he hadn't noticed.

But Peter was watching her too closely, his brow furrowed, his eyes filled with worry. "Ava … you're in pain." His voice was firm but gentle, as he sat up quickly, leaning over her. "What happened last night? You didn't answer my calls. I was freaking out."

She forced a weak smile, feeling his guilt mixed with concern. "I'm okay. It's nothing serious."

He shook his head. "You've been out for hours, and every time you move, you're flinching. That's not *nothing*." His gaze flicked to her abdomen, the area where she instinctively held her hand. "Did someone hurt you? Let me see."

Ava gently pushed his hand away, her movements slow and deliberate. "It's fine, really. Just a dumb accident. Just sore. Besides, with you here, the pain's pretty much gone."

"What kind of accident?"

She bit her lip, trying to come up with something believable. "I was walking outside, and I wasn't paying attention. I tripped over some roots in the woods and fell pretty hard." She hesitated before adding, "I landed on a rock. It's just a bruise, nothing serious."

"A bruise?"

"It's fine."

He exhaled a shaky breath, his eyes laden with guilt. "I'm an idiot, Ava. I don't deserve you," he muttered, his voice thick with regret. "I was a jerk for what I said, and I should've made you stay. If I had been there—"

"You couldn't have stopped it from happening. It wasn't your fault." She hoped that would ease his mind, even if it didn't ease her own.

"Still, I'm sorry."

She didn't want to talk about apologies, didn't want to confess that she didn't deserve him either. Not after what she had done. Instead, she rested her hand on his shoulder, holding it there, hoping that the moment would be enough to quiet both their fears.

Later, when Ava returned to the Manor, every step felt heavier than the last. Her Enchanter genes helped her heal faster than an Ephemeral ever would, but the wound still throbbed with every movement, a constant reminder of what she had done. *I killed them.*

As she entered the Manor, the murmur of voices drifted from the library. A part of her longed to join them, to lose herself in the comforting chatter and pretend everything was normal. But another part—the part shackled by guilt—just wanted to wash the night away and hide.

Despite the stabbing pain, she forced herself to climb the stairs, her hand brushing against the banister as if seeking support. Once she finally reached her room, she moved to the bathroom, avoiding her reflection in the mirror. She couldn't bear to see the evidence of what had happened.

She grabbed a washcloth, soaking it in warm water, and carefully wiped her face and neck, her movements slow and deliberate, avoiding any motions that would aggravate the wound. The warmth soothed her, but each time her hand brushed near her injury, it was like a blade jabbing in her thoughts. Jonah's face flashed before her. Those cold, lifeless eyes staring back at her. *I killed him.* And Drew. She was a murderer. *What's wrong with me? Is this who I'm becoming?*

Her thoughts spiraled, dark and relentless, pulling her deeper into self-loathing. Her mother's voice echoed in her mind. *Your destiny awaits, Ava.* The vision of standing beside Corbin, a symbol of the Cimmerians, haunted her. *Was this what destiny looked like?*

She slid down to the cold bathroom floor, her body trembling as silent sobs overtook her. Tears streamed down her cheeks, each one a reminder of the person she feared she was becoming. She hated herself. Hated what she had done. But the worst part—the part that twisted the knife in her chest—was that Jonah and Drew didn't deserve to die.

17

EXPOSED

To keep up appearances, Ava forced herself to eat dinner at the table, even though it was optional. Most nights, she ate with her dad, Mrs. Arrington, and a few others, so skipping would raise suspicion. So far, she'd managed to keep the attack a secret, and no one had questioned her odd behavior. Melissa had done a good job convincing people that Ava had just had a bad dream and stayed over at her place.

As she reached the top of the stairs, she paused. The descent loomed like a challenge, knowing each step would be a painful reminder of her secret. Times like these made her wish for Gabriel's teleporting ability or Peter's presence to numb the pain. But this was something she had to face on her own.

Clenching her teeth, Ava gripped the railing and descended one agonizing step at a time, fighting through the sharp, stabbing pain in her side. When she reached the bottom, she paused again, taking slow, steady breaths before stepping into the dining room.

"Well, hello there, sleepyhead." Her father grinned, pulling the chair beside him out for her.

She forced a smile, lowering herself into the chair gingerly. "Sorry, didn't get much sleep last night."

"I'm just teasing." He winked.

Colden entered with steaming casserole dishes, and soon, others joined the table. Gabriel, Joss, and Eric joined her as her father served creamy noodle and beef casserole to everyone, amidst a chorus of gratitude.

Ava stared at her plate, the savory smell reaching her nose, but her appetite had vanished.

"How was school?" Joss asked. "I bet people are even more depressed after that mall shooting and the two boys who died the other night."

Ava's heart nearly stopped. Her stomach lurched. She tried to keep her expression neutral, but panic buzzed beneath her skin. *What was Joss talking about? How did she know?*

"What?" she managed to ask, her voice tight.

Her father lowered the newspaper he'd been reading, turning it so she could see the headline. "Didn't you hear?" he asked. The words *"Two Teens Dead in Scuffle"* screamed at her from the page.

The smell of the casserole suddenly churned her stomach, and guilt twisted like a knife deep in her gut. Without thinking, she shoved her plate away, the harsh scrape of it against the table louder than she expected. Her breathing quickened, chest tightening as she gripped the edge of her chair. Nausea swirled, threatening to rise. She swallowed hard, forcing it down, but the unease lingered.

Her father looked at her with concern. "Something wrong with the casserole?"

"No," she muttered, barely able to control her emotions.

"You're looking pale. Are you feeling okay?" His brow furrowed in concern.

"Yeah, I think I'm coming down with something."

"Tis the season," he chuckled.

"I guess you didn't know the two guys," Joss added. "I wonder what they were fighting about."

Gabriel leaned forward. "Wait, let me see their faces." He grabbed the newspaper, and Ava's pulse quickened. *He's going to recognize them.*

Ava shifted uncomfortably in her seat, her fingers trembling.

"Aren't these the guys from Thomas's house fire?" Gabriel studied the photos.

Ava nodded, her voice stuck in her throat. She kept her eyes glued to the table, refusing to meet Gabriel or Joss's gaze.

"Those poor parents," her father sighed. "One of the boys lost a sister in the bombing."

Ava clenched her jaw, the guilt consuming her. *What have I done?*

"Are the kids at school still giving you all a hard time?" Eric asked, oblivious to the tension brewing inside her.

"Yes," she whispered, her voice barely above a murmur.

Her father reached for her hand, but she pulled it away. She wasn't sure why. Maybe because she didn't want him to feel how clammy and shaky she was, or maybe because she couldn't bear for anyone to touch her right now.

"Ava, are you sure you're okay?" he asked, his concern deepening.

"I'm fine," she said, a little too sharply. She had to get out of there. Gabriel and Joss knew. They both knew.

Pushing back her chair, she stood abruptly, biting back a cry as the pain in her side flared, sharp and stabbing. "I'm going to lie down."

"Do you need anything?" her father asked.

"No," she said, her voice shaky. Avoiding his eyes, she hurried out of the dining room, blinking back the tears that threatened to spill. *Keep it together, Ava.*

As soon as she reached the stairs, a warm, wet sensation spread across her side. Ava glanced down, her stomach dropping in horror. Blood had seeped through her shirt. *The stitches.* Panic surged through her chest as she stepped onto the first stair, but before she could take another step, a hand clamped down on her arm.

"Ava, come with me," Gabriel's voice was quiet, but firm as he pulled her away from the stairs.

"What are you doing?" She winced when Gabriel's grip tightened.

"You're bleeding."

"I'm fine," she snapped. She couldn't go back to the hospital. *And she definitely couldn't face Savina.* Not after everything that had happened. What she had done. Ava yanked her arm, trying to break free, but Gabriel's hold didn't budge. In a blink, the air shifted around her. When she opened her eyes, the familiar space of Savina's parlor surrounded her.

No. No, no, no.

"I can't be here." Panic clawed up her throat as she stumbled back toward the door, only to find Gabriel blocking her path.

"Ava, you obviously need healing. Just let me help you." His hand reached out, the touch gentle yet firm, but she twisted away from him, her breathing erratic.

"No. I don't want her to know."

"Ava—"

"Let me leave!" She shoved against his chest, though it felt like hitting a stone wall. Her arms trembled with the effort.

Gabriel didn't move, his expression softening. "She's not here."

Ava froze, her mind struggling to process his words. "What?"

"She's not here," he repeated, his brows knitting together in concern as his eyes, usually so guarded, flickered with something softer. "You need to heal."

The pain in her side overwhelmed her senses, making her lightheaded, like she was losing her grip on reality. She bit her lip, the coppery taste of blood mingling with her panic. "Then what are we doing here?" she whispered, her voice weak, barely holding on.

"Healing you." Gabriel moved toward a shelf hidden behind a heavy black curtain, revealing rows of vials filled with liquids, pastes, and herbs. He grabbed a small vial from the top and turned back to her. "Savina keeps these for emergencies or when she's away." Uncorking the vial, he held it out to her. "Here, drink this."

She eyed the vial warily. "What is it?"

"A healing potion. I don't know exactly what's in it, but I know it works. Trust me."

Her whole body trembled as pain twisted deeper into her side, but she shook her head. "No. I don't deserve to heal."

Gabriel blinked, clearly taken aback. "What?"

"Why do you care? I thought you hated me."

For a split second, something flickered in his expression— surprise, maybe regret. His jaw clenched, and his voice came out firmer, but with an undercurrent of something gentler.

"Take the damn vial, Ava. You're about to pass out. Maybe afterward, you'll be able to think straight."

Her mind swirled, teetering on the edge of collapse, but the pain … it was unbearable. Reluctantly, she took the vial from him, her hand trembling. The liquid slid down her throat, its taste tart and bitter, making her gag as she forced it down.

"Yeah, sorry about the taste," he said.

Ava barely registered his words. A strange tightening sensation coursed through her side, almost like invisible hands stitching her back together. She lifted her shirt and peeled back the blood-soaked bandage, watching in disbelief as the stitches dissolved, the skin knitting itself together before her eyes. The pain disappeared, leaving only a faint ache. She felt Gabriel's gaze on her and quickly tugged her shirt back down, her fingers trembling slightly.

But the relief was fleeting. The moment her physical pain faded, her guilt crashed back down like a tidal wave, threatening to drown her. Jonah's face flashed in her mind. His cold, dead eyes staring back at her. Drew's terror as she ended him. *I killed them.*

Gabriel stood, his stoic expression masking any hint of emotion, but his unwavering gaze remained fixed on her. He was watching, waiting, but his usual guarded demeanor seemed softer, more open. "Ava," he said gently, his voice a low murmur in the quiet room. "You don't have to tell me anything, but I'm here if you need to talk."

Her throat tightened, a lump of emotion rising that she couldn't swallow down. She didn't want to talk. She didn't want to explain, relive what she had done, or admit the darkness growing inside her. All she wanted was for the ground beneath her to open up and swallow her whole, to disappear from the crushing guilt.

"Thanks." She avoided his eyes.

"You don't deserve to suffer like this."

But his words fell on deaf ears. No potion could heal the wound deep inside her. The one that kept reminding her of the lives she had taken. The guilt followed her like a shadow, always lurking, always waiting. No magic could make that go away. *I'm evil. Reckless.* The thoughts circled like vultures, picking away at the last shreds of her self-worth. And as much as she wanted to run from it, the truth clung to her, relentless.

"What is wrong, dear?" Colden's soft voice reached Ava's ears, but instead of calming her, it sent a wave of panic through her. She spun around to face both him and Gabriel, her resolve crumbling. She was seconds away from falling apart, and didn't know how to stop it.

"Ava?" Colden's tone was gentle but laced with concern. He looked frail, weaker than she remembered, which only added to the anxiety swirling inside her. "I assure you, you are safe here. We can keep a secret if you desire."

That was it. The floodgates opened.

"I-I didn't mean to do it," she cried, her voice shaking as she finally let go of the control she'd tried so hard to maintain. "I swear, it all happened so fast."

Gabriel's arms were around her, guiding her gently toward the center of the room. Colden quietly closed the door behind them, sealing them off from the rest of the world. Ava's breath hitched. *This was a mistake.* She couldn't tell them. What had she been thinking?

"We're here to help you," Colden said, his voice soothing. "Please. You are hurting."

She shook her head, sliding to her knees. "No, no, no," she sobbed, pushing Gabriel's hands away. "I can't, I can't." She didn't deserve to be comforted. She was a killer.

"You are safe." Colden kneeled beside her.

Ava drew a shaky breath, her mind spinning, but she couldn't hold it in any longer. "I killed them. I didn't mean to, I swear."

"Who?" Colden asked.

"Drew and Jonah," Gabriel answered for her, his eyes flicking to Ava with understanding.

"Yes." Ava gripped the floor as if it could anchor her. "I thought I was just knocking them unconscious, but … they didn't deserve to die."

"They shot you, didn't they?" Gabriel's voice had a sharper edge now.

"Yes," she whispered, the memory flashing in her mind like a cruel replay.

"Then it was self-defense."

"I could have just injured them and left it at that. I didn't have to kill them. Their families are already hurting."

Colden exchanged a glance with Gabriel. "What do you mean, Ava?"

"Jonah's sister died in the bombing. He kept blaming me. I tried to stop him, I swear, but then Drew grabbed the gun and shot me."

Colden's brow furrowed. "Ava, you had nothing to do with the bombing."

"I know. But now I'm just like them. Like a Cimmerian. What if Marcel was right? What if it's in my blood?" The words tumbled out revealing her deepest fear.

Gabriel moved closer, his gaze intense. "Ava, don't do this to yourself. You're not a Cimmerian."

"How can I not think that? I've been having dreams … and thoughts," she admitted as she looked away from them both.

"What kind of dreams?" Colden asked.

"Ever since Marcel told me my mother stood next to Corbin, I've been dreaming about her death … but from the killer's perspective. And I've had thoughts about … hating Ephemerals. Wanting to kill them."

The room fell into a heavy silence.

"That doesn't make you a Cimmerian," Gabriel said, his voice steady.

"He's right," Colden added. "Marcel's visions aren't always clear. Your mind is overwhelmed by all that's happened, which is why these fears are haunting you."

"But it happened to Corbin, didn't it?" Ava asked. "He was good before he left for Caprington, and when he came back … he hated Ephemerals."

Colden sighed, his posture slumping slightly. "Corbin had demons he couldn't outrun. The Hunters' betrayal … his sister's danger … they consumed him. But you are not Corbin, Ava."

She took a breath, bracing herself. "Colden, was my mother a Cimmerian?"

He studied her. Finally, he spoke, his voice soft but filled with regret. "I don't know, dear."

Ava's anger boiled over. "*Someone* has to know! Did she betray anyone? Is there someone taking Corbin's place?

Because I know there are Cimmerians watching us. I had a vision right before Drew and Jonah dragged me into the woods. It was Trudy McVaine. What are you hiding from us?"

Colden remained calm. "There is nothing out there, Ava. You need rest. Your mind is overwhelmed, and that's why you're imagining the worst."

She clenched her fists. "Easy for you to say."

"I promise, you are safe," Colden said. "Savina and Aaron would never withhold information if it meant putting you in harm's way."

"They did before. When I mentioned Xavier, no one believed me."

Colden placed his hands on her shoulders, his touch warm and steady. "You are like a daughter to me, Ava. I understand your fears, but you must trust me. You are safe."

"I haven't felt safe in a long time," she whispered.

Gabriel squeezed her hand.

Colden's expression softened. "I am sorry for that, truly. But you have my word. No harm will come to you. Not while I am here."

Ava nodded, though her fear and guilt still lingered. "What's going to happen to me now? I killed Ephemerals. Am I going to be banished?"

"They didn't leave you much choice," Gabriel said. "You were defending yourself."

"I could have stopped before killing them," she said.

"You can't save everyone, Ava," Colden said gently. "You did what you had to do to survive. And no, you will not be banished for protecting yourself."

She felt a glimmer of relief.

Colden hugged her briefly. "If you need to talk, I am here. But for now, rest."

As Gabriel led her out of the room, Ava turned to him. "How do you get past the guilt?"

He glanced at her, his expression unreadable for a moment before it softened. "You don't. But you learn to live with it."

She wanted to ask more, to understand what burdens he carried, but she wasn't ready for that conversation. Not yet. "I wish they'd been Hunters. It would be easier to accept. But they were just kids … angry, hurting."

"They weren't innocent. Don't forget that."

His words echoed in her mind as they walked down the hall. She stole a glance at him, a strange tension brewing inside her. For the first time, she wondered if Gabriel was truly protecting her. Or did his quick judgment of the Ephemerals reveal something darker within him?

The thought unsettled her, but she pushed it aside for now, too tired to confront it.

In the darkness of her bedroom, Ava tossed and turned, her thoughts suffocating, pressing down like a heavy blanket. Nightmares of Drew and Jonah, their terrified faces, the guilt piercing her like a sharp blade. And that cold and commanding voice still whispered in the corners of her mind: *Kill them.* Every time she closed her eyes, it was there, urging her. She couldn't rest.

Frustrated, Ava threw off the covers, the cool air hitting her skin as her bare feet padded across the wooden floor. The Manor was silent, save for the occasional creak of the old house, the shadows stretching long and eerie in the faint sliver of moonlight filtering through the large windows. Everything felt too still, too oppressive, as if the walls themselves were closing in on her.

She wandered down the hall and down the stairs, lost in her thoughts, her steps quiet but purposeful. Turning a corner, a soft glow caught her attention. The library. Curious, she peeked inside.

Link sat at one of the desks, the small lamp beside him casting a warm circle of light over piles of books. His brow was furrowed in concentration, flipping through pages with an intensity that matched the turmoil in Ava's chest.

He glanced up at her. "Can't sleep?"

"No." She pulled out a chair and sat across from him, her fingers playing nervously with the edge of the table. "What are you reading?"

"Little bit of everything. Origins, transformations, abilities, dark magic." He motioned to the scattered books. "Trying to piece together ... something."

Ava tilted her head. "Dark magic?"

"Yeah. Xavier didn't turn me into an Enchanter. I'm trying to figure out what or who changed me. Maybe he used something more ancient, more dangerous. Maybe even Necromancy." His voice dropped to a hushed tone, as if each word held immense significance.

"Necromancers?" she echoed, feeling a chill run down her spine. He'd mentioned them before.

Link nodded. "I've been digging into what they can do, why they have that kind of power. It's all connected somehow."

"Don't necromancers only communicate with the dead?"

"No. They can manipulate spirits, control them even. Some of the more powerful ones are said to have the ability to influence the living, especially those with certain vulnerabilities."

Her throat tightened. "Vulnerabilities like what?"

"Emotional instability, trauma … or just having a powerful magical presence. The stronger your abilities, the more you might attract attention from … certain forces."

She swallowed, her pulse quickening. His words made her think back to that night. The voice in her head, the overwhelming surge of power, the uncontrollable rage that had taken over. She had been herself, and yet … not herself at all. Was it possible someone had reached her? Manipulated her? "Can they make someone do things they wouldn't normally do?"

"It's possible. I've read stories where Necromancers, or even dark magic users, can push people into acts of violence, or make them feel like they don't have control. But that kind of influence doesn't come out of nowhere. It usually preys on something that's already inside you. Which is why I'm trying to figure out if that's why Xavier chose us."

Ava bit her lip. Was that what had happened to her? Had something—or someone—used her darkness, her confusion, to push her into doing the unthinkable?

"I've been having … thoughts lately," she said carefully, not meeting his eyes. "Like … dark thoughts. Ones that don't feel like mine. I guess I'm just trying to figure out where they're coming from."

"You've been under a lot of stress lately. The Cimmerians could be messing with your head, too. They're not above manipulating our emotions, making us feel things that aren't real."

"Do you think it could be them?" Ava asked, desperate for some sort of explanation, that wasn't just her losing control.

"Maybe. Or it could be something else. Necromancers, or anyone with ties to dark magic, could exploit someone's inner turmoil. They thrive on emotional chaos." He paused, his gaze softening. "Why do you ask? Are you worried about something happening to you?"

She hesitated. "I wonder if my mom is trying to communicate with me. But I don't know if that's even possible."

"It is. Necromancers can connect people to the dead, to memories, to something beyond. If your mom is trying to reach you, there could be a reason. It's worth exploring."

Her heart raced at the thought. *Could Mom be trying to protect me?* But a darker question danced on fringes of her mind: *What if she's behind the voice that urged me to kill Drew and Jonah?* The thought made her stomach churn.

She needed to know, even if the truth was terrifying. And if it meant seeking out a Necromancer, then she would.

"Could you help me find one?" she asked.

Link hesitated. "I … can. But we have to be smart about it. We can't just rush into something like this. It's dark magic. It has a cost."

Ava nodded, her mind swirling with possibilities and dangers. But whatever the cost, she knew one thing for certain: she couldn't live with the uncertainty any longer. She was tired of living in fear. She had to find out the truth about her mother, about the voice in her head, and about herself. No matter where it led her.

18

QUEEN OF HEARTS

"Seth wants to go to the Halloween dance." Peter dropped his tray on the table. Seth sat across from him with an eager grin.

Ava barely reacted, her eyes tracing a faint line on the table as her heart sank. Did Peter actually want her to go? Or was he just mentioning it for Seth's sake? The idea of a dance, of pretending everything was normal, felt foreign. Like a life she didn't belong to anymore.

Melissa dipped a celery stalk into dressing and took a casual bite. "They're still having that? I mean, in light of everything that's happened?"

Nicole shrugged, tearing open a bag of chips. "Guess they're trying to keep things normal. Or, you know, help people grieve."

Ava poked at her salad, hardly registering the conversation. She stabbed a cherry tomato, missing the center, and it shot across the table, bouncing off Melissa's arm.

Melissa gave her a halfhearted glare, flicking the tomato back onto Ava's tray. "Okay, seriously. You've got to stop sulking. Eat something."

Her words stung more than they should've, but Ava knew Melissa meant well in her own way. Still, no one else knew the truth. No one knew that it wasn't everything happening around them. It was the blood on her hands. Gabriel had healed her injuries, but nothing could heal the memories. And as much as Melissa had kept quiet, the guilt was like a heavy current pulling her under. She hadn't eaten in days. Not really. Every time she tried, it was like drowning. Her throat closed as if the water from her powers was still there, suffocating her.

Her nightmares and constant thoughts of what she had done only grew worse. She spent most of her time studying Necromancers with Link, using schoolwork as an excuse. No one seemed to notice. Not even Peter.

"I'm not hungry." She pushed away her plate.

Peter leaned in. "Ava, you have to eat. You've barely touched anything for days."

"I know."

He frowned. "Are you sick?"

Ava grabbed onto the excuse, desperate to avoid the real conversation. "Yeah, something like that."

Melissa raised an eyebrow. "If you're not feeling well, you should let Savina check on you."

Their worried looks bore into her. She quickly tried to steer the conversation away from herself. "I will. Why are we even talking about going to this dance?"

"You want to do normal human things, right?" Peter nudged her playfully. "Here's your chance. Besides, you could use a night to relax."

Her gaze met his. How could he say that so casually. Relax? She hadn't relaxed since that night. But Peter's soft smile, the way he was trying to reach her, pull her out of her shell, made her falter. He was still trying. He still cared. Even if she didn't deserve it.

"Will you go with me?" His voice was warm, hopeful.

With a heavy weight in her chest, she mustered a small smile. "Sure."

"Great, so we're all going," Seth said, clearly excited. "I've been leaving Amanda notes all week in her locker. I know she'll be there."

Melissa popped another celery stick into her mouth. "She'd be dumb not to show up."

Link shook his head. "I don't know, man. I don't feel like going."

"Yeah, same," Nicole said. "Too many eyes on us."

Ava's stomach twisted, her thoughts drifting to Drew's empty desk, the ghost of his presence haunting her classes. What right did she have to go to a dance, to play dress-up, when people had died because of her? She had killed him. Her fingers tightened around her fork, her mind flashing back to the moment—water closing in around him, his panicked gasps. She'd suffocated him. "And you all still want to go to this dance?"

Melissa shrugged, her usual nonchalance back in place. "One night of fun. We need it."

Peter leaned closer, his arm brushing hers. "It'll be like a date."

Ava managed another thin smile, though it felt like a mask. "Hopefully it'll go better than the last."

Melissa rolled her eyes but smirked. "Then maybe you won't ruin one of my dresses this time."

Ava wanted to laugh, but it felt hollow.

Peter kissed her cheek, the gesture warm but unable to reach the coldness settling in her chest. "It'll be better."

"Gag," Melissa muttered, pulling a face, though her teasing didn't carry its usual bite. Even she seemed to recognize the need for something, anything, that felt like normal.

But normal felt like a distant memory to Ava. As much as she wanted to escape, to have one night where her guilt and fear didn't sit on her shoulders, the thought of walking into that gym full of Ephemerals made her feel sick. The blood on her hands was invisible to everyone else, but she felt it. Maybe, just for one night, she could let it go. Maybe Peter was right. One night wouldn't change what she'd done, but it might help her forget, if only for a few hours.

Ava stared at her reflection in the full-length mirror, aghast. How had Melissa talked her into wearing this? The red velvet bustier barely covered her, with its off-shoulder top clinging to her in all the wrong places and a wide skirt that was far too short for her comfort. Sure, there was a black underskirt that fell to her ankles in the back, but the front left her legs exposed far more than she'd ever planned.

The sheer, knee-high stockings itched against her skin, and she was already dreading the three-inch heels. As for the top, it gaped slightly where someone more voluptuous would have filled it out. How was she supposed to feel confident like this? Wouldn't a bed sheet ghost costume have been so much easier?

A knock at the door pulled her from her spiraling thoughts, and she sighed. *Might as well get this over with.* Ava opened the door, her breath catching as Gabriel stood on the other side. His gaze traveled down her figure before settling on her eyes, an unreadable expression crossing his face.

Heat flared under her cheeks. "Don't laugh." The blush spread. There was something in the way Gabriel looked at her, something that made her feel exposed in more ways than just the outfit.

"I'm not laughing. You look … great."

She shifted awkwardly, feeling self-conscious under his gaze. "I shouldn't be wearing this. I feel ridiculous."

He chuckled, low and easy. "It's just one night. Besides, I think every guy at that dance will be staring at you."

"Great. So, I look provocative. Maybe I should change."

Gabriel stepped closer, his eyes never leaving hers. "You look fine, Ava. More than fine. You're beautiful. Trust me, no one's going to be thinking that. Just go with it."

His words made something flutter inside her, though she quickly pushed it aside. Why was she so flustered? It was just Gabriel. Her friend. And yet, the way his eyes lingered on hers, the way he reassured her was different. More than she was used to.

But something deeper nagged at her, something she couldn't shake. She hesitated, looking away. "I don't know if I can do this," she said, more to herself than to him.

"What is it? It's not just the costume, is it?"

She looked down, her fingers nervously picking at the edge of the fabric. "It's everything. Ever since that night with Drew and Jonah... I don't feel like I deserve to have fun, Gabe. I keep seeing them in my dreams ... it's like I can't escape." Her voice trembled. "Maybe this is a bad idea. Maybe I shouldn't even go."

"Hey. What happened that night—it wasn't your fault."

She shook her head, her throat tightening. "I don't know that. I killed them, Gabe. How am I supposed to just ... go to a dance and pretend everything's fine when I—" Her voice broke, and she quickly turned away, blinking back tears.

"Ava." He placed a hand on her shoulder. "You didn't want to hurt anyone. You were defending yourself. They attacked you."

"I know. But it still feels wrong. I didn't mean to hurt them ... but I did. And now I don't know if I can just forget that."

His grip on her shoulder tightened. "You're not supposed to forget it. But you're not supposed to carry it alone, either. You have to give yourself a break. You've been through hell, and you're still standing. That says a lot."

She met his eyes then, searching for the comfort he offered. His words made something ease in her chest, though the guilt still lingered. "But I don't know if I can just ... let it go."

"You don't have to let it go. You just have to live. You deserve to have fun, to be with your friends, and to be yourself. What happened with Drew and Jonah was tragic, but it doesn't make you a bad person. You didn't choose this."

Ava swallowed hard. She still wasn't sure she believed him completely but hearing him say it, and knowing he was on her side, made her feel a little braver. "I'm just scared. Scared of myself."

"I know. But you don't have to be. Not tonight. Just ... let yourself have this one night. You deserve that."

"Maybe you're right."

He offered a gentle smile. "I know I'm right. The Queen of Hearts didn't let anyone get to her, right? Neither should you. Just be confident, even if you don't feel it."

She glanced down at her costume, doubt still gnawing at her, but Gabriel's encouragement gave her strength she hadn't felt in weeks. "Yeah, well, I'm not exactly the Queen of Hearts."

"You can be, for tonight. Besides, Peter's waiting downstairs."

The mention of Peter snapped her out of the moment. "I really don't want anyone in this house to see me like this."

He tilted his head, studying her. "Why? You look amazing."

She blushed again. "I just … I don't want anyone to see me." The idea of walking through the Manor, past everyone's eyes, made her want to crawl back into her room.

He took her hand, and in a blink, they were outside, transported away from prying eyes.

"Thanks. Now I just have to face everyone at the dance."

He grinned, something almost playful dancing in his expression. "You've got this. Just have fun tonight."

"Thanks, Gabe."

His smile deepened, his eyes lingering on her for a moment before he turned away. "I'll go get Peter." He disappeared into the night.

As she waited for Peter, she took a deep breath, feeling both anxious and relieved. For the first time in a while, she felt like maybe she could let herself breathe again, if only for one night.

She felt a smile tug at her lips as Peter stepped outside. Dressed as a gangster, he wore a slick silver vest over a crisp white button-down shirt, the sleeves casually rolled just above his wrists. A fedora sat on his head, completing the look. He looked effortlessly sexy.

"Wow, you look amazing." His eyes traveled appreciatively over her outfit before pausing with a hint of confusion. "What are you?"

"Queen of Hearts. I guess it isn't so obvious."

"It's different. But you look great. Ready?"

She took a deep breath. "Yes." Tonight was about forgetting everything. The pressure, the guilt, the secrets. She'd have fun. A night dancing with Peter, and that was all that mattered.

He opened the car door for her, and she slid in, feeling a mix of nerves and excitement. Peter got in on his side and started the car.

Ava fidgeted with the hem of her dress, her palms sweaty. She didn't understand why she was feeling so nervous. It wasn't like she hadn't been around people since everything happened. Still, her secret, the guilt she carried, tortured her.

"You're going to tear a hole in your lip if you keep chewing on it," he teased.

"Sorry," she muttered, trying to shake off the nerves.

"Are you okay?"

"I'm just … nervous." Her fingers fiddled with her dress again.

"About going to the dance?"

"Yes," she lied. She couldn't tell Peter she killed two Ephemerals. She feared his rejection and judgement.

His smile returned, warm and reassuring. He slowed the car to a stop and leaned over the stick shift, pressing a soft kiss to her cheek. His lips grazed her neck as he pulled back slightly. "Still nervous?"

Some of the tension eased. "No."

"Good." He grinned, giving the car more gas as he continued down the road.

She glanced out the window, her mind still half-buried in thought. "Where are we going? The school's the other way."

"I'm picking up Seth. I figured it would be okay since this is all for him."

Her heart sank a little. So, it wasn't really a date after all. "Oh." She tried masking her disappointment.

"What?"

"Nothing."

"Ava."

"I just thought this was a date."

Peter frowned as he pulled into Seth's driveway. "Seth didn't want to go alone. Come on, don't be like that."

"I'm not being like anything." But she couldn't help feeling a little deflated. Dressing up, preparing for the night, thinking it would just be the two of them now felt like she'd gotten her hopes up for nothing.

He reached over, squeezing her hand. "I promise, we'll still have our date. We're just giving him a ride, nothing more."

"Okay," Ava replied, forcing herself to relax. She wasn't going to ruin the night over something small. She had promised herself to let go of the tension, at least for tonight.

Seth climbed into the car a few minutes later, dressed in blue scrubs, radiating nervous energy. Ava gave him a tight smile as they drove to the school, her earlier excitement dimmed.

When they arrived, Melissa and Lance were already there. Melissa's long blond hair was curled, and she wore a short black knit dress with a high wing collar cape. Fishnet stockings and knee-high boots completed her vampire look, while Lance's Dracula costume was classic.

"Vampires?" Seth asked as he took in their costumes.

Melissa grinned. "Yep. I tried to get Lance to put some glitter on, but he wouldn't."

Lance rolled his eyes. "That's because vampires do not glitter."

Ava laughed. "Some do, apparently."

They walked into the darkened gym, which was lit only by black lights. Dance music reverberated off the cement walls, vibrating through the air. Streamers and fake spider webs hung everywhere, and mannequins posed as bodies sat in chairs, stuck out from closed-up bleachers, or hung from the rafters. The sight of them was unsettling. Ava couldn't help but wonder if anyone else would have flashbacks to the bombing.

Peter slid his hand into hers, pulling her towards the dance floor where a group of people moved to the music. The beat was loud, chaotic.

"What are we doing?" she shouted over the music.

"Dancing," he yelled back, smiling as he pulled her closer. "I know the music sucks, but we can make the best of it." He turned and passionately kissed her, the taste of his lips lingering on her tongue. The sudden surge of energy took her by surprise, her heart pounding in her chest as a rush of adrenaline coursed through her veins. It was intoxicating, like a heady scent wafting through the air. As they swayed to the music, a discordant melody that filled the room, she could feel his hands, warm and firm, gripping the small of her back, pulling her closer. She lost herself in him, the world around them fading away. Under the dim glow of the black lights, their bodies moved in perfect harmony. This was what she had been craving. The pulsating beats, the touch of Peter's hands, it all ignited a fire within her. Ava felt alive in a way she hadn't felt in weeks, a surge of liberation washing over her as they danced beneath the ethereal glow of the black lights.

"I can't believe you," someone yelled from behind them.

Ava and Peter broke apart, turning to see Valerie and Amanda standing there, both dressed as glowing angels. Their wings shimmered under the black lights, but the look on their faces was anything but angelic. Arms crossed, lips curled in disgust, they glared at Ava with thinly veiled hatred.

"What?" Peter asked, confusion and frustration flickering across his face.

"You're dancing with *her*," Valerie spat. "The devil worshipper. She and her freak friends are responsible for the bombing. What the hell is wrong with you?"

Ava's stomach churned with the familiar sense of dread. Her hands clenched into fists, trying to hold back the fury rising inside her. "I do *not* worship the devil," she snapped, her voice steady despite the storm of emotions brewing inside her. "And we had nothing to do with the bombing."

"Do you even know who you're with?" Valerie asked Peter. "She's a killer, just like the rest of them. She and her cult put a spell on you and Seth. We all know it."

Ava's blood boiled, her heartbeat pounding in her ears. *Killer.* The word echoed in her mind, twisting the knife deeper. Valerie had no idea how close to the truth she was.

Peter exhaled. "No, they didn't. I'm sorry I haven't been around, but there's a lot going on."

Valerie's eyes blazed with anger. "Yeah, a lot going on because of *her*." She pointed at Ava. "She's cursed. Her mother's dead, her father almost died, and now you're next. What's going to happen to you if you stay with her? You'll end up dead, too."

Something inside Ava snapped. Her vision blurred with red, her hands shaking. Valerie's words echoed in her head, louder and louder. *Cursed. Killer. Dead.* The heat surged through her, overwhelming every rational thought. Her fist struck Valerie's face with a sharp, resounding thud.

Valerie stumbled back, her eyes wide with shock as she crumpled to the floor. Blood gushed from her nose. Amanda screamed, and gasps rose from the crowd gathering around them.

Peter knelt down beside Valerie, his face stricken with worry. "Are you okay?" He pressed his tie against her bleeding nose.

Ava froze, her hand still trembling from the punch. Guilt and shame crashed over her like a wave, drowning out the rage. She couldn't breathe, couldn't think. All she could do was watch Peter tend to Valerie, the girl who had insulted her, belittled her, and yet, there was Peter, rushing to her aid without a second thought.

"I think she broke it," Valerie moaned, wincing in pain.

"I'll take you to the hospital." As Peter stood, he helped her to her feet. He handed Ava his car keys without meeting her eyes. "Take my car home. I'll be there soon."

The words stung, cutting deeper than Valerie's insults. Ava stared at the keys, their cold metal biting into her palm. "Is that really necessary?"

Peter's jaw clenched, his eyes hard with frustration as he turned away, leading Valerie toward the door.

The realization of what had just happened slammed into Ava's chest. Her breath caught in her throat, a sharp ache spreading through her like wildfire. She had ruined everything. The crowd's judgmental stares bore into her as she stood frozen, the reality of what she had done sinking in. She had let Valerie get to her, let her anger take control. She had become exactly what Valerie had accused her of being.

Valerie was right. Being around her really was *dangerous*. She was a *killer*. Reckless.

Her heart raced as she spun on her heels and bolted for the exit, Melissa calling out after her. "Ava, wait!"

But she didn't stop. The night air hit her like a slap in the face as she stormed into the parking lot, her body trembling from head to toe.

The dance was supposed to be an escape, but instead, she was left with the same haunting truth: no matter how hard she tried to outrun it, the darkness inside her always found a way to surface.

And this time, Peter had seen it too.

"What happened?" Melissa's voice was closer now, her footsteps quickening to catch up.

Ava fumbled with the keys, ignoring the cold as she slid into Peter's car. "I punched Valerie in the face."

Melissa's eyes widened in shock as she opened the passenger side door and climbed in beside her. "You *punched* her? What the hell—why?"

Ava jammed the keys into the ignition, her voice tight as she started the engine. "Because she wouldn't stop. She kept accusing me of manipulating Peter, called me a killer, said I was bad luck. That I'd get him killed." Her voice cracked as she slammed the door shut. "I just … I couldn't take it anymore."

Melissa pushed out a breath. "I'm sorry. She's been horrible, and you've been through enough. I don't blame you for snapping." She hesitated. "But punching her? You know we can't afford that kind of attention. We're already under a microscope. Now you've given them a reason to watch us even more closely."

Ava gripped the steering wheel tighter, her knuckles white as they drove off. "She deserved it."

"I get it, trust me," Melissa said gently, but there was an edge to her voice. "But we're supposed to be better than that. Remember what happened when Thomas lost it on Peter? We're not like them. We can't just lash out, no matter how much they push."

Guilt twisted inside Ava, mixing with frustration. "I know, but … it's not just Valerie."

"What do you mean?"

Ava's hands shook as she turned onto a road. "It's everything. I feel like I'm losing control, Mel. My thoughts … they're getting darker. Every day, it's like I'm fighting to stay myself, but I don't know if I'm winning."

"Why didn't you tell me sooner?"

"I didn't want to admit it," Ava confessed, her voice wavering. "I didn't want to face it. But now … I don't know what's happening to me."

Melissa reached over, placing a comforting hand on Ava's arm. "You need to talk to Savina. You can't keep carrying this on your own."

"Colden knows."

Something cold grazed against her neck and she shivered. Her hand shot to her neck, fingers brushing against something cold and hard. "What the—" she gasped, swatting at the air.

"What's wrong?" Melissa's voice rose in alarm.

"I don't know," Ava choked out. The cold sensation wrapped tighter around her throat, like icy fingers pressing down, cutting off her air. Panic surged through her as her vision started to blur.

The car swerved wildly as she slammed her foot on the brake, but her foot slipped, and the world outside the windshield tilted.

Everything went black.

Ava blinked, disoriented, her mind swimming through a haze. Darkness surrounded her, except for the flashing memories—dark eyes, black hair, pale skin. And her mother, standing beside Corbin with a smile on her face. Her mother raised her hand, an icicle forming from the water at her fingertips, and drove it through the chest of a woman kneeling before them.

A deafening crash shattered the vision, and the sound of screeching metal pierced Ava's ears as the car spun out of control. Glass exploded around her, sharp fragments raining down like deadly shards. Her body lurched violently, the seatbelt digging into her chest as the car flipped. The world tumbled into a chaotic blur. Up became down, and her stomach twisted with every jarring roll.

When the car finally slammed to a stop, Ava dangled upside down by the seatbelt, her hair falling into her face. The metallic scent of blood mixed with burnt rubber filled the air. Her head pounded with a fierce, throbbing pain, and something warm and sticky trickled down her cheek. Every breath was a struggle, pain tearing through her side like fire, making her ribs scream with each inhale.

"Mel," she croaked, twisting her head painfully to the side. Melissa was unconscious, her body slumped against the door. "Melissa!"

Her own body ached, but she had to move. She had to get them out. With trembling hands, she unbuckled the seatbelt, falling hard onto the roof of the overturned car. She let out a sharp cry, the pain in her ribs unbearable.

Ignoring the pain, Ava crawled toward the broken window, dragging herself through the shattered glass. Her hands bled from the shards, but she kept going, every movement a fight against the agony wracking her body.

Once outside, she collapsed onto the cold ground, gasping for air. "Help," she whispered, though no one was around to hear.

She looked back at the car, her heart stopping at the clump of blond hair near the backseat. Trudy McVaine. Ava's breath hitched in her throat. How had she gotten in the car? Had it been her invisible hands choking her?

Ava's thoughts raced, but she couldn't afford to think about it now. Melissa needed her. She started crawling back toward the car, her body trembling with each painful movement.

The sound of glass shattering caught her attention. A man dragged Melissa's limp body through the broken glass.

"Stop!" Ava forced herself to stand on her good leg.

The man with whitish blond hair and strong features stood over Melissa, his hands raised in mock surrender. "I'm trying to help." Something in his eyes unsettled Ava.

"Where did you come from?" she demanded.

"I was camping just up the hill and heard the crash." He gestured toward the woods.

Ava narrowed her eyes, her instincts screaming at her that something wasn't right. There was no sign of a campfire, no sounds of other people. Just the eerie stillness of the night.

"Put her down." Water coiled down her arms, pooling in her hands.

The man's smile widened, a devilish glint in his eyes. "I'm helping you."

"Leave her alone."

"You don't understand." He inched forward. "I'm trying to save you."

She raised her trembling hands, summoning every ounce of strength she had left, and shot a powerful stream of water at the man. The force of it slammed him backward, knocking him off balance as he dropped Melissa's limp body to the ground. Her vision swam for a moment, and her arms felt heavy as the power drained her energy. She wanted to rush to Melissa, but her legs wouldn't respond. She was too weak, her body protesting every movement.

"Who are you?" she demanded, her voice barely steady as she fought to stay upright.

The man scrambled to his feet, his face darkening with anger. "Someone who's about to teach you a lesson," he snarled. "Where do you come off attacking someone who's trying to help?" He charged at her again, moving with terrifying speed.

Ava forced her hands up, willing another stream of water to surge forward, but it was weaker this time. She could feel her energy slipping away. He dodged the blast and tackled her to the ground. The impact sent shockwaves of pain through her body, stealing her breath and what little strength she had left.

She cried out, her ribs screaming in protest as his weight pinned her down. Her muscles burned, her limbs felt like lead, and her vision blurred as exhaustion crept in. She squirmed beneath him, trying to break free, but her power had drained too much of her strength. She was too depleted.

"Would you just listen to me?" His dark eyes bore into hers, cold and unrelenting. "I'm trying to save you. You and your friends. You belong with us, Ava. You don't even know it yet, but you do."

She stilled, her body too weak to keep fighting. "With who?"

"Havok." The name cut through the night like a knife.

Her blood ran cold. *Havok.* The name Devon had whispered in his final moments. Her thoughts were muddled.

The man leaned down, his lips brushing her ear. "It's your destiny. And deep down, you know it's true."

Her stomach churned, but her limbs refused to obey her. *No,* she thought, trying to push away the doubt creeping in. It couldn't be true. She wasn't like them. She was *good.* But her body was betraying her, the exhaustion making it harder to think, harder to fight the fear. Her actions, Drew, Jonah, crushed her, threatening to suffocate her resolve.

"I can see it in your eyes," the man said, his breath hot against her skin. "This is who you are, Ava. Just like your mother."

The mention of her mother snapped something inside her. Even with the last flicker of her energy fading, rage surged. She gritted her teeth and, with the last of her strength, kneed him hard in the groin.

He let out a strangled groan, rolling off her. Ava's body screamed as she pushed herself on top of him, her limbs heavy and trembling. She could barely focus, but she didn't hesitate. She tapped into the last dregs of her power, imagining him drowning in her mind. His body convulsed beneath her, gasping for air, his eyes bulging as water filled his lungs.

He choked, his body jerking violently, then he went still. His eyes, now lifeless, stared into the dark sky, unseeing.

Ava collapsed beside him, her body trembling uncontrollably. Her vision dimmed as exhaustion washed over her. She twisted around, desperate to check on Melissa. Trudy was gone. Her heart slammed against her ribs in panic. Had Trudy taken Melissa? Were others coming for them?

Her mind raced, but her body was too drained to move. She pressed her palms to her forehead, her fingers icy cold. The wind rustled through the trees, and the leaves scraped across the road, but it all sounded distant, muted.

Ava forced herself to crawl, her limbs protesting every movement. She dragged herself toward the other side of the overturned car, each breath a struggle as pain pierced through her ribs. By the time she reached Melissa, she could barely think straight.

Ava grabbed her friend's arm and pulled her close, her entire body shaking with effort.

Melissa moaned weakly, her eyelids fluttering open.

"You're awake," Ava breathed, her voice breaking with relief. She pressed a shaky kiss to the top of Melissa's head, feeling the sticky warmth of blood in her hair.

The moonlight cast long shadows across the road, and the air had grown bitterly cold. Ava was too weak to conjure any heat, too exhausted to do anything but hold Melissa close. She squeezed her eyes shut, hoping, praying, that help would come soon.

Her mind spiraled again, thoughts flashing back to Valerie. Had punching her triggered all of this? Was this her punishment? But Trudy had been in the car, hiding, waiting. This had been planned, hadn't it? Ava's heart twisted. What did the Cimmerians want? Why had they targeted her?

And the vision. Why had Trudy shown her mother killing someone? Was it real? Had her mother been a Cimmerian? Ava couldn't shake the hollow feeling that settled deep in her chest. Was Marcel's vision coming true?

Her head pounded, each thought more confusing than the last. She wasn't sure if she could keep it all straight anymore. Exhaustion clouded her mind, weighing her down.

In the distance, headlights pierced the darkness, cutting through the night like beacons. Ava's breath hitched, her body frozen in fear. There was no way she could summon the strength to protect them, no way Melissa could make them invisible.

The car slowed to a stop, its lights illuminating the wreckage of Peter's car. Ava braced herself, holding Melissa tighter as two men stepped out of the car, their figures looming in the light as they approached.

19

HEART OF DARKNESS

"Ava?" a voice shouted, filled with worry.

She tightened her grip on Melissa, but Ava recognized the voice instantly. *Lance.* He stepped in front of the blinding headlights, and she let out a breath of relief. Tears welled in her eyes. She had never been so happy to see him.

Lance and Seth hurried over to her, their faces etched with concern.

"What happened?" Lance asked, his voice tight. "Is she okay?"

The dull roar in her head muffled their voices. Each shallow breath sent a searing pain through her chest, like knives twisting between her ribs. Her vision blurred, and she fought to stay conscious, but the agony made it nearly impossible to focus.

"She's alive," Ava rasped. Her throat felt raw, each word a struggle. Breathing was like trying to draw air through a thin straw, each inhale shallow and tight as her broken rib screamed. "We … have to get out of here."

Lance wasted no time, scooping Melissa into his arms while Seth carefully lifted Ava. Every jolt of movement sent fresh waves of pain through her body, her broken leg throbbing in sync with her ragged breaths. She gritted her teeth, trying not to cry out, but it was unbearable. Seth carried her to the car, and as soon as the door shut behind them, Lance hit the gas, speeding down the dark, quiet road.

Ava slumped against the seat, her head resting on the cool window. She closed her eyes for a moment, desperate to block out the pain, but every time she inhaled, it felt like her ribs were stabbing into her lungs.

"That was Peter's car, wasn't it?" Lance asked, his voice rough with tension. "Where is he?"

Seth looked over his shoulder. "Who was that guy back there? What the hell happened?"

Ava swallowed, her throat burning. She couldn't answer them. Her body felt battered and broken. The once-elaborate Halloween costume she had worn was now nothing but torn fabric and bloodstains. She licked her lips, tasting blood. Every second she fought to stay conscious, but her eyelids grew heavier with each breath.

Her mind raced with questions: *How will I get into the Manor without Dad knowing? What if Peter finds out about the crash? How can I explain Peter's overturned car?*

"Take us to the library," she rasped.

Lance frowned. "The library? Ava, you're hurt—"

"My dad … can't know."

The rest of the ride was silent. When they finally reached the Manor, Lance carried Melissa inside while Seth supported Ava, carefully guiding her through the heavy doors. The warmth hit her like a wave, but it did little to ease the cold settling in her bones.

By the time they reached the library, Ava couldn't keep her eyes open. Joss and Gabriel were talking, but they felt distant, muffled through the haze of pain.

"We found them like this," Lance said. "Get Savina!"

Joss darted from the room, her footsteps echoing down the hallway.

Ava's head swam. "Peter's with Valerie at the hospital."

Seth's eyes widened in shock. "What? Valerie? Is Amanda with her?"

She nodded weakly.

"I've got her." Gabriel gently pried Ava's hand from Seth's shirt. With gentle hands, he lifted her and brought her closer to the crackling fire, settling on the floor with her nestled in his arms. He smelled like juniper and something woodsy, and it calmed her.

She rested her head against his chest. Tears spilled over, her body too weak to contain the emotion any longer. All she could see were fragmented images. The man holding her down, telling her it was her destiny to join them. Trudy's invisible grip choking her. The vision of her mother standing beside Corbin.

Gabriel tightened his grip on her. "I'm right here."

The door burst open, and Savina swept into the room with Colden right behind her, their expressions grim.

"She can't breathe," Gabriel said, his voice filled with alarm.

"Help … Melissa…" Tears slipped down her cheeks, but the pain was too much. She couldn't fight it.

"Ava, I'm going to heal you." Savina's voice cut through the fog. "This will hurt for a moment, but you'll be able to breathe soon. Gabriel, hold her still."

He held her as Savina's hands glided over her ribcage. A sharp, searing pain enveloped Ava, and she screamed, but the pain quickly faded as her ribs healed. Next, the pain in her leg dulled, and the cuts on her skin sealed over. She gasped, drawing in a deep, steady breath for the first time in hours.

"Melissa?"

"She's awake," Savina said. "Upstairs resting. And you need to rest as well."

Ava let out a relieved sigh but still clung to Gabriel. She looked down at his shirt and gasped from the amount of blood she'd gotten on it.

"It's okay," he said.

"What happened?" Colden asked.

Gabriel helped Ava into a sitting position as she steadied her breathing. "Trudy McVaine."

Savina's face hardened. "That's impossible. We haven't seen any Cimmerians since we killed Devon. Are you sure it was her?"

Ava gritted her teeth. "Trudy was hiding in Peter's car. She attacked me. I crashed. I wouldn't be here if Lance and Seth hadn't found us."

Gabriel stiffened beside her.

Savina's green eyes narrowed, her disbelief evident.

"Why would Trudy try to kill Ava?" Joss asked.

"There was another man, too," Ava added, her voice growing steadier. "A blond-haired man. I killed him."

Colden's expression darkened. "Did Trudy die?"

"No. She disappeared before I could stop her."

Savina's jaw tightened. "Gabriel, Joss, Eric—go to the crash site. Find Trudy, if she's still there. And take care of the body."

Gabriel hesitated, his eyes locking onto Ava's. "Are you going to be okay?"

She nodded, though her heart ached. "I'll be fine. Just … please don't tell anyone about this."

Savina shook her head firmly. "Ava, you can't be serious—"

"Please. I don't want my dad to worry."

Savina's stern expression softened, just slightly. *You are not weak,* she mind-spoke to Ava. "Fine," she said aloud. "But we will discuss this tomorrow."

Gabriel gave her one last, concerned look before vanishing with Joss and Eric.

Ava sagged into Colden's arms, exhausted beyond belief. "I let her inside my mind."

His face softened. "Did she show you something?"

"She showed my mother … with Corbin."

"You couldn't have known she was there."

"You were angry earlier," Savina said. "Did that affect your ability to block her?"

Ava met her gaze. "I thought this was over. You said Trudy wouldn't come back."

Savina sighed. "As I said before, Trudy shows you what she wants. Be cautious of what you believe."

"Was my mother a Cimmerian?" Ava's eyes burned with unshed tears.

Savina hesitated for a moment too long. "Trudy wants you to believe that. Don't fall into her trap."

"That's not an answer! You're keeping secrets—"

"I am here to protect you. Not everything is as it seems." With that, she turned and left the room, leaving Ava standing there, breathless and full of doubt.

She turned to Colden, her voice trembling. "Please. Tell me the truth. Was she a Cimmerian?"

Colden's eyes softened, and he took a deep breath. "Yes."

20

BAD BLOOD

A whirlwind of motion engulfed Ava as her surroundings spun wildly. She clutched Colden's arm, desperate for something solid as her vision blurred, her breath caught in her throat. *Her mother was a Cimmerian.* The words slammed into her chest like a battering ram, swirling in her mind, refusing to settle. She had felt the intuition, the whispers, the fear, but hearing the truth, spoken aloud, shattered her in ways she hadn't expected.

"Why didn't you tell me before?" She trembled as the revelation choked her.

Colden steadied her. "I'm sorry, Ava. Savina didn't want me to tell you."

"Why? Why would Savina hide this from me?"

"She was trying to protect you."

"Protect me? By keeping secrets? How does that protect me? I had a right to know!"

His eyes were filled with guilt. "Savina feared you would seek vengeance for your mother. She believed you were already thinking about it from the moment you learned she was murdered. You have a fierce heart, Ava. You don't shy away from confronting your enemies."

"Vengeance?" The word sounded foreign in her mouth, yet familiar, too close to home. As she carried the burden of those buried thoughts, a fiery desire for retribution burned within her. "How … how is it even possible that she was a Cimmerian? Was she forced? Compelled? Does my dad know?"

"I don't think he ever knew. It was a long time ago. Long before you or your father came into the picture."

"All this time…" She squeezed her eyes shut, her mind spinning. "I thought my mother was good, that she was … perfect." The word felt jagged now, painful. "Now I don't even know who she was." Her breath hitched, the pain of betrayal tearing at her chest. "Does this mean I'm going to become a Cimmerian? Is that why I've been having these thoughts? There are days when I can't stand to be around Ephemerals. When I went to the dance earlier, I was fine, but some days…"

"Your mother was born a Cimmerian. It's all she ever knew. But you … you're not her. You have a choice."

"But how do I know that? How do I know I won't end up like her? I can't stop the thoughts, Colden. The darkness. What if it's inside me, waiting for me to slip?"

He placed a hand on her shoulder. "That's not who you are. You're strong. You're good."

"But I don't feel strong. I feel … broken. Confused. I've killed people. How can I be good after everything I've done?"

"We all have our demons. Your mother's path was her own, but it doesn't have to be yours."

Sorrow pressed down on her chest like an anchor, and for a moment, Ava wasn't sure she could breathe. She wanted to believe him but doubt lingered.

"Let's get something to eat," he said.

Ava followed him to the kitchen, where she sat numbly at the table. Colden returned moments later with a plate of steaming shepherd's pie. The rich aroma filled the room, and despite her swirling emotions, Ava's stomach growled. She ate in silence, the familiar taste offering a strange comfort.

"Savina won't tell me anything," she said. "Would Aaron? How did my mother just … show up one day and switch sides?"

"She was abandoned by the Cimmerians. Or at least, that's what we were told."

"Abandoned? Why would they abandon her?"

"Perhaps she was seen as a liability. Or maybe she knew too much."

"They mentioned Havok tonight. That it's my destiny to join them."

Colden's jaw clenched, the muscles in his face twitching as his expression darkened. "That vile woman," he muttered, venom dripping from his voice. "She tried to murder you."

Ava flinched. She had never seen Colden so upset before. It unnerved her, watching the composed man unravel, even if just for a moment.

"And those Ephemerals," he spat, shaking his head. Sweat gathered at his brow, his skin paling to an alarming degree. He looked as though he might be sick.

"Are you okay?" she asked.

He nodded but winced as if the action caused him pain. "Havok doesn't exist," he said, his voice strained, as if every word cost him something. He struggled to breathe, his chest rising and falling with difficulty.

She pushed back her chair. "Do you need me to get Savina?"

"No." He raised a trembling hand to stop her. "I'm fine, dear. It'll pass."

But she wasn't convinced.

His breathing slowly steadied, and the color returned to his face.

The tension didn't leave her. "What was that?"

"It's nothing. Do not concern yourself with me."

Ava frowned but didn't press further. Not yet.

"Now, as for this Havok business," Colden continued, his voice regaining some of its strength. "Devon called himself that, but he's dead now. Perhaps Trudy and the man you encountered are acting out of revenge."

"Revenge? For killing Devon? What if they're the ones who burned down Thomas's house? Or … what if they manipulated the Ephemerals to do it?"

"I don't know who burned Thomas's house. But another uprising? I don't think so. Security in the Cruciari is tighter than ever. They're even building an electric wall around it."

"But do you think it could happen again?"

"Revolutions…" he paused, his tone thoughtful, as though searching for the right words. "Revolutions have always happened. Throughout history. It's inevitable. It's not a matter of if. It's when. That's why Savina was right. You need to be prepared. You and the others. You need to practice more."

Ava nodded, though her thoughts were already drifting to the bigger question burning in her mind. "Colden … do you know who killed my mother? I saw a woman … at the

Cruciari. She claimed to be the one, but was it really her? Who is she?"

His expression darkened, his lips pressed into a thin line. "I don't know," he said at last, though there was something in the way he spoke that told Ava he wasn't saying everything. He opened his mouth as if to add something, but closed it, shaking his head.

"What? What is it?"

"I shouldn't be telling you these things."

"Like what? Please, Colden. I need to know the truth. You can't keep this from me."

He let out a long, conceding sigh, his resolve crumbling. "You must keep this between us, Ava. No one else can know."

She sat up straight, her heart pounding in her chest. "Absolutely."

"If Savina won't give you the answers you seek," Colden said slowly, his voice hushed as if the very air around them held secrets, "there are … other ways to obtain the information."

"What do you mean?"

"There are ways to contact those who are no longer with us."

A chill ran down Ava's spine as she processed his words. "You mean … the dead?"

His eyes met hers, steady and unflinching. "Yes."

Gabriel, Joss, and Eric entered the room, their faces shadowed with concern. Colden rose from his chair.

"We couldn't find Trudy," Gabriel said, his voice taut with frustration.

"And the man Ava killed … he used to reside in the Cruciari," Joss added, her words hanging heavy in the air.

Ava froze, and a wave of icy dread washed over her. How could this be happening all over again? It was like the past was repeating itself. Cimmerians, somehow, escaping again.

Corbin and Devon had been after her and the Elementals to create the strongest army. But they were both dead. So why were the Cimmerians still hunting them? What did they want now? And who was Havok?

Her thoughts coiled and tangled with confusion and fear. And what had Colden meant about talking to those who weren't there? Was he suggesting Necromancy? Talking to the dead? Ava couldn't even ask him now. He had already left to take the news of Trudy's escape to Savina.

She hardly noticed the sound of the chair being moved until she felt a soft touch on her shoulder.

"Are you okay?" Gabriel's voice was soft, concerned.

"No." She stared blankly at her hand as she slid off her opal ring, the one her mother had given her. The weight of it felt wrong now, like it didn't belong to her anymore. Why had she even kept it? Her mother was a liar. A fake.

"Do you want to talk about it?" Joss asked.

Ava shook her head. Words felt futile. Everything felt too heavy. Too overwhelming.

She stood and left the room, her footsteps hollow against the floor. Her room felt no better than a cage as she shut the door behind her. The ache in her chest tightened, as if the walls were slowly closing in on her.

She crossed the room and sank onto the edge of her bed, her movements mechanical, drained of life. The opal ring gleamed in her palm, a reminder of the lies, the betrayal. She opened the nightstand drawer and placed the ring inside, the cool metal slipping from her fingers.

Why would she want a reminder of her mother's bad blood?

None of it felt right, and she couldn't even hide behind the excuse of Cimmerian blood. That wasn't who she was, or at least, that wasn't who she thought she was.

But the thoughts wouldn't stop. They churned inside her like a storm, dark and endless. She had always known she was different from the rest of her coven. But was joining the Cimmerians really her destiny? Was that what all this was leading to?

Tears pricked her eyes, but she didn't fight them this time. She let them fall. Ava caved into the flood of emotion, her chest tight as sobs wracked her body. She closed the drawer slowly, the sound muffled by the raw ache inside her.

With trembling hands, she turned out the light. Darkness enveloped the room, but it didn't comfort her. The questions, the guilt, the fear were all too much.

Her mother had left her with more than just memories. She had left her with doubts, with a bloodline that Ava couldn't ignore.

And now … she had to figure out how to live with it.

21

AN UNDERSTANDING

The pale morning light filtered through the thin curtains, casting muted shadows across the room. Ava's eyes, gritty from a sleepless night, tracked the slow brightening of the world outside, though it did little to lift the heavy feeling pressing down on her chest. The lingering weight of the previous night settled on her like a thick, suffocating fog.

Every muscle in her body ached, as if the tension of her thoughts had burrowed deep into her bones. The memory of Trudy's invisible hands around her neck sent a chill down her spine. A lingering coldness that felt like it had seeped into her very soul. Peter hadn't come back last night, and her frustration with him simmered beneath the surface.

After everything she'd been through—the accident, the pain, the fear—he hadn't shown up. But the anger quickly gave way to something heavier, darker. What if he was right to stay away? Maybe he had sensed what she was only just realizing. She was dangerous.

Her chest tightened, her breath catching. She'd nearly killed herself and Melissa in that car crash, and worse, she had Drew and Jonah's deaths on her conscience. The voice in her head echoed: *Kill them.* She squeezed her eyes shut, trying to shake the thought. What if next time, Peter got caught in the crossfire?

She glanced at her phone. One missed call from Peter, no messages. *Of course not.* Her frustration deepened. He had to know about the accident. Seth would've told him. Or maybe Valerie had kept it from him.

Her phone buzzed, jolting her out of her thoughts. Thomas had texted, asking the group to meet at the cabin. She sighed, pulled on some jeans and a sweater, and tugged on her boots, far more comfortable than the heels from last night.

When she opened the door, Peter stood there with guilt painted across his face.

"Hey," he said quietly.

"Hey." She crossed her arms.

"Sorry I didn't come back. It was late."

"Yeah." She wasn't sure what angered her more: that he didn't come back or that he didn't seem to care enough to call.

"I tried calling. Didn't think you wanted to talk."

"You didn't even leave a message."

"Why are you acting like this?"

"Why? You took care of Valerie. She's milking her minor injury for all it's worth."

He sighed. "Why are you so angry with her? You broke her nose, Ava."

She swallowed hard, her knuckles turning white as she clenched her fists. *I suffered broken ribs and a leg, and almost lost*

Melissa. She forced herself to stay calm, but her voice came out sharp. "Did you even hear what she said?"

"They're just words. Why do you let her get to you like that?"

"Because you didn't defend me. If anyone had said that about you, I would've stood up for you. But you … you didn't say a word."

He dragged his hands down his face. "I think you already did, considering you punched her. If someone had said that about me, I would've gotten over it."

Her anger flared. "Is that why you've been struggling at school? Because you just 'get over it'? Maybe I care because there's some truth to what Valerie said."

"I'm not going through this again."

"Go through what? That she thinks I forced you into this and that I'll kill you?"

His jaw tightened. "She didn't say that."

"Why are you defending her? Is there something you're not telling me?"

He took her hands in his. They were warm but unsteady. "Ava, I didn't become an Enchanter so I could be with Valerie. I love you."

Her heart clenched at his words, but they did little to ease the hurt. "If that's true, then why weren't you here last night? I was in an accident, Peter. Seth knew, and Valerie probably did too, but she didn't tell you, did she? Because you were with her."

His face twisted in shock. "What? What are you talking about?"

"I totaled your car. I was in a wreck, and I spent the night in pain while you were off playing nurse to Valerie."

"I didn't know. I tried calling—"

She jerked her hands from his. "Once! You tried once, and when I didn't answer, you stayed with her. Valerie needed help more than me, I guess."

"What was I supposed to do, just leave her?"

"You're my boyfriend, not hers." A tear slipped down her cheek, her voice faltering. "You made me feel like I didn't matter."

"I didn't know. I'm sorry. But why didn't you tell me about the accident earlier?"

"Because you didn't give me a chance. You were too busy with Valerie."

He reached for her again, his touch soft but unsure. "I love you, Ava. You."

Her heart wavered, the resentment still simmering. She hated how much they fought. Was it always going to be like that? Was she pushing him away like she had done with Thomas? "I don't want us to keep doing this. I don't want us to always be at each other's throats. Is this how it's going to be forever?"

"It won't be. We'll figure it out."

"Will we?" She paused, looking at him closely, the memory of how torn she'd been before she fully became an Enchanter surfacing. She could see it now, the way Peter was caught between his old life and this new, overwhelming reality. Just like she had been.

But the realization didn't soothe her hurt. Not yet.

"I know you're still trying to find your way between being an Ephemeral and being an Enchanter," she said, her frustration ebbing as the truth settled in. "But I'm hurting too. I need you, and it feels like you're always somewhere else."

"I'm not trying to be."

"I just … I don't know how much more of this I can take."

"I'm with you, Ava. I promise."

She looked up at him, trying to decide if she believed that. "I hope that's true."

The heavy wooden door creaked as they stepped inside the dimly lit cabin, the faint smell of smoke and ash lingering. The crackling fire was the only source of light, casting flickering shadows across the room. Gillian, Jeremy, Seth, Link, and Nicole stood clustered behind the couch, Melissa and Lance lingered in the kitchen, their faces tense. Thomas paced in front of the fireplace, the flames reflecting in his eyes. His anxiety rippled through the room like an electric current, and their necklaces glowed a deep red, feeding off his agitation.

"Are you okay?" Gillian nervously played with her hair, twisting and untwisting the curls with each breath.

Thomas clenched and unclenched his fists, his gaze fixed on the floor, his movements restless. The silence felt thick, stifling, as if the air itself had become laden with gravity of whatever he was about to say.

"We're all here, man," Lance said. "What's going on?"

Melissa tilted her head. "Did you find out who burned your house?"

Thomas stopped pacing for a moment, his eyes drifting from Ava to each of them. His face had a pallor, a ghostly hue, as if sleep had evaded him for countless nights. Shadows etched deep lines, giving his visage a worn, haggard appearance. "It was me."

Ava's breath caught in her throat.

His words seemed to suck the air out of the room. "I killed my dad, and I almost killed all of you."

Gillian gasped, her hand flying to her mouth.

Ava exchanged stunned glances with Melissa and Lance, the shock hitting her like a physical blow. Peter's grip tightened on her hand.

"What?" Lance asked, his voice full of disbelief.

Thomas resumed pacing, his hands tugging at his hair in frustration. "It was me. I've been dreaming for weeks that my dad was a Cimmerian. The dreams were so real. So powerful. That they convinced me he was evil. That he needed to die. I don't even remember doing it, but I know I did. And now … now I don't know why."

The room fell into a stunned silence. The crackling of the fire filled the room, the only sound to break the heavy silence after Thomas's confession.

After a long pause, Gillian cleared her throat. "I've been having dreams too." She blushed, wrapping her arms around herself. "About my mom."

Ava's stomach twisted. Could they all be connected to the Cimmerians? Was it happening to all of them? Savina had kept too many secrets, but this … this felt like betrayal. Her throat tightened. It was time. "My mom … was a Cimmerian."

Peter dropped her hand. "What? Why didn't you tell me?" His voice was full of hurt and disbelief.

"I just found out last night." Her gaze fixed on the floor. She couldn't bring herself to meet his eyes, to see the shock and disappointment written there. "When I went to New Orleans, one of Joss and Gabriel's friends, Marcel, had a vision of my mom. And last night … I had one, too. That's why I lost control of the car."

Gillian's eyes were wide. "A vision of what?"

"My mom … standing next to Corbin, like she belonged there."

"It was Trudy." Melissa stepped closer to Ava. "She gave you the vision."

Link frowned. "How did you find out about your mom?"

"Colden told me."

Jeremy turned to Thomas and Gillian. "Does this mean your parents were Cimmerians, too?"

Thomas resumed his pacing, his jaw tight as he spoke. "I don't know. But I *killed* my father. I wanted to kill him. I didn't care what it cost me."

"No, Thomas," Ava said. "It wasn't you. The Cimmerians are controlling us. They're planting these thoughts in our heads, making us see things … making us dream things."

"It makes sense," Gillian said. "I've been having horrible thoughts about Ephemerals. Angry, hateful thoughts. It's probably why I haven't been nice to you, Peter." She gave a guilty glance in his direction.

"Is that why you punched Valerie?" Peter asked Ava.

She couldn't handle his accusatory tone right now. "I don't know. But … I'm the one who killed Drew and Jonah."

A collective gasp filled the room. Ava's hands shook, her heart racing as she fought the urge to run from their judgment.

But Peter's disappointment, his shock, his disgust consumed her through the bond.

"What?" he stared at her, stunned. "Why would you do that?"

Tears welled in her eyes. "I didn't mean to. I swear. They attacked me, they…"

Melissa gripped Ava's hand. "They shot her, Peter. They thought she was responsible for the bombing. They threatened to come after all of us."

His eyes widened in shock. "You were *shot*?"

"Yes, I didn't … fall. I was attacked. I … I didn't mean to kill them. I was defending myself."

"You didn't have to kill them. You could have knocked them out."

Jeremy glared at Peter. "They *shot* her. What did you expect her to do?"

She blinked back the tears. "I'm sorry. I never wanted to kill anyone. But in that moment, I wanted to. It had to be the Cimmerians."

"We're supposed to protect them," Peter said coldly. "I warned you that you'd lose control."

With clenched fists, Thomas moved forward. "Give her a break. You act like you're better than all of us. Why are you even here? You clearly regret becoming an Enchanter."

"Thomas, stop," Ava pleaded.

Peter squared his shoulders, facing Thomas. "I belong here just as much as any of you. The Cimmerians tortured me, too. They know what I'm capable of."

"I did it!" Gillian's anguished scream cut through the air as tears streamed down her face.

"Did what?" Melissa asked.

"I compelled Trent to kill those people … then himself."

A heavy silence settled over the room as her confession left everyone stunned. Ava's heart sank as she realized the full extent of the Cimmerians' control. They were breaking them from the inside.

Thomas cursed, slamming his fist into the wall, leaving a jagged hole in the wood. "The Cimmerians are making us do these things. We have to stop them."

"We have to tell the Elders," Jeremy said.

Ava shook her head. "No. I don't want them to know."

"We can't handle this alone," Melissa argued. "We need help."

"What about Marcel?" Thomas asked. "Do you think he could tell us more?"

Ava shuddered at the thought of seeing him again. "I don't know … his visions aren't always clear."

"But it's worth a shot," Thomas said. "We need to know if we have Cimmerian blood, and what they want from us."

Ava sighed. "I'll ask Gabriel. Maybe he can take us."

Thomas nodded grimly. "We can't let them win."

22

BREAKTHROUGH

Thick strain filled the small space between Ava and Peter during the drive back to the Manor. Silence stretched, heavy and uncomfortable, only broken by the soft patter of rain against the windows. Outside, the autumn trees blurred into a swirl of orange and red, while droplets chased each other down the glass, mirroring Ava's spiraling thoughts.

She glanced at Peter, his jaw tight, eyes fixed on the road ahead. His silence hung in the air, heavy and suffocating. It was far from how she imagined telling him about Drew and Jonah. She had tried to hold it in, but the secret had eaten at her, and now she didn't know if Peter could ever forgive her.

Melissa twisted around from the front seat, her green eyes wide with worry. "Ava, the night of Thomas's house fire … Gillian was acting strange, like she was under some kind of influence. I didn't want to jump to conclusions without more proof, but now it's clear the Cimmerians have been controlling us."

Ava nodded slightly, her gaze returning to the rain-splattered window. Could the Cimmerians really be manipulating all of them? The idea seemed both terrifying and painfully possible.

Lance slowed the car to a stop outside the Manor. "Whatever they want from us, it's not good. They're making us do things we'd never do."

Peter crossed his arms and exhaled sharply.

When they got out of the car, Peter didn't linger. He headed straight for Ava's car, signaling that he wasn't staying the night.

She hesitated for a moment, then followed him. She hated the silence between them. She was sick of it.

As she pulled out onto the main road, Ava turned to him. "Please talk to me."

Peter kept his eyes on the road, jaw tight. "I don't know what to say. You killed Drew and Jonah. Thomas killed his dad. Gillian ... compelled Trent to murder. And now, we're all finding out that half of your parents might have been Cimmerians. What are we supposed to do with that?"

Ava's grip tightened on the steering wheel. "Are you mad at me?"

"I'm not mad ... I'm just—Ava, you killed people. I just ... I need time to wrap my head around it."

"I never meant for it to happen. I didn't want to..."

"But you did it. Why didn't you tell me?"

"I was scared of how you'd react. I didn't want to hurt you or push you further away. I hate myself for it. I didn't want anyone else to know."

"I'm not just anyone. You should've told me. I thought we were in this together, but you keep shutting me out. You're always hiding behind your wall."

"And you don't? You've been absent for months. It feels like you care more about your old life than anything here."

"Are you serious right now? Don't change the subject. You're the one who keeps me in the dark. You could've been honest with me, Ava. If the Cimmerians are messing with your mind, why wouldn't you tell me? And you were shot … I can't believe you never told me that."

Her throat tightened. "You were already struggling. I didn't want to make it worse, didn't want you to feel like they'd get inside your head too." She hesitated. "And I guess I let my jealousy over Valerie and Amanda get in the way. It just felt like you resented me."

"Ava, I love you. I became an Enchanter for you. But I've been scared—scared of all of this. I thought maybe if I ignored it, I could hold on to something normal for a while. I'm sorry for pulling away. I never meant to make you feel like you didn't matter."

Her chest tightened with guilt. The weight of her mother's mistakes pressed down on her, making it hard to breathe. She had done exactly what her mother had done to her father—kept secrets. "I'm sorry, too."

Ava pulled into his driveway and shifted the car into park.

He reached for her hand, squeezing it gently. "About Valerie … she's my friend. But I'll talk to her. She needs to understand that you're my girlfriend, and I'm not leaving you."

Ava felt her heart soften at his words, the tension between them loosening slightly.

He cupped her face, leaning in to kiss her softly, and she melted into the moment.

When he pulled back, he brushed a strand of hair behind her ear and kissed her forehead. "We're in this together, okay?"

Ava nodded, blinking back tears. "Okay."

Peter got out of the car and jogged to his front door. Why couldn't she just tell him everything? Maybe if she had been honest with him from the beginning, his reaction wouldn't have been so bad. She hated how much they fought now, and she couldn't help but wonder if things would always be this hard between them.

But for now, at least, they were in it together, even if things were messy.

Ava returned to the Manor, her mind heavy with what she had to do next: ask Gabriel to take them all to New Orleans, but as she walked through the dim hallway, she spotted Colden. He looked better than he had the night before, though there was still something off about him. His skin seemed paler, and the usual liveliness in his eyes had dulled.

"Good evening, dear." He greeted her with a warm, albeit weary smile.

"Hi." Ava tried to sound casual, but her voice came out tight.

"How are you?"

"Okay, I guess. Can we talk?"

"Of course. Let's go to the parlor."

Following him down the corridor, her thoughts raced. How was she supposed to bring up what he'd said the previous night? As they entered the cozy parlor, Colden closed the door behind them and gestured for her to sit in one of the high-back chairs by the fire.

She clenched her hands together, the familiar anxiety building in her chest as she tried to gather her words. The warmth of the room did little to ease the tension knotted in her stomach.

"What's on your mind?" Colden settled into the chair opposite her.

She hesitated, biting her lip. "About last night … What did you mean when you said I could contact those who aren't here?"

Colden's expression darkened, and he closed his eyes briefly, as if weighing his response. "I shouldn't have mentioned it."

"Please, Colden. I've been reading about Necromancy. Is that what you meant?"

"Ava…"

"Please. No one thinks I can handle the truth except you. You wouldn't have said anything if you didn't want me to know."

He pressed his lips into a thin line. "I made a mistake."

"You didn't. I need to know. Where can I find a Necromancer? Or … I could try a séance myself, if you won't help me."

His eyes narrowed, a flash of concern crossing his face. "Absolutely not. That's far too dangerous for you. Necromancy is only for advanced Enchanters."

"Then tell me where I can find one." She hated threatening him, but she was at the end of her rope. She needed answers about her mother, about the Cimmerians, about everything.

His shoulders slumped. "There is one … in New Orleans."

New Orleans. The same city where Marcel was. A plan started forming in her mind.

"But Ava, you must promise me you won't go alone. Necromancers deal in dark magic. They can be very dangerous."

Her heart raced. She could barely contain her excitement at the prospect of communicating with her mother, of finally getting the answers she'd been seeking. "Of course. I'll be careful."

Colden's gaze lingered on her, his expression troubled. "Do not tell the Elders about this. And don't mention my name. I won't admit to helping you."

"What exactly will happen when I see the Necromancer?"

"He will call upon your mother's spirit. But I warn you, it may not be a pleasant experience. Don't linger. Get what you need and leave."

Ava swallowed hard, her throat tightening. His warning stirred doubt within her, but she pushed it aside. "Okay. Are Necromancers Cimmerian?"

"They practice dark magic, but they don't pledge loyalty to anyone. People fear Necromancers because they can call upon spirits, good and bad, and bend them to their will."

A shudder rippled through her "I'm surprised Corbin didn't have one on his side."

"He did. Corbin forced a Necromancer to summon spirits during the war. It was madness."

Her stomach twisted at the thought. "What happened to them?"

"When Corbin died, the Necromancer disappeared. They're reclusive by nature." Colden's gaze shifted uneasily. Ava knew he didn't want to divulge more than necessary.

"How do you know where one is?"

"I've come across certain people over the years. Not always by choice."

"Why are you more open with me than Savina is?"

Colden smiled faintly. "Because I see a lot of myself in you. You don't let being different stop you. Corbin kept Savina and me in the dark about so much. When he betrayed us…" His voice trailed off, sadness creeping into his tone.

"What was it like? Growing up without powers?"

"It was difficult. Savina was loved for her healing, but I was seen as an outsider in both worlds. Too human for the Enchanters, too different for the Ephemerals. I tried to win my father's approval with my blacksmith skills, but it was never enough."

"That's awful. He treated you poorly because you didn't have powers?"

Colden nodded, his face etched with old pain. "He was disappointed. To him, I was too much like a human."

They sat in silence for a moment, the weight of Colden's past settling between them. A pang of sympathy for him struck Ava, realizing just how deep his wounds went.

"Thank you for trusting me," she said. "I won't let you down."

Colden gave her a tired smile, but his face contorted with pain. He grabbed his chest, his breathing becoming labored.

"Colden!" She shot out of her chair and kneeled beside him. "What's wrong? Do you need me to get Savina?"

He shook his head, waving her off. After a few agonizing moments, he exhaled and relaxed, though his face remained pale. "I'm fine, dear. Just … tired."

"Are you sure?"

"I just need rest." He gave her a weak smile. "Go, Ava. Seek the answers you desire. But be careful."

She helped him to his feet, guiding him to his room. He seemed frail, and she couldn't shake the fear gnawing at her. "Are you sure you don't want Savina?"

"I'm sure." He lay on the bed. "I'll manage. You've done enough."

Ava hesitated, watching him for a long moment before nodding. "Okay. Get some rest."

As she left his room, her mind whirled with conflicting thoughts. Colden had given her what she needed, but the cost felt high. Was he hiding something about his health? She couldn't lose him. Not now, not when he was one of the few people she could trust.

And now, with the knowledge of the Necromancer in New Orleans, she had to convince Gabriel to take them there. She could already feel her plan taking shape. She'd use the trip as cover to find the Necromancer. Finally, the answers she so desperately craved were within reach.

23

NO REST FOR THE WICKED

Ava slammed her locker harder than she intended. The sharp metallic sound echoed down the hallway, drawing a few glances her way, but she didn't care. She didn't want to be there. Too many things weighed on her mind. Killing two Ephemerals, almost killing her best friend, and now the looming trip to New Orleans to see a Necromancer. School felt trivial in comparison.

"Do we really have to be here?" she asked.

Peter leaned casually against the locker next to hers and shrugged. "It's not that bad anymore. At least it's a distraction."

"I need a bigger distraction, then."

He smiled, his eyes glinting with mischief. "Maybe I can make it worth it."

"Oh yeah? How?"

He caged her between his body and the locker. His lips met hers in a soft, teasing kiss. Her fingers curled around the collar of his sweater, pulling him in for more, but he broke the kiss, smiling.

"After each class, I'll give you a kiss," he said.

"That's my incentive?"

"Not good enough?" He raised an eyebrow, feigning innocence.

With a playful grin, she grabbed the neck of his sweater and pulled him into another kiss, this time more intense. His hand slipped to the small of her back, pulling her closer as the heat between them grew.

"It's plenty good enough," she whispered when they broke apart, breathless. "But I can kiss you anytime."

Peter cleared his throat, looking down both ends of the hallway before grabbing her hand. "Good point. Come with me."

They darted into an empty bathroom, and he locked the door behind them. His lips were on hers, the kiss deeper this time, filled with a hunger that sent shivers down her spine. He pressed her against the counter, lifting her up onto it. The cold marble under her thighs contrasted with the heat of their closeness, the intensity surprising her, but she liked it.

His lips, warm and velvety, traced a path along her chin, leaving a trail of tingling sensations in their wake. As they traveled down to her neck, she savored the delicate touch, her eyelids closing in bliss.

A loud, resonating bang on the bathroom door shattered the moment, followed by a muffled complaint from someone outside, barely audible over the rush of blood in her ears.

Peter groaned, but Ava kept him in place, her heart pounding. She didn't want to stop, but another series of impatient bangs made it clear their stolen moment was over.

"Maybe you can come over after school," she suggested breathlessly.

"I have to work."

"Then come over after."

He avoided her gaze. "I can't. I'm busy."

"Busy with what?" She hated the sinking feeling in her stomach.

"Nothing." He moved to the door, pulling her along.

She yanked her hand back. "What is it?"

He hesitated. "I have to go check on Valerie."

"What?" Her heart sank.

"Please don't get upset. I'm just trying to maintain some civility with Valerie and Amanda. They're my friends."

"Were you not going to tell me?"

"I didn't want to upset you."

"Keeping it a secret is definitely not the way to avoid that." She brushed past him, unlocked the door, and stormed out into the hallway. Whoever had been knocking was gone, but the frustration boiling inside her wasn't.

"Ava, don't be like this," he called after her, but she didn't stop. She pushed her way through the crowded hall, anger swelling inside her. Why wouldn't he just tell her the truth? What was he hiding?

The noise of lockers slamming, phones chiming, and idle chatter grated on her nerves. Ephemerals talking about nothing, completely unaware of the world that existed beyond their own. She clenched her teeth. They were so oblivious, so weak. Why was it her responsibility to protect them? Why did she even care?

Then, suddenly, she couldn't hear anything at all.

The silence hit her like a wave, making her halt in the middle of the hallway. She looked around, watching students walk by, mouths moving in conversation, phones in hand, but no sound reached her ears. Panic flickered through her. Why couldn't she hear?

A hand touched her shoulder, and she jumped, spinning around to see Melissa standing there, her lips moving. But Ava couldn't hear her either.

Just as fast as it had vanished, the noise returned, flooding her ears with an overwhelming rush of sound.

"Earth to Ava," Melissa said. "What's wrong with you?"

Ava shook her head, trying to shake off the disorienting sensation. "Sorry ... just spaced out."

"Yeah, no kidding. You okay?"

"Not really. I don't want to be here."

Melissa shrugged, linking her arm with Ava's as they walked down the thinning hall. "Not many people do."

What had just happened? Losing her hearing, the anger that kept bubbling up inside her... Was she going crazy? Or worse, were the Cimmerians messing with her mind?

"So, what are we calling this new soap opera of yours? The Secret Life of a Teenage Witch? Or maybe Spellbinding Drama?"

Ava rolled her eyes. "Peter's going to see Valerie after school. And he wasn't going to tell me."

Melissa winced and sucked in a sharp breath through her teeth. "Ouch."

"He said he didn't want to upset me."

"Which, clearly, he succeeded in doing."

"It's because he kept it from me."

"Look, I get it. Valerie's a bitch, but you gotta let it go. Peter's with you, not her. He loves you, and he's trying to hold onto his old life. There's nothing wrong with that."

Ava sighed. Melissa was right, as usual, but it still stung. "He doesn't need to keep things from me."

She shot her a knowing look. "You're certainly one to talk. You haven't exactly been open with him about a lot of things."

Guilt hit Ava. Melissa had a point, but the fear of Peter's reaction had kept her silent. "Because … you saw how he reacted."

"Sure, but he'll come around. He loves you. Let him in. Don't shut him out. We're all struggling right now. He just needs you to trust him."

Ava hated that Melissa was right, hated that she let her anger cloud her judgment.

"Have you asked Gabriel about Marcel yet?" Melissa asked. "Thomas is getting pretty antsy."

"No, not yet. But I did talk to Colden last night. I think something's wrong with him."

"Wrong how?"

"He looked pale, and he's been having trouble breathing. He gets tired a lot."

"Does Savina know?"

"She has to. But she won't say anything, just like she wouldn't tell me about my mom."

Melissa shook her head. "Why is she keeping so many secrets? She wouldn't tell Thomas about his dad, either. Also, where has she been lately?"

"I don't know." A sliver of doubt crept in. "Maybe … maybe she's not who we think she is."

"Wait, do you actually think Savina's hiding something more? Like … betrayal?"

"No. I don't know. I'm just tired of all the lies."

Melissa placed a hand on Ava's arm, her voice soft. "Don't jump to conclusions. There's always more to the story. You'll get your answers."

The bell rang, signaling the start of class, and they parted ways. As Ava took her seat, her eyes fell on Drew's empty chair, her thoughts pulling her down again. Could she ever stop the dark thoughts, the growing resentment toward Ephemerals?

She hoped the Necromancer would have the answers she needed, before she lost herself completely.

As soon as school ended, Ava needed something to occupy her mind, something to pull her thoughts away from Peter being at Valerie's house. Checking on her, spending time with her. She clenched her fists. What if Valerie kissed him?

She shook her head. *Stop being jealous.*

The library seemed like a good escape, and maybe Gabriel would be there. She wasn't sure how to approach him about going to New Orleans to see Marcel but at least being surrounded by books would soothe her.

The familiar scent of old paper and ink greeted her as she stepped inside the library, the quiet hum of the space calmed her nerves. The rows of books, the shelves stretching high above her, felt like a comforting shield from the chaos in her life.

"Hey," a voice said, startling her.

She turned and found Gabriel seated in one of the plush chairs, his book resting on his lap.

"Sorry," he chuckled. "Didn't mean to scare you."

Ava's gaze dropped to the book in his hands. *A Hero of Our Time*. "How ironic."

He grinned, his crystal-blue eyes crinkling at the corners. "How was school?"

She dropped into the chair beside him, sighing. "It was school."

"What's wrong"

"Let's just say I've been playing the Queen of Hearts role a little too well lately."

He tilted his head, waiting.

"I punched one of Peter's friends the other night, and now it's like he's at her every beck and call. He's at her house right now, but he wasn't going to tell me."

He raised an eyebrow. "You punched an Ephemeral?"

"She causes so much drama. She said Peter would wind up dead if he stayed with me. That my mom being dead and my dad almost dying was proof. I lost it. And Peter consoled her." She shook her head, feeling the anger boil up again. "I was so angry."

"I'd have hit her too, honestly."

"You? You're like the calmest person I know."

He smiled faintly. "I didn't used to be. I had a pretty bad temper once upon a time."

Ava tried to picture it, but Gabriel's demeanor was so composed, so steady. "I can't even imagine."

"Why do you feel so threatened by this girl?"

"I don't know. Maybe I'm not threatened. I guess … it's just … the night of my accident, Seth told Valerie to tell Peter what happened, but she left that part out. Kept him with her all night. It's like he doesn't see through her bull. He defends her over me. Every time."

"Maybe he's just trying really hard to hold onto his old life. The Ephemeral part."

"That's what Melissa said. But I feel like he hasn't fully committed to being an Enchanter. I know it's a hard transition, but he wanted this. And now ... I can't even talk to him about the dark thoughts I've been having. I finally told him about Drew and Jonah, and he freaked out." Her voice cracked. "I didn't mean to kill them. I didn't know my own strength. And now, with everything about my mom being a Cimmerian, I was afraid if I told him, he'd just ... pull away."

Gabriel's gaze sharpened. "Wait ... your mother was a Cimmerian? Do you know this for sure?"

She froze. She hadn't meant to tell him that. But Gabriel had a way of making her feel at ease, like she could say anything. "Yeah. Colden told me."

"Damn. I'm sorry, Ava."

Now seemed like the perfect time to bring up Marcel. She shifted in her seat. "So ... a few of us who've been having Cimmerian-like thoughts. Thomas and Gillian. We were hoping you could help us with something."

"What is it?"

"I told them about Marcel. They want to see if he can help. We need to know if one of their parents was Cimmerian. Could you take us to see him?" She braced herself for his reaction, expecting resistance.

"Sure," he said without hesitation.

"Really?"

"Of course. I don't mind helping. You all need answers, and it's not like Savina's been forthcoming with information. Marcel is my friend. Just ... make sure they know what to expect with him."

"I will. Thank you." Relief flooded her.

"You're welcome." His eyes lingered on hers for a moment, an intensity there that made her feel exposed, vulnerable.

She looked away, her cheeks warming. "How's the book?"

"It's good. I've read it before."

The silence stretched between them, charged with something she couldn't quite name.

"Have you got anything going on this afternoon?" he asked.

"You're looking at it."

Gabriel stood, tossing the book into the chair. "Come on."

"Where are we going?"

"It's a surprise." He offered his hand with a mischievous smile.

She hesitated but placed her hand in his. Seconds later, they stood in an empty parking lot in the middle of a bustling city.

"Where are we?" She still clutched his hand.

"Baltimore." He pulled her toward a large gray building across the street.

Ava's eyes landed on the engraved sign above the entrance: *Enoch Pratt Free Library*. "Why are we here?"

He grinned. "You like reading, so I thought you'd enjoy this."

Ava stared at him in surprise, her heart warming at the gesture. He had always been so thoughtful, and yet she hadn't expected something so … sweet. "I don't know what to say."

Inside, the library was breathtaking. The warm, golden rays of the sun poured through the expansive, glass-paneled ceiling, bathing the lobby in a radiant glow. Smooth, creamy marble columns enveloped the main hall, creating a sense of grandeur and elegance. Positioned at the heart of the room, a small desk, its surface worn by time, beckoned visitors to approach.

As Ava ascended to the second floor, the scent of old paper, wood, and a faint trace of polished brass filled the air, giving the library an inviting, timeless atmosphere. She paused for a moment, taking it all in. The grandeur, the history, and the sense of calm that contrasted with the storm of thoughts inside her head.

"This is incredible," she murmured, her voice barely a whisper in the cavernous hall.

"Wait until you see the rest." He motioned for her to follow, leading her deeper into the library, where the whispers of the past seemed to mingle with the present.

"What do you want to be when you grow up?"

"A teacher."

For a moment, she imagined it. Serious yet kind, his blue eyes filled with passion for literature. "You'd make a great teacher."

"Thanks." His smile widened.

As they descended a staircase into a quiet room, Gabriel led her to the *Special Collections* section. Her eyes widened as they approached a display filled with relics from Edgar Allan Poe—letters, personal items, even locks of hair.

"This is incredible." She leaned over the display case. "That's actually his hair?"

"Yeah. They kept it, hoping it would help them figure out how he died," he replied, a flicker of mystery in his eyes.

"It was rabies, wasn't it? That's what I've always heard."

His expression remained serious. "I think he was turned into a vampire."

"You're kidding, right?"

"Think about it."

"They don't even exist," she countered, waiting for him to break into a smile. But Gabriel's gaze was steady, alive with the kind of quiet conviction that sent a shiver down her spine.

"If we can do what we do, then why can't vampires exist?"

A laugh escaped her. "Your imagination is wild."

His eyes glinted with amusement, but there was something darker beneath, something unsaid. "Imagination helps when reality's too much."

The words hit Ava in a way she wasn't expecting. "I can't even imagine what your childhood must have been like." The second the words left her mouth, she regretted them. Gabriel's past was scarred, and she'd opened a wound without thinking. "I'm so sorry, Gabriel. I didn't mean—"

"It's okay. It was a long time ago. I've had time to come to terms with it." He winked, but it didn't fully mask the old hurt behind his eyes.

She nodded, but the knot of guilt tightened inside her. "How did you do it? I mean, how did you survive all that? Being on your own…"

"I didn't have a choice."

"What happened? If you don't mind talking about it."

His gaze flickered, as if debating how much to share. "I was really young when my parents died. My uncle took me in, but … he didn't understand what I was. He wasn't an Enchanter."

"Your parents were mixed like mine?"

"Yeah. My uncle wasn't … part of that world. So, when I turned sixteen and my powers started to show, he didn't know how to handle it. I couldn't control them, and he was scared. He … kicked me out."

Ava's heart sank. She couldn't imagine what it must have been like to be abandoned like that. "He just left you?"

Gabriel's jaw tightened, and he looked away. "Yeah. He didn't understand me. Thought I was dangerous."

She reached out, squeezing his hand as her chest tightened. "I'm so sorry. That's awful."

He gave her a small smile. "It's fine. I figured things out eventually. Found people who understood." He paused, his eyes darkening. "But it took a long time to stop feeling like an outsider."

Ava felt a surge of empathy. She knew that feeling too well. The isolation, the confusion about where she fit in. "You're not alone anymore, though."

"No. I'm not. And neither are you."

His words hit deep, and she didn't know how to respond. His intense gaze bore into her, making her feel seen in a way she hadn't before. She swallowed hard, looking away.

"I'm glad you found them. They would never abandon you."

Gabriel squeezed her hand back, a small comfort in the quiet space around them. "And I won't abandon you either, Ava."

With a smile, she found comfort in that. "I don't think I could've lasted as long as you. And here I am complaining about such trivial things."

"I hardly consider being ambushed by Cimmerians trivial. Or everything else you've been dealing with."

"I just meant Peter."

"I know."

"I don't know what to do about him. Everything's just … complicated now. We're constantly fighting, and I keep wondering. Did I make a mistake by pushing him to become an Enchanter?"

"Do you really think that?"

"I don't know. Ever since he changed, it's like we're not on the same page anymore. We've both changed so much."

"It's not easy, transitioning between two worlds. Peter was an Ephemeral his whole life, and now … he's in this world of magic, power, danger. It's overwhelming."

"I know. But it feels like I'm losing him. He spends all his time with Valerie or avoiding training. And … we don't connect the way we used to."

"Give it time. He loves you."

She nodded.

"I know things between you and Peter are tough right now," he said. "But I see how much you care about him, and how much you're struggling with everything happening. I'm here for you."

A blush crept up her cheeks and she looked away. "Thanks. Should we head back?"

"Sure." He took her hand, and instinctively, Ava closed her eyes.

When she opened them again, she expected to see the familiar surroundings of the Manor, but instead, they stood in an open field beneath a blanket of gray skies. A cool breeze swept through her hair, and Ava's stomach dropped as she recognized the scene. She turned in place, her eyes locking onto the patch of blackened grass and the lone clothesline swaying gently in the wind.

It was her former home. The exact spot where her mother had died.

She jerked her hand out of his grip. "What are we doing here?"

His eyes widened, confusion flashing across his face. "I don't know."

"Why would you bring me here?" she yelled, her voice trembling with a mix of panic and anger.

"I didn't. I swear, I didn't." He took a step back. "This is what Aaron warned me about."

Her heart raced, her breath coming in short gasps. "Did you know this would happen? Did you do this on purpose?"

Gabriel's face fell, and for a moment, genuine hurt flicked in his eyes. His lips parted as if he wanted to say something, to explain, but the words never came.

Ava froze at the slightest rustle from the tree line. A group of people, ten, maybe more, emerged from the woods, their forms dark and ominous as they closed in around her. Panic surged through her, and she spun back toward Gabriel, only to find…

He was gone.

Vanished.

24

TIDAL WAVE

Water dripped down Ava's arms, cold and slick, coiling around her wrists like living tendrils. She focused, watching her opponents closely, just as Gabriel had taught her. But he wasn't there now. He had abandoned her. Was he getting more help? Or worse, was he a traitor? Ava's mind flashed through possibilities, but there was no time to dwell on it.

A tall man with wild red hair charged toward her. Ava raised her hands and blasted him with a surge of water, sending him sprawling unconscious on the wet ground. Her heart pounded in her chest, every pulse a reminder that she was on her own.

Another witch ran at her, and Ava knocked her out just as swiftly. But more were coming. Emerging from the shadows of the trees. Ava's stomach twisted. How many were there? How long could she hold them off? She wouldn't die there, not in the same place her mother had fallen. She wouldn't let them win.

There were too many for her to take down all at once. She needed more. More water, more power, more help. Her chest heaved as she inhaled, feeling the water trickle down her arms. It wasn't just water anymore, it was energy, thrumming inside her, sparking against her skin. The warmth spread through her veins, as calm settled over her. She was ready.

Water surged from the ground, swirling around her legs, lifting debris in its current. As the witches closed in, Ava raised her hands, and the water obeyed, building into a roaring tidal wave above her head. She didn't just want them defeated. She wanted them drowned, swallowed by the darkest ocean.

With a flick of her wrist, the tidal wave crashed down, a thunderous roar shaking the earth. The witches were caught in its wrath, their bodies tossed like rag dolls. The ground trembled beneath Ava's feet as the water swept through, swallowing them whole. Their screams were muffled beneath the roaring water. Ava's heart raced, her chest heaving. This was her message.

She wanted them to know that she was done playing games.

The world dimmed. Everything went black. Ava's vision blurred as she swayed on her feet. She heard the gasps of the witches as the water slowly receded, the storm inside her subsiding. Her legs buckled, and she fell to her knees, drained. The water pulled back, leaving the field soaked and littered with bodies. Some witches stirred, others lay motionless.

As she tried to catch her breath, a voice pierced through the eerie silence.

"Surprised?"

Ava's head snapped up. Xavier Holstone stood before her, a sneer twisting his pale lips. For someone who had been tortured for months, he looked surprisingly well. Too well. His ashen skin, his cocky stance ignited something cold and furious in her.

She staggered to her feet, water forming around her fists. She wasn't afraid of him anymore. "Not really. I knew you'd crawl back."

"Smart girl. And yet, you're still standing." His black eyes gleamed, but there was no warmth behind them.

"Why should I be scared of you? You've had plenty of chances to kill me. Yet here I am."

Xavier's grin darkened. "Havok will have your power soon enough, and when he does, I'll enjoy watching you break."

"Is that why he wanted Devon? To absorb all the Elemental powers?"

"That didn't exactly go to plan, did it?"

"Why doesn't Havok come for us himself? What's he so afraid of?"

"You don't know much about Havok, do you?" Xavier clicked his tongue, mocking. "He's a soul reaper. When he has all the powers inside an Absorption Enchanter, then … well, let's just say, you'll wish you were dead."

"Who's your new guinea pig now that Devon's gone?"

Xavier's wicked grin widened. "Lance, of course."

"It won't work. Absorption Enchanters can only take one power at a time. You'll fail again."

"I take back what I said. You're dumber than I thought. But you'll learn soon enough."

The water around her hands swirled. Her patience was wearing thin. "Why are you here? What do you want?"

Xavier's smile faded, replaced with cold intent. "Havok wants you to give yourself over to him. You, your little group, and your protector."

Protector. How did he know about Peter?

"Don't act surprised, Ava. We know everything about him. That's why no one could control you. Not me, not anyone. That's why torturing Peter was useless. But don't worry, you have until the new moon to give yourself to Havok. Otherwise, we'll bring the war to you." He started walking away.

"Is that it? You come here with your lackeys, fail to kill me, and expect me to surrender? You're a coward, Xavier."

He stopped, turning to face her again. His cold, dark eyes glinted with amusement. "Tempting, but you're not much use to me by yourself."

"If you take me now, they'll come for me. Then you'd have us all."

Xavier smirked. "Are you so desperate to leave them?"

"No, I'm tired of this game. None of us will give ourselves to whoever this Havok is. Not ever."

His smile grew, but it didn't reach his eyes. "You will, Ava. It's your destiny."

Her blood turned cold. "What do you know about my destiny?"

Xavier's laughter echoed through the clearing. "You poor girl. Still don't know. Your mother promised your soul to Havok. You belong to him."

Ava's world tilted. Her mother ... *promised* her? "That's a lie."

"She's been sending you signals. Haven't you noticed?"

Fury burned inside her. She raised her arm to strike him.

"I wouldn't do that," Xavier warned. "Your friend here is suffering. I wouldn't want him to get worse."

Ava's gaze snapped to where Xavier gestured. Gabriel. He appeared, bound by what seemed to be crackling ropes of lightning, bloodied and barely clinging to consciousness. Her heart lurched. "Gabriel…" she whispered.

Xavier stepped closer. "I wouldn't trust him if I were you."

"Let him go."

"As you wish." Xavier made a motion, and Ava blasted him with water, hitting him square in the chest.

A hand grabbed her arm, and in the blink of an eye, the world shifted. She was no longer in the clearing but in a forest, alone, with an injured Gabriel at her side.

25

HEALER

Ava stood poised for an attack, her heart hammering in her chest as her eyes darted around the darkening forest. The trees loomed tall and twisted, their gnarled branches creaking in the sharp wind. Every rustle of leaves or snap of a twig sent her pulse racing, her senses on high alert. The thick air tasted of damp earth, and storm clouds gathered overhead, their heavy shadows casting the woods in an eerie half-light.

Water slithered down Ava's arms, cool against her heated skin, forming droplets that pooled at her fingertips before falling onto the cracked, dry leaves below. But there was no one else around.

Just her and Gabriel.

Her necklace burned against her skin, glowing faintly beneath her shirt. She turned sharply toward Gabriel and her breath caught. He was hunched over, blood streaming down his arms, soaking his once-white shirt, now stained deep crimson. He looked pale, drained.

Panic tightened her throat. "Gabriel."

He met her gaze, his blue eyes full of pain. The sight of him, normally so composed, now broken and bleeding, rattled her. Ava rushed to his side, her mind racing. Their phones buzzed somewhere, but the world had narrowed to just this moment. She grabbed his arm, and the water around her responded, rushing to his wounds. Her power shifted, changed, as it wrapped around him, sealing every cut, every gash.

When the last wound closed, she stumbled back, staring at her hands in disbelief. Her fingers still trembled with energy, but now, there was fear. "What did I just do?"

Gabriel looked down at his arms, still catching his breath. His eyes, wide with disbelief, locked onto hers. "You healed me."

"I … I didn't mean to. I've never—never healed anyone before."

He slowly stood, his movements careful, as though he was afraid the healing might unravel. "Your water—you're a Healer, Ava. I had no idea."

She had healed him. But if she could heal … what else was she capable of doing?

"You're shaking," he said softly, edging closer. "Are you hurt?"

Ava shook her head, overwhelmed by the storm of thoughts and fears churning in her head. The adrenaline from the fight had worn off, leaving her raw and vulnerable. Tears blurred her vision, her breath coming in short, jagged gasps. The world felt like it was closing in on her, the dark forest pressing in from all sides.

He pulled her against him, holding her tightly.

She buried her face in his chest. "I thought you abandoned me. All those witches were closing in, and you weren't there."

"I was," he murmured, his voice soft, full of regret. "They put up a barrier. Wrapped me in ropes. I saw everything, but I couldn't do anything to help you. But Ava, you—" He pulled back just enough to look her in the eyes. "You were incredible. You're getting stronger."

"I didn't know I could do any of that."

"You did what you had to."

Their phones rang again, but it felt distant, unimportant.

"How do they keep getting out?" she asked. "How do they keep finding us?"

"I don't know. But we have to tell the Elders."

She flinched, pulling away from his embrace. She hated the idea of facing Savina and Aaron again. "I need time to think."

"Ava—" His tone was urgent, but gentle. "What did Xavier say?"

She couldn't hold back the tears any longer. "He said my mother promised my soul to Havok."

"That's not true. Xavier's trying to mess with your head."

"But what if it is? The visions, the dreams … someone is in my head, Gabriel. They're following us, watching us."

He placed his hands on her shoulders. "Don't let him get to you. You can't let him make you doubt everything."

"Xavier said if I don't give myself to Havok and convince the others to do the same, they'll declare war. We have until the new moon."

Gabriel pulled her into his arms again. "We'll figure it out. But we have to tell the Elders. They need to know what's coming."

Ava nodded against his chest, though a part of her felt defeated. They couldn't go to New Orleans now, not with a threat of war looming over them. She needed answers, but she needed to stay alive more. "Can we hold off until after we see Marcel? Everyone still needs answers."

"We'll tell the Elders first, then I'll take you to Marcel. Deal?"

Ava met his eyes, her heart still heavy with doubt. She didn't understand why Gabriel helped her, why he always came back. But in that moment, she was grateful for his strength. "Deal."

As they began walking back through the forest, the ground wet beneath their feet, Ava couldn't shake Xavier's words. *"You can't trust him."*

She glanced at Gabriel walking beside her, his blue eyes scanning the path ahead. He had always been there for her. But if Xavier knew more about Gabriel's past than she did, what could that mean? Could Xavier be playing with her mind again?

The wind rustled through the trees, the chill in the air cutting through her as sharply as her uncertainty. But for now, she pushed it aside. Gabriel was there. That's what mattered, at least, for the moment.

A wave of tension greeted them as soon as they arrived at the Manor. Several coven members gathered near the entrance, their faces etched with worry.

"What happened?" Melissa scanned them for any sign of injury.

"Are you okay?" Joss rushed up to them.

"We're fine." Gabriel's voice was firm but tired.

Natalia crossed her arms, her gaze lingering on Gabriel's blood-soaked shirt. "Your shirt says otherwise. What happened?"

"I'm fine. Really. But we need to talk to the Elders. Now."

Eric shifted uncomfortably. "I'm not sure this is a good time."

Ava frowned. "Why not?"

"Colden's really sick," Eric replied. "He's been coughing up blood all day."

Her stomach clenched. *Why hasn't Savina healed him?* Something was off. "What's wrong with him? Why hasn't Savina done anything?"

Joss shrugged, her brow furrowed. "We don't know. She's been with him, but it doesn't seem to be working."

"This can't wait," Gabriel said.

Thomas raked a hand through his hair. "We all felt it, you know, whatever happened to both of you. What's going on?"

Ava glanced at Gabriel before speaking. "Xavier Holstone escaped."

Gasps rippled through the group, and Melissa's face paled. Joss took a step back, shock settling in. Even Natalia seemed rattled.

"You've got to be kidding me," Thomas muttered. "How the hell did he escape? And what does he want now?"

"He wants us to give ourselves to someone named Havok before the new moon," Gabriel answered, his jaw tight. "Otherwise, they're declaring war."

"Havok?" Eric asked. "Who is that?"

Ava's voice wavered, the revelation settling over her. "We don't know exactly. But Xavier, Trudy, and Devon mentioned him. They said he plans on using Lance to absorb all of our powers."

Joss gasped. "This sounds like Corbin all over again. You should tell the Elders. Now."

Gabriel nodded, and they headed inside the Manor. As they neared Savina's parlor, they stopped abruptly when Aaron emerged from the shadows, holding a pot. Ava caught a faint whiff of something metallic. Her stomach churned. *Blood.*

"Hello," Aaron said, his voice calm, though there was a flicker of concern in his eyes. "What's going on?"

"We need to talk to the Elders," Gabriel said. "Urgently."

Aaron studied them for a moment and sighed. "Given the urgency in your voices and what we felt earlier, I assume this is serious." He glanced down at the pot in his hands. "Let me take care of this first."

Ava's gaze followed Aaron as he walked into the kitchen. She sneaked a glance inside the pot, catching a glimpse of dark red liquid as he poured it down the drain. Her pulse quickened. *Is all of that Colden's blood?* Something was deeply wrong. *What is Savina doing?* Her unease deepened as Aaron returned, wiping his hands on a towel.

Aaron led them into the parlor, where Savina and Maggie were already waiting, their faces a mix of concern and exhaustion.

Savina wiped her hands on a black cloth and looked up. "What—good heavens, Gabriel!" Her eyes widened at the sight of him. "What happened?"

"We're fine," he said. "But Xavier is out. One of the Cimmerians got inside my head and forced me to teleport to Ava's old home. He said we have until the new moon to give ourselves to Havok, or they'll start a war."

Savina's brow furrowed. "Xavier? Are you sure?"

Ava nodded. "He told me Havok plans to use Lance to absorb all of our powers so Havok can control them."

"Who is Havok?" Maggie asked.

"We don't know," Ava said. "But this isn't some empty threat."

Savina's face tightened. "That's impossible. Lance can only absorb one power at a time. They're bluffing."

Ava's anger flared. "How can you say that? Xavier *escaped* the Cruciari! This isn't a joke."

Aaron said, "I weakened him. His powers shouldn't be functional."

"Well, he has them back," Gabriel said. "We were ambushed. Cimmerians tied me in electric ropes. Ava fought them off."

Savina began pacing. "This doesn't make sense. Havok … this could be a ruse. Maybe someone morphed into Xavier."

Ava's frustration bubbled over. "Why do you keep denying this? They've attacked us repeatedly. We can't ignore this."

Gabriel placed a calming hand on Ava's shoulder. "It was Xavier, I assure you."

A violent cough sounded from behind a black curtain, harsh and rattling. Aaron immediately excused himself, disappearing behind the curtain where Colden lay hidden from view.

Savina exchanged a glance with Maggie. They whispered to one another, keeping their conversation private.

Ava clenched her fists, anger swirling in her chest. *They're keeping something from us. Again.*

Maggie finally spoke up. "Tomorrow, we'll start preparations."

Aaron returned, his face paler than before. "We need to call the other Aureoles."

Savina hesitated, her lips pressed into a thin line. "There's no need."

"We cannot take any chances, Savina. If Havok is truly trying to do what Corbin did, we must be prepared."

Reluctantly, Savina nodded. "Fine. Contact Gustav and Maya." Savina turned to Gabriel, concern etched across her features. "Let me heal you, Gabriel. You're still bleeding."

He shook his head, glancing at Ava. "I don't need it. Ava healed me."

Savina's eyes widened, surprise and curiosity mixing in her gaze. "Ava?"

"Her water healed me. I don't know how."

Savina stared at Ava, her voice soft with awe. "You're a Healer. I had no idea. Healers are incredibly rare."

Ava shook her head, still processing. "But why didn't I heal myself when I was hurt before?"

"You have to direct it," Savina explained gently. "The water must come from within you."

Her mind flashed back to her past injuries, the burns from Thomas, the welts from Trudy. She hadn't realized that her own water could have healed her all along. "I wasn't thinking about healing Gabriel. I just wanted to stop his pain. I had to get him here as fast as I could."

Savina smiled softly. "And your water listened."

But her mind raced with darker thoughts. "What would the Cimmerians do if they found out I'm a Healer?"

Aaron's voice interrupted her thoughts. "They would want you even more. If Havok is anything like Corbin, you would be a prized possession."

A cold dread settled in her chest.

"We won't let that happen," Savina promised, but Ava wasn't sure she believed her. Too many secrets had already been kept.

Savina's voice softened. "There is something else I need to ask you."

Aaron gestured to Gabriel. "You're free to go. But no more teleporting until we know it's safe."

Ava's heart sank as she exchanged a glance with Gabriel. *How will we get to New Orleans now?*

As Gabriel left the parlor, her resolve hardened. She had to find another way to see Marcel. She bit her lip. "What do you want to ask me?"

Savina crossed the room, her thin fingers cool as they settled on Ava's shoulders. "Colden is very sick. His body won't respond to my healing … but perhaps it will to yours. Would you help us?"

Her pulse quickened. Doubt crept in, tightening her chest. *What if it doesn't work?* She wasn't an expert. She barely knew how she'd healed Gabriel earlier. *What if I make things worse?* But Colden needed help, and she couldn't say no. "I'll try."

Every muscle in her body ached. The fight with the Cimmerians had drained her, and the surge of energy it took to create the tidal wave had left her feeling hollow. Her legs felt weak as she followed Savina down the hall. But there was no turning back now.

Savina gave her an encouraging nod and turned, leading the way through the darkened hallways. Ava's hands shook as she followed, dread weighing heavy in her chest. When they reached a small room, Savina raised her hand, and the candlelight inside flared, casting long, flickering shadows.

Colden lay on his side, his pale skin glistening with sweat. He groaned softly, his breaths labored, a bloodstained rag near his mouth. Ava's stomach churned at the sight. He looked far worse than she had imagined. Gaunt and fragile, and his body shook from the effort to stay alive.

"Colden." Savina placed a gentle hand on his forehead, the way a mother soothes a sick child. "Ava is here. She's a Healer."

His eyelids fluttered open. His lips twitched, as if he wanted to smile, but even that small motion seemed to exhaust him. "How … extraordinary," he rasped, his voice barely audible, hoarse and rough.

"I've asked her to help you."

He managed a weak nod, his eyes filled with hope despite his suffering.

Ava's throat tightened. Her hands were trembling again as Savina extended her own hand to her, a gesture of trust.

"Do not be afraid," Savina said. "If this doesn't work, at least we will have tried."

Easy for you to say. Her pulse thudded in her ears. The weight of responsibility crashed down on her. Colden looked like he was on death's door, and Savina was asking her to perform a miracle. *What if I hurt him?*

Her body ached, her energy low, but she had to try.

"Take a deep breath," Savina instructed, guiding Ava's hand to rest on Colden's arm. "Will your water to heal."

She closed her eyes, trying to focus, but her head felt foggy, her body drained. She reached deep within herself, calling on the water, but it felt sluggish, like trying to pull water from a dry well. *Come on, please work.* Colden needed her.

Slowly, she felt a trickle of water forming at her fingertips, cool and soft against her skin. She opened her eyes to see the water wrap around Colden's arm, its shimmer catching the light. The color began to return to his face, his breathing easing as the water spread over his body.

Ava's heart soared. *I did it.* She had actually healed him. Despite the weariness that clung to her bones, a rush of pride and awe swelled in her chest. Twice in one day. She had healed Gabriel and now Colden. The realization filled her with something she hadn't felt in weeks: hope.

"This is incredible," Savina murmured.

Ava smiled, unable to contain her excitement. But just as she started to pull her hand away, she froze. A strange, unsettling tugging sensation anchored her hand in place, as though something, or someone, was pulling the water back. Panic flared in her chest, and she yanked her hand free, her heart racing. Had anyone noticed?

She glanced around, but everyone seemed focused on Colden's miraculous recovery, unaware of the weird pulling sensation she had felt.

"How do you feel?" Aaron asked, his brow furrowed in concern.

"I feel … wonderful." Colden sat up slowly. His movements were stiff, but the pain seemed to have left him. "A little tired, sore even, but I can breathe again. I'm not in pain."

Savina beamed with pride. "The soreness will fade in a few days. You'll need rest." She turned to Ava with a grateful smile. "Thank you. You've done something truly remarkable."

Ava's mind still spun from what she'd just done, and yet a thrill of awe coursed through her. She had healed him—truly healed him. The sense of power, of control, was exhilarating, even though her body was weak and trembling with exhaustion.

"You're welcome," she said, her voice soft, the thrill mixing with a deep fatigue that weighed heavily on her.

Savina embraced her, the hug warm and reassuring. "I have much to teach you about Healing. We shall begin tomorrow."

Ava nodded, but the moment she stepped back, the adrenaline faded, and exhaustion slammed into her like a wave. Her legs felt like jelly, her hands still trembling slightly. But despite the weariness, she couldn't help but feel amazed by what had just happened.

I did it. She had healed Colden. The weird pulling sensation tugged at the back of her mind, but she was too drained to think about it right now. She just wanted to hold onto the feeling of accomplishment.

As she left the room, her legs wobbled beneath her. Her head throbbed, and her vision swam slightly, but nothing could dim the sense of awe that still buzzed in her veins. *I have to tell Dad.* Her heart fluttered with the desire to share the good news. And somehow, she would tell him about her mother too.

But for now, she needed to rest. She had done more than she ever thought possible, and even though her body was drained, her spirit felt stronger than ever.

26

UNDER CONTROL

The knife glinted in the sunlight that streamed through the window, casting a warm glow across the room. Ava sat perched on the bench, her reflection barely visible in the glass as she made a small, deliberate slit in the palm of her hand. Blood pooled instantly, dark and rich. Without hesitation, she conjured water, feeling it rush from within her, cool and soothing. The liquid swirled around her hand, sealing the wound effortlessly.

She could heal. The thought sent a thrill through her, a quiet pride that stirred deep inside her chest. Despite all the chaos surrounding her, Xavier's threats, the tension with Peter, knowing she was a Healer brought her a sense of peace. She couldn't wait to show Peter, her father, and the rest of the Aureole what she could do. But the Cimmerians couldn't know. It had to stay a secret.

The thought of Peter, though, quickly dimmed her excitement. He hadn't reached out since yesterday at school. It felt like an eternity since she'd last seen him. *Hadn't he sensed my distress?* She wondered if he was still trying to avoid his Enchanter life or worse, if he was spending more time with Valerie than her.

But it was her eighteenth birthday, and the last thing she wanted was to be weighed down by doubt and anger. *It's going to be a good day,* she told herself firmly, no matter what.

Ava dressed quickly, pulling herself out of her thoughts, and headed downstairs, a determined smile tugging at her lips. The dining room was already bustling with activity. Her father and a few others sat around the long wooden table, and the warmth of their voices greeted her as she entered.

"Good morning." She slid into the seat next to her father.

Her father gave her a small, thoughtful smile. "Happy birthday, Ava."

"Thanks." Her smile widened, but there was a flicker of concern in his eyes that made her heart tighten slightly.

Joss looked up from her bowl, her eyes lighting up. "It's your birthday?" She turned to Gabriel, playfully smacking his arm. "Why didn't you tell me?"

"Ow! sorry," Gabriel said. "I thought you knew that was why I took her to the library. Early birthday surprise. But you know … Xavier had other plans."

His thoughtfulness surprised Ava. It had been a nice trip, before everything fell apart. "Thank you. It really meant a lot."

"You're welcome." Gabriel's gaze held hers for a beat longer than usual, making her heart stutter slightly before she looked away.

The kitchen door swung open, and Colden entered with a large pot, his face lit with pride. "Tunisian Chickpea Breakfast Soup." He set it on the table. "Chickpeas, loads of spices. You can garnish with whatever you like." He gestured to a row of small ramekins filled with cilantro, cumin, croutons, and more. He squeezed Ava's shoulder as he passed her. "And a very happy birthday to my hero."

"Hero?" Natalia raised an eyebrow as she sat beside Gabriel.

"Ava is a Healer," Colden announced, his voice filled with admiration.

Joss's jaw dropped. "What!"

"She healed me last night," Colden continued, as though recounting a miracle. "And Gabriel, too."

"You did that?" Ava's father asked, his eyes widening with surprise and pride.

Ava's cheeks burned as all eyes turned to her. She nodded. "Yeah, I guess I did."

Her father beamed. "You never cease to amaze me, Ava. I'm so proud of you."

The admiration in everyone's eyes was overwhelming. Ava fidgeted in her seat, not used to this much attention. It felt good, but also … strange. She wasn't one to enjoy the spotlight.

"That's awesome!" Joss practically bounced in her chair, her violet eyes wide with excitement. "We should celebrate! It's your birthday, and you're a Healer! We have to do something."

"We could have a party here," Eric suggested.

"Or," Thomas interjected with a grin, "we could go to New Orleans."

"Ooh, great idea!" Joss clapped.

Ava's pulse quickened, a mix of excitement and apprehension at the thought of a trip to New Orleans.

Natalia shot Thomas a withering glance. "We're on the brink of a war, and you want to go to New Orleans?"

"They gave us until the new moon," Thomas said. "We deserve one night of fun."

Natalia sipped her coffee, unimpressed. "I doubt the Elders will let you all go."

Joss rolled her eyes dramatically, sprinkling cumin over her soup. "They'll never know we're gone. Gabriel can have us back here in a blink."

He shook his head. "I can't teleport. Aaron's orders."

Thomas scraped his spoon against the bowl. "Sounds like a road trip then."

Ava caught Gabriel's eye, silently thanking him for trying to make it happen. But as she sat there, surrounded by her friends, a pang of sadness hit her. Peter hadn't even called to wish her a happy birthday. She hoped he'd show up at school.

"We'll figure something out," Gabriel said.

When Ava finished her soup, she hugged her father before leaving the table. Despite the strange mix of emotions swirling inside her—excitement for what she had accomplished, anxiety about Peter, and the looming threat of war—she was determined to make the most of her birthday.

As she made her way to the front door, Gabriel fell into step beside her. The morning air was crisp and refreshing, the sky a soft, muted blue. She glanced at him out of the corner of her eye, noting how his usual confident stride seemed slightly subdued today.

"You okay?" she asked, her voice quiet but filled with genuine concern.

Gabriel looked at her, a hint of surprise in his eyes before his expression softened. "I'm fine. Still a little sore, but nothing serious. Thanks to you." He smiled.

"I've never healed anyone before. I didn't even know I could."

"I figured. It's pretty amazing, though." He paused. "You saved me."

She swallowed, her heart tightening at the sincerity in his words. She remembered the panic that had surged through her when she'd seen him bleeding, trapped in those electric ropes. The relief she felt now that he was okay was almost overwhelming. "I'm just glad you're all right."

They walked in silence for a few moments, the sound of their footsteps muffled by the fallen leaves beneath their feet. Ava bit her lip, glancing at him again. "By the way … how did you know it was my birthday?"

Gabriel's lips curled into a smile. "I overheard your dad mention it a while back. Figured it was something worth remembering."

Ava's chest warmed, but her mind flashed back to Xavier's warning. *Don't trust him.* A small chill prickled at the back of her neck. Had Gabriel really just overheard her dad, or was there something else she didn't know? She forced a smile, pushing down the unease. "You remembered?"

"Of course. I know it doesn't always seem like it, but … I pay attention."

Her heart thudded a little harder in her chest. Was Gabriel just being thoughtful, or was there more going on beneath the surface? The unease gnawed at her, but she didn't want to let Xavier's words poison everything. Gabriel had been there for her. He had helped her. And yet … that flicker of doubt lingered.

"I wasn't sure if you were okay after everything yesterday," she admitted, shifting slightly. "It was a lot."

Gabriel shrugged, though she could see the tension still lurking in his shoulders. "I'll be all right. And you? How are *you* holding up?"

She hesitated. Peter. Gabriel. The Cimmerians. Her mother. "I'm … managing. It's my birthday, so I guess I'm just trying to focus on that."

He studied her for a second. "That's fair. You deserve to enjoy today."

"Thanks. And thanks again for yesterday."

"It was nothing. I wanted you to have a good day." As they reached the gate, he paused. "You sure you're okay heading to school? You don't have to go if you're not feeling up for it."

She looked at him, the concern in his voice making her chest tighten again. "I'll be fine." But part of her wasn't sure if she believed that. "I'll see you later?"

"Yeah. Happy birthday, Ava."

She smiled, but as she turned to walk away, the seed of doubt Xavier had planted tugged at her, refusing to let go completely.

Peter waited by her usual parking spot, his face etched with guilt. As Ava got out of her car, he pulled her into a tight embrace, his arms wrapping around her as if afraid to let go.

"Ava, I'm such a dipshit. I'm so sorry I wasn't there last night. Melissa told me everything. I felt you for a second. Like something was wrong, but I thought you were fine. I didn't … I didn't think."

She stepped back slightly, keeping her hands on his shoulders, searching his face. His eyes were clouded with regret. She wanted to be angry with him, but everything they were facing made it hard to hold onto that anger for long. "I forgive you. But you have to take this seriously now. We're on the verge of a war, Peter. I need you by my side. I don't want what's happened between us to drive a wedge. I love you. I just need to know if you're really ready for this, for us, for everything."

"I am. I'm going to start practicing and training again. I just … I've been terrified."

Ava placed her hands gently on either side of his face, her fingers brushing his skin. "We all are." Leaning in, she kissed him with urgency, feeling the warmth and familiarity of his lips. He held her close, and for a moment, their troubles faded into the background.

His lips moved to her jaw, trailing down her neck in a way that sent shivers down her spine. Her heart raced, and she breathed heavier, her body betraying the calm she tried to maintain.

"We should probably skip if we're going to keep doing this," she whispered.

He pulled back slightly, a smile tugging at his lips. "I can't believe I've been such a dick to you."

"It's in the past. Let's leave it there." But there was a lingering fear that they might not be able to escape it entirely.

"I haven't been there for you like I should have. But I want you to know, Ava, I love you. I've never stopped loving you." He reached into his pocket and pulled out a small box, handing it to her. "Happy birthday."

Ava blinked in surprise as she opened the box, her breath catching at the silver bracelet inside. It was simple yet elegant, the words engraved on it reading *without you, I'm nothing* in delicate script. "Peter…" She lifted the bracelet from the box, the metal cool against her fingers. "It's beautiful." She wrapped her arms around his neck and pressed her lips to his. "I love you. Thank you."

"I'm glad you like it." He tipped her chin up to look into her eyes. "Whatever you're going through, whatever you need to do … we're in this together."

"Okay," she whispered, hoping he meant it.

Peter studied her face, his brow furrowing. "You've been smiling all morning, despite everything. Is there something you're not telling me?"

She leaned closer, whispering in his ear. "I can heal."

"What? Are you serious?"

She nodded, the excitement bubbling up again. "I healed Gabriel and Colden yesterday. I had no idea I could, but now … I can. We have another Healer if we go to war."

His jaw dropped, clearly awestruck. "That's incredible. How did you find out?"

"When Xavier attacked us, Gabe got hurt, badly. My water … it just healed him. It was like nothing I've ever felt before."

They began walking toward the building.

"And you never knew you could do that?" he asked.

"No. If I had known, I could have saved Jonah and Drew." Her voice grew quieter, the guilt creeping back in.

"What happens now?" he asked. "Are we going to war for sure?"

"I don't know, but we have to be prepared."

Peter's face fell.

"Let's not talk about that today. Tonight, we might be going to New Orleans for my birthday celebration."

He raised an eyebrow. "Is that such a good idea?"

"We have until the new moon. It's just one night."

"How many times have we said that?" he teased, though there was a serious edge to his voice. "And how many times did it turn into chaos?"

She laughed softly, playfully nudging him. "Don't jinx it."

As they reached her locker, Peter's fingers intertwined with hers, their hands a quiet promise to each other. But even as they stepped into class, Ava couldn't help but wonder: could they really escape the chaos, even for one night?

Ava barely heard the drone of the lecture over her own thoughts. She was already in New Orleans in her mind, her thoughts racing with the possibilities. No one knew the real reason she wanted to go, and she wasn't about to tell them. The Necromancer might finally give her the answers she craved, the chance to reach her mother, to find out the truth. The thought of facing her mother's spirit both thrilled and terrified her. What if her mother had betrayed her? What if she had promised Ava's soul to Havok, just as Xavier had claimed?

The weight of it pressed down on her, making it impossible to focus on anything else. But excitement pulsed beneath her fear. Soon, she might have the truth. Her fingers drummed on her desk, her eyes locked on the slow-moving hands of the clock, willing them to move faster.

A soft whisper broke through her thoughts, sending a shiver down her spine. "*Join us. It's your destiny.*"

Her heart skipped a beat. The voice was soft but unmistakable. She snapped her head up, scanning the room. Everyone was either taking notes, falling asleep, or sneaking glances at their phones. No one seemed to have noticed anything.

"You know it's the right thing to do."

Her pulse quickened. She swatted at the empty air next to her, feeling nothing. Was she imagining it? She shivered as an eerie presence, icy and disturbing, grazed against her skin.

"You're so weak now. Think of what you can become if you give yourself to Havok."

Ava shot out of her seat, ignoring the curious stares of her classmates as she bolted from the room.

"You can't run from me." The voice followed her, each word a dagger to her mind.

Trudy McVaine.

Ava's fists clenched, her teeth grinding together. If Trudy wanted to play, Ava was ready.

She slammed open the bathroom door, the sound of it smacking against the wall echoing through the small room. Two gasps followed, and she found herself face-to-face with Valerie and Amanda.

"You hate them." Trudy's voice slithered into her ear. *"You want to kill them."*

"What the hell is your problem?" Valerie glared despite the white bandage stretched across her bruised nose. Despite her efforts to conceal it, fear tinged her eyes.

"Get out," Ava demanded.

Amanda crossed her arms. "Or what? You gonna punch me too?"

"I don't want to hurt either of you."

"Kill them," Trudy's voice urged. *"Your mom would be so proud."*

Ava's vision blurred with rage. "Shut up!"

Valerie and Amanda exchanged nervous glances. Ava could see the doubt in their eyes. They thought she was losing it. Maybe she was.

"You seriously need help," Valerie said. "There's a hospital not far from here that can lock you up for good. Away from Peter. You've ruined him, but I'm helping him."

A sharp pang of jealousy and guilt hit her as Valerie's words sliced through her.

"You know you want to drown them. Just like Jonah and Drew."

Drew and Jonah's lifeless faces flashed in her mind, their dead eyes staring at her.

"I said shut up!" Her hands trembled.

"Are you too scared?" Trudy's voice mocked. *"I'll start it for you."*

Amanda rolled her eyes and turned to leave, but Valerie froze, clutching her throat. Her face flushed, her eyes wide with panic as she struggled to breathe.

"Val, what's wrong?" Amanda's voice wavered.

Valerie's mouth opened, but no sound came out. Her hands clawed at her throat, her face turning an alarming shade of red.

Trudy was choking her.

Panic rose in Ava's chest. "Stop it!"

Amanda's eyes darted to Ava, horror filling them. "What are you doing? You're strangling her!"

Ava's heart pounded in her ears. She couldn't let Trudy win. She had to act fast, even if it meant risking everything.

Water trickled down her arms, cold and responsive. She raised her hands and blasted the mirror behind Valerie. The glass shattered, sending shards flying through the air.

Amanda screamed, dragging Valerie down as the fragments rained around them.

Ava held her breath, hoping she'd hit Trudy. The room fell silent except for the sound of Valerie gasping for air and Amanda sobbing.

Amanda's wide, terrified eyes locked onto Ava. She knelt beside Valerie, holding her as if she might break. "Wh-what did you just do?" Tears streamed down both of their faces.

Ava fumbled for her phone, her hands shaking as she dialed. "Peter, I need your help." Her chest tightened. She hadn't meant for things to go this far. The look of fear in Amanda's eyes, the shattered glass, and Valerie's shaking form twisted in her gut. Trudy had pushed her, but now, as she stood there, her hands still wet from the water she'd conjured, it didn't matter who was really to blame. All anyone saw was the destruction she had caused.

27

ERASED

"She tried to kill us!" Amanda clutched a dazed and pale Valerie.

Standing in the middle of the room, Ava crossed her arms under the gazes of Aaron, Savina, Peter, and Seth. Their eyes burned with judgment, suspicion, and confusion. Peter and Ava had brought Valerie and Amanda to the Manor after they both broke down in hysteria, and Seth had hoped Savina could help them calm down. But now, things were spiraling out of control.

"What happened?" Savina asked, her voice calm but concerned.

Ava bit her lip, her arms tightening around herself. "Trudy McVaine was there. She kept whispering in my ear. I went to the bathroom, and I found Valerie and Amanda. Trudy was strangling Valerie."

"Are you crazy?" Amanda asked. "There was no one else. You tried to kill us!"

"No—"

"You—water—came out of your hands." Amanda's eyes were wide with terror, her words barely coherent through her sobs. "Who are you people? What do you want with us?" Her tears flowed freely, her grip on Valerie tightening, as if she could protect them both by holding on.

Seth reached out, his expression soft. "Amanda, listen—"

"Don't touch me!" She recoiled from his hand. "Get away from us!"

Aaron stroked his goatee thoughtfully. "So, now Trudy is following you?"

"I don't know," Ava said, her voice growing small under his scrutiny.

"Did you actually see her?"

Ava shook her head, feeling her heart drop. "No, but I know it was her. I know her voice." She silently pleaded with Savina to believe her, hoping her mentor could sense the truth in her words.

Savina's gentle voice filled Ava's mind. *I do, my child.*

"Why did you bring them here?" Aaron turned to Seth.

Seth's eyes were rimmed red, unshed tears barely held at bay. He remained silent, his jaw clenched tight.

"Oh dear," Savina muttered.

"What?" Ava asked.

He wants their minds erased. Of him, of Peter. Completely.

Ava's breath caught in her throat, and she spun toward Seth. "You can't do that."

Seth's gaze hardened, but there was a deep sadness behind his eyes. "It's the only way."

"You can't take away everything. They're your friends."

"It's the right thing to do," Seth replied, his voice cold and distant.

Ava turned to Peter, searching his face for some sign of resistance, but he looked down, his expression torn. "Peter, you can't agree with this. They deserve to know the truth, not be erased."

He sighed, rubbing the back of his neck, avoiding her gaze. "Ava, we don't have a choice. We're on the verge of war, and if the Cimmerians come after them, they'll use them as bait. It's the only way to keep them safe."

"It should be their choice," Ava argued.

Seth shook his head. "Valerie was attacked today, and now that the Cimmerians know they've been with us, they'll be hunted. I won't let them die because of us."

Ava's chest tightened. She knew he was right. She had seen what the Cimmerians were capable of, how close they'd come to killing Peter. But the idea of wiping Valerie and Amanda's memories, them never knowing Seth and Peter, felt too cruel.

"What are you going to do to us?" Amanda demanded, her voice trembling as she looked from Seth to Savina.

Savina turned to Seth and Peter. "Are you both certain this is what you want?"

Peter nodded, though he looked pained by the decision. "It has to be done."

Ava's heart sank, feeling his agony. "There has to be another way. Can't you just erase today? Not everything?"

"They'll still ask questions," Peter said. "It's better this way. They need to be far away from all of this."

"Very well," Savina said. "Say your goodbyes, and I'll erase their minds." She and Aaron left the room, leaving the others in tense silence.

Valerie's eyes were wide, her lips trembling. She looked utterly terrified, and it made Ava's stomach churn with guilt.

Unable to watch, Ava turned on her heel and stormed outside, her chest heaving with the effort to hold back her tears. She wandered into the garden, the vivid orange, red, and yellow flowers swaying gently in the breeze. The beauty of the place felt like a cruel contrast to the turmoil inside her. Her hands clenched into fists, and her body trembled.

"Are you okay?" Kira's voice came softly from behind her.

Ava turned to see Kira standing with a water bucket, her white hair flowing in the wind, her face as flawless and unreadable as ever. Ava had never spoken to her much, but Kira's reputation as someone who could kill with a single touch preceded her.

"I'm fine," Ava lied.

Kira raised an eyebrow, her gaze steady. "You're lying."

Ava stiffened. "Excuse me?"

"It's okay to lie to yourself, but you're not very good at lying to others."

Ava turned to walk away, but Kira's next words stopped her. "I heard what you did for Colden. It was a brave thing."

"I didn't have a choice."

"You did." Kira smiled. "But you made the right one. Thank you for saving him."

Ava didn't know what to say, so she nodded, her throat tight.

"You're braver than you give yourself credit for," Kira added. "You should work on that."

The door opened, and Seth and Peter emerged, their faces pale, their eyes red-rimmed. Seth stormed ahead, but Peter walked slowly, his body sagging.

Ava rushed to Peter, wrapping her arms around him tightly. "I'm so sorry."

"It's not your fault," he whispered, but it felt hollow.

"Why did you make them forget everything? Why both of you?"

"They don't deserve to be caught up in this. After what the Cimmerians did to me, I couldn't let that happen to them."

"Savina was going to do the same to you. I wanted you to stay with me, but I also wanted to protect you. I never forgave myself for what they did to you because of me."

"None of that was your fault. And they'll never hurt me again."

Ava wasn't sure she believed him, but she held him tighter, hoping that for once, he was right. "I'm here for you. I'll always be here."

He drew back. "I know. But I need some time. Seth and I are going for a drive."

"Do you want me to come with you?"

"Not now. Savina and Aaron are taking Valerie and Amanda home. Seth and I just need to get away for a bit."

She shouldn't have felt rejected, but she did. Seth impatiently gestured toward the car, and Peter kissed her cheek.

As they drove off, her heart felt heavy with guilt and sadness. She wanted to be there for Peter, but she understood that sometimes, even love wasn't enough to take away the pain.

Ava had dinner with her father and a few others, but her heart wasn't in it. Even though it was her birthday, she felt hollow, detached from the celebration around her.

Melissa had texted, wanting to take her out, but Ava declined. Instead, she retreated to her room, hoping for some peace.

Dropping onto the window bench, she leaned her head against the cool glass. Ava stared out into the dark. The wind outside had picked up, blowing the last few leaves from the branches. The clouds moved swiftly across the sky, barely veiling the waning moon.

It had started as a good day, but deep down, she knew it wouldn't last.

Valerie and Amanda were attacked today. Trudy tried to manipulate her into killing them. The thought clawed at her insides. Would her mother have been proud? Was her mother really the cruel, manipulative person Xavier made her out to be? The memories she had of her mom didn't align with the version Xavier painted. But if her mother had truly promised Ava's soul to Havok, what did that make Ava? A pawn? A sacrifice?

She shook her head, wrapping her arms around her knees. If Havok had existed this long, why had the Elders never mentioned him? And why did the Cimmerians kill her mother if she had been working with them?

The questions felt like a storm in her mind, no answers in sight. She was desperate to talk to the Necromancer and uncover the truth no matter how dangerous that might be. Maybe she should go alone. Maybe she needed to face her mother, whatever the cost.

A sudden knock on the door startled her.

"Come in." She wiped the back of her hand across her eyes.

The door creaked open, and Gabriel stepped inside. "Hey. Are you okay?"

Ava's eyes darted to him, taking in his crisp white button-down and the fresh cut of his raven hair. He looked almost too put-together, and the intensity of his crystal-blue gaze made her heart race.

She shrugged, trying to downplay her emotions. "I guess."

Gabriel crossed the room and sat on the edge of her bed. "I heard what happened."

"Lucky me, huh?"

"I'm sorry."

"It's fine. I just wish I knew the truth."

His brow furrowed. "Would it really change anything?"

"Of course, it would. I could understand myself better. I could understand why I've done what I've done. Maybe I could even understand my mom. If your parents had promised your soul to Havok, wouldn't you want to know why?"

"You have to stop obsessing over this, Ava. It'll destroy you."

She sighed. "I think it already has."

"So, how do you plan on finding out the rest?"

Ava hesitated. She hadn't told anyone about her plan, except Colden. "A Necromancer. I could talk to my mom directly."

Gabriel's expression shifted, his eyes widening. "Whoa, Ava. No. Don't even think about it. It's dangerous." His tone sharpened, as if the very idea terrified him.

"You sound just like Savina."

"You really don't want to do this."

"Why not? What could be worse than not knowing the truth?"

His gaze darkened, and for a moment, she thought he wouldn't answer. But he sighed, his shoulders slumping slightly. "Because Necromancers … they don't just pull spirits from the beyond. They mess with your emotions, your mind. They take memories and twist them, feed on your deepest regrets and fears. They dredge up things you might not want to relive."

Ava blinked, taken aback by the rawness in his tone. "Is that what happened to you?"

"I went to a Necromancer years ago, when I was desperate for answers about my sister's death. I thought I could get closure, but all I got was pain. When the Necromancer called her spirit, she was trapped in this … endless loop of her last moments. Screaming for help, over and over again. I had to watch it. Hear it again and again." He paused, his voice tight with emotion. "It wasn't her, Ava. It was her pain. That's all that came through. No real answers, just suffering. I couldn't save her then, and I couldn't save her in that moment either. I left there feeling worse than I ever had before."

The idea of Gabriel seeing something so harrowing made Ava's heart tighten. "That's … awful."

"It was. And that's why I don't want you to go through it. Necromancers don't give you peace. They drag you through hell."

"But my mom—what if she has answers I need? What if she can explain why she—"

"Even if she can explain, is it worth the cost? You're already haunted by everything that's happened. Do you really want to add to that? I barely came back from my experience. I don't want to see you fall into the same darkness."

Ava looked down at her trembling fingers. She had been so focused on getting answers that she hadn't fully considered the consequences. Could she really face her mother like that? Could she handle seeing her trapped in the same way Gabriel had seen his sister?

"I don't know. I just want to understand. I need to know if my mother betrayed me."

He gently placed a hand on her shoulder. "You will find answers. But not like this. Not through a Necromancer. There are other ways. You're strong, and you can find the truth without risking everything. You have to trust that. Plus, the Cimmerians will use it against you. They'll take those images and twist them, make you see them over and over. Just like they've done recently."

"It's okay," she lied. "I wasn't really going to go. It was just something Link mentioned once."

His gaze searched her face as if trying to see through her words. "Is this really about your mom? Or is there more?"

She sighed, standing up and pacing by the bed. "It's because I'm a murderer, Gabriel. I killed Jonah and Drew without hesitation. I almost killed Valerie and Amanda. I have Cimmerian blood, and it feels like I'm becoming one of them."

He stood and grabbed her by the shoulders, stopping her in her tracks. He fixed his gaze on her eyes. "Ava, listen to me. *You* control your destiny. No one else. Not your mom, not the Cimmerians. *You* choose which side you're on."

Tears welled in her eyes again. "But what if I'm too far gone? What if I've already done too much damage?"

"You acted in self-defense every time. You saved Valerie and Amanda today. That's not the mark of someone becoming a Cimmerian. That's you being strong. Stronger than you know."

"It's hard to believe that when I let them get inside my head."

"You're not weak, Ava. Look at what you've done. You saved Colden. You healed me. Cimmerians don't heal."

Ava's eyes snapped back to his, confusion in her gaze. "What?"

"They use their powers for darkness. You use yours for good. That's the difference."

She wiped her tears and nodded slowly. Gabriel had a way of cutting through her spiraling thoughts, grounding her when she felt lost. He was a good friend, always challenging her. "I need to learn to block them out. You're good at that. Can you teach me?"

"Of course." A smile tugged at his lips. "It'll take time, but we'll get there."

"I don't care how long it takes. What a birthday, huh?"

"I know. But I have good news. We're still going to New Orleans."

Her heart skipped a beat. "What? How?"

"Colden and Aaron talked. They gave us permission."

"How will you keep the Cimmerians from getting inside your head?"

"I'll be expecting it this time. Plus, there's going to be too many of us for them to pull anything. But we can't stay too long. Colden was pretty strict about that."

"When do we leave?"

"Saturday night."

Ava's mind raced. She was finally going to speak to her mother. As terrifying as the idea was, she needed the answers only her mother could provide. Could spirits lie beyond the grave? Would her mother be happy to see her? Or would it be another betrayal?

There was only one way to find out.

$$\overbrace{\qquad\qquad}^{28}$$

ANTICIPATION

Blood poured from Peter's chest, the deep red staining his torn shirt as he collapsed to his knees. Ava's breath hitched, stepping forward to help, but Gabriel's firm grip on her arm held her back. A knot tightened in her stomach, fear mixing with the heat of battle. She couldn't lose focus. But then, almost as quickly as the wound had appeared, it sealed shut. Peter's breath came out in a relieved laugh, and the tension in Ava's body eased a little.

Maggie's ability to shift her arms into weapons was still astonishing to Ava, but her preferred choice of the three-pronged Sai weapon always left an impression. Peter staggered to his feet, his gray shirt slashed open, blood soaking the fabric but his skin flawless underneath. He gave a lopsided grin, walking back to the group.

"Are you okay?" Ava checked him over.

"I'm fine." He pressed a quick kiss to her forehead. His smile reassured her, but the sight of the blood-soaked shirt sent a jolt through her. *If this were real, if this were battle…* She shook the thought away. No time for that.

They trained relentlessly, fighting until sweat soaked their clothes, muscles aching with the strain of preparation. Every move, every hit felt like a rehearsal for the inevitable war that loomed closer with every passing day.

Ava's mind, however, kept drifting back to New Orleans. The excitement she felt was almost impossible to contain, though she hadn't told Peter the true reason she was eager to go. That secret sat heavy in her chest, mingling with the pressure of everything else.

Gustav and Maya's Aureoles had arrived earlier in the week to train with them. The added presence of the two groups made the reality of war feel even closer. The looming threat wasn't just talk anymore. It was tangible.

Maya Gutiérrez's Aureole, from Spain, was composed of her siblings—graceful, quick, and skilled. Despite their youth, they carried themselves with the solemnity of warriors. There were four of them—Maya, Esteban, Diego, and Lucia—and each moved with an effortless fluidity that left Ava in awe. Their olive skin and thick, dark hair made them stand out among the group. Both Diego and Esteban caught more than a few admiring glances, though they seemed oblivious, focused solely on the training.

Gustav Kovalevsky, an Elder from Russia, was as imposing as the tales of his battles suggested. His body, massive and scarred, had weathered countless fights, and his hulking frame made Thomas look small by comparison. Gustav's Aureole was formidable: Ilya, a shapeshifter with an easy smile and boyish features; Zhan, an older man with striking green eyes and cropped white hair; Konstantin, a tall blond with icy blue eyes; Alena, a petite brunette with strikingly clear skin and sharp features; and Anastasya, an older woman with a scar above her left eye. The Russian group exuded an air of quiet authority, their eyes always scanning, calculating.

Katarina Obolensky, the young Protector of Gustav's Aureole, stood out in her own right. Her short, metallic-blue hair contrasted with her pale skin, and she carried herself with the confidence of someone far older than her years. Ava guessed she was around Joss's age, though her maturity and intensity made her seem older.

The group practiced well into the afternoon, pushing their limits. Despite the exhaustion, there was no room for error, not with only nine days left until the new moon. If war was inevitable, they had to be prepared.

Katarina stepped up to face Maggie. Maggie, known for her speed and precision, was a challenging opponent. Her rapid attacks proved hard to defend against. But Katarina moved like water, her body twisting in ways that defied expectation.

Ava's breath caught when Katarina leaped into the air, flipping over Maggie and grabbing her legs. Maggie hit the ground hard, and before she could recover, Katarina placed a hand on her shoulder. In an instant, Maggie turned as pale as snow, her body immobilized. Katarina released her, and Maggie returned to normal, but the damage was done— Maggie had been defeated.

There was a collective gasp from the crowd. No one defeated Maggie.

Konstantin leaned toward Ava, and spoke with pride in his thick Russian accent. "She can generate radiation. It is impressive, no?"

Ava nodded slowly, still in awe as Aaron's voice rang out. "Ava, you're up."

Her heart pounded. She was supposed to fight the person who had just bested Maggie?

"Don't lose sight of her," Konstantin whispered.

Swallowing the lump of anxiety in her throat, she stepped forward, feeling the familiar cool rush of water forming around her hands.

She locked eyes with Katarina, who stood still, waiting with a calm Ava envied. She was taller, but Katarina's quiet confidence unnerved her.

Katarina didn't move, only watched.

Ava hesitated. Would water be enough?

Katarina was on her. Ava barely had time to react, grabbing the girl mid-charge and slamming her to the ground. Water rushed to her hands, and she sent it flooding over Katarina's face, momentarily disorienting her.

Katarina choked and sputtered but regained her footing, walking back to the group with drenched hair, her expression still unbothered.

Ava took a breath, and Eric appeared next.

His smirk gave away nothing of his plan. He struck, kicking her square in the stomach. The air rushed from Ava's lungs as she doubled over. She kept her eyes on him, trying to anticipate his next move. But he didn't move, at least, not the Eric in front of her. Arms locked around her from behind, choking her. The real Eric had duplicated himself. The cold grip of his clone tightened around her neck, making her vision blur.

She struggled, calling on her water, but nothing came. Her air was running out.

Finally, he released her, the duplicates merging back into his single form. He chuckled as Ava caught her breath, rubbing her throat.

"Gets them every time," he muttered.

Joss stepped in next, her hands crackling with blue electricity. Unfazed by Eric's duplication trick, she sent her electric current through all his copies in a single motion, which amazed Ava.

Eric stood up, his tone light despite losing. "One day, Joss."

Joss giggled. "We'll see."

By sunset, Ava's muscles screamed with fatigue. She was drenched in sweat and ached in places she hadn't known existed. The Elders called for a brief respite before the meeting. As the group disbanded, Ava caught Peter's eye, sharing a brief smile of understanding. They were exhausted, but it was only the beginning.

New Orleans was all she could think about. Answers waited for her there. And soon, she'd face whatever lay ahead.

29

GOING DOWN IN FLAMES

New Orleans pulsed with life on the cold November night, the vibrant energy of the city coursing through the streets. The faint strains of jazz music drifted through the air from the square as Ava and the group made their way to Marcel's. Despite the chill, the warmth of the music and the liveliness of the city provided a stark contrast to the heaviness in Ava's heart.

Once they arrived, the introductions were brief. Marcel, ever the enigmatic figure, welcomed them into his home. His eyes lingered a little too long on Ava, making her shift uncomfortably under his gaze.

"I guess I'll wait for you out here," Peter said.

Ava kissed him lightly on the lips. "Thanks."

Following Marcel inside, Ava, Thomas, and Gillian were ushered into a small, dimly lit sitting room. Marcel quietly closed the double doors behind them, the soft click echoing through the room. The shift in atmosphere was immediate. The distant hum of the city outside was swallowed by an eerie silence. The air felt heavier, as if the room itself was holding its breath.

Ava, Thomas, and Gillian sat side by side on a plush, velvet couch beneath a tall window, the pale moonlight barely seeping through the thick, drawn curtains. Shadows loomed large, dancing along the walls, adding to the room's strange stillness. Across from them, Marcel took his seat in a high-backed armchair, his posture rigid, eyes sharp. His gaze felt piercing, as though he was studying them not just on the surface but trying to reach into their very souls.

"I didn't think I would ever see you again, Ava," he said.

She shifted on the couch. Even now, he still unnerved her. "Well, your vision or whatever turned out to be true."

His lips twitched in something like regret. "I am sorry for what you've been through."

"Do you have anything for us now?" Thomas asked abruptly, his knee bouncing. His voice was tense, as if barely holding back the flood of emotions he had buried.

Marcel's gaze moved to Thomas, but he didn't immediately respond. The room seemed to grow colder with each second of his silence.

"What's he doing?" Gillian whispered. "Why is he just staring?"

"Your father was killed," Marcel said to Thomas.

"Yeah, I know."

"It wasn't entirely you." Marcel's eyes glazed over, the whites glowing faintly. "You were physically there, but mentally … you were persuaded. The Cimmerians used you for revenge."

Thomas jerked back, his fists trembling. "What?"

Marcel's eyes grew brighter. "Your father … he sided with Corbin. He fought for them." His head snapped to the side, as though seeing something only he could perceive. "He went to war with the Cimmerians."

Thomas shot up from the couch, his body shaking with rage. "No, that's not possible! Why would he pretend to be one of us when he was on their side the whole time?"

Marcel's eyes returned to normal, and the haunted look on his face showed sympathy. "I'm sorry."

Gillian leapt to her feet, shaking her head. "I don't want to hear anymore. I changed my mind." She bolted out of the room, her footsteps echoing down the hallway.

Thomas stood frozen, his breaths coming out in short, ragged gasps. "I can't believe this. He hated me. He hated me from the start." His face twisted in a mixture of hurt and fury.

Ava's heart sank. She wanted to comfort him but didn't know how. "Maybe he was jealous of you, Thomas. Maybe that's why—"

"He never gave me to Corbin. Why didn't he betray me sooner?"

She couldn't answer. She was still processing the fact that her own mother had been a Cimmerian. Was this how Thomas felt? Betrayed by someone who was supposed to love him?

"Perhaps he wanted to change," Marcel suggested, though his voice lacked conviction.

Thomas let out a bitter laugh. "Doubtful. He's better off dead."

"Do you really mean that?" Ava asked.

He sighed. "You saw it for years. He never cared about me."

As the door opened, Rene walked in. "I think we should stop for tonight. This is hard news for Marcel to deliver."

Thomas nodded, his jaw clenched as he forced himself to calm down. "Thanks for … confirming it."

Marcel stood, his eyes locked onto Ava's gaze once more. There was a flicker of something unsettling in his eyes. "There is much darkness in you."

She stiffened, her heart skipping a beat. "My mother was a Cimmerian. What do you expect?"

"This is something else. Darkness is growing inside of you."

Her necklace warmed against her skin, a familiar and comforting sensation, but the unease grew.

Thomas placed his hand on her shoulder. "We should go."

"Marcel, let's call it a night," Rene urged.

Ava followed Thomas out of the room, but not without a final glance at Marcel. Darkness? What was he talking about? Did he think she was becoming a Cimmerian? She clenched her fists, hating the way his words wormed their way into her thoughts.

Outside, the rest of the group waited. Jeremy held Gillian close, comforting her while Thomas walked over to join Lance and Melissa. Ava found Peter, who moved to her side.

"You okay?" he asked.

"Yeah," she lied.

Joss and Sophia rushed over. "Now that you're eighteen," Joss said, her voice light and teasing, "we were thinking we could hit up Metropolitan. You know, make up for your ruined birthday."

Ava perked at the mention of the Metropolitan. Colden had told her the Necromancer hid out in the Metropolitan. What were the odds that it was the same club Sophia and Caroline frequented?

"We're not going clubbing," Gabriel said firmly.

Sophia waved a hand dismissively. "Oh, don't be such a party pooper."

Joss's eyes sparkled with excitement. "Come on, Ava, you deserve a night of fun."

Ava hesitated, her heart pounding in her chest. *This is dangerous.* She knew that. Gabriel's warning echoed in her head, his voice a steady reminder of how dangerous seeking answers through a Necromancer could be.

But I need answers. I need to know the truth.

She forced a smile. "You know what? Let's go."

Everyone blinked in surprise, but Joss cheered. "Yay! Let's go before she changes her mind!"

Peter raised an eyebrow. "You sure? You really want to go to a club after everything?"

She nodded, squeezing his hand. "Why not? Let's have some fun."

Gabriel sighed. "One hour."

Joss squealed.

Ava's plan was falling into place too easily, and it unnerved her. The bustling crowd, the loud music was the perfect distraction. She could slip away, get her answers, and be back before anyone noticed. But what if someone did? What if Gabriel followed her? What if Peter or someone else realized what she was doing?

The group made their way through the lively streets, and as they neared the club, Ava clutched Peter's hand tightly, taking deep breaths to steady her nerves. She would have to play along, keep her emotions calm, and act like she was just there for a good time.

Colden's instructions were simple. Ask for Zach and use the code phrase. But simple didn't mean safe. She couldn't shake the fear in her gut, knowing what was coming.

The club loomed ahead, a stark, deserted building in the warehouse district. The streets outside were eerily quiet, save for the long line of people waiting to get inside. The blacked-out windows of the two-story building gave it an imposing, almost sinister feel, and the heavy thump of the bass vibrated in Ava's chest as they neared the entrance. She glanced at Gabriel, who seemed at ease as he walked with the others.

If he knew what I was about to do, would he stop me? The thought gnawed at her, but she had to stay focused.

"Leave this to us," Caroline said as she and Sophia approached the bouncer. He unhooked the velvet rope, allowing them all inside without question. The moment they entered, the sound of the music swelled, shaking the walls with its relentless beat. Strobe lights flashed across the sea of dancers, illuminating faces lost in a drugged-out trance. The overwhelming mix of bodies, sweat, and flashing lights made Ava feel disoriented, like she was descending into some underworld.

How was she supposed to find Zach in all the chaos?

Caroline dragged a reluctant Gabriel to the dance floor, and the others paired off or mingled with the crowd.

Stay focused. You can do this.

"I'm going to get a drink," she shouted to Peter over the deafening music. He nodded, looking as uncomfortable as she felt. Link and Nicole nudged him, motioning for him to follow them, and Ava seized the opportunity.

This was her chance.

Slipping through the crowd, she pushed past writhing bodies and dodged the occasional stray elbow. Her heart pounded as she made her way to the bar, her mind racing. The longer she stayed, the more chances there were for someone to realize something was off.

When she finally reached it, a young boy was laughing with the bartender, his voice slurred, and his eyes glazed over. The bartender, a tall blonde, looked like she'd seen it all before. She was cool, detached, and completely uninterested.

Ava hesitated, wondering if she should ask.

Do it. Get this over with.

"Excuse me," Ava yelled over the blaring music. "I'm looking for Zach."

The bartender's gaze landed on her, and for a split second, Ava thought a flicker of recognition in her eyes. Or was it amusement? The bartender smirked, and she served the boy his drink. The music pounded louder, the room spinning slightly from the flashing lights.

Ava's palms were sweating now. Was this a mistake?

"He'll be here in a minute," the bartender finally said.

Nerves pricked Ava's body. Was it a trap? *Calm down. Just wait.* But every second that passed only made her more anxious. Her mind replayed Gabriel's warnings, the dangers of dealing with someone like this. What if Zach already knew she was coming? What if he didn't want to help? The shadows seemed to press in on her, suffocating.

The boy at the bar turned his attention to Ava. His eyes roamed over her in a way that made her skin crawl. "Why don't you have a drink while you wait, sweetheart?" he slurred, grinning like an idiot. "On me."

"No, thanks," Ava said firmly, but when he grabbed her arm, a jolt of irritation flashed through her. She gripped his wrist tightly, forcing him to let go, her grip strong enough to make him wince. "I said no."

The boy's eyes widened, fear flickering across his face.

The bartender laughed, clearly entertained by the exchange. "Guess she told you."

"Looking for me?" a deep voice came from behind Ava.

She spun around, and a tall, muscular man with a jagged scar running down his neck stood. His eyes gleamed in the dim light, and there was something predatory in the way he looked at her. "Yes."

"What do you want?" he asked.

Her throat felt dry. *Just say it.* "I need a chaotic flower." The code phrase felt foreign and awkward on her tongue. It sounded like she was asking for a drug, but she forced herself to hold her ground.

For a moment, he stared at her, his eyes narrowing as if sizing her up.

This was a bad idea.

He grabbed her arm, his grip firm and unyielding.

Ava's heart skipped a beat, but she didn't resist as he dragged her through the crowd, her mind racing with a thousand worst-case scenarios.

They reached an old elevator tucked away at the back of the club. It looked like it hadn't been used in years, the metal gate rusted and creaking as Zach wrenched it open and shoved her inside.

"Press the blue button." A twisted smile crept across his lips. "Good luck."

She hesitated, her finger hovering over the button. Something wasn't right. But she pressed it anyway, and the elevator groaned to life, descending deeper into the building. The walls closed in around her, and her pulse thundered in her ears.

When the elevator came to a halt, she slid open the gate and stepped out into a dimly lit hallway. Torches flickered along the stone walls, casting long shadows that seemed to move of their own accord. The air was cold, and the hair on the back of Ava's neck stood on end.

At the end of the hallway, a faint blue glow beckoned her. With every step, Gabriel's warning flashed in her head, but her desperation for answers kept her moving forward. She hoped she could live with the consequences.

As she neared the room, the glow intensified, and Ava's heart raced faster. This was it. She was about to face the unknown.

The door creaked open, and inside, the eerie blue glow of candlelight bathed the room. A dark figure stood waiting for her, his face obscured by the hood of his cloak. The air in the room felt thick with something sinister, something ancient.

Long, crooked fingers curled in front of him, their movements deliberate and slow. "Hello," he rasped, his voice like gravel.

"This doesn't seem like the place for a Necromancer."

"That's the point."

"Right. I want to speak to my mother's spirit."

"Very well." He approached closer. "I will need your blood."

She held out her hand, and the Necromancer pricked her finger with a small, pointed blade, letting the blood drip onto the center of the rug. The flames of the candles surged, growing taller than Ava, their blue light flickering like shadows come to life.

"Have you a picture of your mother?" he asked, his voice soft but unnerving.

"No. They were all lost in a fire."

"That's a shame. Think of her in your mind. Focus on her."

Closing her eyes, she pictured her mother—her fiery red hair, her piercing gray eyes, and her familiar smile. But the image shifted, twisting into something darker. Her mother's face morphed, her eyes cold and cruel, standing next to Corbin, reveling in the destruction. Ava's breath caught in her throat, but she forced herself to concentrate.

The Necromancer's voice rose, chanting in a language that felt ancient and dark. The air grew thick, and Ava's heart raced as she felt a presence. Her skin prickled, and the hair on her arms stood on end.

The light flickered, and when Ava opened her eyes, a figure emerged from the shadows. A woman, draped in black, moving toward her with slow, deliberate steps.

"Hello, Ava," her mother's voice echoed, soft but distorted.

"Mom?" Tears stung her eyes.

"Don't be afraid," her mother said, but there was something wrong. Her presence felt hollow, detached.

"Is it really you?"

Her mother smiled, the same unsettling smile from the vision. "Join them, Ava. It's your destiny."

"No, Mom. You promised my *soul* to Havok. Why? Who is Havok?"

"If you don't join him, everyone will die. You must convince the others."

Her mother's apparition began to fade, slipping away into the blue flickering flames.

Desperation clawed at her chest, panic rising like bile in her throat. "No, Mom! Don't go. Tell me more. I need answers!" She reached out, but her mother's figure dissolved into wisps of shadow and smoke.

In the place where her mother had stood, another figure appeared, darker, more menacing. At first, Ava thought it was a trick of the candlelight, but the temperature in the room plummeted. Her breath fogged the air as the icy presence loomed closer, the whispers in her mind growing louder, harsher, commanding.

Let us in.

Her heart pounded, each beat echoing in her ears as a tremor ran through her hands. She stared into the void left by her mother. The room felt suffocating as its walls seemed to squeeze in on her, leaving her gasping for air. The air grew dense and heavy, as if a fog of tension had settled, elongating the shadows and intensifying the silence.

She had to leave, but her feet felt as if they were cemented to the ground. A new presence filled the space, a figure draped in darkness with glowing, hollow eyes. It was not her mother. Its gaze pierced through her. Her limbs grew heavy as her mind clouded with confusion.

It spoke, but the words didn't reach her ears. It was a vibration, a pulse that echoed inside her skull.

Bind yourself to us. Become one.

Kill him. You have chosen your destiny.

Ava's pulse slowed as if her body were no longer her own. Her thoughts became foggy, distant, as though she were watching everything from far away. Her body ached, her head spinning, but a strange calm washed over her. She felt lighter, almost peaceful, as if surrendering to this presence would relieve her of all the burdens she carried.

The darkness moved closer, so close that Ava swore she felt a hand brush her cheek, cold and sharp like ice. But she didn't pull away.

The dark figure surged forward, disappearing into her. Ava's body jerked violently, her vision going black for a split second, and the room snapped back into focus. The candlelight steadied, the whispers ceased, and the eerie calm settled over her once more.

But Ava didn't feel the same. Her skin tingled, and her limbs felt heavy, foreign. She swayed on her feet, blinking away at the dizziness, her head still swimming from the overwhelming encounter.

She pressed a hand to her forehead, trying to shake off the strange sensation. "What … What just happened?" There was something different, something off about her. Yet she couldn't place it, couldn't pin down the shift.

From the shadows, the Necromancer silently observed, his eyes gleaming with a mysterious intensity. He didn't say a word, but the slight curl of his lips sent a chill racing down her spine.

Ava turned away, her heart still racing, but she forced herself to push the fear aside. She had what she came for. Answers, guidance. The feeling of unease was just … the aftereffect. The darkness was behind her now.

She was free.

Or so she thought.

30

TRAPPED

Ava blinked slowly, her mind shrouded in a haze of confusion. Her body ached, stiff like stone, and her head pounded as she slowly came to, eyes squinting against the pale light of the early morning. It took a moment for her vision to focus. She was in the cabin. *How did I get here?* Her mind raced, trying to piece together the fragments of her memory. *The club … the Necromancer … and then … nothing.* Her thoughts hit a wall. She couldn't remember leaving.

She struggled to move, but her limbs felt disconnected, heavy, as if they weren't hers to control. The panic rose in her chest as her body moved, getting up from the bed, but she hadn't commanded it to.

What's happening? Ava screamed internally, trapped within her own body. It was like watching herself from behind a wall of glass, a passenger in her own skin. She had no control. Only the sensation of something else, some other force, guiding her movements.

The door to the room swung open and Peter stood, relief washing over his face. "Ava!" He rushed over, wrapping his arms around her. "Where did you go? We've been searching everywhere. We teleported back from the club last night, but you disappeared. We couldn't even feel your presence."

Her hands clenched into fists, and a surge of unfamiliar rage rushed through her veins. She pushed him away. "Don't touch me," her voice snapped. But it wasn't Ava. It was her voice, but not her thoughts.

Ava recoiled, horrified. *This isn't me. What's happening?*

Peter frowned, taken aback. "Ava ... what is it?"

Her body brushed past him, as though he didn't exist, and walked out of the room.

No! Stop! Ava screamed inside her mind, banging against the invisible walls holding her captive.

But her body moved with a purpose she didn't understand. "Ava, wait!"

As she reached the door, he grabbed her hand, but she pushed him away, causing him to stumble and fall to the ground. "Get away from me," her voice growled. The anger burned like fire inside her, but it wasn't her anger. It was something—*someone*—else's.

Fear drained the color from his face. "Your eyes ... Ava, they're black. What's happening to you?"

"I finally see things clearly." Her hands shook with barely contained fury.

What's happening to me? She wanted to scream, to beg Peter to run, but she was powerless.

Her body moved with a will of its own, slipping into the car and driving away, leaving Peter behind.

The sky was beginning to lighten, casting the faintest glow across the horizon. She didn't have long. Just a few minutes before the sun rose to get to the Manor. She had to kill him.

Heart pounding in her chest, Ava's body moved with cold precision. She was trapped, watching helplessly from within as her limbs carried her down the empty road, faster, more determined with each passing moment.

No, please … I'm going to hurt someone. Stop! Someone, stop me! But her silent plea became lost beneath the dark force gripping her mind, controlling her every move.

Inside her head, she was screaming, clawing for control, but it was futile.

Ava's possessed body moved with purpose, her steps firm as she approached the Manor. She could feel the stirrings of a dark spell swirling in her mind. Words she didn't know but somehow *did*, a language she would never have used but was now poised to speak.

The front door loomed before her, its creak ominous as it opened.

I can't stop.

I have to kill him. The thought wasn't her own. It belonged to something darker. Her possessed body moved with ruthless determination, guiding her down the hallway. Her mind raced, searching for any flicker of control, but her body knew exactly where to go.

Colden emerged from the kitchen, wiping his hands on a towel, his face brightening. "Ava! There you are—" He halted and gasped. "Your eyes—"

Her lips moved, cold and alien, whispering words of power, a language ancient and foreign. The darkness within her grew, thickening with each syllable. The spell took hold, and the temperature in the room plummeted.

Colden froze, confusion flickering across his face, quickly replaced by terror as he realized what was happening. "No…" he gasped, his voice tight with panic as the magic coiled around him like a tightening noose. He clutched his chest, staggering backward, eyes wide with disbelief.

No, no! Please stop! Ava's mind screamed, but her lips kept moving, the incantation rising in intensity, a low, guttural chant.

Colden dropped to his knees, gasping for breath, his body wracked with violent tremors. His skin paled, and it was as if something invisible was ripping his life force from him. "Ava…" His pleading gaze locked onto hers.

Please, stop! I can't do this!

But her lips kept moving, her voice dark and cold as she completed the spell.

Colden collapsed, and his body convulsed as though something was tearing him apart from the inside.

"Ava, stop!" Peter collided with her, tackling her to the ground.

Pinned beneath him, she snarled, the sound foreign in her own ears. "Get off me!" The words spilled from her lips. Her body thrashed violently, striking out with brutal strength. She landed a hard punch to Peter's chest, knocking the wind from him.

Peter, I'm so sorry. I can't stop it…

Her possessed body continued to fight, each movement beyond her control. As she was about to recite the spell again, a blur of motion knocked her from behind, and she hit the floor with a heavy thud.

Eric's duplicates appeared, surrounding her, holding her down as she flailed.

She screamed, a sound filled with fury and desperation, as her body fought against them.

Natalia rushed into the room, pale with horror. She knelt beside Colden, who was barely breathing, his body limp and lifeless. "What did you do?"

I didn't do it! Ava's mind howled, but no one could hear her.

In the distance, Savina entered with a group of others, their faces stricken with fear. Savina's sharp gaze fell on Ava, fear flashing in her eyes. "She's possessed." Her voice rang out, commanding and firm. "Take her to the parlor. We need to exorcise the spirit."

The spirit fought harder, but her body was weak now, drained by the spell.

Eric, his duplicates, and Gabriel dragged her, kicking and screaming, as her vision blurred. Colden's lifeless body burned in her mind. She had killed him. She had become everything she feared.

Once inside the parlor, Eric's duplicates and Gabriel restrained Ava, holding her arms and legs down as she thrashed.

Gabriel, hear me! It's not me! Please, listen!

But no words escaped her lips, only the spirit's dark snarl.

Savina entered, her face grim. "Hold her still. This will be painful."

Ava's father stood in the doorway, his face pale, his eyes wide with fear. He looked helpless, like his very world was crumbling in front of him.

Joss clutched his arm, her knuckles white, her own fear reflecting in her eyes.

Savina knelt beside Ava, her hand hovering above her chest.

The spirit inside Ava hissed violently, its voice cold and inhuman. "Don't touch me!"

But Savina pressed her hand firmly against Ava's chest.

A searing, burning pain shot through her, so intense it felt as though her skin was being flayed open from the inside. Ava's scream was raw, primal, her body bucking against the agony. The magic was tearing at her like jagged glass, burning beneath her skin. It was as if sandpaper was scraping through her veins, shredding her from the inside out.

The pain was unbearable, as if her very soul was being ripped apart. Her vision blurred, dark shapes twisting at the edges, and her screams echoed in the room.

I can't take it. I can't breathe. Please, make it stop!

Savina's eyes narrowed in concentration as her magic worked its way deeper, battling the darkness inside Ava. The spirit fought back viciously, writhing in her body, but Savina's power was relentless. Slowly, inch by excruciating inch, the darkness began to retreat, losing its grip.

After what felt like an eternity, Ava felt the dark presence being torn from her. She felt weightless, like she was floating above a calm, shimmering body of water. Her body went limp, her screams fading into weak gasps. The spirit was gone. Her strength completely drained, her body trembling in the aftermath.

Everything went black.

The sound of crackling fire reached her ears, and warmth brushed against her skin, but the dull ache in her chest lingered, stubborn and unrelenting. Ava's eyes fluttered open, her vision swimming in the soft glow of firelight. She blinked slowly, trying to focus, but everything felt distant, as though she were submerged in water.

Her body felt impossibly heavy, as if lead filled her veins instead of blood, pinning her down. Every movement was an effort. Her fingers twitched at her sides, the only part of her body that seemed willing to obey her command.

As the haze began to clear, she recognized the faint outline of her father sitting nearby, his gaze fixed on the fire. His expression was tense, his shoulders hunched, as if he had been watching over her for hours. She tried to speak, but her throat felt raw, as if she hadn't used it in days.

A soft groan escaped her lips, and her father's head snapped toward her.

His eyes widened, relief flooding his features as he rose from his seat and moved to her side. "Ava," he murmured with relief. "You're awake."

She blinked again, her mouth dry as she struggled to form words. "What … happened?" Her voice came out as a rasp.

He leaned closer, his face lined with worry. "You were possessed. We had to exorcise the spirit. It's gone now, but … you were out for a while."

Ava swallowed hard, the memory of the dark spirit crashing into her like a wave. Her heart raced, and for a moment, panic clawed at her throat. "Colden … is he okay?"

He nodded, his hand resting gently on hers. "He's alive. Weak, but he'll recover."

She let out a shaky breath, the tension in her chest easing just a little. But the guilt, the heaviness inside her, remained.

"Let me get Savina," he said.

Ava shut her eyes, allowing fatigue to overwhelm her.

The scent of oranges wafted, and she opened her eyes to see Savina sitting on the edge of the bed, holding her hand. "You gave us quite a scare."

A tear fell out of her eye and down her cheek as Peter, Gabriel, Joss, and Natalia piled into the room.

Peter sat to her right, his hand resting on her arm, though his gaze was distant.

Gabriel lingered by the fireplace, his face tight with concern.

Joss hovered nearby, her hands wringing together, unsure of what to say.

Natalia stood stiffly by the door, her glare like daggers.

"How did this happen?" Peter asked, his voice filled with confusion and hurt.

Her pulse raced. She couldn't tell them the truth. Not about the Necromancer. "I … I don't know."

Savina's piercing gaze stripped away Ava's defenses, leaving her vulnerable. "Don't lie to me."

Ava recoiled, sensing Savina's presence invading her thoughts, drawing nearer, determined to uncover the truth she desperately attempted to conceal. *No, please… don't.*

But it was too late.

Savina's expression darkened, her eyes wide with realization and horror. "You sought out a Necromancer."

The room fell into a stunned silence.

Peter's eyes widened in disbelief, his mouth slightly open.

Gabriel's jaw tightened, his blue eyes narrowing, locking onto hers with a mixture of disappointment and barely contained anger.

Ava's stomach twisted painfully under his silent judgment, the shame creeping up her spine like a cold shiver.

Natalia stepped forward. "You endangered all of us. She should be punished. Severely."

"No!" Joss moved in front of Natalia. "She didn't know what she was doing. You can't punish her for being tricked."

Natalia glared at Joss. "She knew enough to seek out dark magic. That's more than just a mistake."

Ava's heart plummeted. Her throat tightened with panic. "I—"

"Who told you where to find the Necromancer?" Savina demanded.

"No one," she lied.

Savina reached out and touched Ava's head.

A sharp pain surged through Ava's skull as Savina tore through her memories. *No! Don't look—*

Savina gasped and recoiled. "No. Colden would not have told you this. The spirits must have corrupted your mind."

Guilt twisted Ava's stomach. It had to be the worst betrayal any witch could have ever done to their coven. Why couldn't she have listened to Gabriel?

Because I am reckless. "I didn't mean to hurt anyone. I was just trying to understand. I didn't think—"

"That's the problem," Savina cut in. "You didn't think. And now we're all paying the price. You nearly killed Colden."

Tears welled in her eyes as the gravity of her mistake hit her like a tidal wave. "I never meant for that to happen."

"Intentions do not change the consequences," Savina said. "You made this choice."

Peter's gaze was cold now, his voice low. "How could you do this?" His hand slipped away from hers, and the distance between them was agonizing. He didn't say more, but the betrayal was clear in his eyes.

Her heart shattered at his words. "I'm sorry," she whispered, but she knew it wasn't enough.

"You don't know what you've done," Savina said. "This wasn't just reckless, Ava, it was dangerous. You could've gotten yourself killed or we could be at war now."

Ava's breath caught in her throat. She glanced at Gabriel, hoping for some kind of reassurance, but his face remained stoic. He'd warned her. He'd told her not to go, and she ignored him. She had betrayed them all.

Natalia's voice cut through the thick silence. "She should be locked away. Or better yet, banished. She's proven she can't be trusted."

"She made a terrible mistake, but she's still one of us," Gabriel finally spoke, his voice low and firm.

Natalia turned to him, incredulous. "After all of this, you still defend her?"

His gaze softened slightly as he looked at Ava. "Yes." But his usual conviction was absent.

"You are bound to the Manor," Savina said. "You are not to leave the premises until we've figured out the extent of the damage. We'll need to monitor you closely, Ava. You've opened yourself to something dangerous."

Her father stood, his face still etched with disappointment. "I need to check on Colden." He avoided her eyes and left the room. The sting of his departure was like a knife twisting in her chest.

As the others began to file out, Gabriel lingered by the doorway, his eyes meeting hers for a brief moment. There was something in his gaze, something like understanding. But there was distance too, a gap that hadn't been there before. And with one last glance, he turned and walked away.

Ava was left alone, the wreckage of her choices heavy on her shoulders. *What have I done?*

Ava wasn't sure how long she had been lying there, staring blankly at the ceiling, when the door creaked open.

Peter stepped in, his face pale, his jaw clenched tight. He couldn't meet her eyes. "Why, Ava? Why'd you do it?" His voice was strained, the muscles in his jaw twitching.

She sat up in bed, drawing her knees to her chest, wrapping her arms around them as if they could protect her. "Are you okay? I didn't mean to—"

"I'm fine. I heal, remember?" Despite his gentle tone, an undercurrent of tension hung in the air. He still wouldn't look at her. "What happened, Ava?"

Tears welled up in her eyes as she shook her head. She longed for him to come closer, to comfort her like he always did. But she could feel his distance, not just physically, but emotionally. He was right there, but he was a million miles away. "I'm so sorry," she whispered. "I didn't want to hurt you. I didn't know what was happening. It was like I wasn't in control … like I was trapped in my own body."

He finally looked at her, but his gaze was heavy with hurt, confusion, frustration. "I know it wasn't you. But … why didn't you tell me? Why didn't you come to me first?" He stayed where he was, standing by the door, not moving closer.

"I just … I needed to talk to her. My mom. I thought…" She wiped her eyes, choking on her words. "I thought I could handle it."

He was quiet for a long moment, his hand twitching at his side as if he wanted to reach out but didn't. "Was that your plan all along? Going to New Orleans to find the Necromancer?"

Fresh tears slipped down her cheeks. "What would you have done if you found out your mother was a Cimmerian, and she promised your soul to them? I didn't know what else to do. And now I've almost killed Colden."

His face softened, yet his eyes remained distant and disconnected. "I don't know what I would've done, but you've put everyone at risk. I wish you'd trusted me enough to tell me."

There was a knock on the door, and Gabriel stepped inside. He stood by the door, his posture stiff, his expression guarded. His eyes flicked between Peter and Ava, but his face gave nothing away. "We're having a meeting later." His voice was devoid of warmth. It wasn't harsh, but there was no comfort there either.

A wave of nausea washed over her as her stomach plummeted. She knew what it meant. Her punishment, her fate. Warm tears welled up again, her chest tightening with dread. She didn't dare meet Gabriel's eyes, not after everything. The space between them felt impossibly wide, and it hurt more than she could bear. *I don't belong here. I'm losing them all.*

A ringing in her ears drowned her, and the walls began to close in around her. She inhaled, but no air entered her lungs. Every breath shallow and ragged, as if the air itself were too thick to take in. Her hands shook, first a tremor, then a full shudder, and she clutched at them, pressing her nails into her palms, but the tingling in her fingers only grew worse. It was like her body was no longer her own, a betraying, frenzied vessel she couldn't control.

"What's wrong?" Peter's voice cut through, somewhere nearby, but it was distant and muted, like she was hearing him through water. His hand touched her arm.

His words drifted over her like mist, and she tried to catch them, but they slipped away.

Her heart pounded faster, each beat a sharp stab in her chest. *I'm going to be cast out. I'll be alone.*

Gabriel's hand was on her shoulder, and he sat beside her on the bed, not pressing too close but close enough to anchor her. "Focus on me, Ava. Just follow my breath." His voice was low and even, his breaths slow and deliberate.

She matched them, each one pulling her a little further from the edge.

"You're okay."

Gradually, her vision cleared, and the room came back into focus. Her heart slowed its frantic rhythm, and the crushing weight in her chest began to ease. Exhaustion settled over her.

Only then did she notice Peter standing nearby, watching her with a pained, uncertain expression. His eyes were wide, filled with worry, but also something that looked like regret.

"Nothing's going to happen to you, Ava," Gabriel said. "Yes, you did something reckless, and there are consequences. But Savina won't banish you."

"But I … I betrayed everyone. I nearly killed Colden."

"Yeah, you did." His jaw clenched, and he closed his eyes briefly, trying to hold back his frustration. When he opened them again, there was a deep frown etched on his face, and he exhaled slowly. "But you're still one of us. Savina sees you as family. She's disappointed, but she won't throw you away. Colden will recover."

His words should have comforted her, but they didn't. She was no longer wanted. Maybe leaving would be better for everyone. Natalia had been right. Ava had only thought of herself.

Ava pulled away, hugging her knees tighter. "I should go … I've caused too much damage. I don't belong here."

"You don't get to run away because it's hard," Gabriel said. "Leaving won't fix anything. We've all made mistakes. We fight through them."

"We'll get through this together," Peter said, but kept his distance, still not touching her. "You don't have to do it alone."

But it felt impossible. Peter's calm but distant tone, Gabriel's frustration, and her father's silence all echoed around her, each layer of disappointment crushing her under its weight. She didn't deserve their forgiveness. She had put them all in danger, and the thought of staying felt unbearable.

No one would be safe around her. She was dangerous.

The thought lodged itself in her mind, cold and certain.

She needed to leave. It was the only way to protect them. To keep them safe from the chaos she had brought into their lives.

Her chest tightened as the decision settled deep within her, a bittersweet resolve.

She didn't know where she would go, but she couldn't stay there. Not anymore.

31

BREAKING DOWN

The library used to be a sanctuary to Ava, but now it felt like a courtroom, and she was on trial. The piercing gazes of the gathered coven members bore into her like fiery daggers. Each step she took echoed through the silence, resonating with a sense of impending doom. It felt like she was walking into her own execution.

Aaron stood at the front of the room, flanked by Gustav, Maggie, and Savina. Natalia lingered by the door, her arms crossed and her gaze as cold as ice. Peter, Melissa, and Lance stood beside her, and Gabriel was nearby. Even now, after everything, he was still standing beside her.

"As you are all aware," Aaron began, "something terrible has happened. When the spirits possessed Ava, their dark power overtook her, and they used her abilities to try to kill Colden."

Ava's heart sank lower as he spoke. Everyone's eyes were on her, the judgment in their stares. Her breath hitched, but she forced herself to keep still, swallowing back the urge to cry.

"Colden is in severe condition," Aaron continued. "But we have a plan. Maya has told us about a rare flower with healing properties. Savina, Maya, and I will leave to retrieve it. Maggie and Gustav will oversee everything in our absence. Natalia and Alena will stay with Colden."

"We must save Colden," Savina said, her voice leaving no room for argument. "Nothing will happen while we're gone."

Link frowned. "Do you really think leaving us right now is a good idea? We're on the brink of war."

Savina's eyes narrowed. "Do not question me. This is necessary."

"But we're exposed," Link continued. "We've been kept in the dark about so much already. How do we know we're not being set up?"

Ava flinched at his words. He wasn't speaking for himself. He was speaking for everyone who felt lost, left out of decisions that would affect their lives.

Aaron raised his hand to calm the room. "We will return before the new moon. You will be safe here."

"What about my mom and Ava's dad?" Thomas asked.

"We are going to put them somewhere safe," Savina said. "Away from here."

Ava's stomach dropped. She didn't want her father to leave.

Savina turned her gaze toward Ava. "When we return, we will discuss your fate."

Her cheeks blazed as she felt the intense wave of hatred and anger radiating from everyone around her, consuming her. Her knees grew weak. She couldn't believe she caused all this turmoil, all because she had an insatiable need to uncover the truth. At last, Ava summoned the courage to lift her gaze and meet Savina's unwavering eyes.

I am so disappointed in you.

Ava thought back the only thing she could say, but it would never be enough. *I'm sorry.*

The meeting adjourned, and she could feel everyone's judgment piercing her back as she hastily retreated from the room. She sprinted up the stairs, the sound of her pounding footsteps echoing through the empty hallway. Finally reaching the safety of her room, she shut the door with a resounding thud, the sound reverberating in her ears. Sliding onto the floor, she pressed her trembling hands against her face, feeling the coolness of her palms against her flushed cheeks.

The door opened again, and Peter walked in. He knelt beside her, pulling her into his arms. But the comfort he offered felt distant now, like an echo she couldn't quite grasp.

"I hate what I've done," Ava whispered. "I brought you into this … and now I'm going to be gone."

He held her tighter, but there was a strain in his voice. "You don't know that."

"Yes, I do. You should leave. You deserve better than this. Better than me."

"Don't … shut me out." He sounded uncertain, his words lacking the conviction they once held. "We're in this together. No matter what."

Ava clung to him, her body trembling. She buried her face in his chest, the tears she had held back finally spilling over. "What will you do when I'm no longer part of the coven? I've betrayed them so many times."

He didn't answer right away. His silence stretched for a beat too long, and when he finally spoke, his breath was shallow, almost as if he were choosing his words carefully. "Didn't you hear what Gabriel said? If they wanted to banish you … they would have done it already."

"I don't know what's going to happen."

"Just … don't worry about it right now. Focus on getting stronger. On healing."

She nodded mechanically, but deep down, she wasn't sure if she believed him. If Savina had just told her about her mother, she wouldn't have gone to the Necromancer. The secrets, the lies had pushed her, and now the damage was irreparable.

32

AMENDS

The cold of the Manor clung to Ava's skin as she lay staring at the ceiling, the darkness above pressing down like the weight of a forgotten promise. Sleep had abandoned her long ago, chased away by the guilt that gnawed at her insides like a festering wound. She was drowning in it, choking on the memories of what she'd done, the faces of the people she had hurt flickering in the shadows. Colden's still body. The destruction she'd caused. The hollow emptiness left behind.

The silence in the Manor was thick, oppressive, the kind that made every creak in the floorboards sound like a scream in the dead of night. And yet, within that silence, her mind spun in relentless circles, her thoughts a tempest that refused to settle.

Peter had gone home. He hadn't said much when he left, but the space between them had grown like a widening chasm, one she wasn't sure she could ever bridge. He was slipping away, and she couldn't blame him. How could anyone stay after what she had done?

She couldn't stay. Not anymore. The guilt was suffocating, wrapping its claws around her until there was nothing left. They didn't need her. She was a danger to everyone, and leaving was the only way to keep them safe. Her mother's blood—Cimmerian blood—tainted her, and maybe she wasn't strong enough to fight it.

Ava sat up, her decision made, a chill running through her veins. The walls of the Manor felt like a cage, and the darkness inside her was becoming too much to bear. Her hands trembled as she pulled on her clothes. She grabbed a small backpack, stuffing in a few essentials, because she wasn't coming back.

The quiet of the Manor was thick as she crept down the hallway, the shadows stretching long and sinister in the faint light that spilled from the windows. The walls seemed to watch her, the weight of the building pressing down as if it could sense her betrayal. Every step echoed louder than the last, and the stillness around her felt alive, like the Manor itself was holding its breath, waiting for her to break.

Moving quickly, she descended the stairs, her heart racing with each step. *I need to disappear. If I'm gone, they'll be safe.* The cool night air hit her as she stepped outside, the heavy front door creaking shut behind her. She took a breath, pulling the straps of her backpack higher on her shoulders as her feet carried her toward the metal gate.

This is it. The sky above was black, a deep void devoid of stars, as if the skies themselves had turned their backs on her. The wind whispered through the trees, low and mournful, and her breath caught in her throat as the gate loomed ahead, tall and cold, like the final barrier between her and the world beyond. Her fingers brushed the iron bars.

Something slammed into her. A force she couldn't see, couldn't fight. She stumbled backward, the air knocked from her lungs as her back hit the ground hard. The impact sent a shock through her body, and for a moment, she lay there, stunned, as the realization settled in.

She was bound.

She scrambled to her feet, heart pounding in her chest, her hands trembling as she pressed against the invisible barrier. It was like trying to push through stone, unforgiving, unyielding. Panic rose like bile in her throat. *No. No. This can't be happening.*

But it was. She was trapped.

"Ava," a voice came from behind her, low and sharp, cutting through the stillness like a blade.

She froze, her breath catching in her throat. Slowly, she turned.

Gabriel stood just beyond the gate, his figure half-hidden in the shadows. The faint glow of moonlight illuminated the sharp edges of his face. His eyes were hard, unreadable, and his posture was rigid, like he'd been waiting for this. He inched closer. "You can't go anywhere. You're bound here for a reason."

"I was just—"

"Leaving? You think running will fix this?" He stepped forward again, his figure looming over her, casting a long shadow that swallowed her whole.

Her heart twisted, guilt and shame flooded her chest like poison. "I just—after what I've done, I don't deserve to be here."

"You think that's your choice to make?"

She opened her mouth to speak, but no words came out. The weight of his gaze pinned her in place, and she felt small, insignificant beneath it.

"You think running makes you brave? That it'll make everything better? It's cowardice, Ava," Gabriel's voice was sharp, but beneath the anger, there was something else. Something raw.

"I'm trying to protect you all. You don't understand."

"I understand more than you think. You think I haven't made mistakes? You think I haven't done things I regret?"

"You never tried to kill an Elder! You never killed Ephemerals or betrayed your coven."

"You don't know what I've done." His eyes darkened, a shadow crossing his face.

She flinched, his words like a blow. Her heart raced as she stared at him. "What ... what are you talking about?"

His face twisted with regret, anger, and something deeper. "You think I haven't hurt people I care about? That I haven't crossed lines I can't uncross? I've done things, Ava. Things I'm not proud of. So don't act like you're the only one carrying this weight."

"I didn't know ... I thought..."

"You thought I was different. But I'm not. I've been reckless. I've made mistakes that haunt me every day. So don't think you're beyond saving just because you made a terrible choice." His voice was rough, pained.

Tears stung her eyes. "I'm sorry. I should've listened to you. You warned me. Now Colden might die because of me."

"You made a mistake. Desperation makes us do stupid things. But running won't solve it. Not now. You have to stay and face this. You have to make it right."

"I don't think I can."

He took another step forward, his voice gentler. "You can. You're stronger than you realize."

"And if I can't?"

"You will. Because you don't have a choice."

They stood staring at each other as fear, anger, shame radiated within her.

"Do you hate me?"

His gaze softened. "No, Ava. I don't hate you. I hate the way you've handled things. How you shut us out."

"I know. I messed up."

"You're not alone."

For the first time in days, Ava felt a glimmer of hope, a sliver of belief that maybe she wasn't beyond redemption. Gabriel hadn't forgiven her, but he had given her something more important. A chance to fight. A chance to make things right.

⎯⎯⎯⎯⎯⎯⎯⟨33⟩⎯⎯⎯⎯⎯⎯⎯

BROKENHEARTED

Standing outside her father's bedroom door, Ava chewed on her lip, her heart racing, hands trembling. She had never been afraid to speak to her father. They hadn't spoken in almost a day, and she needed to see him before he left. She had shattered his trust, and she knew there was no way to take back what she'd done. Colden was his close friend, a friend to everyone.

She took a shaky breath and knocked. It was better to face it now than later. A few seconds passed before the door opened, and there he stood, his expression instantly sobering.

"Can we talk?" she asked.

"Of course." He stepped aside, letting her in.

The room was simple, masculine, and familiar in its scent, but it struck Ava how she'd never really been inside before. Her eyes fell on the half-packed suitcase on the bed, her stomach coiling. She didn't want him to leave, even if it was to keep him safe.

She turned back to face him. His gray hair was disheveled, the lines of stress etched deeper than ever into his face. He looked like a man who had carried the burden of raising a teenage daughter alone, especially one like her.

"Dad, I know you hate me," she began, her voice shaking. "I'm sorry for what I did. I never meant for things to go that far. I just … I wanted answers. About Mom. About why I am the way I am."

Her father's face softened, but his eyes remained stern. "Ava, let's get one thing straight. I will never hate you. You're my daughter. I love you, no matter what."

Her chest tightened, and her chin quivered as she tried to hold back tears.

"I know you didn't intend for this to happen," he continued. "But you weren't thinking. That's what I'm most disappointed about. You had to know that seeing a Necromancer was dangerous. You had to know the risks."

"I thought I did. I thought it was just dangerous for me. Colden told me how to find one, and I figured … if he told me, it couldn't be that bad."

Her father's eyebrows drew together, confusion flickering across his face. "Colden … really told you?"

"Yes. He said he felt bad for me because Savina wouldn't tell me the truth about Mom."

"What truth?" She could hear the edge of uncertainty in it.

She cursed herself silently. She hadn't wanted to tell him like this, but now she had no choice. Her necklace warmed against her skin, pushing her forward. "Dad," she began slowly, carefully, "Mom was … she was a Cimmerian."

The color drained from his face, and Ava's heart raced as she braced herself for what would come next.

He stood still, his expression blank with disbelief. "What are you talking about?" His voice was strained, like he was barely holding himself together.

"It's true. Colden told me. And Xavier said Mom promised my soul to Havok. That's why I went to the Necromancer … to talk to her, to find out if it was true."

He stumbled back as if the wind had been knocked out of him, and she rushed to his side, helping him into a nearby chair. His hand gripped hers tightly, his fingers trembling. "What … did she say?" His eyes pleaded with her to tell him it wasn't real.

Ava couldn't hold back her tears anymore. "She said it was my destiny."

Her father's face crumpled, and the devastation in his eyes shattered her heart. The woman he had loved, given up his life for, had betrayed him. The woman they had both lost had deceived them both. "Oh, Ava." He wrapped his arms around her. She hadn't seen him cry like this since the day her mother died, and it broke her. She clung to him, wanting more than anything to take away his pain, to undo what had been done.

But there was more, and she knew she had to say it.

"There's something else, Dad."

He pulled back, wiping his eyes, bracing himself. "What else could there be?"

"I killed Jonah and Drew," she blurted out, her words rushing together. "They attacked me, and I didn't mean to, but I killed them. The Cimmerians … they've been torturing us, and I got so obsessed with finding the truth, I made the worst mistake of my life."

He stared at her, horror and shock clear in his expression. "Ava…"

"I know it's a lot."

He studied her face, the pain in his eyes still sharp, but now softened with sorrow. "I'm sorry. I should have done more to help you through this. I should've known…"

"I just wanted answers."

He pulled her into his arms again, holding her as tightly as he could. "We'll figure this out. When this is all over, we'll talk to Savina. We'll find out the truth together."

After a few minutes, he stood and zipped up his suitcase.

Ava's heart clenched. It was time to say goodbye. "Where are you going?"

"I don't know, and you can't know either. In case the Cimmerians get inside your head."

"I can change, Dad. I can be better. I won't make any more mistakes."

He smiled softly and touched her cheek. "You'll make mistakes. We all do. But the important thing is that we learn from them. I love you, Ava."

"I love you, too. I don't want to say goodbye."

"No goodbyes. We'll see each other again."

There was a knock on the door, and Ava clung to him as tears streamed down her face. She didn't want to let him go, not knowing when or if she would see him again.

"I have to go, sweetie." He kissed her forehead.

She nodded, stepping back as he walked toward the door. Gabriel was waiting, his expression somber.

Her father looked back one last time. "I'm so proud of you, Ava. I love you."

By the time she opened her mouth to tell him she loved him, he was gone.

34

FRAYED

Throughout the training session, Ava couldn't shake the hollow feeling in her chest. She channeled her guilt, frustration, and anger into training, but nothing eased the ache. Each glance from her friends was another reminder of what she'd done, of how far she'd fallen in their eyes. Even Peter had been distant, his silence more painful than words.

After training, she followed her friends to the library. They all looked as exhausted as she felt, shadows under their eyes and weariness in their posture. The air was thick with waiting for war, for answers, for something to change.

"How's your dad?" Melissa asked.

A feeling of unease twisted in Ava's stomach. "I don't know. I can't talk to him or see him."

"That really sucks." She shook her head. "Every bit of this sucks."

Thomas chewed on his fingernails, his eyes darting around the room. "You can say that again."

"Do you really have to do that?" Melissa grimaced, but the tension in her voice betrayed her nerves.

"Yes," Thomas replied sharply, and the group lapsed into silence again.

"It's so weird," Lance said. "It's like we're just sitting here, waiting for something terrible to happen."

Ava nodded. "We are."

Link pulled a chair closer to the table, sitting on it backwards. "Yeah, well, this waiting is getting old. Why can't we just attack them? Hit them before they hit us?"

Thomas perked up, leaning forward. "Exactly. I've been wondering the same thing for days. Savina's supposed to be so smart and strong, but it's like she's just waiting for disaster to strike."

"Colden said she used to be naïve," Ava muttered, deflecting the anger from Savina.

"Used to be?" Thomas snorted. "No offense, but telling everyone to sit tight while she and an Elder go hunt for a random flower isn't the brightest plan."

Ava's chest tightened. She was frustrated, too. Waiting was tearing them apart, but this mess was her fault. Her guilt weighed heavier by the second. "I don't think Savina wants to admit the truth."

"Why are you guys being so harsh on her?" Peter's voice cut through the room, startling Ava. He had been so quiet, withdrawn in the last few days, it was easy to forget he was there.

Ava sighed. "It's not that. I'm just … frustrated. We're all frustrated. Where are Gillian and Jeremy?" Ava asked.

Melissa shrugged. "Gillian's been hiding. Ever since she found out that her dad is really her stepdad and her real dad was a Cimmerian, she hasn't been herself."

"Wait, what? How did she find out?" Ava's stomach twisted again. Had she been so focused on the Necromancer that she hadn't noticed what was happening with her friends?

"She went to Marcel while you guys were … busy."

Thomas let out a low whistle. "A Cimmerian dad? Rough, but she's not the only one. My dad was one. So was Ava's mom." He leaned closer. "Speaking of, that was pretty damn ballsy of you, Ava."

"Thomas," she warned.

"What? I'm serious. What was it like?"

Melissa smacked his arm. "Thomas! Stop."

Ava glanced down at her hands, feeling everyone's eyes on her. "It's nothing anyone should ever experience." A lump formed in her throat.

Natalia appeared at the edge of the room, her eyes hard, cutting through the tense atmosphere like a blade right at Ava. "Colden has been asking for you."

Ava's heart leapt. Relief mixed with fear flooded her chest. Colden wanted to see her. After everything… She wasn't sure she could face him. Her legs felt heavy as she stood, and her breath came in shallow bursts. She squeezed past the others as Natalia led her down the hallway.

Each step took more effort than the last, like she was walking toward her own reckoning. The closer they got to Colden's room, the more her fear grew. What would she say? How could she look him in the eye after what she'd done?

Outside his door, Natalia stopped and fixed Ava with a stern glare. "I'll be right here the whole time. Don't even think about hurting him again."

"I'm not going to hurt him. I didn't mean to last time."

"Whatever." Natalia pushed the door open.

Ava stepped inside, her heart hammering in her chest.

Colden lay in the bed, his face pale and slick with sweat, the faint aroma of antiseptic lingered in the air. But when his tired eyes met hers, a feeble smile graced his lips. "Hello, Ava."

Overwhelmed with sadness, she burst into tears. How could he be so kind to her, after everything? "Colden, I'm so sorry. I don't know what I was thinking."

"Don't apologize," he rasped. "Come sit."

She hesitated, but took the chair beside his bed, feeling her stomach twist with guilt. "Why aren't you angry with me? You should be."

"Anger solves nothing."

"I think most of them hate me. And I can't blame them."

"No, Ava. They're angry, yes. But they won't stay mad forever."

"I was stupid to go. I just wanted to talk to my mother. To find out if she really did … everything."

"Did you get the answers you were looking for?"

"Not really. She kept saying it's my destiny to join Havok. But I won't give in to him."

He winced, clutching his side in pain.

"Can't I heal you?"

"No. You've already given me more than I ever expected."

"What do you mean?"

"I've been suffering for so long. I'm ready to die."

Her body froze in place, as if time had come to a standstill. More tears fell. "What? No. No, you can't say that. Savina will be back soon with the cure."

"I'm glad I got to know you. You've grown into a strong, beautiful young woman. I'm proud of you."

"No. Stop saying your goodbyes."

He reached for her hand, his grip weak but warm. "Don't cry. I won't be suffering anymore."

"I can't lose you, Colden. I've lost too much already."

"You haven't lost everything. You still have your friends. Your family. You're stronger than you think. And you don't have to face this alone." Colden's voice was fading, his breaths growing shallow. "Remember, your mother loved you. She sacrificed herself to protect you and your father."

"What?" Ava's breath caught in her throat. "How do you know that?"

"Savina knows. She'll tell you … when the time is right."

"Will they banish me? I can't do this without you."

His eyes softened. "No. They won't banish you. You're too important. You did what you could. My illness is much too strong, and I've been suffering for years. But you … you have a future. Don't give up."

Ava could barely breathe. The guilt, her fear, everything she had done crushed her. Her stomach was in ropes as she gripped Colden's hand tightly, but his grip loosened as his body grew weaker.

"I don't want to say goodbye."

"No one's ever ready to say goodbye. I love you, Ava, like a daughter. You'll be okay. I know you will."

His words shattered her heart into a million pieces.

Convulsions wracked his body, and his breathing became erratic.

Ava jumped to her feet, panic surging through her veins. "Natalia!" She fumbled with the door as Colden's body thrashed violently.

Natalia and Alena rushed into the room, leaving Ava in the hallway, her heart pounding in her chest.

As the door closed behind them, Ava leaned against the wall, tears streaming down her face. Fear and grief overwhelmed her. Her chest tightened painfully, and she struggled to catch her breath. Losing her mother had felt like the end of her world, and now, it felt like it was happening all over again. The thought of Colden dying because of her was too much.

She wanted to scream, to stop time, to do anything to keep Colden from leaving her. But she knew there was nothing she could do.

FAMILY

Sleep had been elusive for days. Ava had given up on it, her body aching for rest but her mind refusing to cooperate. Exhaustion consumed her, both physically and mentally, as if every bit of energy had drained away. The events of the last few days swirled relentlessly in her thoughts, leaving her restless. She was tired of tossing and turning, tired of hearing Peter's soft snores beside her, tired of feeling completely lost, and tired of being confined to the Manor.

Carefully, she slipped out of bed, not wanting to wake Peter. Dressing in the dim light, her fingers fumbled with her shirt. She touched the bracelet Peter had given her, and a sharp pang of guilt hit her. He was still by her side, but the distance between them was growing, and she could feel it widening with every passing day. She hadn't just betrayed her coven, she was losing him too.

Downstairs, the Manor was silent. But in the dining room, Ava found Kira sitting at the table, a steaming cup of coffee in her hands. Her long white hair was pulled back into a thick braid, and a book lay open in front of her.

Ava paused, not expecting anyone to be there. "Sorry. I didn't mean to interrupt." She turned to leave, but Kira's soft voice stopped her.

"You're welcome to join me."

Surprised by the warmth in Kira's tone, she hesitated before sitting down across from her.

"Can't sleep?" Kira asked.

"No." She fidgeted with the bracelet on her wrist. "I don't think anyone can."

"Understandable. There's a lot on all our minds."

Ava swallowed the lump in her throat, unsure if she'd ever find peace again.

"How are you holding up?"

"I'm fine. Just trying to make sense of everything."

"I'm sorry your search for answers ended the way it did."

"I wish Savina had told me everything from the start."

"She was probably trying to protect you," Kira said. "Or maybe your mother didn't want you to know."

"That's selfish. Did she think Havok wouldn't come for me eventually? Or for all of us?"

Footsteps approached, and Alena stood in the doorway, her face drawn with exhaustion.

Ava expected harsh words or a glare, but instead, Alena's expression softened as she stepped closer.

"She was a spy," Alena said in her thick Russian accent. The petite brunette carried herself with quiet grace, her dark blue eyes sharp and focused. Despite her small frame, there was an undeniable strength in her posture.

Ava blinked in shock. "What?"

"Your mother. She was a spy for the Cimmerians."

Her mother … a spy? The ground felt like it was shifting beneath her again. "Why didn't Savina tell me?"

"Savina never confirmed it, but it was clear," Alena said. "Your mother showed up one day, claiming her coven had been killed. But no one knew her or where she came from. She was working with the Cimmerians, plotting against us. But something changed."

"What changed?"

"She fell in love with your father," Alena said. "She chose him. She chose you. She stopped being a spy and truly wanted to be one of us."

A whirlwind of emotions swirled inside Ava—hurt, anger, confusion, and finally, a glimmer of relief. "If that's true, why would she still promise me to Havok? It doesn't make sense."

Alena sighed, her expression weary. "Maybe she thought it was the only way to keep you safe. Maybe she made mistakes. But I know she loved you and your father."

Ava clenched her fists under the table, her frustration rising. How could her mother claim to love her and still condemn her to such a fate? It felt like betrayal, wrapped in affection, and it was almost too much to bear.

More people trickled into the room, filling it with a subdued energy. Exhaustion hung in the air, weighed down by Colden's impending death. Small groups gathered, sipping coffee and murmuring quietly.

Peter appeared at some point, pressing a kiss to Ava's temple before sitting beside her. His hand found hers, but it felt different, distant.

Ava scanned the room. Joss and Eric shared a quiet conversation, Thomas sat staring into space, and Melissa was curled up in Lance's lap, half-asleep. Gillian twisted a strand of hair between her fingers. Gabriel occasionally glanced Ava's way.

None of them seemed angry or disappointed in her, despite everything she had done. They remained by her side, supporting her, even when she didn't deserve it. The guilt consumed her, constricting her chest. These people had become her family, had made the Manor her home, and she owed them more than she could give.

"Guess we better start training." Link stretched as he stood. The others murmured in agreement, rising slowly from their seats.

Melissa yawned and squeezed Ava's shoulder. "You coming?"

"Yeah, in a few," she said. "I want to check on Colden first."

Melissa gave her a sympathetic smile before heading out with the others.

Peter lingered for a moment, brushing her hand as he stood. "I'll see you outside." He followed the group.

Once the room was empty, Ava finally stood, her body stiff from sitting too long. Her heart raced as she approached Colden's room, her hands trembling as she reached for the doorknob.

Natalia greeted her with an icy glare.

"I just want to see him."

Natalia moved aside.

Ava entered and sat beside Colden's bed, taking his hand. Emotion welled up inside her. For years, Colden shielded her, but now his strength was waning. She wasn't ready to say goodbye. Not to someone else she cared about.

Colden stirred, his eyes fluttering open, and a familiar smile spread across his face. "Ava." How could he still look at her like that after everything? She was grateful for it though.

"Hi. How are you feeling?"

"I am quite rested."

Something was off. His gaze, once warm, now seemed cold, distant. A flicker of unease sparked in her chest.

"Have you said your goodbyes?" he asked, his tone unnervingly calm.

"Goodbyes?"

"We have a long journey ahead," he continued, speaking slowly, savoring each word.

She swallowed hard, panic rising. *He's hallucinating.* "Where are we going?"

A dark grin tugged at his lips. "Caprington."

She stiffened, yanking her hand from his. "Caprington? What are you talking about?"

"You'll soon find out." His eyes gleamed with something dark and dangerous. He pushed the blankets aside and swung his legs off the bed.

Ava leapt to her feet, knocking over the chair in the process. "Colden, should you be getting up?"

He smirked, the eerie calmness more terrifying than an outburst. "You'll find Caprington to be a beautiful place. A place where Enchanters reign. No Ephemerals. No weakness." With each step he took toward her, he seemed to grow taller and more commanding. The room seemed to close in as he leaned closer, his cold hand grazing her chin.

Ava flinched at his touch, and a chill settled deep into her bones. "Why are you saying this?"

"Because it's time. Enchanters will rule again, Ava. You, Thomas, Gillian ... you were all part of my plan."

Her heart raced. "You ... convinced us to kill those people?"

"In a sense. You were all so easy to manipulate. Thomas killed his father out of betrayal. Gillian made Trent murder those innocents. And you—you killed the Ephemerals. It was easy to get inside your heads, manipulate you into killing. Now, you're ready to join me."

"Join you?" Her stomach twisted in horror. "What are you talking about?"

"You've been so valuable to my recovery, Ava. Don't you see?" His lips curved into a dark, eerie smile. "You may know me as Corbin, but those days are over."

Her blood ran cold, and her knees threatened to buckle. "No... You're Havok?"

"I've been trapped inside this body for years, but thanks to you, I'm free. You helped release me, Ava. You were so desperate to learn about your mother... It didn't take much convincing you to see a Necromancer."

Ava stumbled backward, her world spinning. She had set Havok free, and now the consequences of her actions were staring her down.

36

KILL OR BE KILLED

Ava's back slammed into the door, her fingers instinctively curling around the cold doorknob. Her mind spun, trying to process the horrifying truth. Corbin had returned. And it was her fault. She had unwittingly released him.

Colden—no, *Havok*—stepped closer, his hand reaching out. That familiar pull, like the one she'd felt when healing Colden and when she'd faced Devon Maunsell, surged inside her, twisting her stomach.

Panic overtook her. With a desperate burst of adrenaline, Ava kicked Havok hard in the stomach. He doubled over with a grunt, but the sinister grin never left his face. She turned the doorknob and bolted, her pulse roaring in her ears. The hallway blurred as she ran, terror quickening her steps. *Where's Natalia? Alena?* The Manor, usually full of life, now felt like a tomb, eerily silent.

I'm trapped. He's coming for me.

Darting past the library, she glanced over her shoulder. Terror gripped her tighter with each passing second. Havok. *How did this happen? How could I have let it happen?*

She collided with something solid, stumbling back in shock.

A man with dirty blond hair and a scar smirked down at her. "Hello, Ava. Ready for Caprington?" He seized her, his grip like iron.

She struggled, kicking and clawing, but it was as if her strength had abandoned her. "Let me go!" She kicked at him.

His grin widened. "Your powers won't work here."

Panic flared. She lashed out again, managing to land a punch.

As he staggered, a forceful blow struck him from behind, and he crumpled to the ground, unconscious.

Ava looked up, breathless. Relief washed over her as Peter stood, holding a broken piece of wood.

"They're everywhere, Ava." He grabbed her hand. "The war has started."

Her mind reeled. *The war? It had begun?* But there was no time to process it.

Peter yanked her outside into the thick night air, the scent of smoke heavy around them. Screams echoed in the distance, and bursts of magic lit the horizon.

"Peter, where are we going?"

"They're coming for you. We have to get you out of here."

But she stopped, yanking her hand free. "We have to fight." She couldn't run. Not now.

"Ava, listen to me—"

She sprinted toward the battlefield, her heart pounding.

The scene before her was a storm of chaos. Enchanters and Cimmerians clashed, their powers lighting up the night.

The earth trembled beneath her, the sky above churned with magic.

Ava hesitated, overwhelmed by the sheer magnitude of the battle. *This is it. The war we've all feared. The war I helped start.*

Screams erupted nearby, and Ava spun around, her breath catching as Ilya fell, clutching his stomach. Fear shot through her.

"Ava!" Gabriel's voice cut through the chaos as he slammed into her, knocking her to the ground. Her body hit the earth hard, the impact sending waves of pain through her limbs.

She tried to push herself up, but her limbs were too weak.

Peter stood over a lifeless woman, his face contorted in anger and grief. Gabriel had saved her, but Peter had struck the final blow.

"Get her out of here!" Gabriel shouted.

"No!" Ava screamed, her voice raw. "I have to fight!"

But the battlefield mirrored her inner turmoil. Every second felt like a reflection of her failures. Lightning shot toward her, and she barely dodged, rolling aside. A white-haired woman charged, electricity crackling between her fingers.

Ava raised her arms, water swirling weakly around her, but her power faltered. She was too slow. Too weak. Too reckless.

Screams filled the air as more Enchanters fell. Guilt twisted inside her. *This is my fault.*

She countered the woman's lightning with water, but her strength was fading.

The woman convulsed and crumpled to the ground.

Ava's breath was ragged, her heart pounding.

Another explosion knocked her to the ground. Pain shot through her limbs as she struggled to stand.

Peter was battling two Cimmerians. His exhaustion made Ava's heart clench painfully. *He's fighting because of me. Because I failed.*

Determined, she summoned water and hurled it at Peter's attackers. But her efforts felt too little, too late. Another Enchanter fell, and the battlefield felt like a living reminder of her mistakes.

A fiery blast erupted nearby, throwing Ava backward. She fell hard, her body trembling from exhaustion. The dark and stormy clouds above mirrored her emotions. Lightning split the sky in jagged lines.

It's your fault.

A man appeared in front of her. His arms transformed into two large, writhing vipers. The snakes hissed, fangs bared as they struck.

Ava dodged, but one viper grazed her arm. A searing pain shot through her, causing her arm to ignite with a burning sensation. Venom. The second viper sank its fangs into her shoulder, sending her to the ground, gasping. Pain exploded, and Ava screamed, her vision blurring. The venom coursed through her veins like liquid fire. Her arm throbbed violently, a dull ache quickly giving way to a deep, pulsating burn.

Her heart raced, panic flooding her senses. Venom spread throughout her. The muscles in her arm weakened, her fingers trembling as they lost strength. She clutched her arm, trying to fight the growing numbness, but her entire arm was on fire.

The man smirked, his viper arms recoiling for another strike.

Ava's vision blurred at the edges. A wave of dizziness hit her as the venom continued its assault on her body. Her breath became shallow, her chest tightening with each inhalation.

She had to act fast.

The snake's cold, scaly arm coiled tightly around her neck, constricting with a relentless grip. She desperately clawed and grabbed at the sleek appendage, feeling its rough texture beneath her fingertips.

Gritting her teeth, Ava summoned her power, envisioning the man and his snakes submerged under icy, freezing water. Her mind fought to focus through the pain, the venom clouding her thoughts. Cold water surged from her outstretched hand, encircling the man. He gasped, his viper arms twitching as he struggled to free himself.

Despite her weakening body, she summoned all her strength to maintain her grip. The man's eyes bulged, his body convulsing as the cold water enveloped him, choking the life from his limbs. His vipers went limp, sliding off her, their fangs no longer a threat. Finally, with a strangled gasp, the man collapsed, the snakes recoiling back into his human arms as he fell dead at her feet.

Ava staggered back, clutching her wounded arm. Blood oozed from the puncture wounds, and her skin was swelling rapidly, turning red and blotchy around the bites. Her breathing became labored, her heart racing as the venom spread further into her system. Her arm felt like it was aflame, while the rest of her body began to grow cold and weak. *I can't heal myself.* The world spun around her as her legs gave out.

Trudy appeared, smirking down at her. "Well, well, well. We meet again."

Ava lifted her arm, water swirling weakly around her hand, but Trudy easily dodged the attack.

"You can't beat me like this. But don't worry. Havok will be pleased."

Ava's vision blurred again, her entire body trembling from the venom. Her arm felt like dead weight, and her mind was sluggish, unable to form coherent thoughts. She collapsed forward onto the ground, her breathing shallow and strained. She was slipping away, the venom taking its toll.

The darkness enveloped her. "We're here to take you home," Xavier's voice whispered in her ear.

A woman with fiery red hair stepped forward, her face twisted in a malicious grin. The woman struck her across the head, hard. Pain radiated through her skull as blood trickled down her face.

Ava crumpled to the ground as Xavier let her go, her limbs heavy, her vision fading. The last thing she saw was the blur of a figure disappearing into the woods, carrying a limp body with long, thick blond hair trailing behind.

And then darkness.

37

POWERLESS

When Ava came to, her face was still embedded in the dirt. Her body had become a mere silhouette, disconnected from her being. The world around her appeared hazy, with blurred edges, like a dream that had lost its vividness. The distant sound of her own breathing echoed in her ears, a constant reminder of her disconnection. Every muscle felt stiff and heavy. Her arm throbbed with a deep, relentless ache, the venom still burning beneath her skin. A feverish chill ran down her spine, making her shiver.

I can't move.

Her mind screamed for her body to respond, but it refused. She felt trapped within herself, helpless as her own limbs betrayed her.

"Ava!" Peter's voice cut through the fog in her mind, distant at first, but his face appeared above her, blurry but unmistakable. His eyes were wide with panic, his hand trembling as it brushed her cheek. The touch was soft, gentle, and despite the pain radiating through her, it was a small comfort. She tried to reach for him, to show him she was still there, but her arms wouldn't budge. They were dead weights at her sides.

Peter... Ava wanted to say his name, to reassure him, but all that escaped her lips was a shallow, raspy breath.

"Don't move her," Gabriel said. She could barely make out his figure in the background. "Savina, Ava needs you."

Her eyelids fluttered, heavy with exhaustion, as the scene around her blurred again. *Why can't I move? Why can't I heal myself?* Panic threatened to rise within her, but her body remained numb, cold, like she was sinking deeper into herself.

"What happened to her?" Peter's voice cracked with desperation, his hand still lingering on her cheek.

She wanted to tell him it was okay, but the words wouldn't come.

"She's been bitten by Gregor," Gabriel explained. "His snake venom is in her system. Xavier and Sorcha almost had her, but I stopped them, though Sorcha knocked me out briefly. Savina and Aaron arrived just in time."

Peter let out a shaky breath. "Yeah, perfect timing." His voice trembled, barely masking the bitterness.

Ava's pulse quickened. She hated hearing the fear in Peter's voice. Hated that she couldn't do anything to reassure him. *I'm still here,* she thought, willing him to feel her presence. But she was fading again, slipping under the weight of the venom.

Then, a soothing warmth spread over her arm, cutting through the burning pain. Savina knelt beside her, focused, her hands moving carefully over the swollen bite. "Keep calm, Ava. I'm going to draw the venom out."

Ava wanted to nod, to show she understood, but she could only manage the faintest movement. Her vision flickered, shapes blurring into one another as the pain began to dull. The burning sensation in her arm ebbed slowly, turning into a more bearable ache.

With each breath, the world around her sharpened. The haze lifted slightly, and despite feeling weak and drained, her body no longer felt suffocated. But her limbs remained too heavy to move, her energy completely depleted.

"The venom's gone now." Savina stood back. "But she needs rest. Take her back to the Manor." She turned and moved to help others.

Peter gently rolled Ava over, cradling her head in his lap.

"Peter…" She shivered uncontrollably. "You're okay … I feel so weak. It's so cold."

"I know," he said, his voice heavy with guilt. "I'm sorry. I'm going to carry you back. We'll get you warmed up." His arms slid beneath her, lifting her carefully, but his movements were strained. He kissed her forehead and began walking through the woods, his breath laboring but determined.

"What … happened? Are they gone?" she asked.

"They're gone. Savina, Aaron, and Maya scared them off. I couldn't protect you, Ava. I couldn't protect anyone…" His voice broke, and she could hear the tears threatening to spill over.

She wanted to comfort him, to tell him it wasn't his fault, but her strength failed her. She rested her head against his chest as he carried her back toward the Manor.

As they neared the protective barrier of the Manor, a group of bloodied and battered Enchanters stood waiting.

Peter carefully set Ava on her feet, but she sagged against him, her legs unable to support her. She clung to him, still shivering, the cold seeping into her bones. Her mind spun as she scanned the room for Melissa, Lance, Jeremy, Gabriel, Joss...

"Ava!" Thomas rushed over, his clothes torn and bloodied, his arms covered in deep gashes. Ilya, Katarina, and others stood nearby, looking equally battered. "Are you okay?" he asked.

She nodded. "I ... I can't make myself warm."

"Sorcha..." Konstantin said gravely. "She weakened all of us. We are all powerless."

"For how long?" Ava asked.

"I don't know," Konstantin replied, his face grim.

Peter held her closer, his grip tightening as his guilt consumed him. His arms trembled. "I couldn't protect anyone. He's dead, Ava."

Her stomach plummeted. "Who?"

"Seth ... I couldn't save him."

"Oh, no ... Peter..." She pulled him into a weak embrace, her own guilt magnifying the pain. "I'm so sorry..."

A scream pierced the air, and Ava turned. Lance carried a frantic Gillian, her fists beating against his chest as she screamed in anguish.

"Where's Jeremy? Melissa? Joss? Maggie?" Ava asked.

Peter's grip on her tightened. "They're gone, Ava ... kidnapped."

"No ... no..." Her knees buckled, but Peter caught her just in time. Her head swam with the weight of everything. Colden's betrayal, the missing friends, the horrors of the battle. Her breath came in shallow gasps, panic rising in her chest. Gabriel. Was he okay? "Where is he?"

"Who?" Peter asked.

"Gabriel…" Her eyes darted around the faces, but they couldn't seem to find him in the crowd. Was he hurt? She needed to know. "Where's Gabriel?"

"He's fine, Ava. He's still outside, helping. He'll be back soon."

But the reassurance did little to calm the frantic pace of her heart. She swallowed hard, as her chest felt heavy with dread. She needed to see him. She needed to make sure he was okay.

Gillian charged toward them, her face twisted in rage. "You!" she screamed at Peter. "None of this would've happened if you'd done your job!"

Peter's face contorted with guilt.

"Gillian, stop!" Savina stepped in, her voice firm. "This isn't the time."

But Ava could see the judgment in Gillian's eyes, the blame. And in that moment, it all became too much. She screamed, an anguished, primal cry, and tried to pull away from Peter. She wanted to run after the Cimmerians, to fight them, to get her friends back. But Peter held her tightly, refusing to let her go.

"Let me go!" She struggled against him, but her weakened body betrayed her.

"I won't let you get hurt again," he whispered, his voice breaking. "I won't lose you, too."

Ava's screams echoed through the night, but the nightmare refused to end. The weight of everything pressed down on her, suffocating her. Colden's betrayal. Their kidnapped friends. The blood. The loss.

It was too much.

38

HOPEFUL

The air in the library was stifling, heavy with tragedy. Ava sat between her father and Peter, her hands tightly clasped in theirs, though she felt no comfort from their touch. It had been hours since the fight, yet her mind still swam in a fog of shock and exhaustion. The sedative they'd given her hadn't dulled the horror of the nightmare that refused to end.

Aaron stood at the front of the room. "Several of our members have been kidnapped." His words sliced through the silence, but they landed like stones in Ava's stomach, heavy and unyielding.

"Four unfortunately perished: Esteban, Alena, Zhan, and Seth."

Beside her, Peter's hand gripped hers even tighter, his knuckles white with the strain. She turned to look at him, her chest tightening with the shared burden of guilt that hung between them like a dark cloud. She felt his anguish as if it were her own.

Across the room, Anastasya let out a heart-wrenching cry, collapsing into Gustav's arms as he held her, his face a mask of grief. Diego's comforting words to Maya and Lucia were barely audible over the soft murmurs and sobs that filled the room.

"Alena…" Ilya rubbed his face as if trying to wipe away the memory. "She saved me."

"I couldn't protect them," Katarina whispered. "There were too many."

Peter hung his head. "I was able to protect myself … but I couldn't protect anyone else." His words sent a fresh wave of guilt crashing over Ava.

She clenched her jaw, forcing back the tears that threatened to spill.

Savina's voice cut through the murmur of grief. "What happened? What started it?"

Gabriel cleared his throat. "We were practicing, but then we heard sounds from miles away. The sky darkened, and lightning struck. We followed the noise and found the Cimmerians. The battle erupted from there."

"I felt like I was on fire." Ilya shook. "It was so intense that I passed out. Alena … she guarded me."

"I had protection on Ilya," Katarina added. "I don't understand why it didn't work."

Aaron's brow furrowed. "The Cimmerians must have had an Enchanter capable of dispelling protection powers." His gaze softened as his eyes landed on Peter and Katarina. "Don't blame yourselves. You fought bravely. None of this is your fault."

Ava swallowed hard, forcing herself to speak through the knot in her throat. "It was him." Her voice trembled, but she pushed forward. "It was Colden—or Corbin all along. He's Havok."

The weight of their stares felt like a heavy blanket suffocating Ava.

"He controlled us to kill innocent people. Convinced me to see the Necromancer."

The room went still, shock rippling through the crowd.

Savina shut her eyes, her lips pressed into a thin line. "I knew this would happen."

They knew?

Gustav, Aaron, and Savina huddled together, their whispers carrying an air of secrecy and unease.

Ava gritted her teeth. "Tell us what's going on? Stop keeping things from us!"

Savina's eyes locked onto hers, the steel in them wavering just for a moment. She sighed, pacing the room. "When we killed Corbin years ago, Colden reaped his soul. It weakened Corbin enough to eventually kill him, but his soul lived on inside Colden. For years, it festered, corrupting him from within. We didn't know it was possible. We ... we thought we'd won."

Ava felt the blood drain from her face as Savina's words sank in.

"When you went to the Necromancer," Savina continued, "they ambushed you. A spirit possessed you, weakening Colden enough for Corbin to fully take control."

Ava's heart hammered in her chest. It wasn't just Corbin. Colden had been battling him all along. "So, Corbin ... he's back?"

Savina's face was pale. "Yes."

Cries of disbelief echoed through the room.

Ava's head swam, her vision narrowing as the room seemed to close in on her. Her father squeezed her hand, but the warmth did nothing to stave off the ice crawling through her veins.

"It's Ava's fault that Colden died?" Natalia's sharp voice cut through the din, her glare piercing Ava like a dagger.

"No," Savina said. "Corbin convinced her to seek the Necromancer. But whether or not Ava went, Colden's death was inevitable."

The words should have brought Ava some relief, but instead, they felt hollow. She hadn't killed Colden, but she had played a part in his undoing.

"I didn't want to believe it … that Corbin could still be alive," Savina said. "I was so desperate to save my brother, I … I ignored the signs."

Aaron frowned. "We never could have known, Savina."

"But my mother promised my soul to Havok," Ava said. "Does that mean Colden and Corbin were like … like Jekyll and Hyde?"

Savina's eyes darkened. "Yes. And Corbin was the one who controlled Devon. He helped them escape the Cruciari, which has now been completely destroyed."

A fresh wave of gasps filled the room. Everything Ava had known, everything she'd fought for, had crumbled in an instant.

"I should have seen this coming," Savina whispered. "I put my brother's life above your safety, and I failed you all." Her defenses crumbled.

Ava had never seen her so vulnerable, so broken. But they were all broken now. Her vision blurred with tears. She wanted to scream, to fight, to do anything but sit there helpless as her world fell apart. She had lost so much, her mother, her innocence, and now Colden too.

Her father's hand squeezed hers, but it wasn't enough to stop the flood of guilt and grief that threatened to drown her.

Nothing was enough.

Anger, confusion, guilt, and heartbreak churned like a storm inside Ava. She couldn't stop the flood of feelings, and as Peter rubbed her back, his own tension made everything worse.

He stared vacantly at the ground, jaw clenched so tight she thought he might crack a tooth.

Anger radiating from him through the bond, lost in his own guilt, and it crept into her like an unwanted guest.

"I couldn't stop them," Peter whispered.

"It wasn't your fault," Ava said.

He shook his head. "I didn't want to fight. I was scared, Ava. I acted cowardly."

She reached for him, gently turning his face toward hers. She could see the war inside him, the guilt eating him alive. "Peter, you are brave. You saved me. You saved so many of us."

His lips quivered, but he nodded. Still, she felt the shame that lingered, the same guilt weighing him down. "They killed him."

Tears welled in her eyes as she pulled him into her arms, kissing the top of his head. "I'm so sorry."

"We will go after Havok," Aaron said, drawing their attention back to the front of the room where he stood with the other Elders. "But we cannot do this without another fight."

"I'm going," Ava said, her voice firmer than she felt inside.

"Me too," Gillian echoed, her voice rough with determination.

Peter squeezed Ava's hand tighter. "I won't be separated from Ava," he said, though his fear was evident

Link nodded, crossing his arms. "Count me in."

A murmur of agreement spread through the room as others volunteered, but Savina raised her hand, silencing them. "We will all go," she said. "But if anyone does not wish to come, we will understand."

"We cannot leave until everyone is ready to fight," Aaron added. "First, we must heal completely. There are things out there that most of you have never seen. Some of you are not experienced enough yet. We also need to track where they are hiding."

"Caprington," Ava said, her voice shaky as she recalled the name. "That's where Havok said he wanted to take me."

The Elders exchanged grave nods.

"So, how long until we leave?" Ava asked.

"I'm afraid it won't be for a month or two," Aaron replied calmly, though Ava could feel his caution. His russet eyes warned her not to push.

"A month?" Ava's anger flared. Her chest tightened, her heart pounding against her ribs. How could they wait that long?

Aaron didn't respond, but his silence was enough of an answer.

Savina stepped forward. "We will heal your wounds now. We want everyone to remain under the protection of the Manor. The barriers have been strengthened."

"Because you were all placed under Sorcha's spell," Aaron said, "it will take time to regain your abilities. Especially for the younger Enchanters."

"So, we have no powers at all?" Thomas asked, anxiety creeping into his voice.

"Unfortunately," Savina confirmed.

"I still have mine," Peter said, but there was no pride in his voice.

Thomas scratched his head. "When will our abilities come back? They will, right?"

"They will," Savina said. "But it depends on your body. You must be patient and not force it. Your body needs time."

Ava's stomach twisted with unease as she thought about what lay ahead. Would she be ready when the time came? She wasn't sure.

When it was Ava's turn to be healed, she approached Savina. The Elder's green eyes scanned Ava's face, and her expression softened with concern. "Oh, dear."

"What?"

Savina gently unglued strands of Ava's blood-caked hair from her face. "There's a long gash on the side of your face."

Ava's fingers instinctively touched the spot, her necklace warm against her chest. She remembered the fleeting image of blond hair, of Melissa being carried away. The memories stung, and she swallowed the lump in her throat. "I can't feel them," she whispered. "Melissa, Jeremy ... Joss. I can't feel any of them."

Savina's hand cupped her chin, her touch comforting. "They're alive. We will get them back. I've sealed the wound, but it will take a few days to fully heal."

"What's going to happen to me, Savina? What's my fate?"

Savina sighed, her eyes filled with both regret and determination. "While you were reckless, this was not your fault."

"No punishment? But I did something terrible."

"We've all done terrible things. I know why you did it, and I should have told you the truth about your mother."

"Alena said she was a spy."

Savina nodded solemnly. "She was. She kept up the ruse for a long time, but when she met your father, something changed. She wanted to be with him, with you. But she couldn't escape the Cimmerians."

Tears pricked Ava's eyes. "Why didn't they take me when they had the chance?"

"I can only guess Havok wanted to wait until you were stronger, until your powers had developed. He wasn't strong enough then."

"If my mother loved me, why did she say it was my destiny to be with Havok?"

"It could have been a corrupted calling. I don't know, Ava. But we will find out. I promise I won't keep anything from you anymore."

Ava nodded, tears streaming down her cheeks. "I should have trusted you."

"We should have trusted each other." Savina pulled Ava into a tight embrace. "Rest now, and we'll talk tomorrow."

She held on, clinging to the only motherly figure she had left. When they finally pulled apart, her gaze met Gabriel's, and her heart twisted. She needed to know if he was okay. His face was smeared with dirt, and the sight of his bloodied shirt sent a shiver down her spine.

"Are you okay?" she asked. "You're hurt."

He looked down at himself, almost as if he'd forgotten about his injuries. "I'll be fine," he said, though his voice lacked its usual confidence.

"You don't look fine." She had never seen Gabriel so beaten, so vulnerable.

"How are you? You look better."

"I should have trusted you. I should have—"

"Stop. Don't apologize."

"H-how long did it take for your powers to come back last time?"

"It took two months. The abilities will return."

Ava bit her lip. "Thank you, for everything."

"No need to thank me." His gaze lingered on her, searching.

"You were right. When it came down to it, I made the right choice. To fight."

Gabriel's face softened, a rare flicker of something unspoken passing between them. "I'm glad, Ava. And I'm sorry about your mom."

Peter came up and took her hand.

Gabriel's gaze shifted to Peter. "Don't blame yourself at all. You are a fighter just as much as the rest of us."

Peter nodded.

Gabriel turned and walked away.

Thomas guided a dazed and shocked Gillian to her room, his arm wrapped around her trembling shoulders.

Ava's heart ached for her friend. As the room began to clear out, Lance stood near the doorway, his face pale and drawn with exhaustion.

She reached out and caught Lance's hand. Her fingers trembled as they wrapped around his, desperate for some kind of connection in the overwhelming emptiness. He turned, his eyes softening. He leaned down and pulled her into a hug.

Ava clung to him, her body shaking as all the fear, guilt, and sorrow came rushing to the surface. She buried her face into his shoulder, the fabric of his shirt soaking up the silent tears that finally escaped. For a long moment, neither of them spoke, holding each other as the enormity of their losses hung between them.

When he finally pulled back, his hands rested on her arms, giving them a gentle squeeze. "We'll find them. We have to."

Ava nodded, her throat too tight to form words. She wanted to believe him, wanted to hold on to that thin strand of hope. "Of course we will." But the words felt hollow, and her heart still ached with the fear of what they had lost.

Lance gave her one last, lingering look, then released her, stepping back. "Come on. Let's try and get some rest."

Ava swallowed hard, her body heavy with fatigue and sorrow. She nodded again, though her mind couldn't fathom rest in the middle of the storm still raging in her chest.

The three of them walked up the long staircase in silence, their steps heavy and slow. The weight of the night hung between them, thick and oppressive. Ava's mind spun in a blur of exhaustion and heartache, her limbs feeling like lead as she climbed the last few steps. She couldn't bring herself to speak. What words could she even find?

When Peter closed the door behind them, the world outside ceased to exist. The silence was deafening. Ava threw her arms around Peter, clinging to him as if holding on for dear life. The flood of emotions she had tried so hard to keep at bay surged forward, and the tears she had fought all night finally broke free. They streamed down her cheeks as she pressed her face into his shoulder, muffling her sobs against the warmth of his body.

Peter kissed the side of her head, his arms wrapping tightly around her, but Ava felt his tension. It wasn't the comfort she had expected. It was strained, distant, as though he was as lost in his own grief as she was.

She pulled back and met his eyes. There was an unbearable sadness in them, something that twisted her heart even more. He leaned down and kissed her, a desperate kiss that seemed to speak of fear, guilt, and love all at once. She tangled her fingers in his thick hair, pulling him closer, trying to lose herself in the connection, to forget everything they had just been through.

When they broke apart, Peter's forehead rested against hers, and his breath came in shallow, uneven bursts. "Is it so wrong of me to feel relieved?"

Ava shook her head, wiping her face with the back of her hand. "No. I feel it too."

He stepped back, the warmth of his body retreating as he moved toward the bed. He sat heavily on the edge, his face crumpling with anguish. "I thought I was ready. I thought I could protect you. Seth. Everyone. But I couldn't. They overpowered me so fast. I—I wasn't good enough, Ava."

Her heart twisted painfully at the sight of him. The guilt that radiated from him hit her like a wave. She crossed the room and sat beside him, taking his hand in hers, holding it tightly. "Peter, this wasn't your fault. You didn't fail anyone."

"I couldn't save them. I couldn't stop Havok. He took them because I wasn't strong enough."

"No." She his face with both hands. "You saved me. You kept me safe. And you fought. That's all anyone could've done."

He stared at her, his brown eyes filled with tears. He was always so strong, so sure of himself. But now, he looked broken. "I couldn't save Seth. I tried, but I couldn't stop them from killing him."

She pulled him into her arms, resting her chin on his shoulder. "I'm so sorry, Peter," she whispered, her own tears mixing with his. "I'm so, so sorry."

His body shook with silent sobs, and Ava tightened her grip, holding him as tightly as she could, wishing she could take his pain away. Wishing she could take all of it back. But no matter how hard she wished, nothing would change what had happened.

"We'll get them back. We'll find them, and we'll stop Havok. This isn't the end. I won't let it be." She kissed his forehead, then pulled him down onto the bed beside her. "We'll do this together. We'll fight again. I promise."

He wrapped his arms around her, burying his face in her hair as they lay there in the dark.

Ava closed her eyes. For now, in Peter's arms, she found a small measure of peace.

And together, they waited for dawn, knowing the fight was far from over.

PLAYLIST

Letters From the Sky – Civil Twilight

I Will Not Bow – Breaking Benjamin

Ungodly Hour – The Fray

Crush – Jimmy Eat World

The Red – Chevelle

Code Red – Tori Amos

Demons – Imagine Dragons

Weight of the World – Evanescence

How To Disappear Completely – Radiohead

Rusted Wheel – Silversun Pickups

Under Control – Ellie Goulding

The Sinking Night – AFI

Heartless – The Fray

Bleeding Out – Imagine Dragons

The Meddler – Chevelle

Lacrymosa – Evanescence

Leave My Body – Florence + The Machine

Hurt – 2Cellos (Sulic & Hauser)

The Lightning Strike (What If This Storm Ends?)
– Snow Patrol

All I Need – Within Temptation

You Look So Fine – Garbage

ACKNOWLEDGEMENTS

To all of my readers, thank you immensely for your enthusiasm, your kind words, and most of all your support. I couldn't do this without you.

To all the musicians I have ever listened to and who continuously inspire me.

To Jennifer. You are truly amazing. To Chani for all of your editorial advice and support. To Angie, Rachel, Derrick, and Laura. To Paige for everything

To my mom; my dad; Patrick, Morgan, and Alison. You are incredible and I love you all.

READ ON FOR AN
EXCERPT FROM
THE NEXT BOOK IN
THE ELEMENTAL
ENCHANTERS
SERIES

PROLOGUE

Havok inhaled the crisp winter air. From the high rampart of the ancient castle, the hills rolled endlessly, their trees ablaze in reds, oranges, and yellows. The snow-capped mountains on the horizon, with their jagged peaks, stood as a testament to the wild, untamed beauty of his homeland. To his left, miles away, a rocky cliff sent water cascading into the shimmering Crystal River below, the sound a faint murmur on the wind.

A smile tugged at his lips. After so many years, he was finally home.

Caprington. His family's legacy. The town stood as proud as ever, though its people were long gone—victims of countless wars or the quiet decay of old age. Only he and Savina remained now, the last remnants of a once-mighty lineage.

But not for long. Soon, Savina would die too.

"Happy to be home?" Xavier Holstone asked from behind.

Havok turned, regarding the young man who had been at his side since childhood. In many ways, Xavier was more of a son than Colden ever could have been. The thought of his real son's sacrifice stirred the faintest flicker of sorrow. Colden had died to bring him back, and that sacrifice had been for the greater good.

"Yes." Havok inhaled a deep breath. "I had forgotten how clean the air is here. How peaceful. Not a single Ephemeral for miles."

"We've been clearing them out for years," Xavier said, pride coloring his voice.

"Good. Soon we will have all of the Elementals, and the Ephemerals will finally be wiped from this world."

"We're ready to begin."

"Excellent." Havok followed Xavier inside the castle, the air growing cooler as they stepped into the shadows of the stone corridor. Built in the 1200s, the fortress had withstood a myriad of attacks and storms. Its ancient stone walls, once battered by time and war, now stood strong, with the faint hum of modern lights added to their ageless grandeur.

They walked in silence until they reached a pair of towering double doors. Xavier pushed one open, and they stepped through into a grand hall. Havok's gaze traveled up to the high, arched ceilings, admiring the intricate patterns carved into the wood beams above.

They strode down the center aisle, flanked on both sides by crowds of his followers, who kneeled as they passed. At the front of the room, his prisoners stood bound. Their faces were familiar to him: Melissa, Jeremy, Joss, Maggie, Kira.

Melissa held his gaze, calm and calculating. Jeremy's nervous fidgeting betrayed his fear. And Joss... Joss glared at him with those striking violet eyes, her defiance evident even in chains.

A small but mighty woman stepped forward, joining Xavier beside Havok as he spoke to his followers. Trudy. Loyal, fierce, and sharp as a blade.

Havok gave her a slight nod, and she returned it, her gaze flickering over the bound prisoners with a detached curiosity.

A cold, satisfied smile spread across Havok's face. "It is so lovely to see you all. I do apologize for the barbaric means of your captivity." He nodded toward Xavier and Eve, the dark-haired woman at his side, who began untying the prisoners. "Welcome to Caprington. I trust you will come to find it much like home. It is a beautiful place, after all. Alas, I brought you here because Savina has poisoned your minds, and I wish to show you the truth."

"You betrayed us, Colden," Joss said. "How could you?"

Havok's smile faltered for a fraction of a second. Colden. The name grated on him, a reminder of a son who had never met his expectations. "Colden is gone. I am Havok now," he corrected, his voice low and cold. The truth was far more complex, of course—his soul now resided in Colden's body—but there was no need to dwell on that.

Joss's jaw clenched. "You're a monster," she hissed.

Maggie raised her chin, her dark eyes unwavering. "Savina has led us for years, but I've often questioned her motives. Perhaps ... there's truth in what you say."

Havok's brows lifted. "Oh? I was under the impression that the Elders were all so loyal to her."

Maggie hesitated, a slight frown touching her face. "Loyalty to Savina has never been easy, and there are those of us who've wondered if she's kept things hidden for her own benefit. Even now, I can't say I truly understand her intentions."

Perhaps she's useful after all.

"Perhaps you're right, Havok. Perhaps … she's manipulated us all."

"I never trusted the Elders' rules either," Melissa said. "Even with Savina's side of the story, I couldn't understand why she never sided with you."

Havok turned his attention to her, surprised by her calm tone. The Earth Enchanter. Tall, blonde, and powerful. She was a gifted warrior with a talent for invisibility and the ability to turn her body into stone. He had been particularly impressed with her skills in the past.

Havok's interest sharpened as he studied Maggie and Melissa, his gaze lingering on Maggie. "So, you both suspect Savina of treachery? You'd be willing to consider my side of this war?"

Maggie let a faint smile ghost cross her face. "If it means protecting our people, I will consider anything. We were working undercover. Savina only looked out for herself. She's the one who killed many of our people."

Havok narrowed his eyes, stepping closer. He probed their minds with a delicate touch. They weren't lying—they truly meant what they said. "Interesting," he murmured, as a smile crept onto his face. "I had hoped to gather all the Elementals here with me."

Xavier nodded. "We can gather an army and go after them. Sorcha has already weakened them. It'll be easy."

Havok's lips curled in irritation. "The Elders still have their powers, Xavier. Or have you forgotten?"

"No. But we can trick them."

Havok raised his hand, silencing him. "No. Savina has declared war, and they will come. I am a patient man,

Xavier, and when they do, I have plans for them—ones they won't survive."

"We're supposed to just sit here and wait?"

"We will train our new members. And once we have all of the Elementals, we will force the Ephemerals and the renegades to obey us. We will build a better world. The Ephemerals have ruled long enough. It is our time and anyone who stands in our way will be obliterated."

As applause filled the hall, Havok swelled with pride. He would finally complete his family's mission, once and for all.

As the cheers quieted, his gaze swept over the prisoners and his followers. "The Elementals have always believed their power lies in their talents. But real power lies not in brute strength, but in the mind. And I know their minds better than they do."

He turned to Joss, whose defiance wavered. "By the time they arrive, they'll barely know who they are. A nudge here, a whisper there, and they'll doubt their own memories, question their thoughts. Their emotions … their loyalties … all so easy to twist."

Joss's glare faltered, and Havok's smirk deepened. He cast a sidelong glance at Xavier, whose eyes gleamed with understanding. "And that is why we wait," Havok continued. "Let them come here, drawn by loyalty they don't even realize is fragile. They'll shatter—without a single spell or weapon lifted."

Xavier leaned in. "They'll be easy prey."

"Precisely," Havok replied. "When they arrive, they won't even know they're already lost."

Havok's words hung in the air, and the hall erupted once more, the applause echoing off the stone walls. He could almost taste it: the quiet satisfaction of a game he had already won.

ABOUT THE AUTHOR

Carrigan is the author of several young adult novels that make you cry and whisk you to faraway places. Though born in Cullman, Alabama, she grew up in Birmingham and moved to Atlanta at 18. She earned her BA in English and her Master of Arts in Professional Writing at Kennesaw State University. For as long as she can remember, she was always making up stories and characters inside her head, sometimes using her dolls to act out the scenes.

When she's not writing (which is rare), she's spending time with her family and friends, listening to music, playing with her furbabies, Ella and Ozzie, and cheering on her Atlanta Braves.

You can visit her online at www.carriganrichards.com.

www.ingramcontent.com/pod-product-compliance
Lightning Source LLC
Chambersburg PA
CBHW011138310726

48972CB00009B/2757